GUNFIRE ON THE RANCH

BY
DELORES FOSSEN

MILLS & BOON

First Published in Great Britain 2018
By Mills & Boon, an imprint of HarperCollins*Publishers*
1 London Bridge Street, London, SE1 9GF

© 2017 Delores Fossen

ISBN: 978-0-263-26455-5

46-0118

MIX
Paper from
responsible sources
FSC™ C007454

This book is produced from independently certified FSC™ paper to ensure responsible forest management.

For more information visit: www.harpercollins.co.uk/green

Printed and bound in Spain
by CPI, Barcelona

Delores Fossen, a *USA TODAY* bestselling author, has sold over fifty novels, with millions of copies of her books in print worldwide. She's received a Booksellers' Best Award and an RT Reviewers' Choice Best Book Award. She was also a finalist for a prestigious RITA® Award. You can contact the author through her website at www.deloresfossen.com.

Chapter One

Theo Canton wished there was a better way to stop a killer. Anything other than coming here to the Beckett Ranch to disrupt wedding plans. But if his intel was right, there could be another murder—tonight.

Maybe Ivy Beckett's murder.

Hell, maybe her entire family and Theo's sister, since they would possibly all be under the same roof for the ceremony. A ceremony that was to take place tomorrow.

Theo definitely didn't want a repeat of what had happened ten years ago when two people died at the hands of a killer. Just the thought of it put a knot in his stomach, along with bringing back old memories. He had to shove those memories aside, though, because they would only cause him to lose focus.

He had enough Beckett blood on his hands without adding more.

Theo took the final turn to the ranch and spotted the decorations already on the pasture fences. Blue satin ribbon flapping in the hot May breeze. There were no ranch hands out and about. No signs of a killer, either, but the snake could already be there, waiting to strike.

His phone buzzed, and he saw the name flash on the screen. Wesley Sanford, a fellow DEA agent who'd alerted Theo that there could be a problem, that a killer could be headed to the ranch. Theo kept his attention on the road, on his surroundings, too, but he hit the answer button to put the call on speaker.

"Anything?" Wesley asked right away.

"No, not yet. How about you?"

"I'll be at the Blue River sheriff's office in just a couple of minutes. I'll tell the deputies what's going on. I might even get the chance to speak to Gabriel himself."

Gabriel, the sheriff of the ranching town of Blue River as well as Ivy's brother. Well, one of them, anyway. Her other brother, Jameson, was a Texas Ranger.

"But I'm guessing that the sheriff won't be working this late the night before his wedding?" Wesley added.

Theo had no idea. He hadn't kept up with news on the Becketts. They were more of those old memories, and wounds, that he hadn't wanted in his life. Besides, the Becketts wouldn't want him keeping up with them. Or even want him around, for that matter. They'd made that crystal clear ten years ago. Theo had had no choice but to come tonight, though. Once the danger was over, however, he'd get out of there as fast as he had a decade ago.

"If Gabriel is at his office," Theo told Wesley, "remember not to say anything in the police station. Take him outside to talk." If their criminal informant had been right, the killer could have managed to plant a bug in the building. And in the sheriff's house. "I don't want this clown to know we're onto him. I want to catch him."

Wesley hadn't especially needed that reminder, but

the stakes were too high for either of them to make a mistake. The last time Theo had made a mistake with the Becketts, Ivy's parents had been murdered. Maybe by this same killer who was after them now.

Or maybe by Theo's own father.

But if his father had actually been the murderer ten years ago, then tonight Theo was dealing with a copycat. Because his father was miles away behind bars in a maximum-security prison. Still, a copycat could be just as lethal as the original one had been.

Too bad Theo couldn't just sound the alarm and alert Ivy's brothers and the ranch hands, but that possible bug in Gabriel's house meant the only secure way for Theo to contact the Becketts was outside, face-to-face.

"Whether the sheriff is here or not, I'll let someone know there might be a bug," Wesley assured him. "Call me when you can."

Theo hit the end-call button on his phone just as he reached the top of the hill, and the ranch house came into view. Well, one of the houses, anyway. From what he'd learned, there were now four on the grounds. One for Gabriel. Another belonging to Jameson. The third was one Gabriel's deputy and longtime friend, Cameron Doran, had built.

It was the fourth house, though, that contained the bad memories.

Because that was where Ivy's parents had been murdered. No one lived there and hadn't since, well, since that night.

According to the quick check Theo had done before he'd left for Blue River, Ivy's house was hours away in a rural area near Houston. Apparently, Theo wasn't the only one who'd left Blue River after the murders.

Other than her address, there hadn't been a lot of info to find on Ivy, though she had listed herself as widowed on the tax documents for her small ranch. So she'd not only moved on physically but also emotionally with another man she'd married and lost. Theo felt a hit of the jealousy before he quickly reined it in. Ivy wasn't his, hadn't been for a long time, so of course she had moved on. That's what normal people did.

Theo hadn't considered himself *normal* in a while now.

He stopped his truck beneath a cluster of trees only about twenty yards from Gabriel's house. Theo drew his gun and made his way to the side of the wraparound porch. There were plenty of shrubs where he could hide and have a line of sight to all four houses. However, he'd barely gotten into position when he heard something he didn't want to hear.

"Drop your gun," someone snapped.

Hell. How had a person managed to get so close without him noticing? And it wasn't just any ordinary someone, either. Theo recognized that voice even after all these years.

Ivy.

He turned, slowly, and he spotted her at the back corner of the house. Thanks to the light coming from one of the windows, he had no trouble seeing her face.

And the rifle she was pointing at him.

Apparently, she had no trouble seeing him, either, because she whispered his name on a rise of breath. What she didn't do was lower her weapon.

Theo said her name, and it had far more emotion in it than he wanted. Of course, any drop of emotion was too much right now, since he didn't want their past playing into this. She was his ex-lover, emphasis on the *ex*. All he wanted now was to do his job and get the heck out of there.

Ivy didn't say anything else, but she started walking toward him. Her attention volleyed between his face and his gun, which he lowered to his side.

"I was getting something from Gabriel's office when I glanced out the window and saw you," she finally said. "We didn't expect you. Judging from the way you were sneaking around, you didn't want us to see you."

No, he hadn't wanted the killer to see him.

"I had to come," he told her. "I found out…something."

Ivy flinched a little and came even closer until she was only about a foot away from him. She hadn't changed much in the past ten years. She was almost thirty now and still had that thick, dark brown hair that fell just past her shoulders. Still had the same intense eyes. He couldn't see the color of them in the darkness, but he knew they were sapphire blue.

Despite Theo's not wanting to feel anything, he did. The old attraction that for some stupid reason felt just as strong as it always had. But he was also feeling something else. The anger. That's why he kept watch around them.

"I guess you heard about the wedding. Are you here to see your sister?" she asked.

"No." Best not to get into the fact that he hadn't seen his kid sister, Jodi, in a long time. Because that was a different set of bad memories. Not because he didn't love her. He did. But Jodi was a reminder that he'd failed her, too. She'd nearly gotten killed the same night as Ivy's folks, and he hadn't been able to stop it. Now, all these years later, she was marrying Gabriel Beckett.

So obviously Gabriel and Jodi had managed to work through their shared painful pasts. He guessed they'd found their "normal."

"It's not safe for us to be out here," Theo explained. "We need to get in my truck so we can talk."

She didn't budge, but she did follow his gaze when he looked around again. "You heard about the threatening letter," Ivy said.

No, he hadn't, but it got his attention, and Theo shook his head. "What letter?"

Ivy huffed, and she finally lowered her gun. "The latest one had a warning that my brothers, my sister and I would all be murdered on the anniversary of our parents' deaths."

Which was only two months away.

Ivy's tone practically dismissed the threat her family had gotten. But Theo wasn't dismissing anything. "You get a lot of letters like that?"

"Enough. Emails, too, and the occasional phone call from blocked numbers. If you didn't know about that, then why are you here?" she asked without hesitating. "And why did you say it wasn't safe for us to be out here?"

"Because it's not." He took a deep breath. "You know I'm a special agent in the DEA?"

Her mouth tightened, and she nodded. "Gabriel says you're what law enforcement calls a joe."

That was the slang term for it all right. An agent who went into deep cover, sometimes years at a time. Just as Theo had done. In fact, he was less than a month out of a three-year assignment where he'd infiltrated a militia group to track the sale of drugs.

"Yes," he verified, "and I have access to criminal informants who give me intel from time to time. According to one of those informants, there's a killer coming here to the ranch tonight."

Her eyes widened. Then narrowed just as fast. She looked ready to bolt, of course, but he saw her quickly rein that in. "How reliable is this so-called intel?"

Good question. "Reliable enough for me to come to a place where I know I'm not welcome."

She stayed quiet a moment. "You could have just called," Ivy pointed out, confirming his notion about his not being welcome.

He shook his head. "According to the informant, the killer managed to bug both the sheriff's office and Gabriel's house."

Theo saw another punch of concern on her face, maybe some skepticism, too, and she had another look around as Theo did. "This killer is connected to my parents' murders?"

"The informant says the killer is." Theo paused. "But the informant also said this is the same guy who murdered your folks."

Ivy groaned. Mumbled some profanity under her breath. "We know who killed them. Your father, Travis Canton. And he's sitting in jail right now because there was more than enough evidence to prove he'd done it."

No, there was more than enough evidence to *convict* him. That was splitting hairs, but since his father couldn't remember if he'd murdered the Becketts, Theo still had his doubts.

"Travis hated my parents," Ivy reminded him as if he'd said those doubts aloud. "He threatened them just hours before the murders. And when the deputies found him by the creek, he had my father's blood on his shirt."

All of that was true. What she could have added was that Travis was an alcoholic who'd experienced blackouts, both that night and others. He could have killed the Becketts in a drunken haze and not even remembered.

Or someone could have set him up.

Someone waiting to finish the job by killing the Becketts' children.

"Your father was the sheriff at the time of his murder," he continued. What he was about to say would be old news to her, but he wanted to remind her that everything might not be black-and-white here. "Your mother was a former cop. They had plenty of enemies because of the arrests they made over the years. One of those enemies could be coming after you tonight, and that's why you don't need to be standing out here."

There was a bit more worry in her eyes this time when she glanced around. But she still didn't budge.

Now it was Theo's turn to mumble some profanity. "Look, I know Gabriel, Jameson and your sister, Lauren, won't want me inside—"

"Lauren's not here and won't be coming. She left town around the same time you did and hasn't been back."

Theo couldn't fault her for that. Lauren was the

youngest, had been barely eighteen when she'd been made an orphan. Like Theo, she had no doubt wanted a fresh start.

"I'm sorry," he said, because it sounded as if Ivy was hurt that Lauren wasn't there. It was a hurt he understood. "Hell, maybe my own sister won't want me here, either. But can we at least sit in my truck while I convince you that this threat could be real?"

"And how will you do that?" she asked. Yeah, he'd been right about that skepticism.

"I've got a recording from the criminal informant. He knew some things about the night of the murders. Things that weren't revealed to the press. He says the killer told him those things."

Her attention slashed toward the house. "Gabriel will need to hear this." And now there was some urgency in her voice.

Yes, he would. Jameson, too. And Jodi. "But not inside. Remember, there could be listening devices. If the killer knows we're onto him, it could send him back underground where he could prepare for another attack. And next time, we might not get a heads-up from a CI."

He could see the debate going on inside her, and with each passing second, Theo's unease escalated. It really wasn't a smart idea for them to be outside.

"Your brothers don't trust me," he added. "I get that."

Man, did he. Because for a short period of time after the Becketts were murdered, Theo had been a suspect.

His father wasn't the only one who'd had bad blood with Ivy's parents.

Just hours before their murder, Theo had had a run-in with Ivy's father, Sherman, and Sherman had told him in no uncertain terms that he was to stop seeing Ivy, that she didn't need a bad boy in her life. Theo had been furious, even though Sherman had been right—Ivy had deserved something better.

"Yes," Ivy whispered as if she knew exactly what he was thinking. "But let's not allow old water and old bridges to play into this. Gabriel needs to hear this recording and decide if it's something we should be worried about."

Yes, and her brother *would* be worried once he heard what the CI had to say.

Ivy motioned for him to follow her. Not to his truck but rather to the back of the house. She hurried, thank God, which meant it had finally sunk in that she was in danger. But since she was clearly taking him inside, Theo had to speak up.

"Remember the part about a possible bug. When we're inside, whisper." That might not be enough if the listening device was sensitive and had a wide range, but at this point he just wanted her out of the line of possible fire.

She led him onto the porch and through the back door, but Ivy stopped in a mudroom, where there were raincoats on wall pegs and cowboy boots stashed beside a wooden bench. A reminder that this was indeed a working ranch. Gabriel wasn't just a sheriff, but also raised cattle and horses. There were cans of paint and what appeared to be scaffolding, as well.

"There was a fire last month," Ivy said, following

his gaze. "An attack. That's why I want to make sure another one doesn't happen."

He wanted the same thing, especially since Theo had read about that attack. His sister had been the target, and even though the guy was now dead, he'd clearly left his mark.

"I'll have Gabriel come back here." Ivy put the rifle on the top shelf of the storage closet, took out her phone from her jeans pocket and sent off a text.

Theo had another look around, shut the back door and then glanced out the single window that was in the small room. Ivy reached for the light switch to turn it on, but he stopped her. Of course, that meant touching her, and he got another sucker punch of the old heat.

A third sucker punch when their gazes met.

She didn't say anything, but Theo thought maybe she had felt it, too. He also thought maybe she was fighting to push it away as hard as he was. Yes, she was a widow, but after everything they'd gone through, she probably didn't want to have another round with him any more than he did with her.

"It's not a good idea to be this close to a window," Theo insisted. And yes, he whispered. "We should at least get down."

She clamped her teeth over her bottom lip for a couple of seconds. A gesture he'd seen her do so many times. Nerves. But she finally ducked down so that her head wouldn't be anywhere near the glass. Theo ducked, too, but he stayed high enough so he could continue to glance out and make sure the killer wasn't sneaking up on them.

The moments crawled by, and with each one of them Theo became well aware of the close contact between them. It was hard to fight the attraction and the old memories when they were this close. And when he caught her scent.

Hell.

For just a split second, the image of her naked body flashed into his head.

Thankfully, the image didn't stay. It vanished when he heard the voice and the sound of footsteps. It was yet another voice he recognized. Gabriel's.

Theo braced himself for whatever Gabriel might dole out. He could just order Theo out of there, but Gabriel barely spared him a glance when he stepped into the doorway. That's because he was on his phone, and he took his sister by the arm and moved her out of the mudroom and into the adjacent kitchen.

Once Gabriel had done that, he finished his call, slipped his phone back into his jeans pocket and finally looked at Theo. This time, it was more than a glance.

"What the hell did you do? Who did you bring with you?" Gabriel demanded. But he didn't give Theo a chance to answer. "One of the ranch hands just called. He spotted an armed man crawling over the back fence, and the man's making his way to the house right now."

Chapter Two

Ivy's heart slammed against her chest. She had already been feeling so many emotions, including dread and fear, but this was a different kind of fear.

There's a killer coming here to the ranch tonight.

She hadn't exactly dismissed Theo's warning, but Ivy had prayed he was wrong. Apparently not, though. Because she doubted an armed intruder had good intentions. And according to Gabriel, he was on his way to the house. Ivy would have bolted toward the front stairs if Gabriel hadn't taken hold of her arm again.

"I've already told the others to lock up and get down," her brother said. "They're fine." He slapped off the kitchen lights and tipped his head to the back door where Theo and she had entered. "Lock that," he added to Theo. Theo did, and Gabriel used his phone to arm the security system.

"There could be listening devices planted in the house and at your office." Theo hurried into the kitchen with them. "Who else is here?" Theo asked at the same moment that Gabriel threw out a question of his own.

"What do you have to do with the armed guy?"

Judging from the glare Gabriel aimed at Theo, her brother felt his question had priority over Theo's. Theo must have felt the same way, because he started talking.

"I don't know who he is, but I have a recording of a CI who says that a killer is on the way to the ranch. I didn't call because supposedly this killer had managed to plant bugs in the house and the sheriff's office, and I didn't want to tip him off that we were onto him. But obviously we're past the point of being worried about tipping him off."

"Yeah." A muscle flickered in Gabriel's jaw. "How long had Theo been here before you texted me?" he asked her.

"Just a few seconds." That was possibly true. Ivy honestly had no idea how long it'd been. Time had sort of frozen when she'd come face-to-face with the man she'd never expected to see again.

Gabriel stared at her as if he might challenge that, but then he growled out, "Follow me."

Ivy was certain that put some renewed panic in her eyes, certain that her brother saw it as well, but Gabriel kept moving, anyway. "We'll go into my office."

Not upstairs. Though that's where Ivy wanted to go. "Nathan," she said.

"He's in the guest room with Jameson and Jodi," Gabriel quickly answered. "They moved him into the bathroom and will make sure he's all right."

That steadied Ivy a little. Jameson was a lawman, and Jodi had been trained as a private security specialist. Still, Ivy didn't want a gunman anywhere near the house or anyone in her family.

"Nathan?" Theo asked.

"Ivy's son," Gabriel said before she could answer. "If this gunman makes it to the house, he'll be seriously outnumbered. But it might not even come to that, because I have three armed ranch hands headed out to stop him."

Gabriel must have made those arrangements shortly before he'd come to the mudroom. Good. Ivy wanted every precaution taken. Correction: she *needed* it, because she had to keep Nathan safe.

"You have a son?" Theo asked, his voice practically a whisper now.

"Yes." She didn't give any other details. No time. Because Gabriel spoke again.

"I want to know everything about the recording," Gabriel insisted, glancing at Theo again. "I want to hear what this CI has to say."

Theo nodded and followed Gabriel into his office, which was just off the family room on the bottom floor. There were plenty of windows here, but Gabriel had already shut the blinds and drapes. He also didn't turn on the lights. No doubt because it would alert anyone close enough to the house that there was someone in that particular room.

However, her brother did go to one of the windows that faced the back of the house, and he opened the blinds just enough so he could keep watch. Theo did the same to the window across from Gabriel. That one would give him a view of the side of the house. While the inside of the house was practically dark, there were security lights on the grounds, so maybe they'd be able to see this monster coming.

"Is there an extra gun in here?" Ivy asked.

"Bottom right drawer," Gabriel quickly provided. It was locked, but he rattled off the combination, and she took out a Glock he had stashed there. She wasn't an expert marksman, not by any stretch of the imagination, but she would use it to defend her son if necessary.

"The CI is someone who regularly gives me intel," Theo started. "I'll write down his name for you later. In case the place really is bugged, I don't want to compromise his identity. The other person you'll hear on the recording is a federal agent. He's the one who sent me this, and the voices have been altered—again so that no one will be compromised."

While still keeping a grip on his gun, Theo took out his phone and hit the play button. He held it up so that Gabriel would be able to hear it, and it didn't take long before the man's voice began to pour through the room.

"I heard some stuff," the man said. "Stuff about them Becketts. I figured I oughta tell you because that family's been through enough."

Yes, they had been. The murder of their parents. Also the near murder of Gabriel's bride-to-be, Jodi. It had changed their lives forever.

It was still changing them.

"There's a killer coming after them," the man went on. "I don't know the fella's name, but I heard him talking at the Silver Moon Bar over on St. Mary's Street. He said he'd been hired—and these are his words, not mine—*to put some more Becketts in the ground.* He said he was going to the Blue River Ranch tonight to finish off as many of them as he could."

A chill slid through Ivy, head to toe, and she felt her stomach clench into a tight knot. "God, will this never end?" she said under her breath.

Ivy clearly hadn't said that softly enough, because it caused both Theo and her brother to look back at her. Theo hit Pause. He stared at her as if he might need to intervene in some way. Definitely not something she wanted. Nor did she want to give in to the fear. So she went to the window next to Theo in order to help him keep watch.

Theo continued to look at her while he volleyed glances out the window, but he finally hit the play button again.

"Describe the man who said that." It was a second person on the recording. Theo's fellow agent, no doubt. "And did he say who hired him?"

"Didn't mention a word about that," the CI answered. "Of course, it wouldn't have been too smart if he had. And I couldn't exactly ask him without maybe gettin' my own self killed. But he was tall, bulky. Built like one of those navy SEALs or something."

Theo looked at Gabriel then, and her brother nodded. "That matches the description of the man the ranch hand saw."

"How do you know this hired gun is for real?" the agent asked the CI.

"'Cause he knew things, that's why. Things about Sheriff Sherman Beckett and his wife, Millie, who got killed ten years ago. It was all over the news, but this fella told me there was something the news didn't mention. Something that the cops kept out of the papers. He said the killer took Sherman Beckett's watch. Pulled it right off his dead wrist. And that he took Millie's necklace. It was a heart-shaped locket and had pictures of her kids in it."

It was true. All true. Those items had indeed been missing, though they hadn't been found on the killer, Theo's father, Travis. Ivy had always assumed that Travis had dropped them or hidden them somewhere, but how would this man have known that?

That didn't help the knot in her stomach, and Ivy had to fight to hang on to what little composure she had left. She had prayed this was all some kind of misunderstanding, that the CI had been wrong, but apparently no such luck. There really was a killer headed to the house who had plans to finish them all off.

"Did this hired gun say anything else?" the agent pressed. "Anything that would help us figure out who's paying him to do this?"

"Nope, but I figure it's gotta be Travis Canton. Yeah, I know he's in jail, but something like this could get him out from behind bars."

Theo didn't say anything, but even in the near darkness, she saw his jaw tighten. "I've already checked with the prison," Theo volunteered, "and other than his lawyer, my father hasn't had any visitors in the past week. Plus, he doesn't have the funds to hire a hit man."

So maybe this was the work of some kind of psycho groupie. There'd been so much interest in the murders, partly because Jodi had also been attacked and left for dead in a shallow grave. And all that interest had attracted some very sick people.

"I know you gotta tell this to the Becketts," the CI went on a moment later, "but you oughta be careful when you do it. The fella at the bar said he'd put bugs in the sheriff's place and his house. So if you say anything to them, sure as hell don't mention my name. I don't want that SOB comin' after me."

"That's the end of the conversation," Theo told them. "But you can see why I had to come."

Yes, she could. Since the CI had been right about the hired killer, maybe he was right about that bug, too. It sickened her to think that someone had been spying on them, listening to their every word. Someone who now wanted to kill them.

Her brother must have realized that, too, because he cursed and fired off a text. Several seconds later, his phone buzzed. He set it aside and put it on speaker, no doubt to keep his hands free for his gun.

"Sorry, Gabriel," the caller immediately said. It was Aiken Colley, one of Gabriel's ranch hands. "But we lost sight of the guy."

That was not what Ivy wanted to hear, and she made a frantic search of every part of the grounds that she could see. No signs of a gunman. No signs of anyone.

Gabriel cursed. "Where was he when you last saw him?"

"By the south barn."

That wasn't that far from the house. Worse, there were other outbuildings and fences between the house and that particular barn, and this man could use those to conceal himself so he could get closer.

"I never had a clean shot of him," Aiken went on. "The guy was running, and every few seconds, he would duck behind cover. Jake and Teddy are out here with me, and I've alerted the other hands."

Jake and Teddy were two other hands, and while none of the hands were in law enforcement, they all knew how to handle guns. But apparently this hired killer knew how to dodge those guns.

"If possible, I want this guy alive," Theo said.

Gabriel didn't disagree with that. Probably because a dead man couldn't give them answers, but at the moment Ivy cared only about keeping this monster away from Nathan and everyone else in the house.

"Kill him only if necessary. And be careful," Gabriel warned the ranch hand.

"We will. We'll keep looking for him until we find him," Aiken added before he ended the call.

Ivy got back to keeping watch. Not that she hadn't been doing that, but she adjusted her position just enough so that she could try to take in more of the yard and the pastures. Still no sign of him, but she could almost feel him closing in on them.

Who the heck was putting this monster up to this?

The CI had said it was Travis, and perhaps it was. Maybe he'd somehow gotten the money. But there was also another possibility. One that had been a thorn in her family's side since Travis had first been arrested.

"Could your uncle August be behind this?" Ivy asked

Theo. "Because August has been adamant that Travis is innocent."

August was Travis's half brother. A hothead. In the past ten years, he'd never turned to violence to free his brother, but August could be getting desperate since Travis had exhausted all his appeals.

"I haven't spoken to August since I left Blue River," Theo answered. "I tried to call him, but he didn't answer. If he had anything to do with this, I'll deal with him."

Judging from Theo's tone, that would not be pleasant. Not a surprise. There was no love lost between Jodi and their uncle, and it appeared to be the same for Theo. Of course, that was probably because August was not an easy man to like, and he was always saying that Travis's "ungrateful kids" weren't doing enough to help their father.

Theo's phone buzzed. "It's the agent who recorded the conversation with the CI," Theo relayed to them, but he didn't mention the guy by name. However, as Gabriel had done, he put the call on speaker. "The gunman's here," Theo told the agent right off. "Not in the house, but it appears this is where he's headed."

The agent didn't jump to answer. It seemed as if he took a moment to process that. "You want me out there?"

"Not yet. This goon could fire shots at you as you drive up. Plus, I don't want to send him running."

Part of Ivy wanted him to run. To get as far away from Nathan as possible. But Theo was right. If the guy ran, he could possibly just regroup and come back for a second attempt.

"Did you find any bugs in the sheriff's office?" Theo asked.

"Not yet, but the deputies are looking. One of them spoke to Gabriel a little while ago. He stepped outside to do that."

"Cameron," Gabriel provided. "He called the moment the agent showed up at the office."

Of course he had. He wouldn't have kept Gabriel in the dark about something this big. That meant Gabriel had been plenty busy in the short time since all of this mess had started with Theo's arrival.

"The deputy wants to know if you need backup," the agent continued.

"Not yet," Gabriel answered before Theo could say anything. "But keep watch, because there might be more than one hired gun. Whoever's behind this could have sent someone there."

Oh, mercy. She hadn't even considered that. But if someone had indeed wanted to put the Becketts "in the grave," then the person might have gone looking for Gabriel at work.

"I just got a call," the agent continued. "The CI is dead."

Other than hearing she had a son, Theo hadn't seemed surprised by much of what had happened. But he was clearly surprised now. And riled. "How the hell did that happen?"

"We're not sure yet. We had a tail on him, just in case he tried to follow the hired gun or something, but the tail stayed a safe distance back. He saw someone dressed all in black gun the guy down."

Ivy doubted that was a coincidence, and that meant... Oh, God.

"Was this all a setup?" she asked. Neither Gabriel nor Theo jumped to deny that, and that only caused her heart to pound even harder. "You think the hired gun wanted Theo to come here?" she added.

Again, they didn't deny it. "If so, it worked," Gabriel mumbled, and he tacked on some profanity.

Yes, it had. But what did it mean? It didn't take Ivy long to come up with something that she didn't want to consider.

All the "survivors" of the murders were now under the same roof. Gabriel, Jameson, Jodi, Theo and her. Along with their sister, Lauren, all five of them had been either in the house where her parents were murdered or on the grounds. Which meant they had all been possible witnesses to the crime.

Possible, but they actually hadn't been.

Ivy had been in her upstairs bedroom with her headphones on. And crying. Because of the blowup that Theo had just had with her folks. The music had been so loud that she hadn't heard her mother and father being murdered in the room just below her. Some people had told her that it was a blessing she hadn't heard because if she had, she would have gone downstairs and possibly been killed, too. But Ivy wished she had heard. Because she might have been able to save them.

Jodi hadn't heard the murders going on, either. She'd been outside, coming back from Gabriel's house, which was a short distance away. She'd been attacked that night. Not by the killer, though. But rather by her ex-boyfriend who'd been in a rage over their breakup. Since he was now dead, he was no longer a possible witness.

Jameson and Gabriel had been at their own houses, but they were close enough to the main ranch house that they could have seen something. They hadn't. But maybe the killer hadn't known or believed that.

"What could your father or August possibly hope to gain by eliminating witnesses?" Ivy came out and asked.

"They wouldn't," Theo answered.

She looked at Gabriel to see if he would argue that. He didn't. "If they wanted to clear Travis's name," Gabriel explained, "they could be desperate enough to arrange a murder. But Theo and Jodi wouldn't be the targets."

Because Travis still seemingly loved his children. Of course, that didn't exclude Travis's brother. August wasn't fond of Jodi or Theo. "This could all be something August put together."

"If August had come up with this plan to make my father look innocent," Theo went on, "he would have hired someone to stab his victim."

The way her parents had been killed.

Ivy was about to say that could be the hired thug's plan. But then she heard a sound that stopped her cold.

"Get down!" someone shouted. Aiken.

But there was no time to do that. Because a bullet came crashing through the window where Ivy was standing.

Chapter Three

Hell. Theo hadn't even seen the shot coming.

But he sure as heck heard it. Felt it, too, when the glass flew through the room and a piece of it sliced across his cheek. It stung, but he ignored it and scrambled toward Ivy so he could pull her to the floor. She had already started in that direction, but Theo helped her along by hooking his arm around her and dragging her about five feet away from the window.

Good thing, because another bullet tore through what was left of the glass.

"Stay down," Theo warned her, and he put her behind a huge leather chair so he could hurry back to the window. He didn't get directly in front of it but instead kept to the side.

This was exactly what Theo had been trying to stop. Ivy and her family had been through enough, but apparently that moron outside didn't feel the same. He was adding to their misery, and in doing so, he was putting an innocent child in danger. Theo didn't know how old Nathan was, but it was possible he was a baby.

"Do you see him?" Gabriel asked. He came to the

window next to Theo and peered out through the edge of the blinds.

Theo looked over the grounds as best he could, but there were too many places their attacker could use for cover. A barn, several vehicles, shrubs and trees. However, it became a little easier to narrow down a hiding place when the next shot blasted through the air. Like the other two, this one slammed into the wall near the door, and it allowed Theo to pinpoint the man's location.

"He's on the right side of the barn," Theo relayed to Gabriel. "I can't see him, but I can see a rifle barrel."

Gabriel didn't waste any time. He tossed Ivy his phone. "Text Aiken and tell him to stay back from the barn." And like Theo, Gabriel took aim in that direction.

Theo didn't look back at Ivy, but he could hear the clicks on the phone as she wrote. However, they were soon drowned out by another shot. This time, it went through the window near Gabriel.

That must have been the final straw for Ivy's brother because he cursed, took aim at the barn and fired. Theo did the same, all the while watching to see if their attacker would show his face. He didn't. And he didn't seem put off by being shot at, because he continued to fire, as well. However, something was off because Theo could no longer see the rifle.

"I think he's trying to make a getaway," Theo mumbled. "I'll go after him." He didn't allow Gabriel or Ivy a say in that. Keeping low, Theo hurried toward the door. "Disarm the security system so I can go out front but reset it as soon as I'm outside."

Theo had only been in Gabriel's house a time or two

even though the man had lived there for going on thirteen years. Gabriel hadn't exactly been a fan of Theo's when he'd been dating Ivy, but Theo had dropped by a couple of times to pick her up there. That's why Theo knew the general layout, and he ran up the hall and through the family room to get to the front door.

Gabriel must have turned off the system because the alarm didn't go off when Theo eased open the door. However, he did hear a sound he didn't especially want to hear.

Footsteps behind him.

It was Gabriel. "You'll need help," Gabriel growled.

"You should stay with Ivy," Theo growled right back.

"She's the one who insisted I go with you." Gabriel didn't seem especially pleased about that.

This was part of that "old water, old bridge" thing between Theo and the Becketts. Still, Gabriel was a lawman, and he knew it was a stupid time to discuss this or anything else, especially all that old baggage. Gabriel rearmed the security system, this time using the keypad on the wall, and he shut the door. He then tipped his head to the left side of the house.

"I'll go that way," Gabriel said, "and make my way to the back. As soon as I get to the porch, I'll fire at the barn, but I'll keep my shots low to try to avoid a kill shot. You do the same from this side of the house. Ivy's texting the hands to let them know we're out here so they won't hit us by mistake."

Good. Gabriel had been thorough. Now, if everything played out as planned, they could catch this snake and get him to talk. If August or his father was involved, then there'd be hell to pay. Not just from Theo but from the Becketts.

Theo made his way to the side of the porch and peered around the edge. He was careful, but the gunman must have been looking for him because he sent a shot right at Theo. It smashed into the wood siding, tearing a hole in it.

That caused Theo to curse again, and he hoped like the devil that none of those shots made it through the wall where Ivy was or upstairs to the others. If the shots went in the direction of her son, Theo was almost certain that Ivy would go running up there, and in doing so she might get herself killed.

Theo waited, giving Gabriel a couple of seconds to get into place, and even though those seconds seemed to crawl by, he knew Gabriel was hurrying. And the next sound Theo heard was a shot coming from the direction where Gabriel had said he would be. Their attacker would obviously soon know that Gabriel was back there.

Theo leaned out, aiming low, and he fired two rounds. Almost immediately, he ducked back behind cover. Good thing, too, because the gunman fired off two rounds of his own at Theo. But Theo could also hear the man cursing. Maybe because he'd been hit. Perhaps because he realized that coming here alone had been a stupid mistake.

That last thought had no sooner crossed his mind when Theo felt that bad feeling crawl up his spine. It was a feeling that had saved his butt a few times, so he didn't ignore it. He pivoted, looking around him.

And spotted the second man near Theo's own truck.

He was dressed all in black, armed with multiple weapons on an equipment belt. He had one weapon in his hand, as well. That's the one he aimed at Theo.

Theo fired first.

He double tapped the trigger, the shots slamming directly into the man's chest, and the guy dropped to the ground. Maybe dead or dying, but it was equally possible that he was wearing a Kevlar vest and had simply had the breath knocked out of him. If so, he could still be dangerous.

"There's a second gunman," Theo called out to Gabriel. "And there might be others."

Of course, Gabriel didn't need him to add that last part, but it was also, hopefully, a reminder for everyone inside to stay down. Especially Ivy. She was on the bottom floor and could easily be hit by bullets meant for Gabriel and him.

The guy by the barn fired another couple of shots, one of them in Theo's direction. At least one went toward Gabriel's office, though. Maybe the guy had thermal equipment or something because he seemed to know that there was still someone in that particular room. When the goon sent another shot at the office, Theo knew he couldn't wait.

He leaned out and fired.

Not low this time.

Theo sent some rounds in the area of the shooter's chest. And finally the shots stopped. Just like that, it was quiet again. Theo didn't hear any moaning or sounds of pain. Definitely didn't hear anyone trying to run away.

It was a risk. Anything he did at this point could be, but Theo left the porch and ran toward his truck, where the second gunman was still on the ground. He kept his gun ready, kept watch around him, too, but as he approached the man, he didn't see any movement.

But he did see blood.

It was on the ground around the guy, which meant he hadn't been wearing Kevlar after all. Theo touched his fingers to the man's neck.

Dead.

He didn't curse, though that's what he wanted to do. Maybe the other one was still alive.

Using shrubs for cover, Theo started making his way to the barn. "I'm back here," he called out to Gabriel.

But calling out to him wasn't necessary because Theo soon spotted the sheriff at the back of the house. Gabriel was closer to the barn now, heading toward the first gunman. And he wasn't alone. There was another man with Gabriel. One of the hands no doubt.

"Are the hired killers dead?" Ivy asked, and that's when Theo realized she was at one of the blasted-out windows.

"Get down!" Theo ordered her.

He hurried past Ivy but not before he got a glimpse of her face. She was too pale and had a death grip on the gun she'd taken from her brother's desk, but she appeared to be unharmed. Physically, anyway. This had to be triggering flashbacks of her parents' murders. Also triggering new fears of the danger to her son and family.

Gabriel and the hand got to the gunman ahead of

Theo, and Theo braced himself for Gabriel to say the guy was dead. He didn't.

"Ivy, call an ambulance," Gabriel shouted. "Tell the medics to hurry."

Theo soon figured out why the hurry part was necessary. Just like the guy in the front yard, this one had gunshots to the chest, and he was bleeding out fast. Theo kicked away the guy's weapon just as Gabriel got right in the man's face.

"Who hired you?" Gabriel demanded, sounding very much like the lawman that he was.

The guy shook his head, and he opened his mouth as if to answer. But he didn't. His eyelids drifted down, and his head flopped back, prompting Gabriel to check for a pulse.

"He's still alive," Gabriel said, glancing at Theo. "Go back in and check on Ivy and the others. Ivy still has my phone so tell her to disarm the security system. Also let Jameson know what's going on."

Theo didn't like leaving Gabriel out there with just the hand, but he soon saw two other men making their way toward them. Not gunmen. These were dressed like ranch hands.

"I heard Gabriel," Ivy volunteered. Which meant she was still too close to the blasted window. "I turned off the alarm."

Good, because the sooner Theo got in the house, the sooner he could chew her out for taking a risk like standing too close to the window. But he didn't get a chance to even start the chewing out. By the time he was through the door and into the foyer, Ivy was already headed up the stairs. Theo shut the door and followed her.

She stopped at the top of the stairs, looked at him, and he saw that her bottom lip was trembling. Actually, she was trembling all over.

"There really could be others?" she asked. Her voice was as shaky as the rest of her.

"Maybe." And he hated that he even had to say that to her because it certainly didn't help with her frayed nerves. "We just don't know who or what we're dealing with right now."

She nodded. But didn't budge. "I need a second to calm down. I don't want Nathan to see me like this."

Theo understood that. As a single mom, she probably wanted to be strong for her kid. But she took more than a second, and the trembling seemed to be getting worse. He figured it was a mistake, but since Theo didn't know what the heck else to do, he put his arm around her.

Ivy automatically stiffened. Maybe because the last time she'd been in his arms, they'd still been lovers. But there was no trace of that attraction now, and Theo heard her try to choke back a sob.

She pulled away from him, hiking up her chin. Or rather, trying. She wasn't doing a very good job of it until one of the doors opened and Jameson stuck out his head.

"Are you okay?" Jameson asked, his attention going straight to his sister.

She gave another nod. "Gabriel's with one of the gunmen, the one who's still alive. The other guy's dead. Theo had to shoot him."

Jameson's attention went to Theo then, and he stepped back when Jodi came out of the room and into the hall. She didn't hurry to Theo. She didn't curse him, either. Considering that he hadn't contacted her in a while, he deserved the cursing.

Ivy didn't linger in the hall, though. She pushed past all of them and hurried into the room, no doubt to see her son.

"You came because of these gunmen?" Jodi asked him.

"Yeah," Theo verified. "I tried to stop this."

Jodi made a sound of understanding, and this time she went to him. Just as he'd done to Ivy, Jodi hugged him. For a couple of seconds, anyway. But then she eased back and punched him in the arm.

Hard.

"That's for not calling me." She punched him again. "That's for letting me think you might be dead or dying somewhere."

The emotion surprised him. So did the tears that sprang to his sister's eyes. Jodi wasn't the crying sort. Or at least she hadn't been the last time he'd seen her. But she hadn't been engaged to Gabriel Beckett then. Obviously, his sister had taken her life in a new direction.

"I love you," Jodi added. "And you're bleeding." She used the sleeve of her shirt to wipe his cheek.

Theo hadn't forgotten about the glass cutting him, but he also hadn't figured it was serious since he wasn't hurting.

"Who's with Gabriel?" Jodi asked.

"Three ranch hands."

Jodi glanced back at Jameson, and that seemed to be the only cue the Ranger needed to get moving. Maybe Jodi wanted her soon-to-be husband to have as much backup as possible.

"Wait here with them," Jameson said to Theo as he headed down the stairs. "And don't let them go outside until I say so."

Theo doubted Ivy would want to venture out of the house as long as that gunman was out there, but since his sister was already nibbling on her bottom lip and looking around, she might try to disobey Jameson's orders. Just in case that's what she had on her mind, Theo took Jodi by the arm.

"Is there a bathroom in here so you can get me a cloth for this cut on my cheek?" he asked. Not that he particularly wanted to do that, but it would give Jodi something to do.

"Yes, this way."

Theo followed her into the bedroom and then to the attached bathroom. It wasn't that big, but it still took Theo a moment to spot Ivy because she was in the corner next to a claw-foot tub. She had a boy clutched in her arms.

Definitely not a baby.

This kid was older, school-age, and he was looking up at Ivy as if to comfort her rather than vice versa.

Jodi froze, practically in midstep. Ivy froze, too, but the boy turned and faced Theo. And Theo felt as if he'd just been punched in the gut. Because he knew that face. Or rather he knew the features, because he saw them every time he looked in the mirror.

Hell.

Ivy must have seen his reaction then, because she shook her head. Not a denial, exactly, since there was no way she could deny what Theo had just realized.

He was looking at his own son.

Chapter Four

Ivy could have sworn her heart stopped beating for a few seconds. Theo knew. God, he knew.

From the moment she'd seen Theo by the side of the house, Ivy had feared this might come. In fact, at first that's why she had thought Theo was there, that he'd found out about Nathan. It would have been safer if that's why he'd been there. But it wasn't going to be easy to deal with the storm that was brewing behind Theo's narrowed eyes.

"Who is that?" Nathan asked, his attention suddenly fixed on Theo. "He's not one of the bad men, is he?"

On the surface those were easy questions, but neither Ivy, Jodi nor Theo jumped to provide him with answers. Ivy wasn't even sure she could speak yet, and she doubted Theo could, either, because his jaw was clenched so tight.

"Uh, this is my brother, Theo." Jodi finally spoke up. "And no, he's not a bad guy. He's sort of a cop like your uncle Gabriel and uncle Jameson."

Because Ivy still had her arms wrapped around Nathan, she felt his muscles relax a little. It would probably be a while before he completely relaxed. Even when he did, this had changed everything for him. Her little boy had heard those gunshots, had felt the terror that went along with him.

There'd be nightmares.

Ones similar to hers, ones she'd been having for a decade. And Ivy silently cursed the gunmen for that. Silently thanked Theo, too, for warning them, or those two thugs might have made it all the way into the house. Then her son might have to deal with more than fear, tight muscles and nightmares. They could all be dead.

A thought that sickened her to the core.

At the moment, though, Theo probably wouldn't want her thanks. For anything. In fact, his shock had morphed into a glare that he was now aiming at her.

"How old are you?" Theo asked. His glare softened significantly when he looked at Nathan.

"Nine," her son answered, meaning Theo could narrow down the date he'd been conceived.

Theo clearly wasn't surprised by her son's answer. Not after seeing Nathan's face. In fact, Theo might even be able to remember the exact date of Nathan's conception. Because it was the same night of the big blowup between her parents and him. A blowup that'd happened because her mom had found ~~Nathan~~ THEO and her in bed together.

All of those feelings came back, too.

Ivy pushed them aside, that mix of pleasure and grief, and she got to her feet. It was obvious there were some things she needed to say to Theo. Obvious, too, that he had some questions for her, and she didn't want him asking those in front of Nathan. Eventually, her son would have to know the truth, but now wasn't the time. He wasn't ready for it. Heck, *she* wasn't ready for it.

"I'll stay with Nathan," Jodi volunteered. "He'll be okay."

Even though Ivy hadn't said anything to her, Jodi and she were on the same page about what needed to be done. But Ivy didn't want her explanation to Theo to come at the expense of her son's safety.

Theo didn't say anything, either. He just followed Ivy out of the ensuite bathroom and into the bedroom, and he pulled the bathroom door shut behind them. She didn't go far, just a few feet away. Hopefully close enough so she could still get to Nathan if there was another attack but far enough away from Theo so that they weren't in each other's personal space. Even though it did seem a little late for that since they'd once been lovers.

He stood there staring, and she could see he was trying to work out what to say to her. Hopefully, he wasn't going to yell at her, since she didn't want Nathan to overhear something like that. At least at the moment Theo wasn't yelling. In fact, he wasn't saying anything. Theo put his hands on his hips, shook his head and turned that glare on her again.

"Why?" he finally asked, and he did keep his voice at a whisper. An angry one that dripped with emotion.

Since that simple word could encompass a lot of territory, Ivy went with a simple explanation. "I couldn't find you to tell you I was pregnant."

Ivy watched him process that, and she knew it wasn't

something he could dispute. Theo had vanished shortly after the attacks. Jodi had been in the hospital, still recovering from her horrific injuries, and she certainly hadn't known how to get in touch with her brother.

"I left because you told me to leave," Theo reminded her.

She couldn't dispute that, either. Ivy had indeed ordered him out of her house and her life after the argument with her parents. In part, she'd done that for Theo's own safety. Because she'd been afraid her father was going to beat him up or have him arrested for something. No way would Theo believe that now, though. And even if he did, it would only make him madder than he already was. He wouldn't have wanted her fighting those kind of battles for him.

"Does Nathan know the truth?" Theo snapped.

Ivy shook her head, and she prayed Theo didn't rush out and tell him.

"How about your late husband?" Theo again. "Did he know?"

"Yes. His name was Chad Vogel, and Nathan was eleven months old when I married him. But Jameson, Lauren and Gabriel didn't know I was pregnant or that I had a child. Neither did Jodi. At least they didn't know until I came back to Blue River two days ago."

Now Theo cursed. "One of them should have called me. And don't say they couldn't find me, because Jameson's a Texas Ranger. He could have tracked me down if you'd asked him to do that."

"Yes," she repeated. "And FYI, Jodi said I should tell you after she finally met Nathan day before yesterday. I just thought it was best if I waited until after the wedding to do that."

Judging from his still-tight expression, Theo didn't agree. And maybe he was right. Maybe she should have searched harder for him, especially after her husband passed away.

Theo glared at her a few more seconds before he finally glanced away and cursed some more. "Is Nathan healthy? Is he okay?"

It seemed petty for her to hesitate even a second to give him that info. But she knew that with each new bit, Theo would only want to know more and more. Then he would want Nathan to know who'd really fathered him.

Theo. And not Chad.

Of course, Nathan didn't have a lot of memories of Chad anyway, since he'd died after losing his battle with cancer when Nathan had been only five.

"I'm sorry," she said. It didn't seem nearly enough, but there wasn't much else she could say or do at this point.

There was a sound outside the window, a car engine, and Theo hurried to look while motioning for her to stay put. Just like that, her heart revved up again. Not that it'd gone back to normal, and that might not happen for a long time.

"It's just the ambulance," Theo told her. He stayed at the window with his gun drawn.

She was glad that it'd arrived. Now maybe the medics could save the gunman so they could find out what the heck was going on. And soon. It was probably too much to ask to find the person responsible for this attack and get him behind bars so that Gabriel and Jodi could get on with the wedding, but Ivy prayed that would happen. Her brother and Jodi deserved to have their special day.

"Did you love him?" Theo asked.

The sound of his voice cut through her thoughts, and it took Ivy a moment to realize that he probably wasn't talking about Nathan. Of course she loved him. But Theo knew that and was asking about Chad.

"Yes. I did."

In some ways that was a lie, but Ivy wasn't about to get into that now. Besides, what Theo probably wanted to know was how she could go so quickly from him to another man. Especially when she'd had Theo's child. But it was because of Nathan that she'd agreed to marry Chad. Once Theo got past the initial kick of anger, she'd maybe tell him more.

More that he wasn't going to want to hear.

"Does it look as if the gunman is still alive?" Ivy said. It was definitely time for a change of subject, because whatever was going on outside that window was critical to their situation. A situation that didn't necessarily have to include Theo.

He nodded. "The guy's moving, clutching his chest."

Probably because he was bleeding and in pain. She wasn't certain of the details of his injury, but Ivy had heard Gabriel's quick phone chat that he'd had with Jameson.

And now she moved on to the part about Theo not having to be in Nathan's or her life. "For the record, I don't expect anything from you," Ivy continued a moment later. "We were practically kids when I got pregnant, and the feelings you once had for me are obviously long gone."

Theo gave her a look that could have frozen the hottest levels of Hades. "I'm not leaving," he spat out. He stared at her as if he might repeat it, but then he shook his head. "I just need to stop whoever sent those thugs, and then I can deal with everything else."

That sounded like some kind of threat. And Ivy wasn't immune to it. She'd never had to share her son with anyone. Not even Chad, who had been a "father" in name only, had been able to spend much time in the parent roll because of his health problems. She didn't feel ready to share Nathan with Theo, either.

"Yeah, we were kids," Theo went on, "but we sure as hell aren't kids now." He paused again, those jaw muscles stirring like crazy. "You should have found a way to tell me."

Ivy huffed. "You can say that now," she argued. "But we were in a different mind-set back then. Remember?"

"Of course I remember. Your mom caught us in bed. Your dad blew a fuse when she told him, and he ordered me to stay away from you. That should have been the time you backed me up, but you didn't. You agreed with him and told me to get out of the house."

Ivy had indeed told Theo to leave, but she darn sure hadn't agreed with her father. Sherman Beckett could be a hard man sometimes, and he hadn't approved of Theo and his minor run-ins with the law. Ironically, her dad had thought Theo would get her pregnant and then run out on her. Strange how all of that had worked out. Strange, too, that Theo had become a lawman, the last thing her father or she would have expected him to become.

"Then you and your brothers actually considered me a suspect in your parents' murders," Theo added. Judging from his tone, that was still an extremely sore spot for him.

It was for her, too.

Because she hadn't stuck up for Theo. That had obviously been the straw that had broken the camel's back. As soon as Theo's name had been cleared, he'd left Blue River.

Ivy was about to put an end to this conversation, or a temporary end at least, but she heard the footsteps in the hall. Both Theo and she pivoted in that direction, and she felt herself gear up for another fight. If a gunman had actually made it into the house, he wasn't getting to Nathan.

"It's me," Jameson called out.

The relief came, but it didn't completely wash away the adrenaline punch she'd gotten when she thought they could be near another attack. A moment later, the door opened, and her brother came in.

Jameson's attention went to her first, and he no doubt saw her tense body. Perhaps saw a whole lot more than that, though, when his gaze shifted to Theo. Then to the bathroom door where he knew Jodi—and Nathan— were waiting. It didn't take Jameson long to piece everything together, and he cursed under his breath.

"Just in case there's a bug in the house, I'll whisper," Jameson said. "How much trouble is this situation with Nathan going to cause the two of you?" he asked. He didn't specifically direct the question to either of them, and neither of them answered.

However, Theo did ask a question of his own, and it was indeed meant for Jameson because he was staring at her brother. "Did the gunman say anything about who sent him and why?" He, too, kept his voice at a whisper.

Ivy figured that he hadn't, but Jameson nodded. He took a deep breath, and that's when she knew this was not going to be good news.

"The gunman died right after the medics put him in the ambulance," Jameson said.

Now Ivy wanted to curse. She didn't. Over the years, motherhood had taught her to rein in the profanity, but still this was a situation that warranted some cursing.

"He didn't know who hired him," Jameson went on. "Or at least that's what he said. According to him, it was all done through a third party. A San Antonio thug everyone just called Mack. I've never heard of him, and I know most of the CIs and other informants in the area. And yeah, I've already made a call about him."

That didn't sound very promising, especially since it wasn't a name her brother knew, but Ivy got the sinking feeling that it wasn't his not knowing Mack that'd put that troubled look on his face.

"The gunman said something else," Jameson continued a moment later. "This Mack hired other men. At least three more." He turned to his sister then. "And, Ivy, they have orders to use whatever means necessary to kill *you*."

Chapter Five

"Ivy's the target?" Theo immediately asked Jameson. He figured it was a question that Ivy wanted answered, as well.

Jameson lifted his shoulder. "That's what the guy said." Like the rest of them, he continued to keep his voice at a whisper. "That doesn't mesh with what the CI told you, though, does it?"

Theo had to shake his head. "But maybe the person behind this changed his mind and decided to go after one of us at a time. He or she might think Ivy would be the easiest to pick off."

Ivy made a soft gasping sound, and Theo wished he hadn't voiced that aloud. Still, it was true. Since they didn't know the person's identity or motive, anything was possible.

"Are you okay?" Jameson asked his sister. He gave her arm a soft pat.

She shook her head as if pulling herself out of a trance. "Yes." Ivy fluttered her fingers toward the bathroom. "I just need to check on Nathan."

"Give yourself a couple of minutes," Jameson advised her. "You're as pale as paper right now, and Nathan will pick up on that."

The kid probably would. Then again, Nathan and Jodi both had to be on edge waiting for news.

"Are you okay?" Jameson repeated. Not directed at Ivy this time, but at Theo.

Theo lied with a nod. He was far from okay. His mind was whirling. Hell. He'd thought this would be a quick in-and-out trip back to the Beckett ranch, but there was no way that was possible now.

He had a son.

And if that wasn't enough to get him to stay, someone wanted Ivy dead. Of course, the gunman could have been lying when he'd said that Ivy was the target of would-be assassins, but the attack had been real. Bullets had actually been shot into the house, and even if she was the sole target, that didn't mean others couldn't have been caught in cross fire. Nathan and anyone else could have been killed.

"Look, I know you two have plenty to work out," Jameson went on, "but you need to leave it here for now. Gabriel wants to take everyone to the sheriff's office. The medics will need to take a look at that, too."

It took Theo a moment to realize Jameson meant the cut on Theo's cheek. "I don't want a medic," Theo insisted. "But someone should check on Jodi and Nathan."

It wasn't the first time he'd said his son's name aloud, but for some reason, it hit him like a punch to the gut. Theo actually had to take a moment just to regather his breath.

"Yeah," Jameson mumbled. Whatever the heck that

meant. "You both stay here, pull yourselves together, and I'll go in and talk to Nathan and Jodi. Be ready to leave as soon as Gabriel has the cruisers in place."

Jameson stepped into the bathroom, shutting the door and leaving Ivy and him alone. Since Theo didn't want to keep glaring at her, he turned his attention back to the window so he could watch for the cruisers.

"Why would Gabriel want us to go to the sheriff's office?" she asked, her voice shaky. "Wouldn't it be safer to stay here rather than risk going outside?"

"No. There could be other gunmen in the area. Plus, he probably wants to set up some security measures here." He glanced at her and saw that didn't do anything to ease the tension on her face. "Gabriel knows what he's doing."

Theo hoped that was true, anyway. There was no love lost between Gabriel and him, but Ivy's brother had been sheriff for nearly a decade now. Maybe that meant he knew how to handle an attempted murder investigation along with keeping Ivy and the others safe. Theo had no intentions, though, of just backing off and letting Gabriel run with this. Not when his son's safety was at stake.

"When I first saw Nathan, he asked who I was," Theo reminded her. "He thinks your late husband is his dad?"

She paused a long time, and it was so quiet that Theo could hear Jameson talking in the bathroom. He couldn't hear what the Ranger was saying. Which was a good thing. Because it meant Nathan wouldn't be able to hear what Theo and Ivy were talking about.

"No. Nathan knows the truth," Ivy finally answered.

"Chad was a widower and a lot older than me. He had a college-age daughter, Lacey, when we got married. Lacey told Nathan when he was about six." Her mouth tightened enough to let him know that was a sore subject. "My stepdaughter and I don't get along that well," she added.

Theo made a mental note of the woman's name. Right now, he needed to look at all the angles to figure out who was behind this, and a riled stepdaughter could definitely have motive for putting this together.

Of course, so could Uncle August.

Theo would be contacting him very, very soon.

August had been a thorn in nearly everyone's side since his brother's arrest for the Beckett murders. For whatever reason, August had become Travis's champion of so-called justice even though Travis had never asked him to do that. In fact, from everything Theo had heard, his father had accepted his fate and was willing to spend the rest of his life behind bars.

His phone buzzed, and Theo answered it when he saw Wesley's name on the screen. "I heard about the shooting at the ranch," Wesley greeted. "I'm still in Blue River, so you want me to head out there?"

"No need. The danger seems to be contained. For now, anyway." Theo didn't mention they'd all soon be going to the sheriff's office since this wasn't a whispered phone conversation. If there truly was a bug in the house, he didn't want to tip off the gunmen's boss about them leaving, since that would mean they'd be out in the open, at least for a little while.

"The deputy here got an update from Gabriel," Wesley went on. "The gunmen didn't ID the person who hired them."

"No. But I've got a lead. I'll tell you about it when I see you."

"A lead?" Wesley practically snapped. "Who?"

"The house might be bugged," Theo reminded him. "The info I got might not amount to anything, but it's a start."

"Text me what you have," Wesley added a moment later.

Theo hadn't thought it possible, but Wesley seemed even more on edge than Theo did. "I will." Theo ended the call so he could do that, but the bathroom door opened before he could even get started on the text.

And Nathan came out.

Jameson was in front of him. Jodi, behind. Both still had their guns in hand. Nathan gave Theo a long look, and Theo wondered if the boy recognized their similar features. If so, he didn't say anything. He just hurried to his mom, and Ivy looped her arms around him, pulling him close to her.

"Gabriel wants us in the cruisers," Jameson mouthed to Ivy and him. "Don't take anything with you in case it's bugged."

It was a good precaution, and while Theo wasn't exactly eager to have Ivy or Nathan outside, he understood why they were in a hurry when they followed Jameson out of the room and to the stairs. There wasn't exactly a peaceful, safe feeling in the house right now.

Jodi paused long enough for their gazes to connect, and he saw the questions in her eyes. How was he handling this? It was too long of an answer and one that he couldn't give her with just a mere glance.

When they made it to the front of the house, Theo spotted the two cruisers that were now parked by the porch steps. There was a deputy behind the wheel of one of them and another deputy next to him, but Gabriel was driving the cruiser in front. "Ride with me so we can talk," Gabriel insisted. He motioned for them to get in with him, and he threw open both the back door and the passenger's side.

"Hurry," Jameson reminded them. "Jodi and I will ride in front. Theo, Ivy and Nathan in the back seat."

Jameson didn't have to tell them twice to hurry. Jodi and he took off running, and Theo got Ivy and Nathan moving fast. Nathan ended up in the middle between Ivy and him, and the moment they were buckled up, Gabriel got them out of there. The deputies followed right behind them, no doubt as backup in case there was another attack.

"Is everyone okay?" Gabriel asked.

Gabriel brushed a kiss on Jodi's forehead, and when his sister looked at her soon-to-be husband, Theo could practically see the love in her eyes. Not really a surprise, though. He had always suspected that Jodi was in love with Gabriel, and despite their painful pasts, it appeared that Gabriel felt the same way about her.

Each of them, including Theo, answered or made some kind of sound to indicate they were okay.

"He's not all right," Nathan said, and he motioned toward Theo. "He's bleeding."

Theo didn't exactly thank him for pointing that out,

because Nathan seemed to be alarmed by the blood. Theo hated to add to the boy's anxiety, but he also didn't want anyone to make a fuss about a small cut. At least he thought it was small. He hadn't really had a chance to look at it, but he did know that his cheek was stinging.

Jameson opened the glove compartment, located a small first-aid kit and passed it not to Theo but to Ivy. "Since Theo said he won't see a medic, you make sure he doesn't need stitches."

That request seemed to add to Ivy's anxiety level, but she opened the kit and took out some gauze and antiseptic cream. She reached over Nathan and blotted the gauze against Theo's cut. It wasn't a very manly reaction, but he grunted from the pain.

"When Mom's fixing up my cuts," Nathan said, "I just think about a computer game or my horse, Willow. You have a horse?" he asked Theo.

Theo shook his head, but nearly cursed when that caused Ivy to press harder on his cheek. He decided it was best to keep still. Best not to make direct eye contact with Nathan, either, since it was obvious the boy was curious about him. Soon, Theo would satisfy that curiosity by telling him the truth, that he was his father. But for now, Theo just let Ivy continue to torture him while he kept watch around them.

Other than the cruiser behind them, there were no other vehicles in sight. Theo wanted to keep it like that. If he'd been alone, however, he would have wanted this SOB to come after him. That way, he could stop him and put an end to this.

No one in the car talked about the attack, though

Theo was certain they wanted to do that. Best to wait until Nathan was out of earshot. The boy had already witnessed enough without having the details spelled out for him.

Two men dead.

Countless shots fired.

And a threat still hanging over their heads because this snake might indeed go after Ivy.

Once Ivy was finished cleaning and bandaging the cut, Theo took out his phone and texted a fellow DEA agent in the San Antonio office so they could get started on locating this thug named Mack. He didn't include Wesley on this, but he would fill him in at the sheriff's office. As soon as Theo was certain there were no bugs in the place. It was bad enough that he had Jodi, Nathan and Ivy on the road, but he didn't want anyone else knowing they were on their way to Gabriel's office.

It wasn't that far from the ranch to town, and Gabriel didn't dawdle. He made it there in probably record time, and he pulled the cruiser to a stop at the back door so they could hurry inside. First through the break room and then into Gabriel's office. Even though it was a good twenty feet away from the squad room at the front of the building, Wesley must have heard them, because he came hurrying back.

Ivy automatically stopped, and she pulled Nathan behind her. Jodi rushed to Ivy's side to shield the boy, as well. Jameson and Gabriel reacted, too, by taking aim at the man.

"This is DEA agent Wesley Sanford," Theo explained. "He's the one who gave me the recording from the CI."

That caused Gabriel and Jameson to relax a bit, but Jodi and Ivy still stayed in a defensive posture. Maybe because Wesley didn't exactly have a welcoming expression. Probably because he'd been in law enforcement most of his adult life, first as a San Antonio cop and then as a DEA agent. The man was tall and lanky with a thin face, and he rarely smiled. He certainly wasn't smiling now.

"You said you had a lead," Wesley reminded him, "and that you'd text me."

"*Possible* lead," Theo corrected. He motioned toward Gabriel. "This is Sheriff Beckett and his brother, Ranger Jameson Beckett. Are you certain the building isn't bugged?" he added to Wesley.

"The deputies and I have gone through the place and didn't see anything."

"I'm having the Rangers bring in equipment to check every inch," Jameson volunteered. "They should be here any minute. Until then, anything we say should be in one of the interrogation rooms."

Good idea. There was minimal furniture, and a person wouldn't have had easy access to those rooms to plant a listening device. Normally, the other option would have been to discuss this outside, but there was nothing normal about this situation.

Nathan was a reminder of that.

"Why don't you stay with Nathan here in Gabriel's office?" Theo suggested to Ivy.

She instantly looked torn, and Theo knew why. Ivy wanted to hear anything about the investigation, but she didn't want their son to be part of it. Neither did Theo.

Jodi must have picked up on their wanting to protect Nathan, because she slipped her arm around the boy's shoulders and led him deeper into Gabriel's office.

"I'll wait in here with Nathan," Jodi offered. "I can probably download a movie or book for him."

"Is everything gonna be okay?" Nathan asked, volleying glances at his mom, his uncles and Theo.

"Of course," Ivy jumped in to say. Jodi, Gabriel and Jameson answered similarly.

Nathan settled his attention on Theo. Maybe because he didn't respond to the boy's question. "Will it be okay?" Nathan pressed.

Theo wasn't sure why Nathan wanted to hear his assurance when they'd only met a short while earlier. Maybe Nathan felt the connection? But Theo knew that could be wishful thinking on his part. He certainly felt a connection to his son, and it didn't matter that he hadn't shared the same years with the boy that Ivy had.

"We're all going to work to put a stop to this," Theo finally told him.

Nathan nodded, apparently accepting that as gospel, and he went with Jodi when she led him to Gabriel's desk. Part of Theo wanted to stay so he could just talk to him and get to know him better, but as long as Ivy was in danger, so was Nathan.

Gabriel motioned for them to follow him to one of the interview rooms just up the hall, and once they were inside, Gabriel shut the door. Each of them re-holstered their weapons. Except for Ivy. No holster for her, so she tucked the gun in the back waistband of her jeans.

"One of the gunmen gave us a first name or possibly

a nickname of the person who hired him," Theo told Wesley. "Mack, someone the gunman described as a thug from San Antonio. Ring any bells?"

Wesley repeated the name, and he nodded. "Maybe. There's a bar. A *seedy* bar," Wesley added. "It's owned by a guy whose last name is McKenzie. I can't remember his first name, but he used to work as a bouncer at the place before he bought it." He took out his phone, stepping slightly away from them. "I'll see what I can find."

"I need to check on my own contacts," Jameson said, taking out his phone, as well. "I also need to keep tabs on anything the ME might find on our dead guys. Anything the CSIs might find, too."

Yes, because those gunmen had gotten to the ranch somehow, and that meant they'd maybe left a vehicle in the area. A vehicle that could contain possible clues as to who had hired them and why.

"I'll get to work on ID'ing the guys," Gabriel said. "Once we have that, then we might be able to find a money trail."

Again, it was a good idea, and Gabriel moved as if he might step to the other side of the room to start on that, but he stopped and looked at his sister. Then at Theo. "I don't want any yelling," Gabriel warned Theo.

That didn't sit right with Theo. Of course, nothing much would at this point unless they found the clown who'd orchestrated all of this. But Gabriel wasn't talking about the danger. He was talking about Nathan.

"You don't think I have a right to yell?" Theo asked him.

Gabriel's eyes narrowed for just a moment. "Maybe.

But it won't happen here. Anything you and my sister have to hash out can wait."

With that "advice" doled out, Gabriel moved away from them and made a call. Of course, that left Ivy and Theo standing there, staring at each other. Theo knew he had his own calls to make. And he wanted to check on this situation with Ivy's stepdaughter to make sure she didn't hate Ivy enough to do something like that. And Theo did pull his phone from his pocket, but Ivy spoke before he could make a call.

"Don't tell Nathan that you're his father," she said. "Let me do it, please."

Theo thought about that for a few moments. "What will you say to him?"

"The truth. More or less," she added. "I don't want to get into specifics. I'll just tell him that it didn't work out between us."

He gave that more thought, too. "I don't want him to think I knew about him and then left. I'm not the bad guy in all of this."

Something flashed through her eyes. Not anger. But hurt. Theo wished he'd phrased that better, but it was the truth. There was only one person who knew Ivy was carrying Theo's child, and that was Ivy herself.

Ivy nodded, finally. "I'll tell him I screwed up," she said, dodging his gaze. But she didn't do the dodging before he saw something else in her eyes.

Tears.

Hell. It was too bad Gabriel hadn't added "no crying" along with the "no yelling." Theo wasn't an ice man—not every day, anyway—and those tears cut away at him. They also brought memories back to the surface. Ivy had been crying the night she'd ended things with him. He hadn't wanted to hold her and comfort her then. Too much anger had been bubbling up inside him. But for some stupid reason he wanted to try to comfort her now.

He resisted.

In part because it truly would be stupid to have her back in his arms and also because her brothers were watching her. Jameson and Gabriel were both on their phones, but they had their attention nailed to their kid sister.

Gabriel finished his call first and came back to them, and judging from his expression he looked ready to blast Theo for making Ivy cry. But Ivy gave a little shake of her head, a gesture for her brother to back off. Gabriel did—eventually.

"They got an immediate match on one of the gunmen's prints," Gabriel explained several long moments later. "Ted Mintor. He has a long record, and they're looking for a match on the second one."

Good. A name could lead them to possible bank records. From what Theo could hear of Jameson's conversation, he was already working on that.

"I'm having the hands beef up security at the ranch," Gabriel went on. He was looking at his sister now. "I'm debating whether to go back there or move Nathan, Jodi and you to a safe house."

"Jodi won't go," Theo quickly said.

Gabriel didn't argue with that. Probably because he knew Jodi well. Jodi was a well-trained security specialist and would consider it an insult if she was tucked away while others were in danger. But maybe Theo could put a different spin on this to get her to go.

"What if Jodi realizes she'd be protecting Ivy and Nathan if she went?" Theo asked.

Gabriel nodded. "That could work. It'd also work if you went with them. That way, I wouldn't have to tie up a deputy."

Theo felt as if Gabriel had just turned the tables on him. He did want to be with Ivy and Nathan. He wanted to protect them. But it would be hard to find the person behind this if he was shut away in a safe house.

Before Theo could respond to Gabriel, Wesley finished his call and joined them. Theo could tell from the agent's expression that he'd learned something.

Something that Theo might not like.

"I just had a tech do a computer search on our person of interest," Wesley explained. "Birch McKenzie. Like I said, he owns a bar in San Antonio, and it's not exactly a five-star place. When I was a beat cop, we were always getting calls to go out to the place. Anyway, SAPD's bringing in McKenzie now for questioning, but the tech found an interesting connection. To you," he added, looking at Theo.

Theo shook his head and was certain he'd never heard the man's name before today. "You think I know McKenzie?"

"No. But your uncle August does." Wesley paused, his mouth tightening. "August lent McKenzie the money to buy the bar."

Gabriel mumbled some profanity under his breath

and took out his phone again. "I'll get August in here right away for questioning. And he'd better have the right answers."

Chapter Six

Ivy tried to put on a brave face for her son's sake, but she felt none of that braveness inside her. She was terrified, not for herself but for Nathan. He was much too young to be caught up in the middle of this.

"How much longer do we have to be here?" Nathan asked her. Considering they'd been at Gabriel's office for well over an hour, she was surprised he hadn't asked that sooner. Maybe, though, that was because he'd been interested in the movie Jodi had downloaded for him.

"We'll be able to leave soon," Ivy told him, and hoped it wasn't a lie. Actually, she wasn't certain how long it would take Gabriel to set up a safe house.

One where Nathan, Jodi and she would apparently be going. With Theo. That caused her stomach to tighten even more than it already was. Because there was little chance that Theo would keep the truth from Nathan much longer.

"But what about Aunt Jodi and Uncle Gabriel's wedding?" Nathan pressed. He yawned. No surprise there, since it was a little past his nine o'clock bedtime. Plus, it'd been the day from Hades what with the attack.

"We might have to delay that a day or two," Jodi answered. She was in the corner of Gabriel's office, working on a laptop. Theo was in the other corner, doing the same. All of them waiting for the deputy to bring in August.

Nathan made a sound of disappointment. In his case it was probably because he'd been expecting cake and party food. But Ivy figured what he felt was a drop in the bucket compared to what Jodi and Gabriel did. They'd waited a long time for this wedding, and now it might have to be delayed indefinitely.

Jodi stood, stretching, and she set the laptop aside. "I'm getting a bottle of water. Anyone else want one?"

Theo, Nathan and Ivy shook their heads. Gabriel had already brought in burgers from the café just up the street, and the only one who'd touched any of it was Nathan. Nothing seemed to dampen his appetite.

Jodi stepped out, closing the door behind her. A precaution no doubt, so that Nathan wouldn't be able to hear anything that was being said in the squad room where Gabriel, Jameson, Wesley and two deputies were working.

"It's like there are a bunch of secrets going on," Nathan said, snagging both Ivy's and Theo's attention. Nathan looked at both of them, probably waiting for them to verify that.

They didn't.

Mumbling something she didn't catch, her son got up from the desk and went to the small bed that Ivy had made for him on the floor. Basically, it was a couple of blankets and a pillow that she'd gotten from the break room. It wouldn't be long before Nathan was sacked out—which was a good thing, considering the loud voice she heard out in the squad room.

Not August Canton.

But it was a familiar voice.

"Lacey," Ivy provided when Theo looked at her.

Ivy got up, and with Theo in front of her, they stepped into the hall. Yes, it was her stepdaughter all right, though it was hard for Ivy to think of Lacey as any kind of daughter since they were practically the same age.

"You did this," Lacey snapped the moment her attention landed on Ivy.

Ivy first checked on Nathan. He was indeed going to sleep, so once Jodi was back in the office with him, Ivy pulled the door shut so this wouldn't disturb him. The trick, though, would be to keep Lacey's voice in the normal range. She looked ready to start yelling.

Gabriel stepped in front of Lacey, but she just tried to go around him. "I want to have a little chat with Mommie Dearest. Because of her, the cops want to talk to me."

"And *I* want to talk to you," Theo snarled right back, and there was no shred of friendliness in his tone.

Lacey peered around Gabriel, and the moment she actually looked at Theo, her eyes widened a little. She didn't smile exactly, but it was close.

"Theo Canton," Lacey provided.

Because Theo's arm was against Ivy's, she felt him tense a little. "How do you know me?"

"I've made it my business to know you and anyone else associated with my dad's wife. Your name and picture were in the papers. You were a suspect in the murders of Ivy's parents." The slight smile stayed on her face.

And Ivy knew why. Even though she'd never told Lacey about Nathan's father, Lacey could no doubt see the resemblance. Of course, the papers that'd covered the murders had gone into the fact that Theo and Ivy had broken up that night and that was his possible motive for murder. It wouldn't be a stretch for Lacey to do the math and realize that Nathan had been born nine months later.

"So," Lacey said, dragging that out a few syllables. Her attention stayed fixed to Theo. "What'd you want to see me about?"

He went closer. "Someone tried to kill us. What do you know about that?"

Despite Theo's harsh tone, Lacey hardly reacted. Instead, she turned to Ivy. "You put him up to this. You want him to suspect me of something I didn't do so you can get me out of the way. Well, it won't work. I'm not stopping the fight to get what's rightfully mine."

Ivy groaned softly. "Chad left everything to Nathan and me in his will," she explained to Theo.

"Because you brainwashed him," Lacey insisted. "I've filed a lawsuit to rescind his will and give me what's rightfully mine."

"Your father didn't want you to have that money," Ivy reminded her. This was old news to Lacey, but Ivy repeated it, anyway. "He thought you already had too much from your mother's trust fund and that you needed to learn some responsibility."

Lacey cursed. "You don't know me, and you don't

have a right to say anything like that to me. He was my dad."

"And he was my husband," Ivy pointed out just as quickly.

"Are you here for your interrogation?" Gabriel asked when Lacey opened her mouth, no doubt to return verbal fire.

Lacey gave him a withering look. "By you? I think not. You're Ivy's brother. And not you, either," she added to Theo. "I won't have Ivy's ex-boyfriend trying to pin something on me."

"What about me?" Wesley asked, standing. "I'm not related to Ivy or Theo. And the sooner you answer questions, the sooner we can clear your name. Or maybe you'd rather I take you into custody now and drive you back to my San Antonio office."

Maybe in that moment it occurred to Lacey that it hadn't been a good idea to come storming into a sheriff's office with wild accusations against the sheriff's sister. She was almost certainly weighing her options, and considering her expression, she didn't like any of them.

"I'm not talking to anyone unless my lawyer is here," Lacey concluded.

"Then you'd best be calling him or her right now," Gabriel said, and he added a glare to it.

Lacey glared back. Cursed. But she took out her phone to make the call to her attorney.

"Get her into the other interview room," Gabriel told Wesley and Jameson. "She can wait for her lawyer there."

When Gabriel looked out the window, Ivy followed

his gaze and realized why there'd been some urgency in her brother's order. That's because August had just gotten out of his car and was making a beeline for the sheriff's office.

Round two was about to hit.

Wesley and Jameson had barely enough time to get Lacey out of there before August came waltzing in. Ivy braced herself for August to unleash some anger on Theo. After all, August had always said that Jodi and Theo hadn't done nearly enough to help clear their father's name. But unlike Lacey, there was no anger on August's face or in his body language.

"Ivy," August greeted. "Welcome home. It's been a long time."

Yes, it had been. Ten years. She would never be able to make her brothers understand why she'd cut them out of her life. Sometimes, she didn't understand it, either.

August was the same as he had been ten years ago, and he still didn't look as if he ran his brother's ranch. He dressed more like a rich businessman, emphasis on the rich. And he was. In fact, he probably had as much money or more than Ivy's family thanks to August's wealthy mother, who'd died shortly after marrying Travis's father and giving birth to August. Travis, on the other hand, had been a cowboy. One with a drinking problem. And despite the fact that August and Travis had been as different as night and day, that hadn't stopped August from spearheading the fight to clear Travis's name.

August turned to Theo next, and while Ivy wasn't sure how the man would react, she certainly hadn't expected him to go to Theo and hug him. Clearly, Theo hadn't expected it, either, because she saw him go stiff.

"Good to have you home, Theo," August said.

Ivy was instantly suspicious. August had always been somewhat of a hothead, and from everything Ivy had heard from Jodi, August had plenty of resentment for Theo.

"Will you be seeing your dad?" August asked when he stepped back from that hug.

"No," Theo said without hesitation.

Now there was that flash of anger in August's eyes that she'd been expecting. He aimed some of that anger at her. "Then why are you here?" August didn't wait for him to answer. "Oh, I get it. You came for Jodi's wedding. That figures. Instead of her saying 'I do,' you two should be helping me. Did you know your dad has been stuck in prison all this time?"

Ivy knew that, of course, but it caused her breath to go thin just thinking about it. She wanted Travis to pay for her parents' murders, but nothing they did now, including Travis spending the rest of his life behind bars, would bring them back.

"I know," Theo answered. "But he was convicted of murder."

More anger went through August's eyes. "On circumstantial evidence. Heck, he doesn't remember anything about that night, and that's why it was so easy for the Becketts to pin this on him."

Since there were three Becketts in the room, August obviously didn't mind letting them know he thought they had railroaded his brother. They hadn't. She started to remind him that when Travis had been found that night, he'd had her father's blood on him. But August knew that, too, and he probably thought they'd planted it there.

Or else maybe August had been the one to do the planting.

"There was another attack at the ranch," Ivy said.

August nodded. "Yeah, whenever somebody goes after you or your kin, your brothers start hauling me in for questioning. They have this warped notion that if I kill one of them, or you, then it'll get Travis out of jail. It won't. The only thing that'll do that is for the truth to come out."

Both Jameson and Gabriel huffed as if this were old news. It gave her a glimpse of what they'd been having to deal with for the past decade.

"So, is that why you told me to come?" August went on. "Because you want to pin this latest attack on me?"

"Yes," Theo readily admitted. "Did you have anything to do with it?"

August tossed him a glare before he gave one to Gabriel, Jameson and her. "No. Of course not." He turned to Theo to finish that. "Your father loves both your sister and you. Why, I don't know, since you rarely go to see him. But if I were going to do something to help him, it wouldn't be by harming one of you."

Gabriel stepped closer to August. "Then explain your connection to the man who hired the two gunmen who came after us."

No glare this time. August's eyes widened. "What the hell are you talking about?"

"Birch McKenzie," Gabriel said.

Ivy carefully watched August's reaction. First, there was more surprise, and then he cursed. "Birch didn't hire those men. Someone's setting him up, and by doing so, they're setting me up, too." He cursed again, snapped back to Theo. "I wouldn't have done this."

August was so adamant about it that Ivy almost believed him. Almost. But then she remembered that his loyalty wasn't to anyone but his brother. Why, she didn't know. Since Travis was a lot older than August, maybe he saw Travis as more of a father than a half brother. Of course, there was another reason, too.

August had had motive to kill her parents.

Like Theo and Travis, August had also had a recent run-in with Ivy's father. August hated him, and there'd been a long feud between them over land rights. Maybe August had killed them, and if so, his guilty conscience could be causing him to do everything humanly possible to free his brother from jail.

That wasn't a new theory, either. Both of her brothers had been investigating it, especially now that the threatening letters and emails had started. Someone was sending those, and it wasn't Travis since he didn't have computer access in his maximum-security cell. Also, his mail was being monitored.

While August stood there still mumbling profanity, the door to Gabriel's office opened. Both Ivy and Theo instantly looked over their shoulders to see Jodi pulling Nathan back into the room.

"Sorry," Jodi said to them. "He woke up and got to the door ahead of me."

"Mom?" Nathan rubbed his eyes and yawned. "When can we leave?"

"Soon," Ivy assured him, and Jodi took him back into the office and shut the door.

But not before August had gotten a glimpse of her son.

Just as Theo and everyone else had done, August saw the resemblance, and he smiled. He moved as if he might go to Nathan, but both Theo and she stepped in front of him.

"So, I guess things weren't as over between you two as you thought," August said. "Are you two back together?"

"No," Theo and she said in unison. It was Theo who continued. "I came back because I got a warning about an attack at the Beckett Ranch. Ivy could be the target." He leaned in closer. "But if she's the target, then her son is in danger, too."

"Your son," August corrected.

Theo didn't confirm that. Didn't deny it, either. "If Travis really doesn't want Jodi and me hurt, then how do you think he would feel about someone harming that little boy?"

Travis's grandson. Theo didn't spell that out, but August clearly understood what Theo was saying. And his eyes narrowed again.

"What will it take to convince Jodi and you that I'm not behind the attacks?" August asked.

"Proof," Theo said. "Proof of who's doing this. And if it's not you, then I'll owe you an apology. For now, though, you have some questions to answer."

"Questions that I'll be asking in the interview room," Gabriel stated, and he motioned for August to follow him.

Thank goodness Jodi had shut the door so that August couldn't get another glimpse of Nathan. It wasn't pettiness on her part. Ivy just didn't want her son to be exposed to his great-uncle until she was certain August was indeed innocent.

Theo looked at her. The kind of look that asked if she was okay. She wasn't. Her nerves were right there at the surface, and Theo must have seen that, because he muttered some profanity under his breath.

"Why don't we go ahead and take Ivy, Nathan and Jodi to the safe house," Jameson suggested. As they'd done in the house, he kept his voice at a whisper.

"It's ready?" Ivy asked.

Jameson nodded. "Just don't expect too much. I didn't have a lot of time to put it together."

Ivy was about to say she didn't care about that, but then it hit her. "What if Nathan gets hurt because of me?" she asked. "The gunman said I was the target."

"And he could have been lying," Theo pointed out just as quickly. He huffed. "I'd rather Nathan and you not be under the same roof as our suspects."

He had a point. Of course, the real culprit could be out there, waiting for them to leave so he or she could attack again. Maybe it was someone who wasn't even on their radar. Her parents' murders had drawn a lot of press, and it was entirely possible this was a sicko who'd glommed on to them. A sicko who was not only sending threatening emails and letters, but a person who could also hire thugs to kill them.

"I'll pull the cruiser up to the back door," Jameson

offered. "Once I have all of you settled, then I can come back here and help Gabriel with the interrogations."

Jameson headed off to do that, but before he made it into the hall, his phone buzzed. "SAPD," her brother said, looking at the screen.

He took the call but didn't put it on speaker. Since this could be an update on the case, Ivy decided to wait to go in and tell Jodi and Nathan about plans to leave for the safe house. She couldn't hear Jameson's conversation, but whatever the caller had said to him, it caused Jameson's forehead to bunch up.

"What?" Jameson snapped a moment later. He paused, listening. "You're sure?"

Ivy glanced at Theo to see if he knew what was going on, but he only shook his head.

"Birch McKenzie's dead," Jameson said when he finally ended the call. "Murdered. A gunshot wound to the head."

Ivy hadn't known the man, of course, but he'd been the link between the gunmen and the person who'd hired them. A link, too, to August.

"Who killed him?" Theo asked.

"SAPD doesn't know. They went out to question him about his possible involvement in this, and they found him dead. The cops also found his phone, and they glanced through his recent calls. The last call he made was to one of our suspects."

"August," Ivy muttered.

But Jameson shook his head. "No, McKenzie called Lacey."

Chapter Seven

As little sleep as Theo had managed to get, he figured
Ivy had gotten even less. After they'd arrived at the
safe house, she'd quickly taken Nathan to the room they
would share, but since Theo's room was right next to
theirs, he'd heard someone moving around in there most
of the night. He figured that someone was Ivy.

He showered and made his way into the kitchen to
get some coffee started, but got confirmation that Ivy
hadn't slept when he saw her at the kitchen table already
sipping a cup. Her eyes confirmed his theory, too. She
looked exhausted.

And beautiful.

Yeah, Ivy was probably one of the few women on
the planet who could have managed that. Despite her
rumpled hair and tired eyes, she still looked amazing.

He felt that old ripple of attraction. Always did whenever he was around her. But he told that attraction to
take a hike. It would only distract him at a time when
he needed no other distractions. And besides, he still
hadn't cooled off from her not telling him about Nathan.

"Are Jodi and Nathan still sleeping?" he asked.

She nodded. "But I figure they'll be up soon. Anything new on the case?" she added. "I heard you talking on the phone a couple of times."

He had, but Theo felt he'd gotten nowhere. "Gabriel questioned Lacey, and she denied knowing McKenzie. Lacey said he called her to set her up."

Ivy groaned, and Theo silently groaned with her. With his coffee in hand, he went to the window to look out. The safe house was on an old ranch, only about thirty miles from Blue River, and it was out in the middle of nowhere. Which was a good thing. The pastures were flat, and he had a clear view of the road. That meant it'd be hard for someone to sneak up on them. Added to that, Jameson had put out a motion detector on the road to alert them if anyone drove up.

"Lacey lawyered up," Theo went on. "So did August. And Gabriel doesn't have enough to hold either of them. That means we're at a stalemate unless SAPD or the CSIs find something to link the attack or McKenzie's murder to someone."

Someone in this case being August or Lacey.

And that brought Theo back to something he'd been wanting to ask Ivy. "Just how much does Lacey hate you?"

She looked at him for a moment before she answered. "A lot. Why?"

He lifted his shoulder. "Lacey said she made it a point to get to know anyone connected to you. It's a long shot, but she could have discovered the link between August and McKenzie."

He was talking softly enough not to wake Jodi and

Nathan, and Ivy got up from the table to go closer to him, probably so she'd be able to hear him better.

"But if she wanted to set up August to take the blame for this," Ivy said, "then why would she have allowed McKenzie to call her?"

"Maybe she didn't allow it. He could have just screwed up. Or it could be he got spooked when he realized someone was trying to kill him and he tried to get in touch with her. Either way, McKenzie would have been a loose end."

That was true even if Lacey or August wasn't behind this. McKenzie had a link to two dead gunmen, and the mastermind pulling their strings wouldn't have wanted to keep McKenzie around.

"August's motive is to clear Travis's name," Ivy whispered. "But Lacey won't inherit her father's money if she kills me." She made a soft gasp and touched her fingers to her mouth. "She'd have to get rid of Nathan, too."

That wiped away the fatigue in Ivy's eyes, and the fear quickly came. Theo had had a similar reaction earlier when he'd thought of how this might all play out.

"God, she can't hurt him," Ivy said on a rise of breath. Tears sprang to her eyes.

Hell. He didn't handle these tears any better than he had the ones the night before at the sheriff's office. This time, though, Theo put his arm around her.

Ivy melted against him.

That definitely wasn't good because she felt soft—and right—in his arms. The years vanished, and for a few seconds, she was his lover again. Thankfully, it didn't go past the thought stage because Ivy pulled away from him.

"Sorry," she said, her voice low. He wasn't sure if she was apologizing for the tears or the reaction they'd just had to each other. And Theo decided it was best if he didn't have the answer to that.

"I'm not going to let anything happen to Nathan," Theo promised her, and somehow that was a promise he'd keep.

She stayed at the window with him, and her gaze connected with his again. "Is there something you aren't telling me?" she asked. "You're not thinking of telling Nathan the truth, are you?"

That was two unrelated questions. "Nathan will eventually need to know," he reminded her.

She kept staring at him. "But?"

"It can wait a little while longer."

He was pretty sure the breath she blew out was one of relief. "Then what's wrong?"

"It's maybe nothing." And that's why Theo hated to even say it aloud. Still, it was bothering him. "It's about Lacey and Wesley. By any chance, did she ever mention him?"

"No." Ivy had the reaction that Theo expected. Confusion and surprise. "Why?"

"Wesley didn't even ask who Lacey was when she came into the sheriff's office. At that point, we weren't expecting her."

"Yes," she agreed after several moments. "But you don't think Wesley could be behind the attack?"

Theo certainly didn't want to believe it, but he just

couldn't shake this feeling. "I've worked with Wesley a long time. In fact, we were teamed up on our last case where a fellow DEA agent was murdered."

She shook her head. "You believe the attack last night could somehow be connected to that?"

Theo scrubbed his hand over his face. "If it is, I can't see it."

That didn't mean he would stop looking, though. He would also be more careful about the info he got from Wesley. After all, it was Wesley's intel about the impending attack that had sent Theo running to the ranch.

"I called a DEA friend this morning," Theo explained. "His name is Matt Krueger, and he's someone I know I can trust. I asked him to look for any connections between Lacey and Wesley. Between Wesley and any of this," he added.

"But why would Wesley want to go after you?" she pressed. "Why would he want to go after you like this?" Ivy amended. "By including our families?"

"This is just a guess, but the attack last night could be the ultimate smoke screen, a way of making sure no suspicion fell on Wesley."

Still, that didn't answer one big question.

Why?

Was it somehow connected to the botched investigation and death of the DEA agent? Theo had spent hours going over every transcript and all the surveillance footage he could get his hands on, and even though he couldn't see anything wrong, he felt it. Deep in his gut. Something about all of it wasn't right.

"Are you thinking that Wesley could be dirty?" she asked.

He had to shrug. "That whole undercover operation had hitches right from the start," Theo explained. He couldn't give her some details because they were classified, but he could tell her the big picture. "There was a militia group dealing arms and drugs, and some of those came from a cache of weapons that'd been seized in a federal raid. The agent who was killed was at the heart of both the bust to seize those weapons and the undercover operation of the militia group."

And now that the agent was dead, there was no way he could answer the questions that were eating away at Theo.

"God," she said. "If Wesley had anything to do with this…"

"Wesley doesn't know the location of the safe house," Theo told her when he realized all of this had put the alarm back in her eyes. "Only Jameson, Gabriel and the four of us know. And just in case something else goes wrong, if someone did manage to follow us, Jameson is working on setting up a second safe house. A backup."

The sound of footsteps stopped him from saying anything else, and Theo automatically slid his hand over his gun in his holster. But it wasn't a threat. It was Nathan.

"Aunt Jodi's taking a shower," he greeted. "Is there any cereal and milk? I'm hungry."

Ivy went to the counter, where there were bags of groceries and supplies, and she rummaged through them. "No cereal, but there are some granola bars."

Nathan didn't seem disappointed with that, and he

opened the fridge to take out the carton of milk. Since he couldn't reach the cabinet and because Ivy was opening the box of granola bars, Theo got a glass for him and set it on the table. Nathan poured himself a glass, all the while keeping his attention on Theo.

"I'm not dumb, you know," Nathan said. "I heard Aunt Jodi and Uncle Gabriel on the phone. She was whispering, but I heard her." He had a big drink of the milk. "You're my dad, aren't you?"

Even though Theo could feel the question coming, it was still a shock to hear it. A shock for Ivy, too, because she stood there, her hand frozen while she reached out to give Nathan the granola bar.

"Yeah, I am," Theo answered. He braced himself in case Ivy was going to blast him for revealing that, but she merely put the bar on the table and sank down in the chair next to Nathan.

Nathan nodded. "We look alike. Aunt Jodi said."

His sister was a regular font of information, but Theo couldn't fault her for that. Nathan was her nephew, and with Ivy keeping that a secret, it meant she'd kept Nathan a secret from all of them.

"We do look alike," Theo agreed, and he turned to Ivy to see if she had anything to add to that.

"Are you mad that I didn't tell you?" she asked Nathan.

While he shook his head, he bit off a chunk of the bar. "I knew Dad wasn't my real dad. Lacey told me, remember?"

"I remember." Ivy's jaw was suddenly a little tight.

Theo waited for Nathan to ask more—such as why

Theo hadn't seen him in all this time—but he continued to eat his breakfast as if this were an ordinary day.

"Are those bad men going to find us?" Nathan finally said.

Theo wished they'd stayed on the subject of fatherhood, but he hadn't expected Nathan just to forget the attack. "No. That's why we're in this house. If we have to stay here long, I'll have one of your uncles bring out some cereal for you."

"Thanks." He finished off the last bite of the granola bar and looked up at Theo. "Will you and my mom be together? You know, like some moms and dads?"

Theo was certain he had the same deer-in-the-headlights look as Ivy, but Ivy didn't seem to have trouble finding her voice. "No. But you will get to see Theo if that's what you want."

"Sure." Nathan stood and cleaned up after himself. "Can I go play a game on the computer now?"

Ivy nodded, and she seemed to release the breath she'd been holding when Nathan took off. However, he quickly stopped and whirled back around. "I think Aunt Jodi's a little sad. Because this was supposed to be the day she got married to Uncle Gabriel."

"I'll talk to her," Theo assured him. That was apparently all the answer he needed, because Nathan hurried to the bedroom.

Theo waited to see if Ivy would start to cry again, but she blew out another long breath and sat next to him. "I thought Nathan would take it harder than that."

Theo made a sound of agreement. And since she'd brought it up—and wasn't crying—he pushed the conversation a little. "When this is over, I want to see a whole lot more of Nathan. I want to get to know him."

She stared at him. "But what about your job? You're rarely around."

"True, but that could change. I've been a joe for a long time, and the DEA would probably like to see me behind a desk for a while."

"You'd want to do that?" She made it sound as if he'd be jumping off a cliff.

Nothing so drastic, but it would be a total lifestyle change for him. One that Theo hadn't thought he'd ever want to make. Then again, he'd never thought he would have a son, either.

"I'm not walking away from Nathan," he warned her. "He'll get to know me as his father, the way he should have from the start."

He hadn't meant for that to sound so harsh, but it was hard to rein in the emotions when it came to the boy. Ivy held all the emotional cards here. She had the history and connection with their son. He was going to have to build it from the ground up.

"Gabriel, Jodi and Jameson will want to spend time with him, too," Theo went on. "After all, Nathan is their only nephew." And he waited for her to dismiss that or accept it.

One way or another, Ivy was going to have to accept it.

He didn't have to wait long. She gave another of those weary sighs. "I didn't plan to keep Nathan from my brothers or Jodi. Or from you. It all got mixed up into one giant mental mess. The murders. Our breakup. Jodi nearly dying. Gabriel and Jameson weren't in a good place mentally, and they had their hands full with the investigation. When I suspected I might be pregnant, I decided to leave." She paused. "They honestly didn't know about Nathan. I made sure they didn't know."

Because Gabriel and Jameson would have gone after her and tried to bring her home. He got that.

"And you didn't stay around, either," she reminded him.

No, he hadn't. "I had to get away, too." He'd had his own mental mess to deal with. "I kept thinking I should have been there to protect Jodi. I shouldn't have let that monster nearly knife her to death. That got mixed up with me being a suspect. Then my father's arrest."

Ivy stayed quiet a moment. "Do you think Travis is innocent?"

He couldn't give her a simple answer. Because there wasn't one. "I thought he was. Then Jodi and the rest of you started getting those threatening letters and emails. I'm a lawman, so I had to look at it from the angle that maybe the real killer was doing this so he could taunt you."

"Or it could be August trying to create doubt for his brother," she quickly pointed out.

Yes, that was more than possible. Still, he doubted his father would have gone along with a plan if it'd actually endangered either the Beckett children or Jodi and him. That meant there was still the possibility of a real killer out there or someone with a sick obsession about all of this.

Theo's phone buzzed, and he saw DEA agent Matt

Krueger's name on the screen. He answered the call while he went to the window to have a look outside.

"Please tell me you found something about that militia raid I was asking about," Theo greeted.

Matt hesitated a moment. "Yes, that. I did go over everything, and I see what you mean about maybe the pieces not fitting. I'm thinking someone could have tipped off the militia about agents having infiltrated them."

That's what Theo had considered as well, but it still twisted at him to think that a fellow agent could have done that. "Is there any proof?"

"Maybe. I just went through the surveillance footage we have, and Wesley made a call about thirty minutes before the attack. Since he was using a prepaid cell, there's no way to trace it. Any idea who he called?"

"None." In fact, that was the point in the assignment, when he, Wesley and the agent who'd died—Ross Callahan—should have been keeping watch for an arms shipment that was about to come in.

"I think it's time for me to ask Wesley about this," Theo added. "I'll give him a call—"

"You haven't heard?" Matt interrupted.

"Heard what?" Theo asked.

"I just got the news a couple of minutes ago. Gabriel apparently took Wesley into custody. Don't know the details yet, but the sheriff found some kind of evidence to link Wesley to those dead gunmen."

Everything inside Theo went still. "What kind of evidence?"

"I'm not sure. Gabriel's holding that close to the vest.

But Wesley claims that you set him up, that you're the one responsible for those gunmen who attacked last night."

Theo cursed. "And why the hell would I have done something like that?"

Matt hesitated again. "Wesley said you did it to get Ivy out of the way so you could get custody of your son."

Chapter Eight

Theo was still cursing under his breath after they got in the cruiser, and even though Ivy hadn't timed it, it'd been well over an hour since his intense phone conversation with Matt Krueger.

During that time, Wesley had accused Theo of attempted murder.

And that's why Theo had immediately started making plans to go to the sheriff's office in Blue River. He did that by arranging for Jameson to come out and stay with Nathan while the deputy, Cameron Doran, drove with Theo as backup into town. Theo and Cameron had been friends since childhood, and Theo trusted him. But Ivy made sure she was in on those plans, too, even though Theo had insisted it wasn't the right thing to do.

Heck, she wasn't sure it was the right thing, either, but she did want to be there when Gabriel interrogated Wesley. And Lacey, as well. Gabriel had had to reschedule her interview so that her lawyer would be there with her.

"If Wesley's the one behind this," Theo said to her,

"then you're not the target. That means there's no reason for you to be there."

Theo had already voiced several variations of that argument to get her to stay at the safe house, and it might be true. The investigation had certainly taken a strange turn, what with Wesley's accusations. Too bad that it might take them a long time to sort it out.

Time they didn't have.

Nathan was okay for now at the safe house with Jodi and Jameson, but Ivy hated the thought of him being shut away. Hated more that her little boy was in danger. Maybe they would get some answers, and soon, and put an end to that.

Theo continued to mumble profanity while he read a text. He did that while volleying glances all around them. So did Cameron while he drove them toward town. Thankfully, it was a rural road with no other traffic, so it should be easy to spot someone trying to follow them. Unfortunately, there were plenty of old ranch trails and even some thick woods between the safe house and Blue River. That's the reason Theo had wanted Cameron to make this drive with him.

"SAPD can't find a money trail for McKenzie and either of the dead gunmen," Theo relayed to her once he'd finished reading the text.

It was frustrating but something she'd expected. None of their known suspects would have left that kind of evidence behind.

"What about the phone call McKenzie made to Lacey?" she asked.

Theo shook his head. "SAPD can't even be sure

McKenzie made that call. There were no prints on the phone. It'd been wiped clean."

Ivy huffed. "That means someone could have killed McKenzie and then used his phone to set up Lacey."

"Yep. And Lacey could have done it that way to throw suspicion off herself. That way, if her name did show up on any of McKenzie's other outgoing calls, then she could say she was being framed."

"And she might be," Ivy admitted. "If someone wants us dead, Lacey would be the perfect patsy since she has motive. Well, motive to go after Nathan and me, anyway. But the person behind this could plan to make it look as if the real target was caught in the middle." She paused. "Of course, we don't know who the 'real target' is."

Theo made a sound of agreement. "About how much money does Lacey think she lost out on with the inheritance?" he asked.

"Four million," she answered after a pause.

That got the reaction she expected. Shock. Yes, she'd married a rich, older man. Practically a cliché. But what was missing from that cliché was that Chad had loved her and had taken very good care of Nathan and her.

"Four million is a lot of motive for murder," Theo pointed out. "You said something about your late husband wanting Lacey to learn to be more responsible. I take it they clashed?"

"A lot. Lacey hated me right from the start and thought I was trying to replace her mother. She died of cancer when Lacey was just a little girl. I think she would have resented any woman her dad married, but it didn't help that she and I are so close in age. She probably would have called me a gold digger, but I had my own money."

Not as much as Chad, but it was close.

"Anyway, Chad divided his estate between Nathan and me," Ivy added. "He left Lacey only a small amount that'll remain in a trust until she's forty."

Theo shifted his position a little until their gazes connected. "Chad loved Nathan."

"He did, in his own way. More like an uncle's love than a father's." Chad had loved her, too, but Ivy figured she didn't need to spell that out. She especially didn't need to spell out that she'd never loved the man who had made her his wife.

"Good," he said under his breath just as his phone dinged again with another text message. The texts had been coming in at a steady rate since the earlier call from the DEA agent.

"Wesley brought my boss in on this," Theo read. "He's also demanding that Gabriel take me into custody."

She was betting her brother wasn't going to do that. Well, unless Wesley came up with some kind of evidence that would force Gabriel's hand.

Theo groaned softly. "I didn't do what Wesley said I did."

"I know," Ivy readily agreed. Theo turned toward her, fast, as if he hadn't expected her to dismiss the charges so easily. "You're not the sort to break the law," she added. "Well, not since you were sixteen."

The corner of his mouth lifted into a smile. One that

lasted only a couple of seconds. But it was nice to see it even for that short time. It brought back memories of other smiles, of happier times.

That seemed a lifetime ago.

"My run-ins with the law were petty," he said. "And stupid."

"Yes. I remember the time you and your friends took my dad's tractor apart and reassembled it in the hayloft. Must have taken you hours."

"All night," Theo admitted. "Your dad had warned me not to touch you when I took you out so I wanted to give him a little payback."

Well, it had certainly struck a nerve with her dad, that's for sure. But then her father had never liked Theo. Sherman had thought right from the start that Ivy could do a whole lot better than the likes of Theo Canton.

She hadn't.

In some ways, no man had ever lived up to him. And that wasn't an especially comforting thought. Things between Theo and her were tense. Maybe not as much as they had been just twenty-four hours earlier, but they were a long way from getting over their pasts.

Something they would have to do for Nathan's sake.

"Has anyone gotten in touch with your sister?" Cameron asked Ivy. "Because Lauren could be in danger, too."

Ivy nodded. "Jameson called her. She didn't answer her phone, but then she usually lets any calls from family go to voice mail."

She met Cameron's eyes in the rearview mirror and saw the flicker of emotion. It was gone in a flash and probably something he hadn't wanted her to see. But Ivy could guess what this was about. Cameron had once been in love with her kid sister, and the murders had torn them apart. Just as it'd done to Theo and her. Now, Lauren had built her life far away from Blue River. Far away from family and friends.

"Lauren is taking precautions in case this guy goes after her?" Theo pressed.

"She texted Jameson back and told him she'd be careful. She has a son now, so I'm sure she will do anything to protect him."

Theo glanced at Cameron, and even though neither man said anything, everyone knew that Lauren was still a raw nerve for Cameron. It probably hadn't helped that she'd gotten married and become a mom. A single mom, though, since her husband had died a little over a year ago. Or so Ivy had heard. Lauren hadn't exactly stayed in touch with her, either.

"So many lives got messed up that night the Becketts died," Cameron mumbled. "Lauren blamed me for a lot of that."

She had. And the blame was partially warranted. Cameron had been a rookie deputy at the time, along with being friends with Theo's family. Just a couple of hours before the murders, Cameron had run into Travis drunk outside the town's bar. He'd taken Travis's keys, but he hadn't arrested him for public intoxication. If Cameron had, then Travis would have been locked up, and he couldn't have committed two murders. She doubted Cameron would ever forgive himself for that.

And neither would Lauren.

"What the hell?" Cameron said, getting Ivy's attention. Theo, too.

She followed the deputy's gaze to the road ahead and spotted a blond-haired woman. Ivy didn't recognize her, but she was on the gravel shoulder, her hands in the air as if she were surrendering.

"You know her?" Theo immediately asked Cameron.

"No. She's not local. I have no idea why she's in the road, but I don't think she's carrying a gun."

Ivy agreed, and since the woman was wearing a body-clinging cotton dress, it would have been hard for her to conceal a weapon. Not impossible, though, and that's probably why Theo motioned for Ivy to get down on the seat. She did, but not before trying to get a better glimpse of whatever the heck was going on.

"You see anyone else?" Theo again, and the question was directed at Cameron.

"No," the deputy repeated, and he slowed the cruiser to a crawl. "Keep the windows up," he instructed—probably because they were bullet-resistant. "She doesn't have on any shoes, and her feet are bleeding. It's possible she got stranded by the river or something."

It was the possibility of that "or something" that troubled Ivy, and when Cameron brought the cruiser to a stop, Ivy could see the woman. She still had her hands in the air. And looked dazed. Her hair was a tangled mess, and while Ivy didn't have a view of her feet, there was also blood and what appeared to be a bruise on the right side of her face. What she didn't do was rush forward.

Strange.

After all, they were in a Blue River Sheriff's Department cruiser that was clearly marked, and both Cameron and Theo were wearing their badges.

Cameron called for an ambulance for backup. He did that because he probably wanted a cop to go with her to the hospital. Then he lowered his window just a fraction.

"Are you all right?" he asked her, sounding very much like the lawman that he was.

She shook her head. "I think I was kidnapped."

Yes, definitely strange. A person should know for certain if they were kidnapped or not, but maybe someone had drugged her. Whoever had done that perhaps caused that injury to her face.

"What's your name?" Cameron pressed. "And who kidnapped you?"

Another shake of her head, and a hoarse sob tore from her mouth. "I'm not supposed to be here."

Cameron huffed. "Then where are you supposed to be, and who brought you here?"

Several moments crawled by, and while Theo was watching her, he continued to glance around. Ivy wanted to help him do that, but she knew it would only make him more on edge if she did.

"I'm sorry," the woman said.

"For what?" Cameron snapped.

But she didn't get a chance to answer. That's because a shot cracked through the air and the bullet slammed right into the woman's chest.

THEO DIDN'T SEE the shooter, but he certainly heard the bullet. And he had no trouble seeing the damage it did.

The blonde made a sharp sound of pain, clutched her chest and dropped to the ground. Theo didn't think she was dead, but she soon would be. The blood was already spreading across the front of her dress.

"We have gunfire," Cameron said to whoever he had called. Probably Gabriel, who would in turn have to hold off on sending in an ambulance.

"Can you pull her into the cruiser?" Ivy asked, as she sat up to get a better look at their surroundings.

Theo was already debating doing just that. It would be a risk, but at this point anything they did would be. The woman had clearly been drugged and was probably part of a trap to get them to stop. It'd worked, but if she was truly innocent in all of this, she could die.

He didn't have long to dwell on his decision, though, because there was another sound. A second shot, and this one didn't go into the woman.

It blasted into the window just above Ivy's head. The glass held though it did crack, but it wouldn't hold for long if the shooter kept firing into it.

And that's exactly what he did.

"You see the gunman?" Cameron asked.

"No. But he must be in those trees across the road." The woods were thick there, and even though the morning sun was bright, the light wasn't making it through the dense branches and underbrush.

Who the hell was doing this?

Theo didn't know, but at the moment their best bet for telling them that was lying on the ground, bleeding out.

"Can you open the window on the front passenger's side just enough to return fire?" Theo said to Cameron.

Cameron glanced back at him, and he didn't look any more certain of this than Theo felt. "You're going to get the woman in the cruiser?"

Theo hoped he didn't regret this, but he nodded. "Get down on the floor," he instructed Ivy. That would not only get her a few inches farther from the window, it would free up the seat so he could drag the woman inside.

"Please be careful," Ivy said, the fear and emotion thick in her voice. It was in her expression, too, and Theo would have liked the time to assure her this was the right thing to do, but there was nothing he could say that would take the worry off her face.

Hell, he was worried, too.

Not for himself and Cameron. But for Ivy. If she was indeed the target, then all of this could be designed to get to her.

Several more shots came at them, each tearing through the window next to Ivy. Obviously, the gunmen were focusing on her. Or else the thug wanted them to think she was the focus. Theo wasn't going to take any of this at face value.

Cameron kept the engine running, but he moved to the passenger's window, lowered it just enough to stick out the barrel of his gun and looked at Theo to give him the go-ahead.

Theo nodded.

And Cameron fired.

The moment the deputy did that, Theo threw open

his door, and he glanced over his shoulder to make sure Ivy was still down. She was. But she was watching him and mumbling something. A prayer, from the sound of it.

Theo moved as fast as he could and hoped he didn't do any more damage to the injured woman when he latched onto her arm and started dragging her to the cruiser. The shots didn't stop. In fact, the gunman picked up the pace, and this time he fired at Theo. The bullets slammed into the ground, kicking up the gravel that was on the shoulder.

The woman cried out in pain, and that's when Theo realized she'd been hit again. This time in the shoulder. Theo hadn't needed any more incentive to move as fast as he could, but that did it.

And he got some help.

Unwanted help.

Ivy scrambled over the floor of the cruiser, and the moment Theo was back at the door, she reached out and helped him drag the woman inside. By doing that, she put herself in even greater danger. Later, Theo would tell her what a stupid thing that was to do, but then he saw the bullets slam into the ground where he'd just been. If Ivy hadn't helped, he could be dead.

"Get us out of here," Theo said to Cameron as soon as he had the woman on the seat.

Cameron was already moving to do that, and as soon as he was back behind the wheel, he hit the accelerator.

The cruiser sped away as the bullets continued to rip through the window.

Chapter Nine

Ivy tried to force herself to focus. There was a lot going on at the Blue River sheriff's office, but she couldn't grasp it all. That probably had to do with the spent adrenaline that had left her exhausted.

Too bad the exhaustion hadn't stopped the sound of the gunshots from echoing in her head. Or stopped the fear that was still racing through her. Mercy, she wanted that gone most of all, because at the moment most of those fears were for her son.

The gunman who'd fired those shots had gotten away. And it wasn't as if no one had looked for him. Gabriel had sent out two deputies almost immediately, but by the time they'd arrived, there'd been no sign of him. That meant the man was out there, probably waiting to attack. Or worse, waiting to follow them to the safe house where Nathan was with Jameson and Jodi.

"How did the gunman even know we'd be on that stretch of the road?" she asked. It wasn't the first time she'd wanted to know that, and Ivy didn't direct the question at anyone in particular.

Theo, however, put away his phone after making

his latest call and went to her. He skimmed his hand down her arm, probably a gesture to try to comfort her, but Ivy figured nothing much was going to soothe her right now.

"There are only two roads leading into Blue River," Theo reminded her. "There could have been a gunman on both."

Yes. And that meant there could have been another woman or hostage to force them into stopping. Or coerced. If so, Ivy hoped they found the person, and the thugs hadn't done to him or her what they'd done to the woman they'd encountered. She couldn't imagine that someone had volunteered to be shot as part of the plan to lure her out into the open.

"Jameson is on full alert," Theo went on. "If anyone tries to get near the safe house, he'll let us know."

She didn't doubt that. Didn't doubt that her brother and Jodi would be vigilant. But this monster could still get to them.

"I just want to rush back to Nathan," she said. Ivy cursed the tears that she was having to blink back. Tears weren't going to help this, and they only put more stress on Theo because it was obvious he was concerned about her. Ivy quickly waved that off. "But I don't want to lead the guy straight to Nathan, either."

Theo nodded to let her know they were on the same page about that. Actually, they were on the same page about several things, and it wasn't all related to the investigation. The attraction that kept rearing its head and the fact that they would do anything to protect their son.

"Any updates on the woman who was shot?" Ivy

asked. Maybe if she talked about the investigation, she could get her mind off Nathan. "Or Wesley?"

Even though the agent was still in the building, he was in an interview room with Gabriel and Theo's boss. Gabriel hadn't wanted Theo to be part of that, maybe because he now had Theo on his suspect list. Even if he hadn't been a suspect, though, it could still compromise things since Wesley and he were fellow agents.

"There's nothing on Wesley," Theo answered, "but whatever he's telling Gabriel is a lie. I didn't have anything to do with this."

"I know," she assured him, and it wasn't lip service. Theo wouldn't do anything to harm Nathan and her. And no, that wasn't the attraction talking. Now, though, she might have to convince Gabriel of Theo's innocence—something she hadn't tried to do ten years ago. That was a mistake she didn't intend to make again.

"As for the woman, I just talked to a doctor at the hospital, and she's still alive," Theo went on. "That's the good news. But she'd been heavily drugged, and one of the gunshot wounds is serious. She's in surgery."

Ivy already knew the woman hadn't said anything in the cruiser on the drive to the hospital because she was unconscious through the entire trip. She also hadn't moved at all when the medics had taken her away on a gurney. Of course, Theo, Cameron and Ivy hadn't waited around to talk to the doctor. It was too dangerous. Instead, Theo had rushed them to the sheriff's office, where they'd been for the past hour.

"The woman didn't have an ID on her," Theo went on, "so we're not positive who she is. But she matches the description of a woman, Belinda Travers, who went missing the night before. From McKenzie's club."

That got Ivy's attention. "She knew McKenzie?"

He lifted his shoulder. "It's possible she just went into the bar, one of the hired guns saw her and decided to use her as bait."

So she could be innocent in all of this. It sickened Ivy to think of how many people had been hurt—or could be hurt—and they didn't know why or by who.

"They did a bug sweep of the sheriff's office and the rest of the building while we were at the safe house," Theo said a moment later. "And they found one."

She could have sworn her heart skipped a couple of beats, and the panic came. It was so strong that she nearly bolted for the door so she could go after Nathan. Theo took hold of her arm and anchored her in place.

"It was by the dispatch desk," he explained, "and it's been removed."

The dispatch desk was also Reception. That meant anyone who'd come into the building could have put it there. Heck, it could have been there for weeks or longer.

"Remember, we whispered whenever we talked about the safe house," Theo reminded her.

Yes, they had. Maybe that had been enough to keep those thugs away from her son.

"Come on." Theo still had hold of her, and he got her moving toward the hall. "We can go to the break room and maybe you can get some rest."

Rest was out, but her legs suddenly felt too wobbly to stand. Maybe she could at least sit down and wait for news about when they could return to the safe house. However, they only made it a few steps down the hall when the interview room door opened, and Gabriel stepped out. Judging from her brother's expression, things hadn't gone well. She got further confirmation of that when Wesley and the other man came out.

Dwight Emory.

Even though Ivy hadn't met the man, she knew this was Theo and Wesley's boss. He didn't look especially pleased, either, but then, one of his agents—Wesley— was accusing a fellow agent—Theo—of a crime.

"Well?" Theo prompted when no one said anything.

"We're sorting it out," Emory answered.

"We're not close to sorting it out," Wesley snarled. He nailed a glare to Theo. "How could you do this to me? We've been partners for years. Friends," he amended. "At least I thought we were, and then you start asking questions. You're treating me like a criminal."

Theo huffed, and his hands went on his hips. "Seems to me you're the one who said I wanted Ivy out of the way so I could get Nathan."

"Don't you?" Wesley challenged.

"No." And Theo moved closer to her, sliding his arm around her waist. He probably did that because she wasn't looking so steady, but it was also a signal to Wesley and Emory that the old baggage between them wasn't as toxic as it had once been.

Ivy wasn't sure when that'd happened exactly. Maybe around the time Theo had been trying to save her life.

Theo volleyed glances between Emory and Gabriel.

"What kind of proof did Wesley produce to make an accusation like that against me?"

"A CI told me," Wesley volunteered.

Ivy wasn't sure who gave Wesley the flattest look, but Gabriel, Theo and even Emory weren't jumping to embrace the so-called evidence.

"We're trying to find the CI now," Emory finally said. "If he confirms Wesley's claim, then we'll still have to consider the source." Emory looked at her then. "As you can imagine, CIs aren't always truthful, and this could be a situation of someone wanting to get back at Theo."

"Yeah, Wesley could be doing that," Theo insisted. "Because he might want to get suspicion off himself."

Wesley howled out a protest, but Gabriel made a sound of agreement. "I got the security footage of McKenzie's bar. It's grainy and there are only a few good camera angles—"

"I didn't go there to pay off anybody," Wesley interrupted.

Ivy glanced at Theo to see if he knew what any of this was about, but he only shook his head. "What happened on that footage?" Theo asked Gabriel.

Her brother took a deep breath first. "When Wesley entered the bar, he took out an envelope from his jacket pocket. And, yeah, he was wearing a jacket despite the fact that it was ninety degrees outside. It gets grainy when Wesley goes to a booth in the corner, but it appears he gives the envelope to a known thug by the name of Nixon Vaughn."

Oh, mercy. That wasn't good, and Ivy immediately

wondered if this Vaughn was a hired gun. Maybe the very one who'd attacked them today and shot that woman.

"He's not on payroll for the DEA or any other agency," Emory added.

Theo's jaw was very tight when he turned to Wesley. "Did you pay off Vaughn?"

Wesley's jaw wasn't exactly relaxed, either. "Yes. Because you told me to."

A burst of air left Theo's mouth. "No, I didn't. And what makes you think I did?"

"I got a text from you." Wesley muttered some profanity under his breath. "You said to give Vaughn five hundred bucks, and that you'd pay me back. You said Vaughn had info about the threatening letters the Becketts had been getting. So I gave Vaughn the money, but he said he didn't know anything about the Becketts."

"The text came from a burner cell," Emory provided.

"Theo uses burners all the time," Wesley snapped.

As the daughter and sister of cops, Ivy knew what a burner was. It was a prepaid phone that couldn't be traced. Theo probably did use them for his job, but in this case someone had used it to set him up.

To maybe set up Wesley, too.

But why would someone have done that?

Maybe the person hoped to get both Theo and Wesley thrown off the case. If so, it wasn't working. Theo wasn't going to let this go whether he was officially on the investigation or not, and she doubted Wesley would just walk away, either.

"Obviously, I need to look into this further," Emory

said. "But at this point, Wesley is going back to his office, and, Theo, the sheriff and I decided you should continue with protective custody for Ivy and her son."

Emory hesitated before "her son," as if he weren't sure whether to include Theo in that parent label or not.

Theo thanked his boss, though it wasn't a very enthusiastic one, and he shot Wesley a glare before he started with her toward the break room. Both Emory and Wesley walked away, but Gabriel stayed put.

"Your dad's lawyer called first thing this morning," Gabriel said, stopping Theo in his tracks. "August visited Travis and told him about Nathan. Travis asked if he could see him."

"No," Theo answered without giving even a moment's thought. Then he shook his head, cursed. "Even if it were safe to take Nathan out, I don't want him visiting a prison."

Both Gabriel and Ivy added a sound of agreement, though they were in tricky territory here. Nathan was Travis's only grandchild, but since Travis was also a convicted killer of her own parents, then Ivy didn't want to give Travis the chance to say anything to the boy that could possibly upset him. Nathan had already been through enough, and she had told him only a few sketchy details about her folks' deaths. She certainly hadn't told him that his grandfather was a convicted murderer.

"The lawyer said he could set up a Skype call with all of you and Travis," Gabriel added. "I told him if you were interested in that, you'd let him know. I didn't tell him that hell might freeze over before that happened."

Theo smiled, muttered a thanks. He turned to get her moving but then stopped again. "What about Jodi's and your wedding? You were supposed to be getting married today."

"Yeah." Gabriel sounded and looked disappointed. "It's still on hold. Jodi and I are okay with that."

They no doubt were okay, but Ivy hated that their plans had been derailed because of some sick monster who wanted at least some of them dead. Of course, all the danger seemed to point to Theo, Nathan and her. At least Jodi didn't seem to be in the path of a killer. After she had already survived not one but two attacks, Ivy didn't want her soon-to-be sister-in-law to go through anything else like that.

Theo led her to the break room, such that it was. It had a microwave, small fridge and a beat-up leather sofa. Theo had her sit, got her a bottle of water from the fridge and then took out his phone. At first she thought he was going to make another of those calls to get updates on the investigation, but when he put it on speaker, she heard Jameson's voice.

"How's Nathan?" Theo immediately asked.

"Fine. Jodi and he are watching a movie. Are Ivy and you okay?"

Since Jameson knew about the attack, he was aware that they hadn't been injured. Not physically, anyway. "I think Ivy will be a lot better if she can talk to Nathan." And Theo handed her the phone.

Other than the initial call to the safe house after they'd arrived at the sheriff's office, Ivy hadn't considered talking to Nathan. She hadn't wanted him to hear the fear in her voice, but the moment her son came onto the line, that fear vanished.

"Uncle Jameson taught me to play poker," Nathan proudly announced.

"Kiddie poker," Jameson corrected.

Ivy figured it was the real deal since her brother favored that particular game, and she honestly didn't mind. Nathan sounded excited as if this were some kind a treat, and that was better than the alternative. Plus, he was getting to spend time with his uncle, something that Nathan hadn't ever had a chance to do.

"Aunt Jodi can't cook at all," Nathan went on. "She burned the toast and cut her finger when she was trying to make a sandwich. But Uncle Jameson can make grilled cheese and popcorn."

"Hey, I'm giving him some fruit, too," Jameson called out.

"Yeah, fruit and chocolate milk," Nathan concurred.

Again, her son sounded happy. "I miss you," Ivy told him. "But maybe it won't be long before Theo...your dad and I can come back."

"Okay. Can you bring some pizza?"

Ivy had to smile. "I'll try." Even after all the food that was just mentioned, she wasn't surprised that Nathan had pizza on the mind. It was his favorite. "See you soon, sweetheart."

Even though she was so glad she'd been able to speak to Nathan, the moment she ended the call, Ivy felt the loss. She had spent so little time away from him that even this short while felt like an eternity.

"I've missed so much," Theo said.

She looked at him, saw the loss on his face, too, but it was far worse than hers. After all, she'd had Nathan all these years that he hadn't. It hadn't been a decision to keep Nathan from Theo. At first, it'd been because of the rift between them and then because she couldn't find him. But after seeing Theo's raw expression, Ivy wished she'd done more.

Theo had indeed missed a lot.

She stood and went to him, and though it wasn't a smart thing to do, she pulled him into her arms. At least that's what she started to do, but Theo did some pulling of his own. Maybe it was the emotion of the moment or the fact that they'd just escaped death. Either way, it was as if he snapped. He dragged her to him.

And he kissed her.

It had been ten years since Theo's mouth had been on hers, but the memories—and the feelings—came flooding back. Ivy hadn't especially needed a kiss to remind her why Theo and she had been together in the first place, but the heat was just as hot as it had been back when they were teenagers.

He'd been the first boy to kiss her, and she had lost her virginity to him. And yes, there was still enough attraction there that she remembered exactly why that had happened. Theo had had her hormonal number then, and he still had it now.

She heard herself make a sound of pleasure, something she often did whenever she was around Theo, and the sound only increased when he deepened the kiss. He added some nice body pressure, too, with his chest moving right against her breasts. It didn't take long for her body to recall just how good the pleasure could be. It also didn't take long for Ivy to find herself wanting more.

Theo was obviously on that "more" page as well because he turned her, moving her so that her back was against the wall. He made the adjustment with her, still touching her with his body. Especially one part of him. In the maneuvering, his thigh ended up between her legs, and the pressure started to build there.

She broke the kiss so she could breathe, and when she pulled back a few inches, Ivy was staring right into his eyes. Those eyes had always had her number, too, and it didn't seem to matter that ten years had passed, because her body was on fire. Still, she forced herself to remember they were in the break room where anyone could come walking in at any second. No way would Gabriel approve of such a thing, and she shouldn't approve of it, either, since they had so many more important things they should be doing.

She repeated that last part to herself. It didn't help. Every inch of her was still zinging from the kiss.

"I should say I'm sorry for that." Theo's voice was husky and deep, and it did nothing to cool her off. It also did nothing to make her want an apology from him or even regret that it'd happened.

But she should regret it.

There were still a lot of unsettled things between Theo and her. Added to that, someone was trying to kill them. The last thing she should have been doing was kissing him. Or wanting to kiss him again.

Which she did.

Ivy might have done just that, too, but the break room door opened, and Gabriel came in. Theo and she immediately stepped apart. She was certain they looked guilty, and equally certain that her brother was aware of what'd happened between them. And yes, Gabriel scowled in a way that only a big brother could manage when he believed his kid sister was making a mistake.

The same mistake she'd made a decade ago.

"I would offer to give you a moment," Gabriel grumbled, sarcasm in his voice, "but this is important."

That got her heart pumping. "Is Nathan okay?"

"This isn't about Nathan. A courier just arrived with some very interesting things that you should take a look at." He turned, headed back toward his office and said the rest from over his shoulder. "Cameron is calling Lacey now to get her in here. She's in town, staying at the inn, so it shouldn't take her long to get here. Once you see this, you'll know why I might have to arrest her."

Chapter Ten

Theo forced his attention on Gabriel and what he'd just told them. It should have been an easy thing to do, what with the investigation and the danger, but he first had to shake off the effects of that kiss.

What the hell had he been thinking?

He had no idea, but Theo knew for a fact which of his body parts had encouraged him to do that, and it was the very part of him that could make stupid choices just like that one. Later, he would owe Ivy that apology he'd skirted around, but it would have to wait for now. Clearly, Gabriel had something important to show them.

"The courier is still here," Gabriel said to them as they walked into his office. "I've put him in an interview room so I can find out more about who had him deliver this. The envelope just has the name John Smith, no address, and the courier only had a vague description of the guy."

It was probably vague because the person hadn't wanted to draw attention to himself. Or could have even been wearing a disguise. If the person who'd attacked them was behind this, he or she probably wouldn't have done something so stupid as approaching the courier themselves. They would have hired someone to do that. Someone who couldn't be traced back to them.

Theo figured Gabriel was going to clarify all of this very soon, but for now he had one big question. "What does Lacey have to do with this?"

"Maybe everything." Gabriel tipped his head to his desk where Theo saw not only a manila envelope, but the item that was lying next to it. It was in a clear plastic evidence bag.

A silver watch.

Hell. What was going on here? The watch face was ordinary, but the band had small copper insets. Theo had only seen one other watch like that.

It had belonged to Ivy and Gabriel's father.

Ivy gasped, pressed her fingers against her mouth and took a step back. She shook her head. "Is that... Dad's?"

"According to this, it is," Gabriel said. He seemed to be struggling with seeing the watch, too. Of course, it didn't help that Sherman had been wearing it at the time of his murder.

And that the killer had taken the watch—probably as some kind of sick trophy.

The watch hadn't been found on Theo's father, though. For that matter, neither had the knife that'd murdered Sherman and his wife.

"It's a lab report," Gabriel said. He didn't touch the paper next to the envelope, but he pointed to it. "Someone claims to have had prints and trace run on the watch." He paused, his forehead bunching up. "There's a small amount of blood. A DNA match to Dad."

Ivy didn't gasp again, but she made a soft, strangling sound, groped around for the chair that was behind her and sank down onto it. "Where's it been this whole time?"

Gabriel shook his head. "The lab report doesn't mention that. Of course, my theory was that Travis had hidden it somewhere. Or ditched it like he did the knife. And maybe he did."

Someone had found the knife, though, hidden it away and then tried to use it to kill Jodi. That'd happened only a month earlier. But the person who'd done that was dead and couldn't have been the one to send the watch.

"I'll have it tested, of course," Gabriel continued a moment later. "Not just for blood but also to verify the partial prints that this report says were on the watch band."

"Prints?" Ivy repeated. "Whose?"

Theo figured it was Travis's prints. Since Sherman's blood had been found on Travis's shirt, it wouldn't be much of a stretch for the prints to belong to his father, as well.

Apparently they didn't, though.

"They're Lacey's," Gabriel said.

Oh, man. That explained why Gabriel had wanted Ivy's stepdaughter brought in, but that was about all it explained.

"Lacey was twenty when our parents were killed," Ivy pointed out. "And she didn't know them. She didn't even live close to Blue River when the murders happened."

"That's exactly why I want to talk to her," Gabriel continued. "If those are really her prints, then she must have touched the watch at some point—either at the time of the murder or afterward."

"*Afterward* could mean someone is setting her up," Theo pointed out. But then there was a problem with that. "Who had the watch to be able to do something like that, and why set up Lacey this way? If someone wanted to tie her to the attacks, there would have been an easier way to do that by just creating a fake money trail."

Obviously, neither Gabriel nor Ivy had answers for that, and if it was a setup, Lacey might not know it, either. But it could mean she'd come in contact with someone who'd been present at the murders. *Could*.

Theo hoped Ivy didn't take this the wrong way, but he had to ask. "Is it possible that your late husband knew your parents?"

She shook her head. But then she paused. "I honestly never asked him. All of that was still so raw and painful when I met Chad, and he seemed to sense that I didn't want to talk about it."

Theo looked at Gabriel, who was already taking out his phone. "I'll see if Chad's name came up at any point during the investigation or the check of the old police records."

That brought Ivy to her feet. "You can't think Chad killed them." She didn't seem to have any doubts about that. "Because he was a gentle man. He definitely wasn't a killer."

Theo took her hand and had her sit again. "I believe you, but it's possible he had some connection to my father. He might have known him, might have sympathized with the feud that was going on between the Becketts and the Cantons. Yeah, it's a long shot," he quickly added, "but we're working with nothing but long shots here."

And that meant Theo might have to talk to Travis after all. Not to have him meet Nathan. Not a chance. But rather to start ruling out any association he could have possibly had with Chad.

"How'd you meet Chad?" Gabriel asked the moment he ended his call.

She narrowed her eyes a little at her brother. Obviously, she wasn't pleased that her late husband was coming into question. Probably because it was too hard to wrap her mind around the fact that she might have been living with the man who'd had some part in her parents' death. And maybe he didn't. Again, this was a long shot.

"I met him at a livestock auction near Houston," Ivy finally answered. "I'd just bought a small place and wanted to buy a horse. Chad sat next to me, and when Nathan started fussing, he started making funny faces at him and got him to stop."

For reasons Theo didn't want to explore, hearing that caused him to scowl. He figured what he was feeling was some old-fashioned jealousy, but hell, it was hard to hear of any man having that kind of interaction with his son when he hadn't had the chance to even see the baby.

Hard to hear about Ivy being with another man, too.

That kiss was responsible for him feeling that. And in this case, the jealousy didn't make a lick of sense. He'd been with other women since Ivy, but then, he hadn't married any of them. In fact, he hadn't even gotten past the casual sex stage. Theo had always blamed that on his job, but after that kiss with Ivy, he knew that his feelings for her were still there, and they had probably been playing into it even after all these years.

Ivy pushed her hair from her face, looked away. "After we met at the auction, Chad asked me out for coffee, and eventually I went…four months later."

So Ivy hadn't exactly jumped at the chance to be with another man. Not that Theo believed she had. Nathan had been nearly a year old when she'd married Chad, and that meant by then Theo had been out of her life for almost two years. She'd moved on. But she'd moved on with a man who could have some connection to the Beckett murders.

"If Chad had known my parents or had anything to do with that watch, why would he have asked me out?" Ivy questioned. "Why would he have married me? Because I can promise you that he never asked a question about my parents, and he certainly never tried to hurt me. So you're wasting your time trying to link Chad to Lacey's prints on that watch."

"You're wasting your time to link me to it, too," Lacey said.

The woman came into the doorway. Cameron was

right behind her, and judging from the deputy's frustrated expression, he'd been trying to hold her back.

Lacey aimed glares at all of them, including Cameron, and her glare was still in place when her attention landed on the watch. "That's why you brought me in here?" she asked Gabriel.

Gabriel gave her a glare of his own. "Your prints are on it. Why?"

Theo carefully watched her expression, and if she was the least bit concerned about the accusations against her, she didn't show it. Instead, she shrugged. "About a week or so ago, I was at the mall, and when I came out, that watch was lying on the hood of my car. I picked it up. I figured someone walking by had found it, thought it was mine and left it for me."

Theo didn't glare, but he was certain he looked skeptical. Because he was. "How'd the watch get from you to here?" he demanded.

"How should I know? I tossed it on the ground, got in my car and left. I didn't want to leave it on the hood because I thought it might hit my windshield and chip the glass."

"And you didn't think it was suspicious that someone would put a watch on your car?" Ivy asked. There was skepticism in her voice, too.

Lacey hadn't seemed to object too much to Theo's question, but she clearly didn't like Ivy's. "No, because like I said, I thought someone believed it was mine. Obviously, it's not my style, and it belongs to a man. I don't even have a current boyfriend."

If Lacey was telling the truth, then someone indeed

had set her up. But Theo wasn't convinced that it'd been the truth that had come out of Lacey's mouth.

"Did you see anyone near your vehicle before you spotted the watch?" Gabriel pressed.

"No. Now, what's this about? Why is that watch so blasted important?"

"It belonged to my father," Ivy answered after everyone paused. "It went missing the night of his murder."

Now Lacey had a reaction. Her eyes widened, and she shook her head. "Oh, no. You're not going to try to pin that on me. It's bad enough that I'm stuck in this cowpoke town because the sheriff here thinks I might be behind the attacks to kill the likes of you. I won't have you accusing me of your parents' murders."

"How about your father?" Theo asked, ignoring the insults Lacey had peppered into her comments. "Could Chad have killed them?" He knew that wasn't going to earn him a kind look from Ivy. It didn't.

Lacey howled out a protest, but she didn't limit it to just Theo. She snapped toward Ivy, too. "You're behind this, aren't you? You think if you can get me out of the way, then I can't get what's rightfully mine."

Ivy blew out a long breath and stood, facing Lacey head-on. "I'm not behind this. If I'd found my father's watch, I would have given it to the cops because it might have some kind of evidence on it. I darn sure wouldn't have put it on your car, knowing that you could toss it."

That didn't seem to soothe Lacey any. The veins in her neck were practically bulging, and her nostrils were flared. "Please. You'd do anything to stop me from getting my father's money."

"Not anything," Ivy argued. "But there is something I can do to make sure my son is safe, and I did it. I had a lawyer redo my will. Since I'm trustee of Nathan's inheritance, I can make decisions about that, too. So if anything happens to Nathan and me, all of your father's money will go to charity."

The color drained from Lacey's face, and she looked at Theo for confirmation of that. He had no idea if it was true or not, but he nodded. "This way, you have no motive to come after our son."

"I never tried to kill him!" she shouted. Then she snapped back to Ivy. "You have no right to a single penny of my dad's money."

"Neither do you." Ivy huffed again, and Theo could see she was having to wrestle with her own temper. "Look, I would give you the money but your father asked me not to do that. It was his dying wish, something he told me many times over, and I'm going to do what he wanted."

Good call, because at this point just giving Lacey the money might not put an end to the danger. It seemed to Theo that Lacey wanted Ivy and Nathan completely out of the picture.

"My father loved me," the woman stated through clenched teeth.

"And he knew you," Ivy agreed. "He didn't think you were responsible enough to handle another large sum of money. Plus, he knew you wouldn't share it with me."

"Because it wasn't your money to have! You brainwashed my father. You got him to fall for you because he'd always wanted a son. Well, your brat kid isn't his son and never will be."

"No, because he's my son." Theo probably shouldn't have blurted that out, but Ivy wasn't the only one having to put a choke hold on her temper. He started to address the brat comment but decided against it. He'd already said too much.

"Like I care whose kid he is," Lacey grumbled. "This isn't over," she added to Ivy, and she turned as if to leave.

"No, it's not," Gabriel agreed. "And you're not going anywhere just yet." He ignored her protest and went into the hall, motioning for Cameron to join them. "I need you to continue this interview with Miss Vogel, and if she refuses, lock her up. Based on what I have here, we won't have any trouble getting a court order."

Lacey fired glances at all of them. "You'll be sorry for this," she spat out, and she slung off Cameron's grip when he took hold of her arm.

However, Lacey didn't head out the front door, something Theo had thought she might try to do. She followed Cameron to his desk.

Gabriel stepped back in his office and shut the door. "You think she's lying?" he asked Theo and Ivy.

"I don't know," Theo admitted when Ivy shook her head. "But I don't trust her."

Both Gabriel and Ivy made sounds of agreement to that.

"Who could have left that watch for her?" Ivy asked, but she didn't wait for them to answer. "August, maybe?

I know he wasn't at our old house the night of the murders, but maybe Travis gave it to him?"

No, August hadn't been at either the Beckett or the Canton house. Instead, he'd been with a woman one town over, and she'd provided him with an alibi for the time of the murders. That didn't mean, though, that August hadn't run into Travis later, since Theo's father hadn't been found until the following morning. Those were a lot of hours when a transfer like that could have taken place, and there was no way August would have volunteered that Travis had had the watch because it would have added another nail to his conviction for the murders.

"If Travis gave him the watch, August wouldn't have turned it over to Gabriel," Theo pointed out. But Theo had some trouble finishing that theory. "Why wouldn't August have planted the watch on someone who's a more plausible suspect, someone we would actually believe could have killed your parents if my father hadn't done it? Or he could have just tossed it in the river, where it probably would have never been found."

Obviously, Theo wasn't the only one having trouble coming up with a reason for August to do this.

"Now, Wesley—yes," Theo went on. "I can see an angle for him on this. If he'd somehow managed to get the watch, then he could have used it to frame Lacey so it would take suspicion off him."

"How would Wesley have gotten the watch, though?" Ivy asked.

Theo had the answer for this one. "Wesley was around during the murder investigation. In fact, he was a San Antonio cop then, and a group of them came out to help comb the area when everyone was looking for Travis. He could have found the watch then."

That didn't explain, though, why a cop would have kept something like that, but maybe Wesley had been dirty even back then. If so, he'd certainly kept his dirty deeds hidden away.

"There's a third theory, though," Theo continued a moment later. One that he hated to even consider. "Someone could be playing a cat-and-mouse game with us. Maybe a person my father has somehow managed to hire." He paused, not really wanting to consider this one as well, but they needed to look at all of the possibilities. However, it was Gabriel who finished that train of thought for him.

"Or your father could be innocent, and the real killer is out there," Gabriel said.

None of them believed that. Or at least they didn't want to believe it. Because if it was true, it would turn this investigation—and their lives—upside down. Again. It also meant Theo had no way of protecting Ivy from a nameless, faceless monster who could have already butchered at least two people and had plenty of others in his or her sight.

Maybe even their son.

If this was truly someone wanting to spill Beckett blood, then Nathan could be a target. Of course, a killer could also use the boy to draw out Ivy and Theo. And it could work, since both of them would lay down their lives for the boy.

Theo hadn't intended to do it, but he slid his hand

over Ivy's shoulder. Gabriel noticed, too. But then he was also the one who'd walked in on Ivy and him shortly after that kiss. Judging from Gabriel's expression, he was about to dole out some big brother advice. Maybe even a big brother warning. However, his phone rang before he could do that.

Theo kept his hand in place, and Ivy looked up at him. Their gazes connected for just a second before Gabriel interrupted them.

"It's the doctor who performed surgery on the injured woman." Gabriel put the call on speaker.

Theo braced himself for the doc to say the woman was dead. That would be tragic not only because she might be truly innocent in all of this, but also because they would lose their chance to question her.

"She's awake," the doctor announced. "And she says her name is Belinda Travers."

So she was the woman who'd gone missing from McKenzie's place. "Did she say anything else?" Theo asked at the same moment Gabriel said, "How soon can I talk to her?"

"Give it another hour," the doctor answered. "By then, she should be a little more alert. And as for the other question—yes, she told me something else. She said someone kidnapped her from a bar. She doesn't know the person who did that, but the reason she was there was to meet August Canton."

Chapter Eleven

Ivy wanted nothing more than to go back to the safe house so she could see Nathan. But there was no way her brother could spare the manpower right now. No way that Theo would let Ivy and him drive back there alone, either. Not after the other attack on the road and with the possibility of hired thugs still being in the area.

So she paced the hall in front of Gabriel's office. Waited.

And worried.

Gabriel had already questioned the courier and hadn't uncovered anything new, but her brother was definitely hoping to learn something from the watch, which he'd already sent for processing. Also to learn something from August. Once the man came in, that is. August had some answering to do over Belinda's accusations that she'd been at McKenzie's bar to meet him.

At least Lacey and Wesley wouldn't be around. Or rather they shouldn't be. It was unnerving enough having August return, and Ivy didn't especially want to be under the same roof with all three of their suspects.

The worries kept coming, too. Because the greatest

danger might not be with August, Lacey or Wesley. Gabriel had mentioned the possibility of Travis being innocent, and if by some serious long shot he actually was, then God knew who'd killed her parents. But whoever it was could want her and the rest of her family dead.

Not exactly a reassuring thought.

That could explain why she and other members of her family had been getting those threatening letters over the years. There'd been details in some of those letters—such as her mother's necklace being taken—and the police had purposely kept those out of the reports. It'd been a way of putting a lid on false confessions. So the person who'd written those threats had either managed to hack into those reports, or else he'd been there that night to take the necklace while he'd murdered her mother.

Ivy had to close her eyes a moment to shut out the images. She'd been the one to discover her parents and had actually stepped in her mother's blood when she ran to the bodies. There'd been nothing she could do, and she didn't even remember making the frantic call to Gabriel. Good thing she had, too, because when he'd run to their parents', he'd discovered Jodi on the path. She was within minutes of bleeding out, and he'd managed to save her.

Something Ivy hadn't been able to do for her folks.

There were times, like now, when she reminded herself that the horror that'd gone on that night could have been even worse. Jodi could be dead, too. Maybe even Gabriel as well, since Jodi's attacker was probably nearby when her brother had found her. Remembering that soothed Ivy a little. But not enough to make the ache fade in her heart.

Theo finished the call he'd just made to the crime lab, glanced at her and frowned. "You can't dwell on it," he said.

It was as if he'd looked right into her mind—something he'd always had a knack for doing—but she didn't care much for it now. In some ways it made it worse that he knew how much she was still hurting. In some ways, though, it made it better. This wasn't a case of misery loving company, it was just that Theo understood how much she'd lost that night. Because he'd lost so much himself.

"How do you forget?" she asked. "How do you push it all aside?"

He stared at her, shook his head. "You don't." On a heavy sigh, he went to Gabriel's fridge, grabbed a bottle of water and brought it to her. "There's no permanent fix for grief. It keeps coming back."

Yes, it did. Like now. It was washing over her.

"Sometimes, it helps if I think about the good stuff," he added. He pushed her hair from her face, his fingers lingering on her cheek. "How close Jodi and I once were. The times I was with you. I just force myself to remember that there were more good times than bad."

Good advice. Too bad she couldn't take it. It was impossible to push away the fear. Or so she thought. But then she looked at Theo, their gazes connecting, and just like that, things were a little better.

And worse.

Because even now with all the bad memories flooding her mind, she noticed him. That rumpled hair. That mouth. Mercy, he had a way of getting right past the fear and into places inside her where he shouldn't be. Like her heart. Of course, her heart wasn't the only problem at the moment. Theo also knew how to stir up things in her body.

Yes, there'd been plenty of good times, and most of those moments had centered on him.

"I would ask you to go to the break room…" he said, arching his eyebrow as if that were a question rather than an attempt at a joke.

Despite everything going on, Ivy had to fight back a smile. "Probably not a good idea."

Theo kept his eyes on her as if waiting for something more. Conversation, maybe? An assurance that she was okay?

Another kiss?

If it was the kiss, then Ivy imagined it would be the kiss that people gave each other when they were used to kissing. When that kiss would suddenly make all the bad things go away. Something that it couldn't do. But it could cause the old heat to slide right through her. In fact, just the thought of kissing him did that to her. It also helped that Theo was so close to her that she caught his scent.

More of that heat came.

"I've seen that look before." He brushed his fingers over the center of her forehead, which was bunched up.

Now she waited, because she wasn't sure where he was going with this. Maybe he had noticed the need in her expression. Or perhaps he was picking up on all the other things—the worry, the fatigue and, yes, the fear.

He didn't take his fingers from her face. Instead, Theo slipped them lower, to her cheek, and his touch—warm and soothing—lingered a moment there. Even though he didn't say anything, they had an entire conversation. About this mutual attraction that was messing with their minds. About what had torn them apart in the past. Even what might bring them back together in the future.

Nathan.

Theo must have realized this wasn't going to be something they could hash out now. Nor should they be doing this. Not with the danger still out there. And that's probably why he stepped back. Not far enough, though. Of course, several rooms over might not have been far enough to get her body to cool down.

"I'm sorry," he said, the frown returning.

Those two words certainly started the cooling-down process. "For what?"

"For not being able to keep you safe."

That's where she thought this was leading, and she didn't like it one bit. "I could be the reason you're in danger," she reminded him. Ivy was about to repeat his apology to him, but then she stopped when an idea went through her head. "Has anyone checked to see if my father was maybe investigating Wesley?"

She expected Theo to look surprised at the abrupt change in conversation, but he merely nodded. "I did last night. All your father's cases aren't digitized, but

Gabriel did a summary of each of them and put the info in a master file and shared it with me."

Now Ivy was the one who was surprised, and she felt her eyes widen. She hadn't known about the master file or the sharing part, and Gabriel must have been able to get over the rocky past with Theo for him to give him that info.

"And?" she asked.

"Your father didn't specifically mention Wesley's name, but he was working on a case that involved SAPD. Sherman had busted some guys for drugs, and he found some guns on them that had been confiscated in a raid in San Antonio. The weapons had been reported as destroyed, but clearly they weren't."

Ivy took a moment to think that through. "So a San Antonio cop sold or gave them the gun?"

Theo lifted his shoulder. "Or it could have been a paperwork error. It happens," he added. "I'll keep digging, but so far I haven't found anything that connects Wesley to the chain of custody of those guns."

And without that, it would be almost impossible to tie Wesley to it—and to her father's murder.

Ivy shook her head. "Maybe I'm overthinking this. Your father was convicted of the murders, and he has never denied doing it." Of course, that was mainly because Travis had been drunk and couldn't remember. "Anyway, maybe Wesley isn't dirty at all. Maybe that drug bust my father made is just muddying already muddy waters."

Theo certainly didn't argue with that. Which meant they were back to Lacey and August. And speaking of

August, Ivy heard the man's voice in the squad room. A very unhappy voice. It wasn't a shock that he was riled about being brought back in again for questioning.

"There'd better be a damn good reason you dragged me back here," August shouted. And yes, it was a shout. "Because I'm sick and tired of being accused of things I didn't do."

Gabriel had been at one of the deputies' desks, but he got to his feet and motioned for August to follow him. Her brother didn't shout, but he was scowling.

Both Theo and she stepped to the side so that Gabriel could lead August into his office. The watch, envelope and report were no longer there. They'd been couriered to the crime lab.

"First things first," Gabriel said to August. "Tell me about Belinda Travers."

"Who?" August made a face. "Never heard of her."

"Well, she's heard of you. She says you were supposed to meet her in a bar in San Antonio, but then someone kidnapped her."

"What?" August howled. "She's lying."

Gabriel and Theo exchanged glances, both of them clearly not happy with that denial. Maybe when the woman was able to talk to them, she could prove that August was the liar.

Gabriel dragged in a long breath and turned his computer monitor in August's direction. "Tell me about this," Gabriel ordered him. It was a picture of her father's watch.

Before August's attention actually landed on the screen, he'd already opened his mouth. No doubt to shout something again about how innocent he was. But he not only closed his mouth, he also moved in closer for a better look.

"Where did you get that?" August demanded.

"I asked you a question first," Gabriel fired back. He didn't add more, maybe because he wanted to see where August would go with this.

It didn't take long for August to respond. He cursed. It wasn't exactly angry cursing, though. His shoulders dropped, and while he shook his head, August sank down on the edge of Gabriel's desk.

"Hell," August mumbled. That definitely wasn't a denial, and neither was his body language. "I need to know where you got the watch," August said, and this time it wasn't a demand. Even though he didn't add a *please*, it was there, unspoken.

"I figured it'd come from you," Gabriel answered.

Since August was a hothead, his normal response would have been to verbally blast Gabriel for suggesting that. He didn't. Mercy, did that mean it'd actually come from August? If so, how had he gotten it, and why had he used it to try to set up Lacey?

"Start talking," Theo ordered him. He stepped closer to his uncle, violating his personal space, and August spared him a glance before his gaze darted away.

"I found the watch shortly after Travis's trial," August explained after a long pause. "It was in the barn at Travis's ranch." He looked up at Theo. "You know that corner where your daddy used to store sacks of feed? Well, there were some loose boards on the wall," he said when Theo nodded. "I looked behind them and saw the watch."

Theo tilted his head, his mouth tightening. Gabriel had a similar expression—one of skepticism.

"SAPD went through that barn," Theo reminded him. "So did Gabriel and Jameson."

August nodded. "So did I, and I didn't see it. Someone had tucked it up behind the boards. I think the only reason I found it was that some of the nails had given way and caused the board to come loose."

Ivy supposed it was possible that Travis had taken the watch and then hidden it there. Well, it was believable if you discounted the fact that Travis had been drunk the night of the murders. Apparently, he'd been so drunk that he'd passed out shortly thereafter.

"How do you think my dad's watch got there?" Ivy came out and asked.

"I have no idea." Now August shifted his attention to her. "But this still doesn't make my brother guilty. The killer could have easily planted it there hours and even days after the crime. Like I said, I didn't find it until after the trial, and that was months later."

"You found it and yet you didn't turn it over to Gabriel?" Theo's mouth was in a flat line now.

"I couldn't see the point of it," August answered without hesitation. "Travis had just gotten a life sentence. I didn't think it would do much good if folks knew a dead man's watch had been found in his alleged killer's barn."

"It wasn't alleged," Gabriel said. "He was convicted. And you should have given the watch to me instead of trying to use it as some kind of ploy to set up Lacey Vogel."

"What?" August jumped to his feet, and she saw that flash of temper that'd been missing the last couple of minutes. "Is that what she said I did? Because I sure as hell didn't."

Theo and Gabriel exchanged more glances. Confused ones. Ivy was right there with them.

"Someone put the watch on Lacey's vehicle," Theo explained. "She tossed the watch aside, and that person then took it and sent it to a lab. It has both Sherman Beckett's blood and Lacey's prints. Not your prints, though. Why is that if you're the one who found it?"

August's gaze slashed between the two lawmen, and his eyes widened before he cursed again. "My prints weren't on it because I used a paper towel to pick it up. I then wrapped it in that towel and put it in Travis's house. In plain view on the coffee table in the living room. I figured if Jodi and Theo came back, they'd see it and turn it in."

Theo huffed. "Why the hell would you do that?"

Ivy wanted to know the same thing. To the best of her knowledge, Theo and Jodi had never gone back to the house. Like her own parents' house, Travis's place had been empty. Abandoned.

"I didn't want the watch at my house," August said as if that explained everything. "I just figured it'd be better if I left it at Travis's."

"Better because it would seem as if someone had put it there to taunt the police," Theo snapped. "You did that to try to make my father look innocent. Or at least that's why you did if you're telling us the truth."

"I am," August insisted.

Maybe he was, but if so, he didn't deny Theo's accusation about leaving the watch to make Travis appear innocent.

"Someone must have taken the watch from Travis's house," August went on. "But why would that person then want to set up Ivy's stepdaughter?"

Ivy didn't know, but she had a theory. "Lacey hates me and would do anything to get back at me. It wouldn't surprise me if she had had someone go through both my parents' and Travis's places. Maybe so she could find something she could use against me. Something to help her win a lawsuit to get her hands on her dad's money."

All three men were staring at her now. Maybe waiting for her to come up with more, but Ivy didn't have more. She didn't have a clue how Lacey would hope to connect the watch to her.

But Theo apparently did.

Still, there was something about all of this that didn't make sense. Ivy gave that some more thought but had to shake her head. "That seems like a lot of trouble to go through just to cast some doubt on my name."

Theo lifted his shoulder. "Maybe it's all she could find and figured she'd use it. By having her own prints on it, too, she might think it takes suspicion off her. It doesn't." Theo shifted his gaze to August. "Nor you. Gabriel could file charges against you for withholding evidence."

August's mouth practically dropped open, and he

snapped to Gabriel. "By the time I found the watch, the investigation and the trial were over."

"Doesn't matter," Gabriel answered. "Anything connected to the case should have been given to me."

"What the hell would you have to gain by bringing charges against me?" August's temper was not only back, but it had also risen a couple of notches.

"Justice," Gabriel answered without hesitation. "Plus, if you'd given me the watch, we'd wouldn't be in this situation now of wondering who's trying to use it and why."

August would have no doubt responded to that with a fury-laced tirade, but Theo's phone rang, the sound knifing through the room. The moment Theo glanced at the screen, Ivy knew from his suddenly tight expression that there was a problem.

"It's Jameson," Theo told her, and he answered the call.

Ivy moved even closer to Theo so she could hear what her brother was saying, but it was a very short conversation. One that ended with Theo cursing and taking hold of her arm.

"We need to leave now," Theo said. "Jameson said there's an armed intruder on the grounds of the safe house."

Chapter Twelve

Theo had been on plenty of assignments where he'd faced down killers, but that suddenly felt like a drop in the bucket compared to what he was facing now.

His son could be in grave danger.

That in itself was bad enough, but in the back of his mind he also had to wonder if this was a trap to draw Ivy and him out for yet another attack. Hell, even that wasn't worse than an intruder going after Nathan.

"Just stay calm," Jodi said from the other end of the line.

She was whispering, something she'd done since she had taken over the call from Jameson. His sister was in the bathroom with Nathan while Jameson was at the front of the house to make sure the intruder they'd seen didn't get inside. She was keeping her voice low so that anyone outside the house wouldn't be able to hear her and pinpoint her location.

"Any idea where the intruder is now?" Gabriel asked from the front seat of the cruiser. He was driving—something he'd insisted on doing—not just so they'd have more backup but also because he'd been concerned that Theo and Ivy were too upset to be speeding down the rural road.

Gabriel was right. Theo was upset. But Ivy was to the point of being panicked. That was no doubt why Jodi kept reminding them to stay calm.

"Jameson just said he spotted the guy again," Jodi relayed. "He's in the ditch near the front of the road."

That probably meant the guy had tripped the motion sensor and that's how Jameson had known he was there in the first place. Maybe now that Jameson knew his location, he could just shoot him or keep him pinned down until they got there. Theo would have liked to have the guy alive, but he didn't want that to happen at the expense of Nathan, Jodi and Jameson.

"The ditch doesn't lead to the house," Jodi added. "Even if the man crawls toward us, the nearest he can get is about twenty yards."

That was still close. Too close. The goon could fire into the house, and the shots could make it through the walls and into the bathroom. Of course, if the gunman lifted his head to fire, Jameson should be able to take him out.

Provided the goon didn't shoot Jameson first, that is. But since that made Theo's own panic soar, he reminded himself that Jameson was a capable lawman. A lawman who was protecting his nephew and his brother's fiancée.

"How did this person find the safe house?" Ivy asked. Her voice was hoarse, no doubt because her throat was tight. Her knuckles were turning white from the grip she had on the seat. "Did he follow us the first time we went there?"

Not likely. Theo was almost certain they hadn't been followed, and it would have been fairly easy to spot someone doing that on this road.

"The listening device," Theo guessed. "Even though we whispered when we were inside, someone still could have heard us. Plus, all three of our suspects were in the sheriff's office and could have overheard something."

Ivy whispered the profanity that Theo was thinking. They'd known about those possible bugs, but they'd gotten so caught up in the danger and investigation that they might not have been as careful as they could have been. Not just with the bug, either. Because it was also possible that someone had sneaked into the parking lot of the sheriff's building and planted tracking devices on the cruisers.

"Is Jameson sure there's just one intruder?" Ivy asked several moments later.

"He thinks just the one," Jodi answered.

His sister could be saying that to calm Ivy's nerves. But Theo figured the only thing that would calm her was for Ivy to see Nathan and make sure all was well. That might not happen for a while. For one thing, they were still a good ten minutes out. For another, the thug might start shooting at them the moment they got there. If he wasn't alone, then Gabriel could be driving right into a trap. That's the reason Theo took out his backup weapon and handed it to Ivy.

"It's just a precaution," he said when her eyes widened.

"Keep watch around us," Gabriel reminded them, and then added to Ivy, "That's a precaution, too."

A huge one. Because this stretch of road had plenty of trees. Ditches, too. More thugs could be lying in wait for them.

Those last few miles seemed to take an eternity, though Theo was certain Gabriel was going as fast as he could safely go. When Gabriel finally reached the turn to the house, he slowed and glanced around.

"Jodi, I'm going to hang up and text Jameson," Gabriel told her. "I've got a visual on the house and the ditch, but I can't see the gunman." Gabriel did text his brother, and it only took a few seconds for Jameson to reply.

The guy is near the mailbox, Jameson responded, and Gabriel read the text to them.

"Get down on the seat," Theo instructed Ivy, and he lowered his window just a fraction. "If you drive up closer, I'll see if I can get this idiot to surrender," he added to Gabriel.

Gabriel did begin to inch the cruiser closer just as his phone buzzed with a call. "It's not Jameson," he said. "It's the hospital, but I'll call them back." Instead, he kept his attention on the ditch.

"Stand so we can see you," Theo called out to the man. "And put your hands in the air."

Theo figured there was no way that would work, and it didn't. Almost immediately, the man got to his feet. But he definitely did not put his hands in the air. Nor did he surrender. Instead he turned, aiming his gun at the cruiser, and he fired. The shot slammed into the front windshield. Just like the other attack, the glass held, but Theo couldn't risk this idiot firing shots that stood any chance whatsoever of hitting any of them.

"Stay down," Theo reminded Ivy, and he lowered the window even more. When the goon lifted himself to shoot at them again, Theo fired first.

His bullet hit the man squarely in the chest.

The goon fell backward, his weapon thudding to the ground next to him. Gabriel didn't waste any time driving the cruiser closer to him. Jameson came out the front of the house as well, but he stayed back on the porch. Probably because there could be other gunmen in the area.

Gabriel stopped the cruiser right next to the wounded man, and Theo opened his door wide enough to snatch up the thug's weapon. Of course, he could be carrying a backup, but at the moment he wasn't reaching for anything. He was clutching his chest.

And he was bleeding out.

Gabriel called for an ambulance, but Theo doubted it would get there in time. That meant anything they could get from the guy, he had to try to get it now.

"Who are you?" Theo demanded.

The guy shook his head. "My name won't mean anything to you."

"Try." Theo kept his gun pointed right at him.

"Morris Carlyn." He groaned in pain, pressing his hands even harder over his wound.

The name didn't mean anything to Theo, but it soon would. Gabriel fired off a text, no doubt to get a background on this guy. Once they had that, they might be able to link him to one of their suspects.

"Who sent you, Morris?" Theo asked.

Another headshake. "There's no threat you can make that'll be worse than what'll happen if I talk."

"Wanna bet?" Theo took aim at the guy's leg. "I can start putting bullets in you. It won't kill you any faster, but it'll make your last minutes on this earth very, very painful."

It was a bluff, of course. He couldn't shoot an unarmed, dying man, but mercy, that's what he wanted to do if it would help them put a stop to the danger.

The guy looked at him, their gazes connecting. "My family could be hurt. That's why I can't tell you. That's why I agreed to do this."

All right. So someone had maybe blackmailed or coerced him. Theo glanced at Gabriel to see if he was already on that. He was. Gabriel sent another text that probably included cops going to this guy's house to check on anyone who might be there.

"How did you find this place?" Theo continued.

"I was just told to come here and kidnap the woman, Ivy Beckett. I was supposed to take her alive."

Hell. That was hard to hear. Obviously hard for Ivy to hear, too, because she gasped.

If the guy was telling the truth, and that was still a big *if*, it didn't rule out any of their suspects. Wesley or Lacey would want Ivy alive so they could use her as a bargaining chip to get whatever it was they wanted. In Lacey's case so she could get the money. For Wesley, it could have been so he could maybe force Theo into a rescue situation so he could kill him. Because there was no way Theo wouldn't go after Ivy if this idiot had indeed managed to kidnap her.

It was ironic, though, that Wesley would be doing that because he thought Theo knew something about that botched militia raid. Other than a gut feeling, Theo had nothing, and you couldn't use gut feelings to make an arrest.

"Protect my family," the guy said, and his eyelids fluttered down. Dead, probably. But Theo wasn't about to get out and check on him.

Apparently, Gabriel wasn't, either, because he sped toward the house, and he pulled the cruiser to a stop directly in front of the porch. Ivy immediately bolted out, running past Jameson and going inside.

"Any sign of other gunmen?" Gabriel asked his brother as they rushed in behind Ivy.

"No. But the sensors are still working because they went off when you got here." Jameson armed the security system and then tipped his head to the ditch. "Is the guy dead?"

"Probably," Gabriel answered, and he went to the window to keep watch while he made a call. No doubt to follow up on the thug's family.

"Go ahead. Check on Nathan," Jameson told him when Theo kept looking in the direction of the hall bathroom. "Once we've regrouped and gotten more backup out here, we'll have to leave, though."

No way would Theo disagree with that. He wanted backup and plenty of it, but he also wanted Ivy and his son out of there. The location had been compromised, and that meant there could be another attack. Or another attempt to kidnap Ivy. Either way, they were all at risk.

The moment Theo stepped into the bathroom, Jodi hurried out, saying that she wanted to check on Gabriel. Theo stood there a moment and watched his sister go to the man she obviously loved. He saw the fear now, on her face and in her body language. The relief, too, that Gabriel was all right.

Theo felt that same relief when he looked at Nathan. Well, what he could see of him, anyway. Ivy had him wrapped in her arms, and even though she wasn't crying, she was blinking hard. No doubt to try to stave off the tears.

"Did you do something to the bad man?" Nathan asked him. He maneuvered himself back just enough so that he could make eye contact with Theo.

Theo nodded and hoped that would be enough of an explanation. He really didn't want to have to tell Nathan that he'd just killed someone.

"Does this mean we have to leave?" Nathan added.

"Yes," Ivy and Theo answered in unison.

Nathan didn't seem upset about that, but he did volley some glances at both Ivy and him. "Will you two get together?" he asked.

It was a repeat of the same question the boy had hit them with earlier. It was understandable for him to want to know. After all, whatever Ivy and he did would affect Nathan's future.

"I mean, since Mr. Chad is dead and you're my parents and all," Nathan added. "I just figured you'd get together."

Considering that Theo's mind was still whirling from the attack, it was hard to switch gears in the conversation. Especially when the switch was this big. Theo looked at Ivy to see if she had an idea of how to answer that.

She didn't.

The blank stare that she gave Theo let him know that.

"We'll talk about that soon," Theo settled for saying. "For now, why don't we go ahead and start gathering up your things so we'll be ready to leave when the other deputies get here?"

Nathan got moving right away, and Ivy and Theo followed him to the bedroom not only to stand watch but to make sure he didn't go near the window. The blinds were down, curtains drawn, but there was no sense taking the risk.

"I can't go to the new safe house with him," Ivy said. Her voice was a hoarse whisper, and he saw that her hand was trembling when she touched her fingers to her mouth. "If someone is truly after me, I can't put him in danger like that."

Theo was already thinking along those same lines, but he doubted that Gabriel had two safe houses ready to go. That would take time.

Ivy turned to him, took hold of Theo's sleeve and pulled him out into the hall. "Just hear me out before you say no," she started.

And Theo groaned. Because he figured he wasn't going to like what would follow that comment.

"I think Jodi and Jameson should take Nathan to the backup safe house. Right away," Ivy added. "The deputies who are coming can follow them as backup. That'll get Nathan out of here in case there are other gunmen."

He couldn't object to any of that, but Theo could practically see where this was going. "You're not going to make yourself bait," he insisted.

"Not bait." She glanced in at Nathan, then pulled Theo even farther away from the room before she repeated those two words. "But we can't let things continue like this. If whoever's behind this can't get to me, they might decide to go after Nathan."

Just the thought of it twisted his gut. So did the fact that Theo couldn't deny that. If this person became even more desperate, then things might escalate fast.

"You're still not making yourself bait," he warned her.

"Controlled bait," Ivy corrected, and she kept on talking despite Theo's protest. "While Nathan is safe with Jodi and Jameson—and you—Gabriel, Cameron and I can go back to Gabriel's place. We can use the ranch hands for extra protection. Maybe even set up some sensors like the ones that are here."

Theo was shaking his head before she even finished, but she took hold of his chin to stop him. "We can make things as safe as we can possibly make them," Ivy added.

That wasn't much of an argument, but then, no place was going to be completely safe. And yes, the ranch hands along with some motion detectors would beef up security. Maybe not enough, though.

"If we can sell Gabriel on this—and I'm not even sure I want to do that," Theo said, "then I wouldn't go with Nathan and the others. I'll be with you since the attack is most likely to happen at the ranch." Just saying that didn't help with the knot that was tightening even more in his stomach. "But first we need to find out if we can find the snake responsible for this before we have to do something this dangerous."

Ivy made a sound of agreement. "You mean talk to Belinda Travers. Gabriel got that call from the hospital, and it's probably about her. Maybe she's talking."

"Wait here with Nathan," Theo instructed, "and I'll find out."

Theo went back to the living room, where he found Jodi, Jameson and Gabriel all standing watch at the window. "Is Nathan okay?" Gabriel immediately asked him.

Theo nodded. "Ivy wants to send him to a separate safe house."

Even though Theo didn't explain Ivy's "controlled bait" idea, Gabriel obviously filled in the blanks because his mouth tightened. What he didn't do was dismiss it.

And that caused Theo to curse. "Belinda's not talking?"

Gabriel gave a heavy sigh. "She's dead."

Hell. Well, there went the notion of questioning her, but it was more than that. From the looks of things, Belinda had been innocent in all of this, and someone had murdered her. That someone wanted to do the same to Ivy, too.

"Please tell me someone didn't sneak into the hospital and finish her off," Theo said.

"No. She developed a blood clot. The doc told me that sometimes things like that happen."

Yeah. Bad things happened all the time. Theo had to make sure now that the bad things didn't continue with Nathan and Ivy.

"I think it's too late for the guy in the ditch, but just in case, the ambulance is on the way," Gabriel continued while he volleyed glances between Theo and the window. "The deputies will be here soon, too."

"What about the guy's family?" Theo wanted to know. "Any idea if they're really in danger?"

"I called SAPD as soon as we were all back in the house," Jameson volunteered. "They're on the way to check on them."

Theo hoped they were all right, but after what had happened to Belinda, it was possible the man's family was also in danger.

"Is there another safe house?" Theo's question got all of their attention. Ivy's as well, since she was now in the hall with Nathan behind her.

"One that's ready now," Gabriel answered. "It'll take me a while to set up another one."

"Wait in your room for just a few more minutes," Ivy told Nathan.

Judging from his pinched expression, that was the last thing Nathan wanted to do. The kid was no dummy, and he must have known that something big was about to happen. Still, he went into his room, and Ivy came closer to them. That's when Theo saw that she was blinking back tears again.

"Look, I don't want to be away from my son. Nor

do I want to die." Ivy's voice was shaking, and one of those tears made it down her cheek. She quickly wiped it away.

Theo went to her and slid his arm around her waist. He doubted it would help. Nothing much would at this point.

"We have to put an end to this—*now*," Ivy insisted. "That means using me to draw out this monster."

Since Theo had already voiced his opinion on this, he stayed quiet and waited for Gabriel to tell her no way in hell was he going to put his sister in danger like that. But Gabriel didn't get a chance to say anything because Jameson's phone buzzed.

"It's SAPD," Jameson said. He answered the call but didn't put it on speaker. Several moments later, he cursed. "The gunman's house has been ransacked, and his wife and two kids are missing." Jameson paused, his attention going to Ivy. "Someone left a note on the guy's door."

"A note about me?" Ivy asked. Theo felt the muscles in her body tense.

Jameson nodded. "The note said, and I'm quoting, 'Tell Theo that Ivy will be next. She dies tonight.'"

Chapter Thirteen

The note had chilled Ivy to the bone. It still did even several hours later. But it had been the final straw needed to convince Theo and her brothers that the only way to end this was to draw out the killer.

Not just for their sakes but for the gunman's family, too.

Ivy now knew that Morris Carlyn's family had indeed been kidnapped, and the cops didn't think it was a staged crime scene, either. The person who'd hired Morris had likely taken them to get him to cooperate. If he'd lived, that is. He hadn't, and Ivy prayed that meant the family would be released soon. While she was praying, she added several for Nathan and the rest of them.

She dies tonight.

If that was true, then she only had five or six hours before this monster tried to come after her. Five or six hours to get everything in place so that at least Nathan would be safe.

"It's time to go," Gabriel said as he disarmed the security system.

That was Ivy's cue to give Nathan one last hug and

kiss before he went off with Jameson, Cameron and Jodi. Ivy trusted all three of them to keep her boy safe, but even though she seemed to be the target, there were no guarantees the culprit might not try to use Nathan the way he or she had used Morris's family.

"It'll be okay?" Nathan asked, but it took Ivy a moment to realize he'd aimed that question at Theo. "You'll take care of my mom?"

Theo certainly wasn't the ice man–lawman right now. His eyebrows were drawn together, and muscles in his shoulders looked stiff. "I will."

Nathan seemed to accept that because he nodded, went to Theo and hugged him. Everyone in the room looked surprised. Especially Theo. He hesitated just a moment before his arms went around Nathan to return the hug.

Ivy had been near tears all day, and seeing that put some fresh ones in her eyes. Over the years she hadn't allowed herself to consider how Theo would be with Nathan, but she could see how much he loved their son.

Theo brushed a kiss on top of Nathan's head, and the boy pulled back, meeting his gaze. "Will you teach me to ride a bull? Because Aunt Jodi said you used to ride them and that you were good at it."

Theo shot his sister a "thanks for nothing" glance. "Maybe when you're a little older," he answered.

Again, Nathan seemed to accept that because he smiled, gave Theo another hug and then hurried to the door next to Gabriel. "I know," Nathan said to him. "We gotta run fast when we get outside."

Since every one of them had mentioned that in some

way or another, Ivy was glad it had sunk in. She went to the door, too, and from the side window, she saw that Cameron had pulled an unmarked police car next to the porch. Earlier, he'd gotten Nathan's things and put them in the trunk, and he'd already opened the back passenger's door.

Jodi and Jameson didn't waste any time getting Nathan outside and into the vehicle. Cameron immediately sped away. A second car with two reserve deputies followed them for backup.

"The new safe house is about ten miles from here," Gabriel said, "but it'll be a while before they get there."

Yes, because Cameron would have to drive around to make sure they weren't being followed. Gabriel had already explained that to her along with the assurance that all the vehicles had been checked and double-checked for bugs and tracking devices. Gabriel and the others had made it as safe as they possibly could, considering that Nathan would essentially be out in the open.

"Now it's our turn," Gabriel instructed.

Another of the deputies, Edwin Clary, pulled a cruiser in front of the house. This one was definitely marked with Blue River Sheriff emblazoned on the side, as was the one behind them that Deputy Jace Morrelli was driving. Along with Gabriel and Theo, that meant there'd be four lawmen driving her back to the ranch.

As Nathan and the others had done, they hurried to get into the cruiser, and Edwin drove them away. Ivy ended up in the middle of the back seat between Gabriel and Theo, and she automatically sank lower since she figured one of them would soon tell her to do that.

However, she kept her head just high enough to help them keep watch.

"We're going straight to the ranch," Gabriel continued, "even if someone follows us."

Ivy had figured that's how things would be, but it still sent a chill through her to hear it aloud.

"What's the plan once we're there?" Edwin asked. The deputy made eye contact in the mirror with Gabriel as he turned onto the road that would take them back to the ranch.

"The hands know we're coming, and they're all armed. Not out in the pastures, though. They've been setting up some sensors and cameras they got from the office to set up motion detectors and surveillance spots on the paths that lead to the house. Once they're finished, I want them out of sight."

It was smart to set up the equipment. Because the road was highly visible from Gabriel's house, but there were two paths that someone could use to get to them. In fact, the man who'd attacked Jodi ten years ago had used one of them. Maybe Travis had as well the night he'd murdered her parents. Those paths were lined with bushes and trees—the perfect place for a person to hide.

"Whoever comes after you," Gabriel continued, "we need to take him or her alive. That's the only way we're going to be able to figure out who's behind this."

Yes, especially considering that Belinda and Morris were dead and Morris's family was missing.

"That's why I want the hands and all of us tucked away. I don't want whoever's coming to see too many guns and turn back."

In other words, Gabriel was going to make it look like it would be an easy attack. Of course, the person behind this likely knew that it wouldn't be and would probably bring lots of firepower.

Ivy looked up at Theo the moment he looked down at her, and she saw something in his eyes that she was certain was in her own. A parent's worry. This was still a fairly new feeling for Theo, and she wished she could tell him that it would go away. It didn't. Even when there wasn't this kind of danger looming over them, she always worried about Nathan.

"Don't worry," Theo said. "I won't teach him how to ride a bull. Not anytime soon, anyway." The corner of his mouth lifted for just a moment.

Ivy was glad at his attempted humor. Glad, too, that it eased her racing heart just a little. She wanted to tell him she was glad he was there, but because he was there, with her, he was also at risk of being killed.

"How does Nathan do in school?" Theo asked. He glanced away from her to keep watch.

It seemed like such a, well, normal conversation. Definitely not the gloom and doom they'd been discussing since his return to Blue River.

"He gets As and Bs," she answered. "He struggles some with math, but he's way ahead in reading. In sports, too. He loves playing baseball."

Ivy realized she, too, was smiling a little, and she understood that's why Theo had talked about Nathan in the first place. That was probably the only thing that could help with the nerves. For a few seconds, anyway. And then Ivy felt the blasted tears threaten again.

On a heavy sigh, Theo slid his arm around her. She had on her seat belt, but Theo didn't, and he eased across the seat toward her. As he'd done with Nathan, he brushed a kiss on the top of her head.

"Thank you," she whispered. She automatically slid into the crook of his arm.

"Don't thank me yet," he whispered back, and she got the feeling they were talking about more than just the danger yet to come.

She looked up at him and got confirmation of that. The heat was still there. Simmering. And the kisses in Gabriel's office hadn't done a thing to cool it down. However, what did help was when Gabriel's phone buzzed, because that quickly got her attention. Theo's, too, since he moved back across the seat.

"It's nothing to do with Nathan," Gabriel said right off. "It's one of the hands. They have everything in place, and they're moving to their hidden positions now."

Good. Because they weren't far from the ranch now. Only a couple of minutes out.

"When we get there," Gabriel went on, looking at her, "I'll have Edwin pull up in front of the porch, and Theo, you and I will go inside. Edwin will leave and drive back toward town, but he'll actually pull off on a trail not far from here so he can make a quick response if necessary."

Ivy hoped it would be quick enough.

"I want you and Theo to go upstairs to the guest bathroom," Gabriel continued. "The hands have put a laptop there so you can watch the security cameras."

It took Ivy a moment to process that, and she didn't like where this was going. "If an attack happens, it'll likely be on the ground level of the house—where you'll be."

Gabriel nodded. "And I'll know they're coming before they even get here. I don't want to make this easy for whoever's after you by giving someone the opportunity to just start firing shots into the place. There's also another cruiser parked out of sight in the barn, and if things get bad, I want Theo to get you there and drive the two of you off the ranch. Don't worry, the hands and I will get out, too."

That caused every muscle in Ivy's body to tense. She didn't want her brother or anyone else right in the line of fire, but that might happen no matter where they were on the grounds. The trick would be to spot a possible attacker and capture him before he could even pull the trigger.

"The hands have made sure someone's not already on the grounds?" Theo asked.

"As much as humanly possible. They've been looking around since I called them a couple of hours ago."

But the hands could have missed a gunman who was hiding. The ranch was huge, and there were a lot of places for someone to stay out of sight of the hands.

"Hell," Gabriel grumbled.

Theo cursed, too, and Ivy lifted her head even higher to see what had caused their reactions. She soon saw the cause. There was a car parked just off the road where they were to take the final turn to the ranch.

And Wesley was there, leaning against the car as if waiting for them.

It wasn't an ideal spot for an ambush since there were no trees nearby, but that didn't mean Wesley didn't have something up his sleeve.

"What the heck does he want?" Theo added under his breath. His gun was already drawn, but he turned it in Wesley's direction.

"Should I stop?" Edwin asked.

The muscles in Theo's face tightened. "Yeah. Stop right here."

They were still a good twenty yards from Wesley, and Theo took out his phone. Since Ivy was sitting right next to him, she saw when he pressed Wesley's number, and when the man answered.

"I'm not going to shoot you," Wesley snarled. "You can come closer."

"This is close enough," Theo snarled right back, and he put the call on speaker. "Why are you here?"

She had no idea how long Wesley had been there, and since he was a good half mile from the ranch, the hands probably had no idea he was there. Still, for someone who'd come out this way to see them, he didn't jump to answer Theo's question.

However, Wesley did mutter some profanity that she could still hear from the other end of the phone line. "I came to apologize. I was wrong to accuse you of anything criminal."

"You were wrong, but you didn't have to come out here to tell me that. How'd you even know I'd be here?"

Wesley lifted his shoulder. "I went by the sheriff's

office, but no one would tell me where you were. I wanted to talk to you face-to-face, and figured sooner or later Ivy would want to come home. And that you'd be the one to bring her."

To most people that probably wouldn't have sounded like a threat, but it did coming from this man. Of course, that probably had something to do with the fact that he was still a suspect.

"I didn't have anything to do with what went wrong with that raid," Wesley went on. "It's important you know that."

"Why?" Theo didn't ease up on the intensity in his voice. Nor his expression, either.

Wesley cursed again, and looked away. "I don't want anybody watching my every move. I don't want people to think I'm a dirty agent."

"Too late. They already think that." Theo paused a heartbeat while he kept watch around them. Edwin and Gabriel did the same. "Let me guess—Dwight Emory has started some kind of internal affairs investigation on you?"

Bingo. Even though Wesley didn't confirm that, Ivy could see enough of his face to know that it was not only true but that Wesley was riled about it. He certainly wasn't looking apologetic now.

"I won't let this ruin my career," Wesley spat out. "Or my life," he corrected. "Just know that I expect you to stop it. You need to tell Emory I did nothing wrong."

Ivy figured there was little or no chance of that happening, which made her wonder why Wesley had really come. Was it to find out if they were at the ranch?

If so, he now knew they were, and if he was the person after them, they might not have to wait long for this to all come to a head.

"Drive," Theo instructed Edwin. "We've wasted enough time here." And with that, he hit the end call button but not before Ivy heard Wesley curse some more. The man continued to curse, too, when Edwin sped past him.

Ivy braced herself in case Wesley took out his gun and fired at them. But he didn't. She watched as he got back in his car, and he drove away—in the opposite direction of the ranch. Of course, that didn't mean he wouldn't just double back.

"What the hell was that all about?" Gabriel grumbled.

Theo shook his head. "I figure Emory put him on suspension, pending an internal affairs investigation."

An investigation that could be connected to the attacks against them if Wesley was indeed trying to silence Theo. Maybe Emory could find something against Wesley before things went from bad to worse.

Edwin took the turn to the ranch and drove through the cattle gate. She didn't see any hands, cameras or sensors, but Ivy figured they were all there. Another thing that wasn't in sight was the wedding decorations that had been on the fences. Someone had taken down the blue bows, a reminder that Gabriel's and Jodi's lives had been thrown into chaos, as well. They should be on their honeymoon by now, and here Gabriel was, preparing to face down a killer.

A ranch hand stood in the opened doorway of Gabriel's house, and the moment Edwin stopped the cruiser, Gabriel, Theo and she rushed inside. Gabriel set the security system.

"It won't be dark for a while," Gabriel reminded them, "but I don't want you two out of the bathroom. If you need something, call me, and I'll bring it to you," he added. "Oh, and you can use the laptops to monitor the security cameras. The motion detectors shouldn't pick up slight movement like a small animal or such, but if you hear a beep, it means we've got someone where they shouldn't be."

Someone who would almost certainly be there to kill them.

Theo and she didn't waste even a second. They went upstairs to the guest bath suite, and they locked the door just in case someone managed to break in.

"Don't turn on the lights." Theo put his hand over hers when she automatically reached for the switch. Both his touch and the warning caused her to look at him. The warning because it was a reminder that they could still be targets here. The touch, well, because even something that simple could cause a swirl of heat to go through her body.

Of course, the timing sucked for that, so Ivy stepped away. It wasn't a tiny space, not with the private toilet area, bathtub and massive walk-in closet all in separate rooms. But she suspected it wasn't the large space that had caused her brother to want them there. It was the natural stone walls in the shower. Like the cruisers, it would be bullet-resistant.

Ivy had been using this bathroom and adjacent bedroom during her stay at the ranch, but someone had added a few things. There was bottled water, a gun with extra ammo, some snacks and a laptop—which Theo went to right away. He sank down on the floor with the computer and booted it up.

"Stay away from the window," Theo added.

She did, though it was impossible to see in or out of it since it was made of glass blocks. Still, it wouldn't stop bullets like the stone.

Ivy watched the laptop, and it didn't take long for the images from the security cameras to appear on the screen. Six total. And while the cameras covered the ranch grounds, that still didn't mean someone couldn't snake their way through the trees and shrubs, staying out of sight of both the cameras and the hands. Though if that happened, maybe the motion sensors would detect them.

"I used to sneak to your old house this way," Theo said. He tapped the screen to the right of her parents' house. No one lived there now, but once there'd been a trail of sorts that led from the road and then coiled around to the back of the place where Ivy met him at the back door and let him in.

"Sneaked him in" was closer to the truth. Her parents had never been keen on her seeing Theo, so to avoid the arguments with them, it was just easier to let them believe she wasn't seeing him.

"I remember. My bedroom was on that side of the house, and sometimes I'd sit in the window and watch for you when you were coming over."

Actually, she'd done that even when he hadn't said

he would be over. Theo had pretty much dominated her thoughts in those days.

In some ways, he still did.

Like now, for instance.

His attention was on the laptop, but in profile she could still see enough of his face to bring back the old memories. Of their first kiss. The first time they'd made love. Ivy had been a virgin—Theo hadn't been—but it had felt incredibly special. Like something that'd never happened between two people before.

She silently cursed just how naive she'd been in those days. Because many couples probably felt that way. Couples who had managed to stay together and not be ripped apart by something as tragic as murder.

Theo went to another screen, this one on the trail that led from the old house to Gabriel's. Something caught her eye, and it must have caught Theo's as well because he zoomed in on a spot on the ground. She sank down on the floor next to him, their backs against the vanity while he made the necessary keystrokes to get the right angle.

Ivy hadn't realized she'd been holding her breath until she got a closer look and then relaxed. "It's one of the blue bows that'd been on the fences. A wedding decoration," she added. "It must have blown off and landed there."

Theo made a sound of agreement but zoomed in even more. Maybe to make sure the bow wasn't covering something like a weapon. But it wasn't. They were able to determine that when the wind blew it again and it skittered against one of the shrubs.

"Blue, Jodi's favorite color," Theo remarked. "She used to plan her wedding to Gabriel when she was just a kid. She had a notebook with pictures she'd cut out of magazines."

Ivy nodded. "I remember. I also remember Gabriel always saying he was too old for her."

"At the time, he was. Five years is a big gap when she was just thirteen, and he was already legally an adult."

Yes. But that hadn't stopped Jodi from making those plans or her feelings for Gabriel. Now, here all this time later, she would finally get to marry the man she'd dreamed about, the man she loved.

"I used to plan our wedding," Ivy mumbled. Oh, mercy. She hadn't meant to say that aloud, so she quickly added, "You know, when I was a kid."

Actually, she'd been a teenager and was still planning it right up to the time of the big blowup and murders.

Theo turned to her, and she got a much better look at his face now that it wasn't just his profile. And she felt that old punch of heat. Definitely not a good time for it, so she looked away.

Theo didn't, though.

From the corner of her eye she could see he was still watching her. Probably because he was stunned by what she'd just said. As a teenage boy, he certainly wouldn't have been into wedding planning and such.

"Did you ever hate me for leaving?" he asked.

Now she was the one who was stunned. "No." It probably would have been a good time for her to at least pause and pretend to think about that. A good time, too, for there not to be so much heat in her voice.

It was probably in her eyes, too. They'd been skirting this attraction since they'd come back to Blue River, but the skirting stopped suddenly.

Theo slid his hand around the back of her neck, pulled her to him and kissed her.

THIS KISS HAD *mistake* written all over it. And worse, Theo had known he was going to kiss Ivy from the moment she sat on the floor next to him. He also had known it would be good.

It was.

But that still didn't mean they should be doing this. For one thing, it was the quickest way for him to lose focus. Of course, Theo's body had a comeback for that—at the moment, there was no danger, and if that changed, the sensors would alert them to it. Still, this wasn't the right time or the right place. Too bad the thing that overrode that solid argument was that while everything else about it was wrong, Ivy was the right woman.

She always had been, and even though it'd been ten years since they'd been together, it was as if all those years vanished. All the old baggage, too. A good kiss could do that.

Along with making him stupid.

Theo should just end the kiss, move away from her and go back to watching the computer screen. But he didn't. Not only did he keep things at the stupid level by continuing the making out, he upped the ante by deepening the kiss and pulling Ivy even closer to him.

Ivy didn't exactly shy away from this, either. In fact,

she was the one who moved the laptop to the counter so that there was nothing in between them. No reason for them not to position themselves so that his chest ended up against her breasts.

Theo kept kissing her, too. Kept moving her until she was practically in his lap. All in all, it was a good place for her to be if they were going to have sex, but he was pretty sure that shouldn't happen. Of course, he felt the same way about the kiss, but that hadn't stopped him.

Ivy finally stopped, though. She took her mouth from his, eased back and met him eye to eye. He figured she was about to apologize or say something else before she moved back to the floor.

She didn't.

"Don't overthink this," she said.

Since that's exactly what he was doing, Theo hesitated and stared at her. Along with the old baggage vanishing, so did the years. Suddenly, he was nineteen again and wanting Ivy more than his next breath. He hadn't had much willpower, but that ate up the rest of it.

Theo pulled her back to him and kissed her.

This time there was definitely no overthinking. Hell, no thinking at all. He just kept kissing her until the fire was burning so hot inside him that he knew sex was going to happen even if it shouldn't.

Thankfully, Ivy was on the same page. Without breaking the kiss, she lowered her hands to his shirt and started to unbutton it. It was not a graceful effort. For one thing, Theo was trying to get her clothes off, too, and their hands kept bumping against each other. Still, he was finally successful at pulling off her top. He flung it to the side, and in the same motion, he turned Ivy and laid her back on the floor.

Because they'd been teenage lovers, they'd rarely had the luxury of a bed for sex. And Theo hated that they didn't have it now. Ivy darn sure deserved better than this, but there was no way he could risk taking her into the bedroom.

"Don't overthink this," she repeated.

She went after his shirt again, succeeded in getting it off him, and then she went after his jeans' zipper. Since things were moving fast, Theo got in some foreplay before the heat built to a point that they'd be beyond that. He took the kiss from her mouth to her neck. Then to her breasts. That brought back some sweet memories, and they got even sweeter when he unhooked her bra, bared her breasts and kissed her the way he wanted.

Ivy made a sound of pleasure and pulled him on top of her. Not a bad place to be, but he wasn't done yet. Theo went lower, dropping some kisses on her stomach while he unzipped her jeans and shimmied them off her.

Her panties went next.

And Theo probably would have kept kissing her for a few more seconds, but Ivy had a different notion about that. She latched onto him, hauling him back up to her so that she could kiss his mouth. And unzip him.

Theo didn't have much of a mind left. Not with his body burning to ash. But he did remember to take the condom from his wallet before Ivy got him out of his jeans. He also remembered how to put it on. No easy feat with Ivy still kissing him and trying to pull him into her.

The moment he had on the condom, he stopped resisting her attempts, and he slipped into her. Hell. He got another slam of memories. Of the first time they'd been together like this, and that slam only fired up his body even more. Definitely not something he needed, because this was already going to end much too fast. The pleasure was always too fast with Ivy, and like those other times, Theo tried to hold on to it.

She lifted her hips, bringing him even deeper into her, and Theo had no choice. There was no holding back, no more trying to draw this out to savor the pleasure. So he took control of the pace. As much as he could, anyway. He kept moving inside her. Kept holding her. Kept kissing her.

Until it was impossible to hold out any longer.

Especially when Ivy came in a flash. She made that sound of pleasure again. Gathered him in her arms. And she gave Theo no choice. He let Ivy take him right along with her.

Chapter Fourteen

Ivy dressed while she waited for Theo to come out of the private bathroom area. She figured he wouldn't be in there long, which meant she needed to try to compose herself before she had to face him.

The sex had been amazing, and while that pleasure was still causing her body to hum, she doubted that Theo would be humming. No. He was probably already regretting this.

He would see it as a lapse in judgment, something that had caused him temporarily to lose focus. Heck, he might even regret it because it was too much, too soon between them. Either way, she didn't want to look as if she expected something more than sex between them.

Don't overthink this, she'd told him.

Well, it was advice she needed to take, as well. What was done was done, and she'd just have to deal with the consequences later. In hindsight, though, Theo and she should have worked out a few things before having sex.

Ivy pushed all of that aside, put on her clothes and sat back on the floor with the laptop. There were still no signs of an intruder. Both a blessing and a curse. Part of her wanted this to come to a quick end so she could see Nathan. Another part of her wished there was a different way. One that didn't involve her brother and the hands in possible harm's way.

Theo's phone was still on the floor, and when it buzzed, she started to tell him he had a call. But then she saw Jameson's name on the screen and hit the answer button.

"Is Nathan okay?" she immediately asked.

Jameson hesitated a moment, maybe because he'd been expecting Theo to answer, and Theo must have heard the buzzing sound because he raced back into the main part of the bathroom. He was dressed for the most part but was still zipping up his jeans.

"He's fine," Jameson answered, and with a huge breath of relief leaving her mouth, she put the call on speaker and handed the phone to Theo. "We're all fine. Jodi and he are eating right now so I stepped into the bedroom to call you. I just got an update on Morris's family. I've already told Gabriel, but he said I should call you because he's basically got you and Theo locked in the bathroom…together," her brother added.

Even though Ivy couldn't see Jameson's face, he'd probably lifted an eyebrow over that. He knew that Theo and she couldn't keep their hands off each other. And they hadn't. But no way was she going to get into that.

"Did the cops find Morris's family?" Theo prompted when Jameson didn't continue.

"Yeah. They were in a motel just off the interstate. A maid found them. They were tied up, gagged and blindfolded but otherwise physically fine."

Ivy was betting that wasn't true of their mental state. Unless they were faking this, that is. "Who do they say took them?" Ivy asked.

"They don't know. The wife said that she and her daughter got back from shopping, and someone was in the house. The person used a stun gun on them. The guy carried them to a car and drove around with them for hours. In fact, he drove so long that he had to stop for gas."

"Certainly the thug made or got a call or two during that time," Theo pointed out.

"He made one call at the beginning of the drive and told the person that he had the 'goods,'" Jameson answered. "Neither the wife nor the daughter could hear anything the caller said, but their kidnapper assured whoever it was that he would keep driving until he got further orders."

All of this had no doubt happened while Morris was on his way to the safe house to attack them.

"The kidnapper received a call right before he dropped them off at the motel," Jameson added. "By then, they must have known Morris had failed and there was no reason to hold his family."

Yes, and the kidnapper's boss could have already started lining up the next thug he or she could use to storm the ranch. Thank God the person had seen no value in killing Morris's family. Of course, there was another thing to consider. If Morris had voluntarily been in on this, then his family could have faked the kidnapping and release. They might not know the truth about that unless they caught the man or woman who was responsible.

"The guy who stun-gunned Morris's family wasn't wearing a mask?" Theo asked her brother.

"No. The wife was able to give a description of the man, but it's a pretty vague one. Not sure we'll actually get much from it."

Even if they did, the guy was probably long gone by now.

"I'll get in touch with you if anything else comes up," Jameson assured them, and he paused again. "I guess you two have plenty to talk over once we're out of this mess. Let me know if I can help with that." And he ended the call before Theo or she could even respond.

Theo put his phone in his pocket, and even though his attention went back to the laptop, Ivy knew he was thinking about what her brother had just said. She certainly was. But she didn't have time to dwell on it because there was a soft knock at the door.

"It's me," Gabriel said.

Since he could have critical information, Ivy hurried to let him in. Theo stood, too, but he volleyed his attention between Gabriel and the laptop. Gabriel's eyes did some volleying as well—between Theo and her.

"Is everything…okay?" Gabriel asked her.

She nodded and hoped it didn't look as if Theo and she had just had sex. But judging from her brother's huff, it did look that way.

"The last time Theo and you tangled, you left town for ten years," Gabriel reminded her. "I'd rather that not happen again. In fact, when this danger is over and done, I want you to consider moving back here. It'd be a good place to raise Nathan."

It would be. Though she'd been comfortable enough at her own ranch, it had never quite felt like home.

"You wouldn't have to move in here," Gabriel added. He must have taken her silence to mean that she needed more convincing. "We could build you a place or you could have the old house."

"Definitely no to the old house. Too many bad memories there."

If she came back for good, Ivy would want a fresh start. Something that didn't add to the weight on her shoulders. Of course, that led her to the next thought that was on her mind.

Where did Theo fit in with this fresh start?

He'd said something about a desk job in San Antonio, but Ivy wasn't sure if he was certain of that or not. It was one thing to love his son and want to spend time with him, but it was another thing to completely alter his life.

"Is something wrong?" Theo asked, his attention on Gabriel now.

Because she'd been so caught up in the conversation, Ivy only then realized that Gabriel probably hadn't come up there to talk about their future. That sent her pulse racing, and it raced even more when Gabriel didn't jump to answer.

"Look at the camera that shows the old house," Gabriel instructed Theo. "You'll have to zoom in."

Ivy practically ran back to the laptop so she could see what was going on, but after frantically searching the screen, she had to shake her head. She didn't see anyone moving around or lurking in the shadows. But she did see an open window on the second floor.

"I'm pretty sure that window was closed last time I checked, and I didn't notice it until a few minutes ago."

It was open, not fully, though, only by a couple of inches. Since there were no lights on in the old house, it was just a gaping dark space. However, Ivy could see the reason for his concern—that window was lined up directly with Gabriel's house.

"The hands searched the place when we were on the way here," her brother continued, "but someone could have been hiding."

Yes, there was a huge attic along with enough rooms and closets that the hands could have missed someone. Someone like a gunman.

"Have you seen any kind of movement in the window?" Theo asked without taking his attention off the screen.

"No. And I considered having a deputy and a couple of hands go down there to check it out, but I decided against it. Too risky at this point."

Definitely, because the deputy and hands would be out in the open and could be gunned down.

"Just keep a close watch on it," Gabriel told them. "I'll focus on the other cameras."

Good idea, because whoever had opened the window could have meant to do that as a distraction. Maybe to lure them out. Or maybe just to take their attention off another hiding place.

Gabriel started to leave, and Ivy followed so she

could relock the door. But Theo said a single word of profanity that stopped them both. With Gabriel right behind her, Ivy went back so she could see for herself what had caused Theo's reaction.

And her heart went to her knees.

Because of what was now in the open window of the old house.

The barrel of a rifle.

FROM THE MOMENT they'd come back to the ranch, Theo had known an attack was possible. Likely, even. But it still gave him an adrenaline spike to see that weapon now pointed at Gabriel's house.

"Get in the shower now," Theo told Ivy.

Gabriel rushed out of the bathroom, no doubt so he could get to one of the windows downstairs so he'd be in position to return fire if it came down to that. Theo locked the door behind him and carried the laptop into the shower with Ivy and him, but not before Ivy grabbed a gun.

Her breathing was already way too fast, and Theo considered trying to do something to help her level it. But if he pulled her into his arms now, it would definitely be a distraction, and he needed to keep his attention on the rifle.

It was already dark, but there was enough of a moon to see the light glint off the barrel. Enough to see, too, when the barrel shifted just a little, and Theo spotted the scope on it. The shooter was taking aim at something, and he hoped it wasn't a ranch hand or deputy who wasn't hidden well enough.

"A shot from there would be able to make it here," she said.

It wasn't a question. She knew it could. But he hated to hear the slight tremble in her voice. Both of them wanted this showdown, but there was plenty of worry and fear, too.

Theo watched as the barrel shifted again, and he steeled himself for what he figured would come next. He didn't have to wait long.

The gunman fired.

Three shots, one right behind the other. Theo couldn't tell exactly where they'd landed, but they'd definitely hit Gabriel's house.

The shooter turned the barrel again, and the goon fired more shots. Not at the house this time. It didn't take Theo long to figure out what had been the gunman's new target.

One of the security cameras.

He'd shot out the one in Gabriel's backyard. That portion of the laptop screen went blank.

"The security system is still on," Theo reminded Ivy when she made a slight gasp. "If anyone tries to get into the house, the alarm will sound."

Plus, there were five other cameras and motion detectors. Theo figured, though, that the shooter would try to take out most of them.

And he did.

The next round of gunfire destroyed the camera on the side of the house, the one that had allowed them to see the rifleman.

"He's setting up an attack," Ivy said, her voice a

little shaky, but she kept a steady grip on the gun she was holding.

Theo hoped like the devil that she wouldn't have to use the weapon. While he was hoping, he added that maybe the ranch hands would spot this snake before he could get anywhere near Ivy.

They lost a third camera with the next shots. This one near the front porch, and it meant they now had a huge blind spot in the area that divided the two houses. Since that was also where the shooter was, Theo doubted that was a coincidence, and it meant the gunman would probably try to make his way to Gabriel's.

The silence came, and in many ways it was worse than the shots. As long as the guy was firing, Theo had known his location. Now he had no idea where the shooter was. However, he kept watch on the three other cameras since someone could be coming from that direction, too.

There was some movement on the screen from the camera on the other side of the house. Not an attacker. It was Al Talley, one of the ranch hands. He was at the back of a shed, and since Theo hadn't spotted him earlier, it meant Al had probably been in the shed itself. Maybe the gunfire had drawn him out.

Hell, or Al could have heard the sound of someone approaching.

Theo was about to text Gabriel to see if he knew what was going on, but the next shot stopped him cold. Because this one didn't go downstairs. It slammed into the window just a few feet from the shower. The bullet tore through the chunk of glass and sent it flying across the room.

"The shooter knows we're in here," Ivy whispered. Her grip tightened on the gun. She made a strangled sound of fear that came from deep within her chest.

Yeah, he did. That probably meant he was using some kind of thermal scanning equipment that could pinpoint them. The next shot proved it, too, because it tore through another chunk in the window, and the gunman kept firing, kept chipping away at it until the entire floor was littered with the sharp glass.

"Why didn't the breaking window trigger the security alarm?" she asked.

"Probably because this one wasn't wired into the system." It couldn't be lifted, which meant it wouldn't normally be a point of entry for someone trying to get in. It still wasn't, not with those jagged shards of glass sticking out all over.

"We'll just stay put," Theo said when the shots moved from the window to the wall. The wall adjacent to the shower. "The bullets can't get through the stones."

He hoped.

But the shots sure as heck could cause debris to fly through the air. It seemed as if the guy was trying to rip his way through the wall.

Theo's phone dinged, and he saw Gabriel's text message pop up on the screen. Are you both okay?

Fine, for now, Theo texted back.

He caught on to Ivy and lowered her until they were lying on the shower floor. It was larger than average size, but there still wasn't a lot of room with both of them in it. They were practically wrapped around each other.

I have a deputy and one of the hands moving in on the shooter, Gabriel added in his text a moment later. I think we can get this snake.

Theo was about to answer, but then he heard a strange sound. Definitely not an ordinary bullet this time. It was something else. Something that was about to make their situation a whole lot more dangerous than it already was.

A small metal canister.

It dropped onto the floor and started spewing tear gas.

Theo tucked the laptop under his arm, yanked Ivy to her feet and they started running. But it was already too late. The tear gas was burning their eyes and causing them to cough. Slowing them down, too. Not good. Because the gunman started firing bullets again, and this time Ivy and he were right in the path.

He crouched as low as he could, making sure Ivy did the same, and Theo somehow made his way to the door. The moment he had it unlocked and opened, he scrambled out in the hall, shutting the door behind them so it would hopefully contain some of the tear gas. Not all of it, though. It was already starting to seep right out at them.

Ivy was coughing so hard that she couldn't catch her breath, and he was certain her eyes felt as if they were on fire. His did, too, but Theo kept moving. Not downstairs, though. He took her to the hall bathroom. It had a tile floor but didn't have the stone protection of the other room. Plus, it had a massive window over the vanity.

It wouldn't take a gunman long at all to shoot through that.

But the last time Theo had checked, the ranch hand, Al, had been on that side of the house. Maybe he'd be able to put a stop to anyone who tried to put bullets or more tear gas into the room.

"Text Gabriel and make sure he's okay," Theo said, handing Ivy his phone. "I'll look on the laptop and see if we have any security cameras left."

They did. Three that were on the opposite side of the house from the shooter. Nothing much seemed to be happening there, but Theo heard more gunfire. This time, though, it came not from just one weapon but two. The gunman and someone else outside the house. Maybe a hand who had finally gotten in position to take out the shooter. Or at least stop him from sending more tear gas their way.

"Gabriel didn't answer," Ivy relayed to him. There was a new round of fear in her voice.

Theo was about to reassure her that Gabriel was probably just keeping watch and that nothing bad had happened to him. But he heard something that made Theo realize that might not be true.

The security alarm went off, the sound immediately blaring. And that wasn't the only sound. He also heard Gabriel's voice.

"Someone's in the house," Gabriel shouted.

Chapter Fifteen

Ivy hadn't thought her heart could beat any faster, but she'd been wrong about that. Just hearing what her brother said caused every part of her to start racing.

Her first instinct was to run downstairs and help Gabriel, but Theo kept his hand on her arm, no doubt to stop her from doing just that. Because it would have been a dangerous thing to do. She could get shot from friendly fire or cause such a distraction that it could get Gabriel killed. Still, it was almost impossible to just sit there and wait when the adrenaline was urging her to fight.

The security alarm went silent. Probably something Gabriel had done so he could hear what was going on. It was entirely possible that her brother had no idea where the intruder was in the house. Neither did she, but she took the laptop from Theo to try to have a look. There weren't any cameras inside the house, but maybe she could spot how the snake got inside.

Theo let go of her and opened the bathroom door a fraction so he could look out. He aimed his gun in the direction of the stairs, but if the intruder made it to that point, it meant he or she had gotten past Gabriel and the others. Rather than think about what that could mean, Ivy forced herself to focus on the computer screen.

And what she didn't see told her loads.

"No open windows or doors on the side, front or back of the house where we still have cameras," she relayed to him in a whisper.

That meant he'd come from the area between the two houses. Since the gunman was no longer shooting tear gas or bullets at them, it was entirely possible that he was in the process of trying to join his intruder comrade for a joint attack.

But how had the intruder gotten past the hands?

If it was just the one in the house, then it would make more sense. One person would have an easier time slipping into the house, especially on the side where they no longer had surveillance.

Ivy tried to pick through the darkness and see if there was anybody else out there. Al was no longer by the shed, and it took her a moment to find him. He was next to some shrubs that were only about ten yards from the back porch. He turned suddenly, taking aim at something on the blind spot side of the house, and he fired. Maybe he'd managed to take out anyone who was trying to sneak in.

Theo glanced back at the screen and muttered some profanity. At first she thought he'd done that because Al had likely killed someone who could have given them answers about all of this.

But no.

Ivy soon smelled more tear gas. And it didn't seem

as if this was coming from the guest bath where they'd been but rather from the direction of the stairs.

"We'll have to get out," he told her.

No way could she argue with that, because Ivy was already starting to cough. It wouldn't be long before they would be so overtaken by the gas that they wouldn't be able to escape.

She wanted to ask him if that meant Gabriel had gotten out, but she soon saw that he had. On the computer screen, she saw Gabriel running from the front porch to the side of the shed where Al had been earlier.

Even though her brother was firing glances all around him, he was also doing something on his phone. A moment later Theo's own phone dinged, and she saw Gabriel's text.

There's a collapsible fire escape ladder on the shelf in my bedroom. Use it to get out the window.

She showed Theo the screen, and he immediately got her to her feet. He took his phone from her and shoved it back into his pocket.

Since he didn't know the location of Gabriel's room, Ivy pointed to the end of the hall. There was a window on the "safe" side of the house where Gabriel was, and they could get out that way.

First, though, they had to make it down a very long hall.

Theo positioned her ahead of him no doubt so he could try to shield her from any attacker who made it up the stairs. If someone was indeed on their way to try to kill them, then he or she had to be wearing a mask since there was now a tear gas mist blanketing not only the stairs but the hall, as well.

Ivy coughed the entire way to Gabriel's room, but with each step also came the fear. At any point someone could come up those stairs and start shooting. If that happened, Theo would be right in the line of fire.

She thought of Nathan and prayed nothing like this was going on at the new safe house. Maybe, just maybe, they could put an end to this tonight. Of course, that meant catching one of their attackers, and right now, that didn't seem probable.

The moment Ivy reached Gabriel's bedroom, she hurried inside. Theo rushed in behind her, closed the door and locked it. Ivy didn't waste even a second. While Theo stood guard, she went to the closet, but since she didn't know exactly where the portable metal ladder was, she had to waste precious time looking for it. She finally found it, folded up like an accordion, and ran to the window with it. Theo helped her with it.

Or at least that's what he started to do.

Before the shot blasted through the bedroom door.

The sound was deafening, and it felt as if it had blasted into her. Despite her shaking hands, Ivy forced herself to stay as steady as possible. Panicking now wouldn't do them any good. Instead, she hooked the ladder frame over the windowsill and let the chain rungs drop.

She spotted Gabriel and hoped he would be able to stop anyone from shooting them while they escaped, but even if he couldn't, Theo and she couldn't stay put.

Especially not when another shot came at them. This one smacked into the wall right next to her.

"Go now!" Theo ordered her. "Leave the laptop so your hands will be free in case you have to shoot." And he returned fire.

Even though there was no way Theo could see the shooter, he obviously had a general idea of where the guy was because of the angle of the shots coming through the door.

Ivy scrambled out the window, and moving as fast as she could, she backed down the steps. Above her, Theo stayed put, volleying glances between the door, her and the yard. When she was halfway down, Theo followed her, and Ivy knew this was probably the best time for their attacker to go to the window and shoot at them.

If that happened, she prayed Gabriel would be able to stop him.

There were more shots from inside the house, and then they stopped. Did that mean the shooter was hurrying outside after them? Maybe. Ivy hadn't needed any other motivation to speed up their escape, but that reminder did it. When she got to the ground, she helped Theo and then turned so they could run to the shed.

But the sound of Theo's shout stopped her. "Gabriel, look out!"

Ivy saw it then. Something she definitely didn't want to see. A ski-masked gunman was behind Gabriel and was taking aim at him.

THEO IMMEDIATELY PULLED Ivy to the ground, though there wasn't much cover here by the side of the house.

The only thing was a line of shrubs, but since bullets could easily go through those, he knew they couldn't stay there for long. Right now, though, there was a more immediate problem.

Gabriel.

Ivy's brother had to dive to the ground, too. In his case it was on the side of the shed facing them. And it was barely in time. Because the masked gunman fired a shot at him, and if Gabriel had stayed put, he would have taken that bullet.

Theo levered himself up and fired the gun, sending the man scrambling out of the line of fire. He didn't want to keep firing in the guy's direction, though, because he didn't know if there was a ranch hand out there.

"There's Al," Ivy whispered. Of course, she was trembling. Terrified, too. And Theo was scared for her.

Theo followed the direction of where she'd tipped her head, and he saw Al halfway between the shed and the barn. The very barn where there was a cruiser. Somehow, Theo needed to get Ivy there since it would be the safest place for her right now. Gabriel and he were obviously on the same page about that, and the text Theo got from him proved it.

I'll keep this thug occupied while you take Ivy to the barn, Gabriel said. It was a group message, and he'd included Al and several of the other hands and deputies.

Good. That way, all the people on their side knew where Ivy and he would be so they were less likely to get hit by friendly fire. Of course, it was the unfriendly fire that they had to worry about.

Gabriel and Al did, too.

Both Al and Gabriel adjusted their positions and got their weapons ready to fire. Theo didn't move yet. He waited for Gabriel to go to the other end of the shed, and he started firing in the direction of where they'd seen the gunman disappear. Al joined him in the shots, and that was Theo's signal to get Ivy out of there.

Theo pulled her to her feet, and while keeping low, they started running. It wasn't that far to the barn, but he knew that each step could be their last. In hindsight, this had been too dangerous of a plan. However, there was no turning back now.

They ran to the end of the house, and Theo paused only long enough to glance around the back to make sure someone wasn't lurking there. If someone was, maybe Al would be able to take them out. Just in case, though, Theo angled his gun as best he could, and then he caught on to Ivy's arm with his left hand. They made it to the barn door, and he pushed it open.

"Stay behind me," he warned Ivy.

Despite the gunfire that was going on in the yard, Theo still took a moment to look around the barn. The overhead light was off, but there was a light on in the tack room, and it gave him some decent visibility. He didn't see a gunman inside, but then, there were plenty of places to hide.

Including the cruiser.

It was impossible to watch every corner of the barn, so Theo turned Ivy so they were back-to-back. Not ideal, since she could end up facing a would-be killer head-on, but at this point nothing was ideal.

"Shoot at anything that moves," Theo told her, because there shouldn't be any hands or deputies in the barn.

Without taking his attention off their surroundings, he reached out and slid the barn door shut. Having the place closed off didn't help with the visibility because it shut out what little moonlight there was, but Theo didn't want to risk one of those stray shots coming in the opening.

"See anyone?" she asked.

He didn't. But that didn't mean someone wasn't there. "No," he answered. "Let's move closer to the cruiser."

Outside, the gunfire stopped, but that didn't give Theo any peace of mind. He hoped it didn't mean Gabriel or Al hadn't been shot. But it could also mean the gunmen were running away. While part of him would have liked that, he didn't especially want to give them a chance to regroup and come at them again.

"I don't see anyone in the cruiser," Ivy said. Theo hadn't thought it possible, but her voice was trembling even more than it had before.

He, too, looked on the seat of the cruiser. No one. Well, unless someone was hiding on the floor. Someone could be on the other side of the vehicle, as well. That didn't help with the bad feeling that was snaking its way down his spine.

"When I open the cruiser door, get in," he instructed. "And slide across the seat so I can drive."

She moved to his side and gave a nod that was as shaky as the rest of her. She also still had a hard grip on her gun. A gun he wanted her to use if there was anyone lurking in the cruiser that they'd missed.

Theo shifted his body a little, and the moment he opened the door, Ivy scooted across the seat. She also locked the door on that side and then looked on the floor of the back seat.

"No one," she told him.

Theo was right behind her, and he locked up as well when he was behind the wheel. Thankfully, the keys were in the ignition, but he didn't start the engine. Not yet, anyway. He didn't want to risk the carbon monoxide building up while he was trying to contact Gabriel. Plus, the sound of the engine might cover up someone trying to sneak up on them.

"Keep watch," Theo reminded her, though he was certain it wasn't a reminder she needed. Still, he wanted to be sure because texting Gabriel would divide his attention for a couple of seconds.

We're in the cruiser, he texted Ivy's brother. And Theo waited for a response.

A response didn't come, though, and after a couple of minutes crawled by, he had to consider that Gabriel might not be in a position to respond. He figured that Ivy realized that as well because her breathing kicked up a notch.

The silence came and everything suddenly seemed so still. As if waiting for something to happen. And something happened all right.

More gunshots came.

All of them slamming into the sides of the barn. Both of them. Theo didn't know exactly where the shooters were, but it felt as if they were closing in on them. He couldn't wait any longer for Gabriel's response. He needed to get Ivy out of there in case these thugs had something more than bullets to launch at them. They could have explosives.

"Hold on," he warned her.

The moment that Theo started the engine, he hit the accelerator, and the cruiser crashed through the barn doors. But almost immediately he had to slam on the brakes. Because there in front of them were two gunmen.

And they had taken a hostage.

Chapter Sixteen

Because she wasn't wearing a seat belt, Ivy jolted forward when Theo brought the cruiser to a quick stop only a few yards in front of the back porch. And she didn't have to figure out why he'd done that.

There were two gunmen on the porch, their backs to the house.

They were both wearing ski masks, and they had their weapons pointed at Al's head. Al was standing in front of the two men, their human shield. They'd no doubt taken up that stance so that Theo or someone else couldn't shoot them.

Ivy's breath froze. Not her thoughts, though. The thoughts and fears came at her with a vengeance. These men were killers. Or that was their plan, anyway, and now the pair had them exactly where they wanted.

She pressed her left hand to her heart to try to steady it. Also tried to rein in her too-fast breathing. If she panicked now, it certainly wouldn't help them. No. She needed to keep a clear head and try to figure out how they could all get out of this alive.

But how?

They couldn't shoot at the men, and if they sped off, then they'd kill Al. At least Theo and she were in a bullet-resistant car, but that wouldn't help anyone else out there—especially Al. Ivy didn't know the hand that well, but he was out here because he'd been trying to protect her. That reminder twisted away at her, and once again she had to remind herself to stay calm.

"Step out of the cruiser," one of the gunmen shouted.

"Stay put," Theo told her, and he didn't hesitate, either. However, he did lower his window a fraction so he could yell back an answer to the men. "Put down your weapons. There's no way you can get out of this alive."

If Theo's threat bothered them in the least, they didn't react to it. They certainly didn't put down their guns. Ivy had to wonder if these men had been in similar situations as Morris. Had their loved ones been taken as well to get them to do this or were they merely hired guns?

Either way, this situation could be deadly.

"Get out of the cruiser," the thug repeated. "If not, we start puttin' bullets in your friend here."

"Hell," Theo said under his breath, and he glanced around, probably looking for Gabriel or the other hands.

Ivy looked for them, too, and she spotted Gabriel still near the shed. He was at the wrong angle to have a shot to stop this, and if he stepped out from cover, one of the gunmen could easily shoot him.

Maybe someone could come through the front of the house to get to the men. But then she had to mentally shake her head. The house was probably still filled with tear gas.

"Who hired you?" Theo called out to the men. "Because whatever he or she is paying you, it's not enough for you to lose your lives. That's exactly what will happen, too, if you don't stop this now."

Even though she couldn't see their faces, Ivy thought the one who'd been doing all the talking laughed. "Just get out of the cruiser. I don't think you want your woman to watch as we shoot this guy."

No, Ivy didn't want to watch that, but she figured the moment Theo and she stepped out, these thugs would gun them down. She didn't want to see that, either, but they didn't have a lot of options here.

"Who exactly is it you're after?" Theo asked. "Me or Ivy?"

The two didn't jump to answer but did have a short whispered conversation. "Ivy. If she wants to save you or anybody else, then all she has to do is open the door and come to us."

"You're not going out there," Theo told her right off. "They won't want any of us alive because we're witnesses."

Because her mind was whirling with fear, she hadn't actually realized that. But it was true. Heck, the thugs probably had orders to kill them all.

But why?

That was the million-dollar question. And they still didn't have the answer. Because any of their suspects could have hired or coerced these men into doing this. It was even possible that their boss was nearby, waiting to make sure his or her orders had been carried out.

"I have men all around here," Gabriel called out.

Her brother had moved his position just a little but was still thankfully behind cover. Or at least he was unless someone came from the back pasture. Hopefully, though, there were still hands out there to make sure that didn't happen.

"So do we," the thug answered back. "And time's up." He lowered his gun to Al's arm. "Either she gets out of the cruiser, or I fire the first shot. Just how much blood do you think he can lose before he dies?"

It was impossible for her not to think of Belinda Travers. She'd been shot and certainly hadn't survived. The same could happen to Al.

"I can't just sit here and watch him die," Ivy said.

Theo cursed again, glanced around as if trying to figure out what to do. "Get lower on the seat," he instructed. The moment she did that, he added to the men, "Give us just a few seconds. Ivy was hurt when we ran into the barn, and I'm trying to stop the bleeding. She's not in any shape to stand right now."

Ivy doubted the men would buy the lie, but it seemed to give them a little time because the thugs had another whispered conversation.

"They're wearing masks," Theo said, but it sounded as if he was talking to himself more than her. "The man who attacked Morris's family didn't wear one."

She considered that for a moment. "You think these are men you know?"

"Maybe." Theo shook his head. "Or maybe they're just cocky enough to think they can kill us all and escape." He turned back to the window. "Ivy needs an ambulance," he shouted to the men.

Theo then took out his phone, and while keeping watch of the situation on the porch, he also sent a text to someone. Probably Gabriel. Because a few seconds later, Ivy saw her brother glance down at his phone screen.

"Put on your seat belt," Theo told her.

Ivy was certain her eyes widened. "Why? What are you going to do?"

"Play a game of chicken to get these guys to scatter so that Gabriel can pick them off. But I want you belted in and as far down on the seat as you can go in case something goes wrong."

And there was plenty that could go wrong.

She managed a nod and did as he said. Ivy also kept her gun ready just in case this situation went from bad to worse.

"Hold on," Theo said the moment they were in place, and he hit the accelerator.

The cruiser lurched forward, but Ivy couldn't see what was going on. However, she could hear it. The men cursed.

And then a shot blasted into the windshield.

THEO HAD ALREADY braced himself for the shot that came right at them. The ones that followed, too. He gave the steering wheel a sharp turn so that his side of the cruiser bashed into the back porch railing. The impact certainly jarred Ivy and him. Seemed to jar the house, too.

But it didn't stop the gunmen.

Four more bullets came crashing into the cruiser's

engine and his window, cracking and webbing the glass to the point that it was nearly impossible for him to see.

He could hear, though.

And what he heard was Gabriel returning fire. Good. It was just as Theo had instructed him to do with that text he'd sent him.

Judging from the angle of the returned fire, Gabriel did indeed have the right angle or at least enough of one to get those gunmen. Maybe that meant Al had scrambled out of the way so they could put a quick end to this.

Since the side of the cruiser was now directly in front of the porch, Theo tried to peer through what was left of the glass. It took him a few seconds, but he saw the gunmen. Both were now in the back doorway of the house and didn't seem to be reacting to the tear gas. Maybe they had some kind of filtering equipment beneath those ski masks.

Both of the gunmen were leaning out from cover to continue firing. The one on the left was shooting into the cruiser. The one on the right was aiming in Gabriel's direction. No doubt to try to pin him down.

There was no sign of Al.

It was possible the thugs had dragged him into the house, and because the lights were off, Theo couldn't see anything in there, much less try to figure out if the man was alive. Later, he would need to do that, but for now he had a much more immediate problem.

There was another round of shots, these going into the engine, and it didn't take long for it to start spewing steam. They'd obviously shot out the radiator, which would make it impossible for Theo to use it for an escape. They certainly wouldn't get far enough away from those gunmen to do any good. Still, he'd known that right from the start. That meant they had to make their stand here and hope Gabriel and the hand could do enough to capture the shooters.

Now that they'd disabled the engine, the shooter shifted back to his window. The bullets tore a big enough hole in the glass that the shots started coming into the interior of the cruiser. He was betting these guys had a lot of ammo, and as long as the one kept Gabriel out of the picture, it meant the other one could continue blasting until he shot Ivy and him.

Another chunk of the glass came flying right at him, and Theo had no choice but to duck down. He didn't stay there, though. He came up off the seat, and he used one of the holes in the window to take aim so he could fire. He double tapped the trigger and sent the thugs ducking back inside.

It didn't last.

After only a few seconds, the thugs started shooting again. This time the glass fell right onto Ivy. She quickly lifted her hand, putting it over the back of her head, but Theo knew that wouldn't be enough to keep her protected.

The shots continued, coming at them nonstop, but there was other gunfire, too. It was coming from the pasture behind the barn. Probably one or more of the hands. Hopefully, that meant they knew that Al was out of the way so that he wouldn't be hit.

"Stay put," Theo told Ivy.

As expected, she lifted her head just enough to make

eye contact with him, and he saw her shake her head. "You're not going out there."

It darn sure wasn't something he wanted to do. Not with bullets seemingly coming from every direction, but he couldn't just sit there and let Ivy be hit. Something that could happen any moment now that the shots were coming into the vehicle.

"I'll use the door for cover," he told her.

She still shook her head and reached for him. Theo wanted to take the time to reassure her, but maybe that wasn't even possible, anyway. He put his hand on the door handle.

And then heard the sound crack through the air.

Not another bullet. It was a tear gas canister, and it smacked onto the ground just a few feet from the cruiser.

Hell.

Theo ditched his idea to open the door and instead try to start the engine to get them out of there. No such luck, though. The gunmen had seen to that. This had likely been their intention all along, and Theo had no choice but to move Ivy.

"We'll go out your side," he told her. "Open the door and get out but stay low. Wait for me, and then we'll run to the shed where Gabriel is."

It wasn't an especially good plan, but he didn't have a lot of options here. Especially not with the tear gas starting to ooze its way into the cruiser. His only hope was that the tear gas would hide his and Ivy's escape. Then he had to hope they didn't collapse along the way.

It wouldn't be a long run, but it would feel like a marathon with that gas burning their eyes and lungs.

Coughing again, Ivy threw open the door, and she practically tumbled out, landing in a crouching position on the ground. Theo kept low since the bullets were still coming, and he crawled toward her.

"Watch out!" Gabriel shouted.

Despite the gunfire, Theo heard him loud and clear, but he had no idea why Gabriel had yelled out that warning. Not until he saw the movement.

Someone was walking out of that cloud of tear gas.

That someone had a gun, and he latched onto Ivy, knocking away her gun. In the same motion, he took aim.

And the man fired.

THE SHOT WAS so close to Ivy that the sound blasted through her head. She braced herself to feel the pain from being hit. But nothing.

Well, nothing other than the pain in her ears from the noise.

From what she could tell, the shot had gone into the ground right next to her. Maybe he'd just missed. Or else it could have been some kind of warning shot. If so, it had certainly gotten her attention.

Despite the man's having hold of her and that fired shot, she was alive, and she needed to do something to keep it that way. Ivy turned, ready to push her attacker away before he could fire again, but she was already too late. He hooked his arm around her and put the gun to her head. Worse, he was in position so neither Theo nor her brother might have a clean shot to take out this guy.

She tried to elbow the man in his gut, but he only tightened his grip on her until he had her in a choke hold. It was already hard enough to breathe because of the tear gas, and that certainly didn't help.

The man, however, probably had no trouble breathing. That's because he was wearing a gas mask. Ivy caught a glimpse of it when she managed to glance back at him.

"Let her go," Theo growled. That's when Ivy realized he had taken up cover behind the back of the cruiser.

Of course, the man didn't release her, and he didn't respond to Theo's demand. He just started dragging her onto the porch. Only a few steps, and he would have her inside where there were at least two other gunmen waiting.

She forced herself to stay as calm as she could. Which probably wasn't very calm. But she needed to think. Needed to do something to make sure no one got killed before she even tried to diffuse this.

"If this is about my husband's money," she said. "We can work this out."

Again, no response. So if Lacey was indeed behind this, then she'd convinced the men not to bargain with her. Maybe by kidnapping their families. Maybe because Lacey had just paid them too well.

The man just kept dragging her, and the moment they reached the doorway, he pulled her inside. Ivy had been right about the gunmen being there. One was on each side of the door. A door they didn't close. They stayed there, no doubt ready to shoot anyone who came after her.

At least the tear gas inside had thinned out enough for her to breathe. But the bad news was that the goon still had her in a choke hold.

"I gave birth to Travis's only grandchild," she tried again. She needed to hit some kind of nerve so she knew who she was dealing with. "He wouldn't like it if anything bad happened to me."

The man still didn't say anything. That didn't mean August wasn't behind this, though. In fact, it didn't rule out anyone.

"Everything's in place," one of the thugs said to her captor.

She didn't recognize the voice, but it made her wonder if Theo would. Ivy peered out through the door but could no longer see him. Could no longer see Gabriel, either, but maybe either he or one of the hands was making his way to the front of the house where the man was taking her.

The lights were all off in the house, but Ivy looked around for anything she could try to grab so she could club the guy. The only thing she could spot was a vase on a table in the family room, but when she reached for it, the man snapped her back so hard that Ivy nearly blacked out from the pain and loss of breath. She couldn't try that again, not while he had her in a choke hold, anyway, or he might kill her. Still, she didn't intend to go with him without a fight.

But where was he taking her?

Better yet, how did he plan on getting her off the ranch?

She soon had the answer to her last question. There was a third masked thug by the front door, and he opened it. When the man dragged her onto the front porch, she saw the black SUV parked by the steps. Maybe this was the vehicle the shooter in the old house had used. It could have been driven up the path between the two houses. Given the limited visibility from the gas fog and the darkness, it would have been hard to see. Still, she couldn't imagine one of the hands not spotting it. Did that mean these thugs had killed them?

It sickened Ivy to think that could have happened, but with all the gunfire going on, it was impossible to know.

There was a new round of shots. This time at the back of the house where she'd last seen Al and those two hired thugs. Gabriel was in that general area, too, and she prayed that none of them had been hit.

In one last-ditch effort to save herself, Ivy dropped down her weight, trying to throw the man off balance, but he just hooked his other arm around her waist and kept going. Straight for that SUV.

"Wesley?" someone called out.

Theo.

Ivy couldn't see him, but judging from the sound of his voice, he was on the side of the house toward the front of the SUV.

As the man had done the other times Theo or she had spoken to him, he didn't say a word, but she felt his arm tense just enough to let her know that Theo had been right. This was Wesley or else someone working for him.

But why would Wesley want her?

"Ivy has nothing to do with this," Theo continued. "This is between you and me."

Again, her captor's arm tensed, but he still didn't talk.

"You don't want me to hear your voice," Theo added. "But I recognized one of your hired guns. He's a criminal informant. I know because I've used him myself. My guess is you got him to do this for cheap or else you threatened him with arrest. Either way, it doesn't matter. This ends here."

The gunmen at the front door came onto the porch, took aim at Theo and fired. Ivy's heart went to her throat, and her breath stalled in her chest until she realized Theo had dropped back in the nick of time. He hadn't been hit.

However, he could be.

In fact, this could end badly for all of them. That's why she had to try to bargain with this man.

"I'll go with you," she told him, "but you need to leave Theo and everyone else here alone."

Wesley or whoever this was certainly didn't jump to agree to that. The man started backing her down the front porch steps, and it would be only a matter of a few seconds before he had her in that SUV. Heaven knew then where he'd take her. Or what he'd do to her. Plus, that would leave the hired guns in place to keep attacking Gabriel, Theo and the hands.

Theo came out from cover again, and he fired at the

gunman who wasn't holding Ivy. The bullet hit the thug and despite the fact that he was wearing a Kevlar vest, he dropped onto the porch. That's when Ivy saw the blood and realized Theo's shot had gone into his neck. If he wasn't dead already, he soon would be.

Her captor mumbled some profanity under his breath and started moving her even faster. It was a mistake. Because it gave Ivy the chance to trip on the last step. She paid for it with pain when he bashed her upside her head with his gun, but that only got him out of position to shoot Theo.

Theo, however, was in position.

Now that Theo had a clean shot, he didn't hesitate; he fired three shots. All three bullets slammed into the guy's chest. He was also wearing Kevlar, but the bullets must have knocked the wind out of him because he fell, his head smacking onto the side of the SUV.

The driver's-side door flew open, and the gunman inside took aim at Theo. However, he barely had brought up his hand when someone fired. Not the gunman or Theo. It was Gabriel. He was now in the doorway of the house, and he'd taken out the thug with a shot to the head.

While Theo ran toward her, Ivy kicked the gun out of the fallen man's hand, and it landed a few feet away. Once Theo reached her, he maneuvered her next to the porch railing, where she'd have a little cover in case there was another attack, and he went to the man. The guy was wheezing and clutching his chest, but Theo ripped off the gas mask.

It was Wesley all right.

He cursed Theo and then smiled, his head dropping back onto the ground.

"You just signed their death warrants," Wesley said.

Theo was no doubt about to ask Wesley what he meant by that, but then she heard something she didn't want to hear.

An explosion.

She whipped toward the sound of the blast. Her parents' old house. And it was now in flames.

Chapter Seventeen

Theo cursed. He hadn't exactly relaxed, but he had thought the worst of the danger was over. Maybe not, though. His instincts were to go running to the old house, to make sure no one was inside, but that could be a trap. Something that Wesley had set up in case he failed here.

Which he had.

The agent was moaning in pain, but he still had that stupid smirk on his face. A smirk that could be there because he'd put someone in that house. Someone who was now dying because of the fire. The flames were quickly eating their way through the place, and even if they could get the fire department out right away, it might still be too late to save it.

"Three of the ranch hands are on the way down there," Gabriel said after reading a text. "And Edwin's just up the road. He'll be arriving at the old house in just a couple of minutes."

Maybe that would be enough, because it was also possible that Wesley had stashed the rest of his hired guns near there. Hired guns who would kill anyone who came their way.

Theo checked the SUV to make sure no one else was inside. It was empty. Theo also picked up Wesley's gun and shoved it in the back waistband of his jeans.

"Where are the gunmen who were at the back of the house?" Theo asked Gabriel.

"Dead," Gabriel answered while he tossed Theo a pair of plastic cuffs that he took from his pocket. "Al's back there, and he's keeping watch to make sure no one else sneaks up on us. The hands in the pastures are reporting that they're not seeing any other gunmen. Not live ones, anyway. They had to shoot a couple of them. Jace has rounded up a couple of them, too."

Theo released the breath he hadn't even noticed he was holding. Of course, there could still be a straggler out there, but maybe that person would just surrender now that his boss had been captured.

From the end of the trail, Theo saw the cruiser lights as the vehicle pulled to a stop near the burning house. Edwin, no doubt. At least now the hands had law enforcement help.

Gabriel made a call to someone else, but Theo didn't wait to hear who he was talking to. He first cuffed Wesley, and since it was still too dangerous for Ivy to be outside in the open where a sniper could pick her off, he put her on the passenger's seat of the SUV.

"Stay down," Theo warned her.

She gave a shaky nod and caught on to his arm when he started to move away. That's when he spotted the marks on her throat. Bruises and scrapes from Wesley putting her in that choke hold. It sickened him to think of just how close she'd come to dying.

And all because of him.

"I'm so sorry," Theo said.

Ivy shook her head, took hold of the front of his shirt and pulled him to her. She kissed him. It didn't last long. Just enough to soothe some of the raw nerves inside him. Still, he wanted to beat Wesley senseless for doing this.

Standing guard in front of Ivy, Theo turned so he could face Wesley. "Who's in the old house?"

"Just tying up some loose ends." The smirk finally faded, and he glared up at Theo. "You might as well go ahead and kill me. You know what they do to former agents in prison?"

Yeah, he did, but since this piece of slime had tried to kill Ivy, Theo didn't care what happened to the man.

"Who are the loose ends?" Theo pressed.

Wesley groaned in pain. Probably because he had cracked ribs. Or maybe the realization of what he'd done was finally hitting him. "One loose end," he amended. "Someone who helped me fund this little operation. Don't worry. I sent proof of the money trail to the sheriff's office so you'll know who paid for all these hired guns."

Hell. That could maybe be August or Lacey. Theo was hoping, though, that it was just a bluff and the only person dead in that house was the guy who'd fired those rounds of tear gas.

"It wasn't supposed to work this way," Wesley mumbled.

"No. If things had gone according to your plan, you

would have kidnapped Ivy and used her to get me to do whatever you wanted me to do."

That could involve anything from destroying evidence to murder. Because Wesley knew that Theo would do anything to get Ivy back.

But there was another angle to this.

If Lacey had been the one to "fund" all of this, then maybe Ivy had been as much of a target as Theo. This attack could have been designed to kill them both.

"The fire department, an ambulance and two more backup cruisers are on the way," Gabriel relayed after yet another call. "I'll stay here with Ivy and you until we're sure it's safe."

Good. But judging from Gabriel's tone and the way his gaze kept darting to the burning house, that's where he wanted to be. So did Theo, but it was too big of a risk to leave Ivy alone. Once backup arrived, Theo could get her out of there. Maybe they'd have more answers by then. Answers that Wesley could give them.

"I had no proof you did anything wrong in that botched raid," Theo told the man.

"Didn't matter. You suspected I had something to do with it, and you wouldn't have let go of it."

Theo shook his head. "I didn't suspect it until the attacks started."

Wesley made a sound as if he didn't believe that. And maybe he was right. In the back of Theo's mind, he'd always felt something was wrong. He wouldn't have let go of it, either, and eventually he would have started digging. That digging would have led him to Wesley.

"Did you think you could kill and silence everyone who could figure out you were dirty?" Ivy asked Wesley.

Wesley turned his head to the side, spared her a glance before making a weary sigh. "Yes. You don't understand. I can't go to jail." He groaned. "I'll die there."

"You didn't mind killing innocent people to save yourself. That makes you a coward," Theo told him. "And Belinda's kidnapping and murder is going to put you on death row."

Gabriel's phone buzzed, and he answered it right away but again didn't put it on speaker. Nor did he say anything. For several slow, crawling moments, Gabriel just listened to whatever the caller was telling him.

"The ambulance should be here any minute," Gabriel finally said, and he ended the call. He looked at Theo. "It's Lacey."

"She came here with Wesley?" Ivy asked her brother.

"Was forced here, according to what she said. She's alive, but Wesley had stun-gunned her and left her in the house with a firebomb that was on a timer before he and the thug came over here. She wasn't burned but took in a lot of smoke before the hands pulled her out."

Now it was Ivy's turn to curse. "Lacey is the one who funded Wesley."

Gabriel nodded. "Wesley apparently went to her with the plan, but she's saying she didn't have anything to do with any deaths. When Wesley tied her up, though, he told her he was going to pin all of this on her by making it look as if she'd died while launching an attack."

Yeah, and it might have worked, too. If they hadn't gotten lucky.

"I had no idea she'd go this far," Ivy said. She tried, and failed, to choke back a hoarse sob. "Nathan could have been hurt, or worse." Another sob. "We all could have been."

Theo kept watch, but he pulled Ivy into his arms for a short hug. It didn't help. Nothing would at this point. That's why he kissed her.

"I love you," he whispered. "And we're going to get through this."

She blinked, clearly surprised by his L-word bombshell. He'd never told her that, and she probably thought it was the adrenaline talking. It wasn't. He'd always loved Ivy. But now hadn't been the time to tell her.

And she certainly wasn't telling him she felt the same.

Definitely the wrong time, because Ivy had enough whirling through her head without adding that.

Theo got a good distraction—he heard the sirens. Lots of them. And he knew it wouldn't be long before he could finally get Ivy out of there. He took out his phone and handed it to her.

"Call Jameson," he instructed. "See if you can talk to Nathan."

The moment the cruiser pulled into the driveway, Gabriel came down the porch steps. "Arrest him," Gabriel told the two deputies who got out of the cruiser, and he tipped his head to Wesley.

Gabriel must have already instructed the ambulance where to go because it sped past them and went to his parents' house. The fire truck was right behind it. The two cruisers, however, came to Gabriel's. Both stopped, and a pair of deputies got out of the first vehicle and a third one exited the cruiser behind them.

Ivy kept watch of everything going on, but she continued her conversation on the phone. Obviously, she'd reached Jameson and could assure him that everything was okay. Well, as okay as it could be considering just how close she'd come to dying.

"Wesley said he sent something to the sheriff's office," Theo told one of the deputies who approached him. Her name was Susan Bowie, someone he'd known since he was a kid.

Susan nodded. "A courier delivered some papers about thirty minutes ago."

Right about the time the attack had started—though it certainly felt as if the gunfire had lasted a lot longer than that. "The papers implicated Lacey Vogel?"

Another nod. "They're records to show withdrawals from an offshore account in Ms. Vogel's name. There were other bank accounts to show where the money went."

Theo was betting they could match the deposits to the dead gunmen scattered over the ranch. Lacey had been an idiot to use a bank to pay for all of this, or else she'd been so hell-bent on revenge that she didn't take precautions. Of course, Wesley wouldn't have helped with those precautions, either, since he'd probably intended to set Lacey up right from the beginning. Lacey had helped him by making herself a prime suspect.

Gabriel stayed right by Wesley until Susan and a male deputy hauled the man into the cruiser. Theo watched, too, and even Ivy got one last look at Wesley before the deputy shut the door. At least Wesley wasn't smirking or smiling now. It had probably set in that he would never be in a position to hurt them again.

Nor Lacey, for that matter.

The ambulance would take her to the hospital, but after that, she'd be arrested. Not only had Wesley ratted out Lacey as funding this attack, Lacey herself had admitted to paying for the thugs used in the attacks.

"Susan, you and Mick go ahead and take Wesley to jail," Gabriel told the deputy. "Read him his rights. Do everything by the book." After Susan nodded, he turned to the third deputy. "I want you to stay here and help Edwin wrap things up. I need to use your cruiser to take my sister somewhere."

Gabriel didn't say where that somewhere was, but Theo figured it was the safe house. There was nothing that would get that look of terror off Ivy's face faster than seeing her son.

Their son, Theo mentally corrected.

He figured it would help settle him down, as well.

Theo hurried when he helped Ivy from the SUV and into the cruiser, and she ended her call with Jameson, probably so she could hear an update from Gabriel and him. As they'd done on their other trips, Theo got in the back seat with her, and as soon as Gabriel was behind the wheel, he took off.

"Please tell me we're going to the safe house," Ivy said.

"We are," Gabriel answered. "I'll drop you two off there and come back here and deal with the investigation."

That wouldn't be a fast or easy thing to do. Heaven knew how many dead bodies there were, and there was a huge crime scene to process. If there were any gunmen left alive, they would also have to be arrested and interrogated. Gabriel would be putting in a lot of long hours and all because of a dirty agent and a greedy stepdaughter.

"Wesley sent bank documents to the sheriff's office," Theo told Ivy and Gabriel, too, in case he hadn't heard what Susan had said earlier. "It should be what you need to bring murder charges against Lacey."

"Murder?" Ivy repeated on a rise of breath.

"Yeah. Because of Belinda, the CI and McKenzie. Since Lacey paid for the attacks, both Wesley and she will be charged."

Ivy stayed quiet a moment, probably letting that sink in. Then fresh tears sprang to her eyes. "It's over." Her voice was mostly breath and filled with relief. So, the tears weren't from sadness this time.

"It's over," Theo assured her.

Gabriel took the turn from the ranch, and once he got onto the main road, he sped up. "The safe house isn't far. Ten minutes or so. That should give you two a little time to…talk or something."

Theo met Gabriel's gaze in the rearview mirror, and even though Gabriel didn't come out and say it, he seemed to be telling Theo to go for it. But what Gabriel didn't know was that Theo already had. He'd told Ivy he loved her, and she hadn't said a word about her feelings for him.

Maybe their pasts were just too painful for her to

put behind her. Hell, maybe she didn't even want him in her and Nathan's lives. Well, tough. He was going to be there. At least in Nathan's, anyway.

"I'm taking that desk job in San Antonio," Theo said. Unlike Ivy's voice, there was no relief in his. But there was some anger. "I could try to put in for a transfer to Houston or wherever you end up—"

She slid her hand around the back of his neck, pulled him to her and kissed him. Hard. That was probably the fastest way to get him to shut up.

"I love you," she said when she broke for air.

Ivy went back for another kiss. Apparently, that was another way to get him to hush, because it stunned him to silence. Strange considering how much he wanted to say to her. But at the moment, he just mentally repeated those words.

And savored them.

Until she'd said it, Theo hadn't realized just how much he'd wanted to hear them. Not just now. But for years. Because that's how long he'd been in love with Ivy.

"I want to stay at the ranch," she continued, her breath as ragged as his was. A good kiss could do that. "Maybe build a house." She paused. "With Nathan and you."

That felt like a punch. A good one. Because it caused a warmth to go through him from head to toe.

"You'd sure as hell better ask her to marry you," Gabriel grumbled. "After all, you did get her pregnant ten years ago. She's crazy in love with you, and Nathan needs a dad. Heck, Ivy needs *you*."

Theo hadn't been certain that Gabriel was listening, but obviously he was. And he was right. That wasn't just Ivy's big brother talking. This was right between Ivy and him, and the past was the past.

"Well?" Theo said, turning to her. "Will you marry me?"

Just in case she had any notion of saying no, Theo kissed her. He made sure it was long and deep. Made sure he poured his heart into it, too. Which wasn't hard to do. Because Ivy already had his heart.

"Yes," she managed to get out before the kissing continued.

Later, they could celebrate. And he could get her an engagement ring. Later, there'd be time for a lot of things—like living the rest of their lives together. But for now, it had to wait, because Gabriel took the turn to the safe house.

The moment they pulled into the driveway, the door opened, and Theo saw something that made this complete.

Nathan.

His boy was there, right between Jameson and Jodi. And Nathan was grinning from ear to ear.

"Mom," he called out to Ivy.

Ivy scrambled out of the car, and before she made it to Nathan, Theo saw more tears in her eyes. This time he knew for certain they were happy ones. She pulled Nathan into her arms, kissed him and kept on kissing him until the boy was laughing.

"Dad," Nathan said when Ivy finally let go of him. He went to Theo and hugged him.

Theo had to blink back some happy tears himself. Not very manly to cry, but he suddenly realized he had everything he'd ever wanted right here. He gathered both Ivy and Nathan in his arms and held on tight.

* * * * *

Look for the next books in
USA TODAY *bestselling author Delores Fossen's*
BLUE RIVER RANCH *series:*

LAWMAN FROM HER PAST
ROUGHSHOD JUSTICE

And don't miss the first book in the
BLUE RIVER RANCH *series:*

ALWAYS A LAWMAN

Available now wherever
Mills & Boon Intrigue books are sold!

Lucas stiffened. Something was wrong.

Charlotte gasped for a breath, her fingernails digging into his palm. "Help…"

He cradled her hand between both of his, soothing her. "You're safe now, Charlotte. You're in the hospital and you're safe." But those four teenagers weren't.

She pushed at the sheets and grabbed the bed rail with her free hand. "I…can't see," she whispered between choked breaths. "I can't see you. I can't see anything."

Lucas's pulse clamored. "You mean you can't see the shooter? You were in the studio, weren't you? Or did you and the girls hide?"

"No…I was there," she cried, her chest heaving. "They stormed in and took them. I tried to save them, but the big one shot me and hit me in the head."

He leaned over the bed and stroked her arm. "Charlotte, it's okay, I know it was terrifying and you wanted to save your students. Just tell me what you saw and we can still save them."

"You don't understand. I can't see. Anything."

SAFE AT HAWK'S LANDING

BY
RITA HERRON

First Published in Great Britain 2018
By Mills & Boon, an imprint of HarperCollins*Publishers*
1 London Bridge Street, London, SE1 9GF

© 2017 Rita B. Herron

ISBN 978-0-263-26455-5

46-0118

MIX
Paper from
responsible sources
FSC™ C007454

This book is produced from independently certified FSC™ paper to ensure responsible forest management.

For more information visit: www.harpercollins.co.uk/green

Printed and bound in Spain
by CPI, Barcelona

USA TODAY bestselling author **Rita Herron** wrote her first book when she was twelve but didn't think real people grew up to be writers. Now she writes so she doesn't have to get a real job. A former kindergarten teacher and workshop leader, she traded storytelling to kids for writing romance, and now she writes romantic comedies and romantic suspense. Rita lives in Georgia with her family. She loves to hear from readers, so please visit her website, www.ritaherron.com.

To my beautiful daughter Elizabeth—who works
tirelessly to help victims of domestic violence and
prevent human trafficking

So proud of you!

Love you always, Mom

Chapter One

Charlotte Reacher knew what it was like to be alone. Without a home or family.

Unwanted. Unloved.

That loneliness had inspired her to start her art program for teenage girls in Tumbleweed, Texas. This particular group of four were all foster kids and needed reassurance and love.

She strolled through the studio smiling at the girls perched behind canvases that had once been blank slates, but now were being transformed. When they'd first organized the group six weeks ago, most of them had painted drab, colorless pictures, all grays and blacks, depicting the despair in their lives.

Not every girl had a bikini body, liked makeup and glamour magazines or cheerleading.

And not every girl had parents with the money to fix her flaws.

The confident ones knew how to socialize, make friends and express themselves, while others wilted on the inside, withdrew and suffered from low self-esteem. Cruel classmates complicated the situation with teasing and bullying, and caused the girls to die a little with every mean word said.

It had been the same for her, growing up in the system.

Her port-wine birthmark had drawn cruel remarks and stares, killing her own confidence.

She brushed her fingers over her cheek. Thanks to a gifted and generous plastic surgeon, who'd offered her services to needy kids when Charlotte was eleven, the skin was smooth now, the birthmark gone.

Still, the internal scars remained. These girls had scars, too. Both physical and emotional.

But here—in her studio, Expressions—everyone was free to paint or draw whatever they wanted with no judgment.

She just hoped the small town of Tumbleweed embraced the teens. So far, the locals had been nice to her. She'd made friends with Honey Granger Hawk, the developer who'd built the small house she lived in. Honey appreciated her cause and had thrown in the studio renovation for next to nothing.

Now Charlotte had a home, a friend and a business. And hopefully a family in this town and her students…

She adjusted the volume of the music playing in the background. Early on, she'd discovered that music relaxed her and the students. Now she allowed the girls to select the CDs they wanted to listen to during their sessions. Today Evie had chosen an upbeat country song.

"Ms. Charlotte, what do you think?" Fifteen-year-old Mae Lynn looked up at her with a mixture of apprehension and hope. She was shy and the most fragile of all of them, but she'd begun to warm up.

"I like the way you've used the colors," Charlotte said. It was obvious the sea of blues and grays represented her changing mood swings. Who could blame her, though? The poor kid had been in and out of more than ten homes in five years.

Two girls who were horse lovers, sixteen-year-old Agnes and her fourteen-year-old sister, Adrian, chatted softly about their portrayals of a big ranch where they hoped to live one day, while thirteen-year-old Evie splashed pinks and blues and purples in a whimsical pattern. Despite the fact that she'd ended up in a group home, Evie had a perpetually positive attitude.

Hopefully, her attitude would rub off on the others.

Suddenly, the front door to the studio opened, and Charlotte glanced up, hoping to see Sally, another foster child she'd invited to the class, but instead four tall masked men dressed in black stormed in, guns raised and aimed at the girls.

Charlotte froze, mentally assessing the situation. She had to protect her students no matter what. Pulse hammering, she stepped forward, placing herself between the men and girls.

The biggest man turned the gun on her. "Don't move."

She stared at the snake tattoo, then noticed a bolt of lightning tattooed on his neck.

Behind her, the girls screamed. Charlotte raised her hands in a submissive gesture. "Please don't hurt them," she said in a choked voice. "I don't keep much money here, but you can take it all."

"We don't want your money," the shortest guy shouted. "Get on the ground."

A sob echoed behind her, then another scream.

"I said get down!" the one who seemed to be in charge barked.

Charlotte dropped to the floor, her gaze scanning the room for something to use as a weapon, but her art supplies and brushes wouldn't do any good against these guns. Semiautomatics. They weren't playing around.

Her phone was inside her purse in her office, too. She didn't have a weapon or an alarm.

Boots clicked on the wood floor as the heaviest man strode to her. With one quick grunt, he slammed the butt of the gun against her head. Stars swam in front of her eyes as the world spun. More screams rent the air, shrill and piercing.

Panic shot through Charlotte. She had to do something. If the men didn't want money, what did they want?

"Leave us alone!" Adrian cried.

"Don't shoot!" Agnes said shakily.

A bullet pinged off the ceiling, silencing them all.

Evie ducked behind an easel while the sisters hunched together beneath a table. Mae Lynn pushed her easel over, paint splattering, and ran for the door, but one of the men grabbed her as if she weighed nothing.

"Please don't hurt me," Mae Lynn cried.

Charlotte pushed to her hands and knees, desperate. "Let her go. Take me if you want, but leave these kids alone."

A bark of sarcastic laughter, sickening in its sound, filled the air as the brute slammed the gun against her head again, then jerked her arm and flung her against the wall. Pain ricocheted through her head and shoulder and, for a second, she thought she might pass out.

Then everything happened at once.

The men charged the girls. Agnes and Adrian kicked and fought. Mae Lynn was sobbing, trying to wrestle free, while Evie scrambled toward the back room to escape, throwing chairs and paintbrushes, whatever she could grasp hold of.

The man chasing Evie tossed the table aside, then snatched her up, laughing as she flailed and fought.

One of them muttered something, but she couldn't understand the words.

Then the men dragged the girls toward the door to the outside. Charlotte couldn't let them get away.

Ignoring the pain in her skull, she grabbed the wall and pulled herself up, then staggered forward.

A second later, a gunshot erupted, then pain seared her shoulder where the bullet had struck. Another bullet zinged by her head and skimmed her temple, and her legs gave way.

She collapsed on the floor, blood gushing from her shoulder. "Let them go!" She crawled after them, but another bullet pinged the floor in front of her, then the intruders dragged the girls through the door.

The biggest brute stood guard, his gun releasing more ammunition across the room to keep her at bay. Bullets pierced the walls and ripped at the canvases, sending paint tubes and containers spilling to the floor.

Her blood mingled with the paint, and the two blended together, the vibrant colors fading to a dull brown. The huge man strode to her and slammed the gun against her head one more time.

A sharp pain splintered her skull, then the world turned black as he disappeared out the door.

SPECIAL AGENT LUCAS HAWK studied the photographs of the missing girls from Waco and Abilene on the white board in the task-force meeting room.

Two kidnappings, two different cities in Texas. Both by a group of masked men who'd abducted teenagers. Female teenagers.

The men's motive hadn't been confirmed, but Lucas suspected what they were doing, and it made him sick to his stomach.

He'd lost his own sister when she was just a kid and he'd been fifteen, and understood the agony these families must be suffering.

"There are eleven victims in Texas so far," Special Agent Tradd Hoover stated.

So far? Implying he believed there would be more.

"At this point, none of the victims have been found.

We have no real lead as to where the men are holding the girls, either." Agent Hoover paused, his expression grim. "Or for how long."

The sheriff from Waco raised his hand. "You don't think they're killing them?"

Agent Hoover shook his head. "If they were, we would have found bodies. We believe this is a highly organized human-trafficking ring. They're bold, aggressive, and the fact that they're abducting groups of teens implies they have orders to fill."

"Any witnesses?" Lucas asked.

"None that have survived," Agent Hoover said. "The kidnappers come armed and dangerous, and have taken out anyone in their path."

The door opened, and Deputy Director Henry Fredericks stepped into the room, rubbing a hand over his bald head. "Just got a call. Another group kidnapping. Four victims." He flicked his pointer finger toward Lucas. "Your hometown, Hawk. Your brother called it in. He wants us there. Yesterday."

A coldness swept over Lucas. The trafficking ring had struck Tumbleweed.

For God's sake, they'd just finally closed the book on his sister's disappearance and death.

With four teenagers from Tumbleweed missing, the town would be in an uproar.

"You hear me, Special Agent Hawk?" the deputy director said.

Lucas jerked himself to attention and stood. "Yes, sir, I'm on my way."

The deputy director cleared his throat. "There's something else. This time there's a witness. She's been shot and needs surgery. But if she makes it, we may have caught a break and she can tell us more about these sons of bitches."

Lucas nodded. If she knew anything, he'd find out. Then

hopefully they could stop this crew before they got too far away with the teens.

The wind whistled as he stepped outside. He jogged to his car and sped from the parking lot. The deputy director had said *if* the witness survived. He couldn't waste time.

He pressed Harrison's number as he drove, tension knotting his shoulders. His brother answered on the third ring.

"I'm on my way, Harrison. The deputy director said you have a witness."

"Hopefully," Harrison said. "She's unconscious now. The medics are transporting her to the hospital."

"How seriously is she hurt?"

"Took a bullet to the shoulder, lost a lot of blood. Looks like one of the jerks beat her in the head with the butt of a semi. Could be serious." Harrison's voice sounded gruff. "Her name's Charlotte Reacher, Lucas. She's a friend of Honey's."

Damn. "Where did it happen?"

"In town. Charlotte's art studio, Expressions. She does art therapy with troubled kids and adolescents."

The injustice of the situation made his blood boil. She sounded like a good woman. She sure as hell hadn't deserved this.

"All four of the teens were foster kids."

Lucas's gut clenched. Most crews slipped in quietly and worked under the radar. These bastards were practically shoving their crimes in the faces of the residents and the law.

They probably thought a small-town sheriff couldn't handle the challenge.

Big mistake. They didn't know his brother.

"We have to find them, Lucas," Harrison said. "This town is having a hard time with the recent arrest of one of our own. A violent attack like this is gonna hit hard."

His brother was right. Lucas tightened his hands around the steering wheel and pressed the accelerator.

Every second the girls were missing gave the kidnappers more time to get away.

AN HOUR LATER, Lucas parked in front of Expressions. Crime-scene tape had already been erected in front of the building and along the sidewalk outside, looking ominous against the soothing pale blue of the studio's exterior.

Harrison's deputy, Mitchell Bronson, was working to keep the growing crowd from crossing the line, but hushed whispers and worried, shocked looks floated through the group.

"I'm going to canvass the neighboring businesses and locals," Deputy Bronson said. "Sheriff said for you to go on in."

Lucas visually swept the street signs and posts. "Surveillance cameras?"

"Afraid not."

Damn, that would have helped. "Be sure to ask if anyone saw the getaway vehicle," Lucas said.

The deputy nodded and addressed the onlookers, holding his hands up to calm the crowd.

Lucas paused in the doorway to analyze the scene. The room was decorated with color palettes and paintings most likely done by students. A brightly lit sign showcasing the name sparkled in deep purple and yellow letters, at odds with the violence that had happened here today.

Worse, the room had been turned upside down in a scene that could only be described as chaotic. Tables, chairs, canvases and paint supplies were scattered across the room. Bullet holes marred the walls and canvases, as if more than one shooter had fired randomly across the space, hitting everything in sight.

Paint tubes, bottles and containers had spilled, the paint

running together, converging on the light wood floors in an ugly brown smear.

Footprints in different sizes that must belong to the girls tracked the paint across the floor, indicating the victims had fought back, and that at least one of them had been dragged.

A female's cowboy boot lay in one corner, obviously lost during the struggle. Beads from a bracelet or necklace were scattered by a bin of paint smocks.

Bloody fingerprints dotted the floor and wall.

"Here's what I think happened," Harrison said. "According to the schedule posted in the teacher's office, Charlotte was conducting a class. Four students." Harrison gestured toward the door. "Looks like the kidnappers just walked in. No sign of forced entry. Door was probably unlocked." He pointed toward the pool of blood on the floor. "Owner of the coffee shop/bookstore next door said Charlotte was giving, kind and dedicated to her students." Harrison ran a hand through his hair, emotion thickening his voice. "Honey would agree to that. She liked what Charlotte was doing here so much that she renovated this space for her at cost."

Lucas clenched his hands into fists. "Have you told Honey yet?"

Harrison shook his head. "No. I'm not looking forward to it, either."

Lucas patted his brother's arm. "She's strong. Tough. She can handle it."

"I know, but I...want to protect that woman from everything bad."

The love in Harrison's voice twisted Lucas's insides. The Hawk brothers had all been loners. He'd never expected Harrison to marry. Then Honey came back to town...

Harrison gestured around the room. "Charlotte obviously tried to stop the men, but judging from the number of bullet holes, they were heavily armed and opened fire. While she was down, the men snatched the teenagers and kept firing to prevent Charlotte from following. She passed out on the floor in that pool of blood. My guess is they thought she was hit in the chest and would bleed to death."

Lucas's stomach squeezed at the sight of the bloody fingerprints where the woman had crawled to the door. Even injured, she'd tried to save the girls.

"Any specifics on the hostages?" Lucas asked.

"Not yet. We're working on compiling that information."

"What about Charlotte? Any family?"

"No. She was alone. That's what drew her to Honey and these adolescents."

Damn. Lucas didn't know the woman, but he already admired her.

He just hoped she survived and could help them. Otherwise, the four teenagers might be lost forever.

Chapter Two

Pain throbbed through Charlotte's head and body. She tried to open her eyes, but a black void swirled around her and a heavy nothingness dragged her into its abyss.

Machines beeped. Low voices murmured. Metal clanged.

Where was she? What had happened?

"Got the bullet," a man said. "Need to stop the bleeding."

Charlotte searched her mind—she must be in surgery… but why?

A burning sensation seeped through her, followed by more darkness and quiet. Then a loud popping sound. Screams. Footsteps pounding. Her paints and canvases crashing.

Her studio, she was back there…the girls were painting, the music flowing, the door opened…

Terror seized her. Strange men stormed in. Men wearing masks. They were dressed in black.

And they had guns…

More screams. She had to save the girls…

The popping sound again. The bullet pierced her. Her head throbbed, colors bleeding together, fading.

Quiet again. Blissful quiet. Except for the voices. Someone touching her. A gentle hand.

"You're going to make it, Ms. Reacher," a woman said. "Just rest now."

Rest? The world twirled, nausea flooded her, then that slow burn again. She tried to move, but her limbs were heavy. Weighted. Something was attached to her arm. An IV.

"The police want to talk to you, but they'll have to wait. Sleep now."

Sleep? Rest? How could she? There was something she had to do. Something important.

The screams echoed in her head again. Her students... they needed her.

Terror and despair flooded her. Adrian, Agnes, Mae Lynn...sweet Evie...they were crying, sobbing, begging for help.

LUCAS PACED THE waiting room, anxious to talk to Charlotte Reacher.

Meanwhile, he phoned Tradd Hoover.

"The art teacher is still in surgery," he told Tradd. "The studio where the attack happened looked like a war zone. Bullet holes everywhere. My brother, Sheriff Harrison Hawk, is supervising the crime-scene unit."

"All four girls were foster kids?"

"That's right."

"That sucks," Tradd said. "As if their lives haven't already been hard enough." Tradd made a clicking sound with his teeth. "In the other two instances, the kidnappers didn't leave a witness behind. First abduction took place at a dance camp. Shot the teacher in the back before she even saw what was coming. More bullets were lodged in the floor near the ballet bar where the girls stretched. Five girls were taken, ages twelve to fourteen."

Good God. Twelve years old? She was just a baby. Innocent. A girl with no idea what the men had in store for her.

"Second attack was outside a Waco high school. Men snuck up on the cheerleading squad as they were walking to their cars after practice. This time they lay in waiting, snatched them one by one. No casualties. Science teacher was leaving about that time and saw the last of the six girls tossed into the back of a black van. Tinted windows. No tag. Driver raced away just as another girl ran around the corner. She was in the bathroom changing or she would have been taken, too."

"Did she see any of the men well enough to make an ID?"

"Afraid not. She was pretty shook up. Said all she saw was a man's back and the gun he was holding to her friend's head."

"You think we're dealing with the same men or factions of a larger trafficking ring?"

"Hard to say at this point. Unfortunately there weren't any surveillance cameras at the dance camp. There were two in the high-school parking lot, but the assailants shot them out."

Of course they did. "None at the art studio, either," Lucas said. Although he'd advise Ms. Reacher to install a security system if she reopened the studio. "How are the families holding up?"

"About like you'd expect," Tradd said. "They've seen enough TV and news stories to speculate on what's happening. None of it's pretty."

No, it wasn't. Most likely they were being drugged and held somewhere until they could ship them out of the country or to perspective buyers. They probably had clients waiting.

His stomach knotted. Too many depraved people in the world, and men who'd pay for sex.

The girls who didn't go to a buyer would suffer an equally harsh or worse fate. They'd be put in brothels, forced to work as prostitutes. Treated inhumanely. Beaten. Raped. Sometimes drugged, chained in a room so they couldn't escape.

"Email me the files, crime-scene photos, information on the victims so I can compare." Not that he thought the victims or their families had anything to do with this. This read like a professional hit. The ring targeted random groups that were vulnerable, easily accessible and fit a certain type and age range.

Otherwise, they would have also taken Charlotte Reacher.

Instead, they'd left her for dead.

THE GIRLS WERE SCREAMING. They needed her. She had to help them. Stop the bad men…

Charlotte blinked and tried to open her eyes, but she was so sleepy she couldn't force them open. A few minutes ago, she'd heard someone talking. The nurse, she said her name was Haley. They were moving her to a room.

She'd been shot. Had a head injury. Had undergone surgery.

She was lucky, Haley said. She was alive.

But what about Evie, Adrian and Agnes, and Mae Lynn?

Tears seeped from her aching eyes and trickled down her cheeks.

A warm hand touched hers. Slid over it and squeezed.

She tensed, then realized it felt good. Comforting.

And she was cold. So cold inside…she shivered.

"Charlotte, my name is Special Agent Lucas Hawk."

A man's voice. Gruff. Almost tender. Another squeeze of her hand and she realized the hand belonged to the man speaking.

"I know you've been through hell today and you're exhausted, but I need to talk to you. Need to ask you some questions."

She blinked, wanting to see his face, but her eyelids slid closed again. The medication must be weighing her down, drawing her back to the darkness. She wanted to stay there, to be numb and forget, to silence the screams.

"I promise you I won't stay long, but you were shot by some men who came into your art studio. They forced the students in your class to go with them."

Her lungs squeezed for air. She suddenly couldn't breathe. She clawed at the bedding, gasping. A machine beeped. Footsteps clattered, then a woman's stern voice said:

"Sir, you're upsetting her. You have to leave."

"I'm sorry," the man said in a gruff tone. "I won't stay long, but we need her help. The men who shot her kidnapped four teenagers. Time is of the essence. The kidnappers might be moving the girls out of the country as we speak."

The woman mumbled something Charlotte couldn't understand, but the agent's words taunted her.

She had to do what she could to help find her students.

She moaned and reached for his hand. He took it and stroked her palm. The contact gave her hope, and she forced her eyes open.

But the room was dark. Completely dark.

"I need you to tell me anything you remember," Special Agent Lucas Hawk said. "Even the smallest details might help—"

His words became garbled as panic seized Charlotte. She blinked furiously, but a cloudy haze of gray and black shrouded her vision. She couldn't see his face.

Couldn't see anything but an ominous black.

LUCAS STIFFENED. Something was wrong.

Charlotte gasped for a breath, her fingernails digging into his palm. "Help…"

He cradled her hand between both of his, tried to soothe her. "You're safe now, Charlotte. You're in the hospital and you're going to be okay." But those four teenagers weren't.

Dear God, he hated to push her, but they had to act quickly. The men could be halfway across the state by now.

She pushed at the sheets and grabbed the bed rail with her free hand. "I...can't see," she whispered between choked breaths. "I can't see you. I can't see anything."

Lucas's pulse clamored. "You mean you can't see the shooter? You were in the studio, weren't you? Or did you and the girls hide?"

"No... I was there," she cried, her chest heaving. "They stormed in and took them. I tried to save them, but the big one shot me and hit me in the head."

She jerked her hand from his and pressed it to her temple. She winced when she discovered the bandage. Her forehead was bruised and discolored, a knot at her hairline, and she had five stitches.

He leaned over the bed and stroked her arm. "Charlotte, it's okay, I know it was terrifying and you wanted to save your students. Just tell me what you saw and we can still save them."

A sob escaped her, painful and heartbreaking. "I couldn't stop them. I tried to."

"Shh, I know you did. I saw the studio, bullets were everywhere."

She grabbed his arm and pulled him closer, then stared up at him with terror-glazed eyes. "I did try, but I failed and they're gone."

"I'm sorry, that's why I'm here. I need your help, though."

"But I can't see," she cried again. "I can't see anything."

"You mean you didn't get a good look at the men?"

She shook her head wildly. "No, I mean my vision is gone. I can't see you or anything in the room."

A cold chill swept over him. She'd suffered a head injury. The doctor hadn't mentioned anything about her eyes, but it was possible…

"I'll get help." He rushed from the room and spotted the nurse. "Get the doctor. Now."

His commanding tone made the woman's eyes widen, then she raced to the nurses station. A second later, a page sounded over the intercom, then she hurried back toward him. He met her in the doorway.

Her disapproving look speared him. "I told you not to upset her."

"It wasn't me," Lucas said between gritted teeth. "She says she lost her vision."

Alarm flashed on the nurse's face, and she rushed into the room. Charlotte was lying so still that it sent a bolt of fear through him.

The nurse gently touched Charlotte's arm. "It's Haley, your nurse, Ms. Reacher. The doctor is on his way."

Charlotte turned her head toward the nurse, but the glazed expression in her eyes remained.

Then silent tears began to slide down her cheeks.

THE VAN THE men had put them in bounced over the ruts in the road and threw Evie against the side of the interior.

She bit back a groan of pain, blinked to stem the dizziness then wrestled with the zip ties around her wrists, but they wouldn't budge. Hands bound behind their backs, Adrian and Agnes were curled together in the dark corner. Agnes was sobbing while Adrian talked in low whispers to comfort her. Mae Lynn was lying on her side, her eyes glazed in shock.

When those nasty men had thrown them in the van, Mae Lynn had been screaming. One of them had jammed a gun in her face and threatened to kill her. Mae Lynn had gone quiet and hadn't moved or spoken since.

Terror gripped Evie's chest in a vise, squeezing her lungs. Ms. Charlotte had been shot. Was she dead?

Tears crowded her throat. No... She couldn't be. Ms. Charlotte was the only person in the world who cared about them. She helped Evie see that she might have a future. That bright colors and light existed. That she could paint beautiful pictures and express herself through art.

And that *she* was beautiful even though no family had wanted her as their child.

Agnes's sobs bounced off the dark walls of the van, drawing Evie back to the situation. She had to stay tough. Do something to get them out of here.

But what?

There were four men, and they were all huge. She barely weighed ninety pounds.

And they had guns.

If she could grab one of those guns, she might be able to force them to release her and the others.

She knew how to shoot. That, she'd learned early on.

Everyone thought she was a weakling. But they were wrong.

She'd survived one foster home after another because she studied people. She didn't know what these men wanted with them, but she had an idea.

A shudder coursed through her, and she squashed the thought.

She'd wait for the right moment, then she'd grab one of their guns. No one knew it, but she'd shot a man once. Foster daddy number five.

She'd had to, or be his bitch. That's what he'd called it when he took the other fosters to bed.

She wasn't going to be anybody's bitch. She'd kill whoever tried to make her into one just like she'd shot that bastard, foster five.

Chapter Three

Lucas gritted his teeth as the nurse shoved him from the hospital room into the hallway. A doctor rushed in, and the nurse joined him, leaving Lucas watching through the small window in the door.

The nurse took Charlotte's vitals while the doctor shined a light in Charlotte's eyes. Silent sobs wracked the petite woman's body, her fear palpable.

Was it possible the only witness to this damn trafficking had been blinded in the attack?

"Lucas?"

His brother's voice dragged him from his somber thoughts.

"What happened? Is she all right?"

"I don't know." Lucas exhaled sharply. "She just woke up from surgery."

"Have you talked to her?"

"I was trying to, but she got upset and the nurse made me leave."

"She's in shock," Harrison said.

Lucas's stomach knotted as the doctor tried to calm Charlotte. The nurse injected something into her IV. Probably a sedative.

Lucas folded his arms. "The head injury may have caused her to lose her vision."

Harrison cursed. "What did the doctor say?"

"He's examining her now," Lucas said. "Before then she was pretty groggy. She didn't say much except that she tried to save the girls, but the men opened fire."

Damn, he didn't like the picture that painted.

"I asked my deputy to notify the foster parents in person and to see if they'd noticed anyone suspicious hanging around their houses. Someone stalking the girls."

"Good idea," Lucas said. "Also, ask him if one of the foster parents seemed suspicious. We had a case once where a stepfather actually sold a girl for money to buy drugs."

"Good God," Harrison said. "What did the mother say when she found out?"

Lucas grimaced. "Hell, she was too strung out to even notice the girl was gone." Lucas and his brothers were damn lucky to have had the family they'd grown up in. In spite of their troubles and trauma over losing Chrissy, his mother had hung in there. If only his father had…

"Find out if any of the girls had computers at their foster homes. If so, confiscate them and send them to the lab. It's possible our kidnappers contacted the girls online. There, they can find out personal information about them, who their friends are, if they belong to a club or group, what their schedules are…"

"So they may be cyberstalking their victims, looking for groups to target?" Harrison said.

Lucas nodded. "Social media has opened up a new hunting ground for predators. People pretending to be someone they aren't. Scam artists. Pedophiles."

"I'll get right on it."

The doctor walked to the door, his expression concerned.

"How is she, Doctor?" Lucas asked.

The older man narrowed his eyes. "Are you family?"

"No." Lucas flashed his FBI credentials and Harrison

indicated his sheriff's badge. "We're investigating the shooting that put Ms. Reacher in here," Lucas said.

Harrison cleared his throat. "We're also trying to find the four girls abducted from Ms. Reacher's studio. If she saw something, it's imperative we speak to her ASAP."

The doctor ran a hand through his thick gray hair. "I understand the situation, but under the circumstances, my patient needs rest. We have to run tests to determine the extent of her injuries. I'm calling in a specialist, ordering a CAT scan, MRI and full neurological."

Lucas glanced through the window and saw Charlotte roll over in the bed to face the door. Compassion for her filled him. She'd obviously been traumatized and needed time to heal.

But every minute that passed meant the trafficking ring could be getting farther and farther away from Tumbleweed. And that any chance of rescuing Charlotte's students would be lost.

CHARLOTTE FOUGHT DESPAIR as she lay in the dark. She needed to do something to help find her students, but she was so groggy from the medication they'd pumped through her that she could barely function.

The doctor said her blindness could be temporary.

Which meant it could also be permanent.

No, she had to hold out hope that she would see again. Even if she didn't, she had to pull herself together and talk to that FBI agent. He wanted to find Evie and Mae Lynn and Agnes and Adrian.

She needed his help to do it more than she'd ever needed anyone in her life.

She hated being needy.

But the girls' lives depended on her swallowing her pride, not wallowing in self-pity and fear.

Still, she was so tired she drifted to sleep. Sometime

later, she woke up and realized she was in the midst of an MRI. She drifted in and out of consciousness through that procedure and the CAT scan, but couldn't keep her eyes open as they wheeled her down the hall.

The nightmares of the day plagued her. The bullets pinging off the floor and wall around her. The girls' terrified screams…

That group was the closest thing to family she'd had in a long time.

She had to fight her way back so she could find them. If she didn't, she'd never forgive herself.

WHILE LUCAS AND Harrison waited on Charlotte to undergo tests, Lucas brought Harrison up-to-date on the abductions in Abilene and Waco.

"Sounds like the same group," Harrison said. "Were the other victims foster kids?"

"No," Lucas said. "One case involved dance students at a ballet camp, the other, cheerleaders from a high school. The ballet instructor was shot and died instantly. No witnesses. Girls at the ballet camp were from various parts of Texas."

"So these guys aren't targeting a specific type, just females between the ages of twelve and eighteen."

Lucas nodded.

"Sick," Harrison muttered.

"Definitely," Lucas agreed. "Human trafficking is a widespread problem and has touched every major city in the US." Although Tumbleweed was just a small town…

Harrison spread pictures of the missing girls on the table in the waiting room. "These photographs correspond with the names of the girls in the class scheduled at that time, but we should confirm with Charlotte that they were in fact the ones abducted."

Lucas's heart hammered as he studied the pictures. All young and vulnerable, mere teens.

Prime targets for predators.

Lucas noticed the nurse slip Charlotte back into her room. He walked over and peered through the window again. Charlotte was agitated, waving her hands.

The nurse rushed to the door, and Lucas braced himself for her to tell him to leave her alone. Instead, she motioned for him to come in.

"She wants to see you. I told her she should rest, but she insists it's important."

Lucas's pulse jumped. Maybe she had a clue to help them find these bastards.

CHARLOTTE WAS SO exhausted that all she wanted to do was fade back into sleep and forget the horror that had happened today. Forget that four of her students were missing, and that she was blind.

The doctor said she needed time for the swelling to go down. The possibility she might need surgery existed, but they wouldn't discuss that yet.

Footsteps sounded and the door to her room squeaked shut. Her lungs tightened.

"Haley? Doctor?"

"No, Charlotte, it's me. Agent Lucas Hawk, Harrison's brother." The footsteps again, soft, as if he was controlling the sound, working to be quiet. "But you can call me Lucas."

Call him Lucas? She didn't even know him. Although she'd seen pictures of all the Hawk men, and Lucas was the most virile, handsome one of the bunch. He was also the most intimidating.

But his gruff voice was soothing, caring…almost sensual.

She thumbed her hand through her hair, self-conscious

when what her fingers connected with was sticky, matted. Blood from her head wound must have soaked the strands. She probably looked a mess.

Not that she should care. But she had the sudden urge to see herself in a mirror, to know just how deep the injury was. To know if she'd have a bad scar.

A dark chuckle bubbled in her chest as she realized she might never be able to look in a mirror again.

Footsteps again, then the scent of the agent's masculine aftershave wafted toward her. A musky odor that was pleasant, sensual, like his voice.

"You told the nurse that you wanted to see me? That it was important." He paused. "What is it, Charlotte?"

"I'm sorry about earlier," she whispered.

His hand gently brushed her shoulder. "You have nothing to be sorry about. You've been through a terrible ordeal today. I hate to bother you, but the longer we wait, the more time it gives these bastards to escape."

"I know," Charlotte said, battling tears. "They could be out of the country. We can't let that happen."

"No, we can't," Lucas said. "Can you tell me the names of the girls they abducted?"

Charlotte twisted the sheets in her hands. "Evie, she's thirteen. Mae Lynn is fifteen. Agnes and Adrian are sisters. Agnes is sixteen and Adrian fourteen." Her voice cracked with emotion.

"All right," he said quietly. "Just take your time and describe what happened. What you saw and heard."

Charlotte sniffed. "We were in the middle of class. I should have had the door locked." Guilt sucker punched her. "But it was midafternoon so I thought we were safe."

"Don't beat yourself up. This was not your fault. Tumbleweed is a small town. Most businesses don't lock their doors during work hours," Lucas said.

Charlotte latched on to his words. "But if I had—"

"Stop," the agent said more firmly. "Again, it wasn't your fault. Playing the what-if game won't help. Let's just focus on what the men looked like, anything they said. There were four of them?"

She stiffened. "How did you know that?"

"Because we believe they're the same group who struck in Abilene and Waco. Could be different hired men, but connected."

The implications he suggested sank in. "It's an organized group?"

"Yes, they're professionals," Lucas said. "Four armed and masked men strike, and kidnap teenage girls. So far they haven't left any witnesses behind."

A chill of foreboding washed over Charlotte. She was lucky to have survived.

They'd probably thought she was dead.

"Can you describe any of the men?"

Charlotte swallowed back bile. The pain was making her nauseous.

He continued in a gruff voice. "Were they tall? Short? Big? Small?"

She struggled to see the men in her mind's eye. "One was a big guy, tall, heavy, he seemed to be the leader. It happened so fast—we were painting, then the men rushed in. The leader ordered us not to move, then I realized they all had guns. I offered them money—"

"They didn't want money," Lucas said bluntly.

She shook her head. "The big one slammed his gun against my head. I fell and was dizzy, then the others started snatching the girls. They're young, but they've been through hell and they're tough." Maybe that toughness would help them survive. "They screamed and fought, and tried to escape. I tried to stop them but…" Her voice trailed off, her throat clogging with tears.

"But they shot you," Lucas said.

She nodded, swiping angrily at the tears that fell. "Then the leader hit me in the head again, and the others dragged the girls out the door. I crawled after them, but I was too late."

THE IMAGE OF Charlotte's bloody handprints on the floor taunted Lucas. She was a petite woman, but she'd made it to the door. Anger shot through him. He wanted to hurt these guys bad.

"You said you crawled to the door," Lucas said. "Did you see what kind of vehicle they were driving?"

Charlotte inhaled a deep breath as if struggling to piece her memory together.

"Was it a car? An SUV? A van?"

"A van," she whispered. "Black. Tinted windows."

Lucas's pulse jumped. The teacher in Waco had also mentioned a black van. "A minivan or full-size?"

"Cargo," Charlotte said in a pained voice.

"That's good, Charlotte. How about a license plate?"

Her brows furrowed together, the bandage on her forehead stark against her ivory skin. "I didn't see a tag."

"Was there any writing or a logo on the side?"

"I don't think so." Her face crumpled. "It happened so fast…"

"You did good, Charlotte." Hopefully she'd remember more as time passed. "Think about the men now. Did any of them have any distinguishing marks? A mustache or goatee? Scar? Tattoo?"

This time she pressed both hands over her face and rubbed her eyes. "The big one, the leader, had a tattoo on his hand. A snake." She paused. "His face was covered with a mask, but I think there was some kind of tattoo on his neck, too. It looked like a bolt of lightning."

"Good work, Charlotte. These details could be helpful."

He quickly texted the analyst at the Bureau the information. Keenan Hart was thirty, smart, and obsessive about details.

She quickly responded with a return text.

Black van reported in the Waco kidnapping. Authorities already on the look for it. Researching tattoos now.

When he looked up, Charlotte's eyes were closing. Sensing she was about to fade again, he hurried to ask his last question. "One more thing, Charlotte."

She moaned softly. "Hmm?"

"Did all of the men speak English or did one of them speak another language?"

She twisted her head toward him as if she could see him, but the blankness glazed her eyes again. "The leader was really the only one who talked. He spoke English."

"Did he have an accent?"

She frowned. "I don't think so. Why? Do you think they're foreign?"

His gut tightened. He'd suspected Columbian or Eastern European. But without witnesses to the other kidnappings, that was a guess.

His phone beeped with a text. Harrison.

Black cargo van spotted outside Tumbleweed at an abandoned warehouse. Meet me downstairs and we'll check it out.

Hope made Lucas's adrenaline spike, and he placed his hand over Charlotte's. Her hand was small and delicate, and her skin felt soft, feminine.

Thankfully, she was tougher than she looked.

"Charlotte, I may have a lead on that van. Harrison and I are going to check it out. Get some rest."

She nodded weakly although she was already drifting asleep.

He smiled at her, then sadly realized that even if she was awake, she couldn't see him. The thought bothered him more than he wanted to admit.

All the more reason he'd track down these sons of bitches and put them away.

Determination kicking in, he hurried to the elevator, rode to the lobby and rushed outside to meet his brother.

Harrison was talking to Honey on the phone. When he hung up, emotions clouded his face. "I broke the news to Honey. She's going to pick up some flowers, then visit Charlotte in a little while."

They hurried to his brother's SUV, and Harrison sped from the hospital parking lot. "Any more word on Charlotte's condition?"

"No. She's trying to be strong, but she's hurting and scared." Lucas tensed. "Doc says the blindness might be temporary. They have to wait on the swelling to go down. That might take a while. Days. Maybe weeks."

Harrison's expression turned grim, and they fell into silence as his brother maneuvered through town then veered onto the road leading to Dead Man's Bluff.

This place held bad memories for them both.

"Those warehouses have been abandoned for so long I'd forgotten about them," Harrison said.

Lucas nodded agreement.

But they would be the perfect place to hold the girls until they could move them to the buyers.

CHARLOTTE'S SHOULDER THROBBED, the pain intensifying as images of the kidnappers flashed through her mind. They had stolen the girls she was in charge of, girls she loved. Girls she was supposed to help.

The door squeaked. Her eyes flew open, but the black nothingness filled her vision.

Then a footstep. And another. So soft that she had to lie perfectly still to hear it.

"Lucas?"

A hushed sound. Breathing. Deep breathing. But no voice.

Terror seized her. "Agent Hawk? Harrison?"

No answer.

She reached for the call button, fumbling along the bed to find it.

The acrid odor of cigarettes wafted toward her.

Dear God, the leader of the kidnappers had smelled like cigarettes.

Had he come back to kill her?

Chapter Four

Cold fear pressed against Charlotte's chest. Lucas said that the men who'd taken her students had struck before and had never left a witness behind.

Had one of them come here to finish the job he'd begun?

She was stone-still and held her breath, hoping whoever was in the room would think she was unconscious and leave. If not for the scent of cigarette smoke and the fact that he hadn't said anything, she might think it was a doctor.

But doctors identified themselves.

Footsteps padded softly. Every cell in her body tensed with anticipation. Her left arm was hooked to an IV. All he had to do was inject her with a drug that would seep into her system and she'd drift into oblivion. No one would ever be the wiser.

She did not want to die.

Another footstep. The tray table made a noise as he pushed it away from her.

His breath punctuated the silence. The bed jarred as he bumped it.

She finally found the call button and pressed it, praying the nurse or a staff member would come quickly.

Her lungs ached for air. She slowly released her breath, straining not to make a sound or rustle the covers.

"Ms. Reacher," a deep voice murmured. "Are you awake?"

She lay perfectly still, careful not to flinch or even bat an eye.

"I hate to disturb you, but my name is Gerald Ingram, I'm with the police. I need to ask you some questions about what happened at your art studio."

He was a cop?

She slowly released a breath. But questions nagged at her. If he was investigating, why hadn't he been with Harrison or Lucas?

In spite of her efforts at control, her breath wheezed out, shaky and rattling in the tense silence.

Being in the dark heightened her other senses. If she could see his face, she might be able to tell if he was lying or out to hurt her.

"Ms. Reacher, I know you were injured and underwent surgery, but the men who shot you kidnapped four of your students. Can you describe them?"

Tears burned the backs of her eyelids, desperate to escape. In her mind, she pictured Adrian and Agnes, and Mae Lynn and sweet Evie. What was happening to them?

If the men planned to sell them as sex slaves, hopefully they wouldn't hurt them, at least not physically. That would mess up their product.

But the girls must be terrified.

Another nudge from the man's hand. "Ma'am, I need a statement about what happened. Did any of the men call each other by name?"

She searched her memory. Had one of them spoken a name?

"You're the only one who can help," the man said again. "Please talk to me. You do want to help find those girls before something bad happens to them, don't you?"

Anger shot through her, and she opened her eyes. Darkness. Not even a sliver of light.

"So you are awake?" he said with a hint of sarcasm to his tone. "Now, what—"

"Excuse me." A woman's voice echoed from across the room, and Charlotte realized the door had opened. The nurse. Finally.

"Sir, you aren't supposed to be in here," Haley said.

"If Ms. Reacher can identify the men who kidnapped her students, she needs to speak up."

Rustling of clothes and footsteps sounded as Haley approached. "Ms. Reacher has cooperated with the sheriff and FBI already. She's just undergone surgery and needs her rest."

The man's hand brushed hers. "Come on, Charlotte," he said impatiently, "give me something."

She blinked rapidly, her head throbbing with confusion, and the memory of the gunshots and girls' cries.

A machine beeped. Her heart monitor? Blood pressure?

This time a softer hand. Haley. "It's all right, Charlotte, it's all right."

"What's wrong with her?" the man snapped. "She's going to make it, isn't she?"

"Yes, but you need to leave."

"But she hasn't told me anything," he protested.

"And she's not going to," Haley said. "Now, either leave or I'll call security."

The man protested again.

"Now," Haley ordered.

Emotion bubbled to the surface, threatening to spill over. Charlotte hated being in the dark, and at the mercy of others.

Footsteps again, then the door closed. Her chest heaved as she breathed out.

Then Haley was back. "I'm sorry about that."

"He said he was a cop," Charlotte said.

"He was no cop," Haley said with a grunt of disgust. "That man is a reporter, and not a nice one. He'll do anything for a story."

Charlotte closed her eyes, grateful she hadn't said anything to him. She'd instantly felt uneasy with him.

Not like she had with Lucas. He'd made her feel safe.

The reporter's name replayed in her head. She vaguely recalled seeing him on the news. Haley was right.

He was ruthless. Had been known to run with a story without verifying the facts or his source. Had interviewed victims of crimes before and implied they were at fault for being victimized.

What kind of garbage would he air about her?

LUCAS SCANNED THE area as he and Harrison approached the abandoned warehouses. They were only a few miles from the cave at Dead Man's Bluff where they'd found his sister's body.

The gruesome image of her bones lying beside two other young girls' skeletons would haunt him forever. The fact that she'd lain there dead for almost two decades made matters worse. All that time they'd searched for her, and struggled to hold on to hope that somehow she was alive.

But her disappearance turned out to be a tragic accident. A mentally challenged boy named Elden had wanted to make friends with Chrissy, but he hadn't realized his strength, and he'd smothered her to death. His mother had protected him. Unfortunately, Chrissy wasn't his only victim.

Harrison's police SUV bounced over the rugged terrain, gravel and dirt spewing.

A row of three warehouses popped into view as Harrison steered the vehicle over a small hill. A rusted-out black cargo van sat by the building.

Except this van had been burned and only the charred shell remained.

Lucas's pulse jumped. If the trafficking ring had brought the girls here to house them until they moved them to buyers, they might have left the girls inside.

The area looked desolate, the warehouses weathered, the steel siding dingy. The Texas sun faded to night, casting shadows across the rugged land.

"It looks deserted," Harrison said.

"We need to check inside the spaces," Lucas said. "You'd be shocked at some places traffickers hold women and children. Boats, storage containers, old barns, the back of cargo vans and trucks. Damn inhumane."

Harrison's mouth tightened as he closed the distance to the warehouses. "Hard to imagine people buying and selling children and women like they're cattle."

Except they might treat cattle with more care. Although if selling the girls at auction to the highest bidder was their game, they would try to preserve the girls' physical appearance.

No visible bruising or injuries.

They'd probably use drugs to keep them under control.

Gears ground, brakes squeaking as Harrison slowed the SUV and swung to a stop. Lucas eased his car door open and slid from the seat, senses honed as he scanned the area between the warehouses.

He and Harrison both pulled their guns, and he braced for trouble as they walked past the charred van then toward the warehouses. Harrison shined a pocket flashlight across the ground.

Lucas did the same, then motioned to Harrison that he spotted tire tracks. He veered right to check the warehouse on the end, while Harrison went left. Gravel crunched beneath his boots as he approached, and he paused to listen at the doorway. He expected it to be locked, but the bolt that had held it closed had been cut and sat in a pile of weeds to the side.

He leaned against the door edge and listened, hoping to hear the sound of girls' voices, something to indicate they were inside.

But he heard nothing.

Frustration knotted his stomach as he eased the door open and aimed the light inside. The space was empty.

Dammit.

Still, he inched inside to search in case there was a room, a box, or a cage hidden in the darkened space.

CHARLOTTE FADED INTO a restless sleep and dreamed that a reporter was in the room snapping photographs of her. She woke, her pulse hammering.

Inhaling to calm her raging heart, she listened for signs the man had returned.

As a child, she'd been self-conscious of her port-wine birthmark. That image of her remained locked in her head, and reminded her that she had once been debilitated by it. No one had wanted her as their child. People had stared and made cruel remarks. Other children had been afraid that if they touched her, that stain would rub off on them.

Tears pricked at her eyes. She blinked furiously to stem them, searching for some semblance of light in the room, but blackness prevailed. Still, she ran her fingers over her cheek, remembering the pain of looking different and wondering if her face or eyes were scarred or appeared unusual.

If the morning paper or news would show her lying in bed, weak and vulnerable, the details of her sordid childhood exposed for the world to see.

Guilt and shame quickly overrode her concern—how could she possibly worry about her looks or people read-

ing about her past when her students needed her? No telling what they were going through.

Her breathing turned erratic again, and she suddenly
felt like her chest was going to explode. Pain shot through
her, stifling and frightening. One of the monitors went
off, the beeping more rapid with the tune of her breathing.

The door screeched open, then footsteps. "Ms. Reacher,
I'm here." Haley's voice, soothing and calm. Her hand gently brushed Charlotte's. "Did something happen?"

Charlotte shook her head. "A nightmare."

"That's understandable. You've been through hell," the
nurse said.

Charlotte gasped for a breath again, that tight sensation returning.

"Just try to relax, take slow even breaths."

"What's happening?" Charlotte asked, her voice cracking as she clawed for air.

"You're having a panic attack," Haley said softly. "It's
not uncommon, especially after suffering a trauma. Try
to imagine yourself in a happy place."

Charlotte nodded miserably and forced herself to do as
Haley instructed. Slow breaths. Think of a happy place.

Her studio. The paints. The vibrant colors. Reds and
blues and purples, shades of violet. Yellow, like the sun-
flowers she adored. Then pastels. The pale yellow of the
moon on a cool night when she gazed at the stars. The
light blue of the sky on a sunny day, of the ocean at sunset.

Except the attack had tainted the image of the studio.
Her happy place was no longer tranquil or peaceful, but
shrouded in the horror of what had happened.

No, she couldn't let those men destroy her place, or the
good that had happened in the studio.

The girls were painting, laughing, talking, listening
to music. Their hearts were opening as they poured emo-

tions onto the canvases, their spirits lifting as they began to trust her and each other.

"It's going to be all right," Haley said.

How could it be when she might never see her students again?

LUCAS SCANNED THE interior of the warehouse space, but it appeared to be empty. Knowing that appearances could be deceiving, he crept inside, senses alert in case the girls had been locked inside a cage or an underground space.

It had happened before. A woman buried in a box beneath the ground. They hadn't found her in time.

He prayed it was different for these young girls.

The flashlight painted a thin stream across the cement flooring, and he inched through the space, crossing to the back. Several barrels were pushed against the wall.

His heart raced as he rapped his knuckles on the exterior. A hollow sound echoed back. Still, he pried open the tops and searched each one.

Empty.

He didn't know whether to be relieved or disappointed.

Satisfied the space was clean, he crept through the back door and outside, then searched the bushes and grounds until he reached the middle warehouse.

Just as made it to the door, a screeching sound came from the interior.

Pulse jumping, he braced his gun and slipped through the opening. It was pitch-dark inside. The noise…there it was again.

A high-pitched wail.

Holding his breath, he aimed his flashlight along the wall, searching for the source. A wooden crate was pushed to the back.

Dear God. Was someone inside?

Chapter Five

The wailing sounded again.

Lucas rushed to the crate, anxious to see if someone was trapped inside. He examined the wood, noting spaces between the slits. It was about a twelve-by-twelve space.

He needed to open the damn thing. He used his hands to pry at the rotting boards. They easily gave way and he yanked off three of them to look inside.

Nothing.

Damn. Where had that sound come from?

He turned and shined his flashlight across the back wall. A pile of rubbish, old cans, wood, storage containers and trash. Determined to find the source of the wailing, he tossed aside all the junk.

Something moved behind the rubbish. Too small to be a person. An animal?

Sweat beaded on his forehead as he stooped down and dug away more debris. A small orange ball caught his eye. Then a low whine, like a baby crying.

A kitten.

Breath whooshing out in relief, he gently reached inside the space and scooped up the tiny feline.

Growing up on the ranch, he and his brothers had taken in stray dogs, but Chrissy had been the cat lover. Pain squeezed at his chest. She would have loved this little bundle of fur.

He nuzzled it next to his cheek. "Come on, little one, we'll find you a home."

Satisfied this warehouse hadn't been used for the kidnapped girls, he carried the kitten outside. Harrison was standing by the last warehouse looking grim.

Lucas's heart lurched. "What?"

"It's empty, but it has been used." Harrison narrowed his eyes at the kitten, but didn't comment, then motioned for Lucas to follow him inside the other space.

The interior was dark, but Harrison illuminated a path with his flashlight, and Lucas followed. In the far right corner, he spotted three old mattresses, discarded paper products from take-out restaurants and several empty water bottles.

But it was the hooks on the wall that made his blood run cold. Metal hooks connected to chains.

A used hypodermic lay discarded on the floor, a sign the kidnappers had drugged their victims.

"There's blood on the chains," Harrison said as he pointed to a dark stain.

Nausea climbed Lucas's throat, anger churning at the images that flashed across his mind.

"Let's collect some of this stuff and send it to the lab. Maybe we can confirm who was here and the kidnappers' drug of choice."

Harrison nodded, yanked on gloves and picked up one of the used fast-food bags. "Food looks crusted and moldy inside."

"They didn't bring Charlotte's students here," Lucas said.

"But there were others," Harrison said.

Lucas gritted his teeth. "Which means this trafficking ring may have been scoping out Tumbleweed a lot longer than we think."

Harrison scowled. "Do you think it's possible that someone in town is part of the operation?"

Good question.

Although none of them wanted to believe that their home town was hiding a ring of child traffickers, they couldn't discount the possibility.

CHARLOTTE WAS DREAMING about the girls again—they were screaming. Then one of the men grabbed her and dragged her toward the door with them.

She jerked awake, her breath choking out. She was still in the hospital. Dear God, she wished they'd taken her, too. At least she could have watched over the girls.

"Charlotte?"

Her fingers dug into the bedding as the sound of the hospital door closing echoed in the cold room. Then footsteps. Soft this time.

The voice had been a woman. Not the nurse, though.

A gentle hand covered hers. "Charlotte, it's me, Honey."

Relief surged through her, and she reached for Honey's hand. She'd met Honey when she was searching for a house, and they'd instantly connected and become friends. She liked Honey's knack for taking crumbling properties and houses and turning them into welcoming, beautiful, loving homes. "I'm glad you're here."

Honey pulled her hand into hers. "I'm so sorry about what happened, Charlotte. How do you feel?"

Honey's concern touched her deeply. Charlotte had been in and out of so many foster homes that she'd never gotten close to anyone.

One family had a scruffy rescue dog that she'd loved. Leaving it had ripped out her heart. Since then, she hadn't allowed herself a pet, either.

"Charlotte, sweetie, talk to me," Honey said softly.

Emotion clogged her throat. Honey was the closest thing

Charlotte had ever had to a sister. "I'm terrified for those girls. They should be laughing and shopping for outfits for school dances, not being terrorized by monsters who want to turn them into sex slaves."

Honey pressed a kiss to Charlotte's hand. "I know, it's horrible."

"I keep dreaming about the girls screaming for help. I can hear them crying, but I can't do anything." Her voice cracked. "I hate being helpless."

"Harrison and Lucas are doing everything possible to find them." Honey stroked Charlotte's hand to calm her. "They won't stop until they bring them back and put those horrid men in prison."

"But they could be on a boat or plane out of the country," Charlotte said. "You hear about cases where young women are kidnapped and never seen again." Evie's face haunted her, followed by Adrian's and Agnes's and Mae Lynn's. "The girls in my group have already been through hell. But this—this could be more than they can bear." Especially fragile Mae Lynn. She'd been a cutter before she'd joined the group.

Honey's quiet breathing whispered in the air. "Listen to me, Charlotte. I know those girls have had it rough, but they're like you and me, they're tough. Survivors. Harrison and Lucas will find them, then they're going to need you." She paused. "So the best thing you can do for them is to focus on your own recovery."

Charlotte blinked back tears. "But all I can think about is Evie and Mae Lynn—"

"Shh," Honey whispered. "You don't know the Hawk brothers like I do. They're the most trustworthy, brave, courageous, strong men I know. When they say they're going to do something, they'll do it."

Charlotte wanted to believe her. But she'd never trusted a man in her life.

Honey released her hand and disappeared for a moment. When she returned she dragged a chair up beside the bed, and dabbed at Charlotte's tearstained face with a tissue.

"Does your head hurt?"

Charlotte licked her dry lips. "Yes, but it doesn't matter—"

"It does matter," Honey said with conviction. "You matter to me, Charlotte." Honey's voice cracked. "I know it must be scary to open your eyes and not be able to see."

"I always hated the dark," Charlotte admitted.

"Me, too," Honey said softly.

Charlotte squeezed Honey's hand and blinked back tears. Maybe her friend was right. She had to be strong. Dig deep. Heal herself.

She wouldn't be any good to the girls if she fell apart.

LUCAS CALLED A crime-scene investigative team to search the warehouses and surrounding area, and to process the interior of the building, where they'd found the chains and blood. He and Harrison had done all they could do, but didn't want to miss anything. Even a partial print or button from one of the kidnappers could help.

His phone buzzed, and he settled the kitten in the SUV. He didn't know what he was going to do with it, but he didn't intend to leave it out here to fend for itself.

Maybe his mother would want it. Or Honey. Or… Charlotte.

Hell, what was he thinking? He didn't even know the woman. She might not like cats. And no telling how long she'd be hospitalized.

"Lucas, it's Tradd."

The agent's voice jerked him back to the present. "What's up?"

"Did you find anything?" Tradd asked.

"We're at some warehouses outside Tumbleweed that

appear to have been a holding place for victims, although judging from discarded food containers, they've been gone a while. We don't think it's the Tumbleweed victims."

"These crews know how to slide in and out under the radar," Tradd said.

"What about you guys?" Lucas asked.

"I'm on my way to the Mexican border," Tradd said. "Got a tip from a CI to check out. Agent Sandino is en route to Miami to look at some containers we suspect the traffickers might be using to transport the human cargo."

Human cargo. Those two words shouldn't be used in the same sentence.

"I'll keep you posted." Tradd ended the call and Lucas hurried to meet Harrison by his SUV. The crime team had arrived and they were combing the warehouse space, processing the charred van and searching the property. If there had been trouble with one or more of the girls or one had escaped, they might find someone in those woods.

The next three hours were grueling as they combed the area. Lucas and Harrison joined in, searching behind trees, rocks, in the ditches and a section of ground that looked as if it had been disturbed.

The dirt was piled high with leaves and brush spread across it. A grave?

Lucas jammed a shovel into the dirt, and proceeded to clear away the soil, leaves and sticks, while Harrison explored another section that had been covered up as if it led to a tunnel or a cave.

Lucas held his breath as he dug deeper and deeper. The shovel hit something hard, and a sick knot clenched in his stomach.

Was it bones? Or a body?

Chapter Six

Praying it wasn't one of Charlotte's students, Lucas dropped to his knees and dug with his hands, tossing aside dirt and leaves. Harrison yanked sticks, leaves and branches away from the space behind him that appeared to be a hidden cave.

Voices echoed from the woods. A coyote howled in the distance.

Dammit, he dug faster. His fingers hit something hard. He felt the surface. Jagged. A large stone.

Not a body.

Thank God.

For a moment, he was so relieved that he leaned his head on his arm and simply focused on breathing.

"Lucas?"

Harrison's voice made him jerk his head around. The grimness in his brother's eyes twisted Lucas's stomach.

"Did you find something?"

"I'm afraid so," Harrison said.

Lucas stood, dread rolling through him. Just a short time ago, he and his brothers had searched a cave not too far from here and found his sister's remains.

"One of our girls from Tumbleweed?" Lucas asked.

Harrison shook his head. "I don't think so. This body has been there too long."

Lucas stiffened. "You think it could have been one of Elden's victims that we don't know about?"

Harrison shrugged. "I doubt it. His mother came clean after we made the arrest. Once we identify her, we can find out if she was a kidnap victim, a runaway or...a victim of another crime."

Harrison phoned the ME while Lucas crossed to the cave entrance and ducked through the opening.

Sure enough, a skeleton was inside, brittle hair rotting along with the corpse.

Lucas shined the light around the bones, searching for any way to identify the girl, but there was no ID or wallet. Her clothes were decaying on her bones, yet he could see that three of her fingers looked broken.

Defense wounds?

Or she'd broken them trying to claw her way out of her chains in that damn warehouse. An image of her escaping taunted him, followed by another image of her being chased in the woods.

Harrison poked his head in. "The ME and CSI are on their way."

Lucas nodded and exited the cave, his anger blending with grief over the dead girl.

He hadn't known her but her young life had been snuffed out way too soon.

CHARLOTTE'S EYES FELT heavy again. "Thank you for coming, Honey," Charlotte said. "I have no idea what time it is, but if you need to go home, please go. I'll be fine."

"I'm not leaving until I hear from the guys." She patted Charlotte's hand again. "But you need to rest, so sleep, Charlotte. I'll wake you when I hear from them."

The need to close her eyes tugged at Charlotte, although even when she did, the darkness grew blacker. She couldn't erase the images of what had happened earlier or the sounds of her students' cries. "Why did they target me and my students?" she asked, thinking out loud.

"I don't know," Honey said. "Harrison said that they're part of a larger group so it was probably random. They probably scope out local businesses or areas where they can find female groups." She brushed Charlotte's hair away from her forehead again. "But this wasn't your fault. No one could have known what they were planning or where they were going to hit. And you certainly couldn't have stopped them."

Funny how Honey could read her mind. When she'd heard Honey's story of growing up in Tumbleweed, Charlotte had instantly been drawn to her. Honey reminded her of herself.

She was a survivor.

Sweet Evie's face flashed in her mind, along with her other students. Those girls were survivors, too.

The throbbing in her head intensified, and she lifted her hand and touched the bandage. The movement caused her shoulder to ache where she'd been shot.

"Do you need more pain meds?" Honey asked.

An image of herself as a child with that port-wine birthmark returned to haunt her. She wasn't a little kid anymore, but she knew her forehead had taken a bashing. "No, I'm okay." She refused to complain and wanted to clear her head. "Can I ask you something, Honey?"

Honey stroked her arm. "Of course, Charlotte. What is it?"

She felt silly for asking, but she had to face the truth. "Is my face, my eyes, am I…going to be scarred?"

Honey sighed softly. "According to your doctor, you have a half-dozen stitches, but they're in your hairline, and the wound should heal." She paused. "I know you've lost your vision for now, but your eyes look normal, Charlotte."

Charlotte blinked back more tears. "That sounded vain, and it's really not important, especially considering my students are in danger—"

"It doesn't sound vain," Honey assured her. "It's only human to wonder. Besides, you and I are alike, Charlotte.

We both have to know what we're dealing with, then we face it head-on."

Charlotte's throat closed. Honey was right.

When she'd first heard how awful some of the locals had treated her friend, she wasn't sure she wanted to settle in Tumbleweed. But Honey's giving spirit had made her want to call this place home.

Only now, her studio had been trashed, her future ripped apart and the kids she devoted her heart and time to help were missing.

LUCAS'S PHONE BUZZED as Harrison drove away from the ranch. Thankfully, his mother had been thrilled to have the kitten. He'd known she was lonely and should have thought of getting her a pet sooner.

Harrison veered onto the road leading to the hospital. Lucas connected the call. Keenan Hart from the Bureau.

"I've been researching those tattoos," Keenan said. "Snakes are common, and I've found several lightning bolts. I need more details. It would help if Charlotte would look at photos—"

"I'm afraid that's not possible," Lucas said grimly. "She lost her sight. The doctor doesn't know if it's temporary or permanent."

"Oh, gosh, I'm sorry. I'll send you the photos of the ones I found and you can describe them to her."

"Good idea." Lucas explained about the body they'd discovered at the warehouse and the charred van. "Also, run background checks on the victims' foster families. Check their financials for trouble."

"You think one of them is involved?" Keenan asked.

"I'm just covering the bases," Lucas said. If a foster parent had been bribed or paid off, he could use that as leverage to push him—or her—for more information about the kidnappers.

Before he hung up, his phone buzzed again.

"Keep me posted," he told Keenan, and then clicked to answer. "Brayden?"

"Yeah, I'm here with Mom. She was upset about what happened in town today."

Everybody in town was probably upset. Missing children had a way of inciting panic and fear.

"Reassure her that we're doing everything we can to find the missing teens," Lucas said.

"I have, but that's not the reason I called. We were watching TV, Lucas, and the story is plastered all over the place. It made national news."

Lucas scrubbed a hand through his hair. Of course it had.

"Some reporter named Gerald Ingram showed a picture of Charlotte in the hospital."

"What the hell?"

"He announced that she was the only surviving witness."

A litany of curse words spewed from Lucas's tongue. "That idiot bastard. He might as well have put a bullet in her head."

"I know. I'm sorry, man. Is there anything I can do?"

"Just stay with Mom for a while."

They said goodbye just as Harrison pulled into the hospital parking lot.

"What happened?" his brother asked as they parked and walked toward the entrance.

Lucas relayed the news about the reporter. "I should have posted security at Charlotte's door," Harrison said.

"I should have thought of it, too." But they'd both been too anxious to track down that van and look for the kidnapped victims. "I'll stay with her tonight," Lucas offered. "Tomorrow we'll assign a detail."

Harrison nodded, and they went inside and rode the elevator to the second floor. With that damn news report on his mind, Lucas scanned the halls and corridors in case one of the kidnappers returned to try and take out Charlotte.

CHARLOTTE WAS ROUSED from sleep again as footsteps echoed in the room. Then voices.

"How's she doing, Honey?"

Harrison. She heard the smack of his lips as he kissed Honey, stirring other emotions inside her. She'd watched those lovebirds with envy the last couple of months.

Harrison was lucky to have found a wonderful woman like Honey. She was lucky, too. Harrison seemed completely devoted to his wife.

"She's been resting some," Honey said.

"That reporter Gerald Ingram just aired the story that Charlotte survived."

This time, Lucas. His voice was slightly deeper than Harrison's. And darker. Intimidating.

"Oh, my God," Honey said. "That's not good, is it?"

"Afraid not," Harrison said grimly.

Charlotte shifted, pushing herself higher on the pillow to prop up. The room blurred into darkness, but she sensed the presence of Honey and Harrison and Lucas.

"I didn't know he was a reporter," Charlotte said. "He said he was a cop."

"Bastard," Lucas said. "He plays dirty."

"It's not your fault," Harrison said. "We should have anticipated that he'd try to sneak in and prevented it."

"The nurse ran him out." Charlotte ran a hand through her tangled hair. "You think one of those men will try to kill me?"

An awkward tense silence followed.

"You don't have to answer that," Charlotte said. "I guess that's obvious."

"We aren't going to let anything happen to you," Honey said.

"She's right," Lucas agreed.

Harrison cleared his throat. "We'll assign a guard to watch your room while you're here."

"I'm going home as soon as possible," Charlotte said. She hated hospitals.

"I'll stay with you when you come home," Honey offered. "We can have a sleepover."

A footstep, then something rustled. "That's not going to happen, Honey," Harrison said brusquely.

Another awkward silence, then whispering.

"Is something wrong, Honey?" Charlotte asked.

A heartbeat passed. "No, nothing's wrong," Honey said.

"What's going on, Harrison?" Lucas asked.

"Maybe this isn't the time," Honey said in a low whisper.

"For heaven's sake, I may be blind, but I'm not deaf," Charlotte said. "What's wrong, Honey?"

"Nothing's wrong." Honey's hand brushed Charlotte's arm. "I'm pregnant, Charlotte."

A light lifted inside Charlotte. "That's wonderful, Honey. I'm so happy for you."

She tugged Honey into a hug, tears dampening her cheeks. Hers? Honey's? Both.

"Congratulations, brother," Lucas said.

She heard motion and realized the brothers must be hugging.

"Have you told Mom?" Lucas asked.

Harrison shook his head. "You're the first to know."

Honey tucked a strand of Charlotte's hair behind her ear. "I'm sorry, Charlotte, I know this isn't the best time—"

"Shh." Charlotte hugged Honey again "This is wonderful timing. We need good news right now. And a baby... there's nothing more exciting than knowing you're having a little one."

"But you've been hurt—"

"Hush." Charlotte set Honey away from her, felt for her hands and cradled them between her own. "I'm happy for you. You're going to be a great mother."

"She will be," Harrison said. "Just like she's a great wife. But it's my job to protect her."

"You're damn right it is," Charlotte said with conviction. "And if having Honey near me puts her and the baby in danger, then take her someplace far away."

"That's not necessary," Harrison said. "But I do want her on the ranch."

"I'll take the first watch here tonight," Lucas said matter-of-factly.

Fear of the kidnappers slithered through Charlotte. But she wasn't about to show it in front of Honey. "Go home, Honey, please. Take care of yourself and that baby."

Honey hugged her again. "You know I'm here for you, Charlotte."

"I know. But I'd never forgive myself if something happened to you and that baby."

"There's nothing more we can do tonight," Lucas said. "Take your wife home, Harrison. Maybe we'll get a lead in the morning."

Shuffling echoed in the room as the men said goodbye, and Honey pressed her hand against Charlotte's cheek. "Call me if you need me."

Charlotte nodded, although there was no way she'd put her best friend in jeopardy.

Voices and footsteps followed as the three of them filed from the room. Charlotte blinked hard, willing her vision to return. Just a sliver of light. A color.

She always associated colors with moods, feelings, emotions. Blue for relaxing and calming, like the ocean. Red, orange and bright yellow for sunsets and optimism. Green for melancholy.

Black—the darkness she saw now—for emptiness. Fear. Uncertainty.

She tugged the covers over her as if they were a safety net. Honey said to trust Harrison and Lucas. Trust had never been in her vocabulary.

Chapter Seven

Lucas walked Harrison and Honey out into the hallway to leave, then slapped his brother on the back. "Congratulations again. You're lucky, bro. Take care of her and that little Hawk."

Harrison wrapped his arm around his wife's shoulders, tugging her close to him. "Don't doubt it, man. I will."

Honey smiled up at him, her eyes glowing. "I hate to leave Charlotte. She acts tough, but she's scared. More for her students than herself, but I'm worried about her."

"We aren't going to let anything happen to Charlotte," Lucas said, surprised at the fierceness of his own voice. He'd barely met the woman, but there was something about the combination of her vulnerability and strength that roused his admiration and respect.

She also aroused parts of his body he couldn't think about. He had no business noticing how beautiful she was when she was lying in the hospital injured and in danger.

"Let me know if you hear anything," Harrison said.

Lucas nodded. "You do the same." He gestured to Honey. "Now take her home. Mom will never forgive us if we keep the mother of her first grandchild up too late."

Harrison chuckled, and he and Honey walked down the hall, hands linked. Their mother would be ecstatic over the news. She'd grieved for Chrissy for nearly two decades. Although at first she hadn't welcomed Honey, she'd changed. Now she adored Honey and would love that child with all her heart.

A seed of envy sprouted inside Lucas. For years he and his brothers had harbored guilt over Chrissy's disappearance.

It was nice to see that Harrison had found a family of his own.

Lucas had never considered the possibility himself.

Do not go there. You have a case to solve. Charlotte Reacher is part of that case, nothing more.

Why the hell was he thinking about this stuff now? He had to keep his mind on the job. Being focused was imperative to being a successful agent.

The missing girls were counting on him. Lives depended on it.

Determined to stay focused, he scanned the hall to make sure no one was lurking around, waiting to hurt Charlotte. Satisfied it was safe, he stepped to the vending machine, got a cup of coffee, then strode back to Charlotte's room.

When he opened the door, the lights were on, but Charlotte was still, her dark hair fanned across the pillow, her eyes closed, her chest rising slowly with each breath.

She looked peaceful.

But the nightmares would return. If not in her sleep, when she woke up in the morning.

Suddenly Charlotte bolted upright. She clenched the sheets, shaking, her mouth parted in a scream.

"It's all right," he said softly.

Her breathing was erratic. "Honey?"

"She and Harrison left." He brushed his hand over hers. "It's Lucas. I'm right here."

"Lucas?"

"Yes, I'm staying tonight so you can rest." But tomorrow he'd push her to describe the tattoos. A sketch artist might help as well.

She exhaled, then rubbed a hand over her eyes, and his heart went out to her. "I'm sorry," she said in a low voice.

"You have nothing to be sorry about, Charlotte, so don't apologize again. Just lie back and sleep. Hopefully you'll feel better in the morning." Either that, or the drugs the doctor gave her would wear off, and she'd be in pain. Reality would be difficult, especially if her world was pitched in darkness.

"You don't have to stay, Lucas."

"I'm not leaving." He eased her back to rest against the pillows. "Now, go to sleep."

She pulled the covers up over her. Lucas gritted his teeth at the sight of the ugly bruise on her forehead peeking below the edge of the bandage. Anyone who hurt a woman was a monster in his book.

Hurting a child was even worse.

He would find these bastards and make them pay for what they'd done.

Charlotte settled under the blanket and closed her eyes, but sadness lingered on her face.

Damn. She was so beautiful he could barely take his eyes off her. He wanted to wipe out her pain and worry.

He wanted to see her smile.

Oblivious to his thoughts, she winced as she rolled to her side. Her shoulder, the stitches…she was uncomfortable.

But she didn't complain. Instead, she closed her eyes and lay in silence.

He flipped off the overhead light, then settled into the recliner beside her bed to stand guard.

No one was going to get to her tonight. Or any other time.

He'd kill anyone who tried.

CHARLOTTE WOKE THE next morning to the sound of rumbling. For a moment she was disoriented.

The noise again. Soft. Masculine.

Reality rushed back, robbing her of breath. Her students were missing…

The sound—snoring, a man's snoring… Lucas Hawk, Federal agent. He was guarding her because those horrible men wanted to kill her.

She jerked her eyes open, a sliver of light causing her to wince in pain. Then a total void again.

Despair threatened, but she tamped it down.

Still, she felt trapped in this room. Trapped in the dark.

She raked tangled hair from her face and pushed herself to a sitting position. Where were Evie and Mae Lynn and Adrian and Agnes? What had happened to them?

The door squeaked open and footsteps echoed.

Rustling. Then Lucas's voice. "I must have dozed off."

"No problem, Agent Hawk." Haley's voice. "I'm going to check her vitals and help her get a bath," Haley said. "The doctor will be here in a minute. A vision-rehabilitation therapist is also going to talk with her about handling her vision loss."

Emotion welled in Charlotte's throat. But she couldn't fall apart.

Like it or not, she had to make adjustments.

"I'd like to ask her a few questions," Lucas said. "And maybe get a sketch artist in here."

Footsteps again, coming closer. Then Lucas's masculine scent swirled around her. "Is that all right with you, Charlotte?" Lucas asked.

"Of course. Although I doubt if I can tell you anything more than I did yesterday."

"The analyst at the Bureau sent pics of tattoos similar to what you described. I was hoping we could narrow down the details."

The door opened again, and Charlotte heard more footsteps. "I have breakfast," a cheery female voice said.

Haley cleared her throat. "Give her some time this

morning," Haley said to Lucas. "Let her clean up and have something to eat then you can come back."

"All right. But I'll be outside the door."

"Lucas, I'm fine here with the nurse," Charlotte said. "Go home. Get breakfast and a shower."

"I'm not leaving until Deputy Bronson shows up to stand guard."

A reminder that her life was in danger.

"But I'll go get some coffee and be right back."

The door closed behind him, then Haley spoke. "How are you feeling this morning, Charlotte?"

Like she'd been run over by a train. "All right. I'm ready for coffee and a bath." Then she needed to focus on recovering her memory of the attack.

She had to do something to help find her students before it was too late.

LUCAS GRABBED COFFEE and a sausage biscuit from the café, then checked his messages as he ate. He hadn't meant to fall asleep, but a few hours rest would help today.

Harrison had asked Deputy Bronson to check out the foster parents yesterday so he punched his number.

"Deputy Bronson, it's Agent Hawk," Lucas said when the man answered. "What did you learn about the foster families?"

Bronson made a low sound in his throat, and Lucas realized he must have awakened him. "Let me grab my notes." Noises echoed, then the deputy returned.

"Okay," Bronson said. "Girl named Evie, thirteen, lived with a single woman named Joleen. She's midfifties, moving to Florida to be near her grandkids so was about to turn Evie back over to the state. She said Evie behaved at her house, but she'd been in some trouble before. Wouldn't talk about it."

It might not be important, but he'd find out what that was about. "Go on."

"Mae Lynn lived with a couple named Ruth and Philip

Cables. According to the couple, Mae Lynn was quiet, withdrawn, depressed. She was a cutter. They thought she needed more help than they could give her and already talked to the social worker about putting her in a residential treatment program."

Poor kid.

"What about the sisters, Adrian and Agnes?"

"Financials indicate that the couple fostering them had money troubles. Husband had been out of work with a herniated disc. Lost his job and disability ran out."

"Were they keeping the girls long-term?"

"They didn't say. The woman seemed concerned about them, said the other foster kids in the house were upset about the kidnapping."

"How many others do they have?"

"Three. All boys," Bronson said.

Maybe the foster father wanted it that way?

THE BATH FELT heavenly and renewed Charlotte's energy. Haley helped her dress in a fresh gown, which made her feel a world better as well.

"Your vitals are normal, and your wounds look good, too," the doctor said. "But it'll take time for you to regain your strength."

"And my vision?"

"Your tests are inconclusive. I'm afraid you'll have to be patient and give your body time for the swelling to go down, then we'll be able to tell more." He patted her shoulder. "Don't give up hope. Meanwhile, our vision therapist is going to talk with you."

"When can I go home?"

A tense pause. "Are you ready to go home? Do you have someone at your place to help you while you recover?"

Charlotte drew in a deep breath. "I live alone, but I'll manage."

Another heartbeat passed. "I realize you're a strong, independent woman," the doctor said. "But you've suffered a trauma and you need to heal both physically and emotionally. Vision loss, even temporary, presents challenges."

She gritted her teeth. "I'm aware of that." Anger at feeling helpless washed over her. She had no idea how she was going to cope. But she couldn't lie in this room in the dark forever.

But like it or not, she was going to need help adjusting. "I'll talk with that therapist about how to handle things at home."

"Good. Work with her and then we'll discuss your release."

Shuffling sounded and he left the room. Charlotte reached for the coffee on the tray that food service had brought, but her hand knocked it over and she yelped as hot coffee spilled onto the table and into her lap.

Frustrated, she pushed away the tray and lifted the sheet from her thighs. Footsteps shuffled, then she recognized Lucas's voice.

"Here, let me help."

Tears burned the backs of her eyelids. "No, I've got it."

But she didn't have it. And the fact that she couldn't have a cup of coffee or eat breakfast without help made her sick inside.

She hadn't relied on anyone but herself for so long. How was she going to live on her own?

Worse, how was she going to help find her students if she was so weak?

EVIE SCOOTED CLOSER to Mae Lynn. She was worried about the girl. She'd stopped crying and drifted into a silent shell. That was worse than the bawling.

Adrian and Agnes were huddled together in the corner on the floor, shell-shocked but alert as if they were waiting for their abductors to return.

Evie had no idea where they were. They'd been traveling for what seemed like hours, over hills and bumps. Once she'd heard water, and felt like they were on a bridge.

In the movies, the people listened for sounds so they could figure out where they were being taken.

But hell, that stupid drug they'd given her had knocked her out and she'd lost too much time. It was so damn dark in here that she didn't even know if it was daytime or nighttime.

She nudged Mae Lynn's arm with her hands. She'd been trying to rip that zip tie off but had only managed to make her wrists bleed. "Stay strong, Mae Lynn," Evie said. "We're going to get out of here."

Mae Lynn didn't budge. Didn't even blink. She just stared into space.

"You know what they're going to do to us, don't you?" Adrian said.

Evie chewed her bottom lip and nodded. "But we're not going to let them. We'll escape."

"How?" Agnes whispered, her voice raw from crying.

"I don't know yet," Evie said. "But we have to stay strong. When the right time comes, we'll find a way." She hesitated. "For now, try to think of what we'll do and where we'll go when we get away."

The girls looked at her as if she was insane. She couldn't blame them. The room or container, wherever they were, was dark and cold and the air felt stale.

But she closed her eyes and imagined Ms. Charlotte's studio. It was the first place where she'd felt happy.

She pictured herself dipping the brush into bright yellow paint and saw herself painting the sunrise. Orange and red came next, then a garden with beautiful wildflowers in pale lavender and purple. Butterflies fluttered above the flowers and grass, an ocean of colors dancing as the butterflies soared around her face.

She'd never seen this place, but she would survive and find it one day. And nothing would stop her from picking those wildflowers and chasing the butterflies in the garden.

Chapter Eight

The next two days were tense and long for Charlotte. Just as he'd promised, Lucas kept someone posted at her door.

The day before, she worked with a sketch artist to describe the kidnappers for a mock-up to show to the public, but she struggled for details that might help and ended up feeling even more anxious.

Between fatigue, headaches and her frustration over losing her sight, despair pulled at her.

But each time her hope slipped, she imagined Evie singing as she painted, imagined Adrian and Agnes chattering about the horses they wanted to own one day, and Mae Lynn with her big, sad eyes brightening when Charlotte praised her knack for mixing colors to create shades that gave her paintings a layered, thought-provoking look. The girl had talent and didn't know it.

The vision therapist had been teaching her tips on coping without her sight. She'd agreed to come to Charlotte's house, help her organize her rooms so she could function independently and be somewhat self-sufficient.

Charlotte was ready to dive in. Anything to leave the hospital and this room.

Last night, when everything grew quiet, the memories of the attack had haunted her. She'd lain awake for hours, wondering where the girls were and what was happening to them.

She was beginning to think Lucas had overreacted to the media coverage of her survival. She wanted to call off the guards, but he insisted on keeping watch.

Having him near her made her uncomfortable. Nervous. Not because she feared him, though.

Because his deep, husky voice sounded sexy and triggered visions of Lucas holding her and kissing her.

She silently chastised herself. Why was she lusting after the man when they hadn't found her students?

The door opened, and immediately Lucas's sultry scent wafted to her. Raw. Masculine. Woodsy.

Her heart fluttered. On the heels of her reaction, reality intruded. "Do you have news, Lucas?"

His footfalls came closer. "I'm afraid not. Harrison and his deputy and I have combed the area and searched a half-dozen abandoned warehouses, ranches and farms, but found nothing."

Disappointment mushroomed inside her. "Then the kidnappers may be long gone."

"It's possible," Lucas said, his own voice rough with frustration.

"How about the other agents?" Charlotte said. "You said they were going to the border and to Miami."

"So far, nothing concrete. If this ring is as organized as we believe, they may have paid off officials to help them cross the border."

Charlotte's stomach twisted. The men—and her students—could be in Mexico or off to another country, where they'd never find them. "I wish I could help more."

"You just need to focus on your recovery."

"I am doing that," Charlotte said. "But that's not enough."

"We're all frustrated and worried," Lucas said quietly. "It might not mean anything, but let's talk about your students again. The report on the girl named Evie hinted that she'd been in trouble before, but the court records were sealed. Do you know what happened to her?"

Charlotte swallowed hard. She did know. And he'd asked her this question before, but she'd deflected it each time. She didn't want to break Evie's confidence.

"Why do you think it's important?" she asked.

"It might not be, but we have to consider the possibility that someone in Tumbleweed or one of the foster parents could be involved."

Charlotte massaged her temple where another headache was beginning to pulse. Evie had shot one of her foster parents.

Could he possibly be involved?

LUCAS SENSED THAT Charlotte didn't want to divulge private information about Evie. But they'd reached a dead end, and he had to explore every angle.

For years, his family had believed that Chrissy had been abducted and taken somewhere far away from Tumbleweed. Yet she'd been right outside town all along.

Not that the two situations were the same. This kidnapping was definitely a professional job. It had to be linked to the others.

Still, someone in town could be part of this group.

"Charlotte?"

"I don't see how it could be connected," she said.

He waited, letting the silence stretch between them, a technique he'd learned to get people to open up.

"Evie is special to me," Charlotte said, her fingers twisting a strand of hair that draped her shoulder. "She's been through bad times, but she always finds a way to be optimistic. Honestly, bringing her into the group was like a ray of sunshine. Mae Lynn tends to withdraw inside herself. I worry about her more than any of them."

"I understand that you care about them," Lucas said.

"But if someone contacted one of the girls on the computer, she may have inadvertently led them to your studio, where they knew a group would be together."

"You checked their computers and social-network sites?" Charlotte asked.

"My analyst is working on it. The people Mae Lynn were staying with didn't have internet access. The couple who were keeping Adrian and Agnes said theirs was limited but allowed us access. So far, the only thing Keenan found was a couple of links to horse camps."

Charlotte pressed her hand to her mouth as if stifling her emotions. "Those girls want to ride more than anything in this world. I just pray we find them and I can help make that dream come true."

Lucas swallowed hard. "We will make that happen," he said, knowing he shouldn't make promises he might not be able to keep. But Charlotte had suffered enough, and he wanted to offer her hope.

Although he was starting to lose it himself.

"Evie's foster mother said Evie didn't spend much time on the computer. She liked to sit outside and draw most of the time."

"That sounds like Evie," Charlotte said, her voice wistful when she said Evie's name.

"The girl you describe, the optimistic artistic one, doesn't sound like the type who'd have a record. Tell me what happened, Charlotte."

Charlotte inhaled sharply. "Promise me you won't judge her or share this information with anyone else."

Lucas brushed his hand over hers to keep her from fidgeting with her hair again. Seeing her touch it made him want to run his fingers through the long, dark strands.

Damn. He was becoming infatuated with her.

"I promise. I would never do anything to hurt you or one of your students."

She nodded, then released a breath. "The fifth home Evie was placed in was not a good experience. The foster father molested another girl and came after Evie."

Lucas gritted his teeth at the images that flashed behind his eyes.

He'd heard this scenario way too many times.

"Then what happened?"

Charlotte lifted her head as if she was looking at him, but a blank expression darkened her eyes. God, he wished she could see him.

"She defended herself," Charlotte said.

He wasn't sure if he wanted to know the rest of the story. But he had to. "Go on."

"She grabbed the old man's gun and shot him with it," Charlotte said.

Good for her. "Did she kill him?"

"No, but he was injured pretty badly. Blew off part of his leg."

So he wouldn't be chasing any more girls.

"What happened then?"

"The wife called the law. They removed Evie from the home and investigated."

"What was this couple's name?" Lucas asked.

"Willamena and Dick Scoggins."

"How did the investigation play out?"

Charlotte toyed with a strand of her hair. "The other girl backed Evie's story so they were both placed in other homes. The social worker felt horrible and worked to get the charges against Evie dropped and her record sealed."

Dammit, he wouldn't have blamed Evie if she'd killed the monster.

CHARLOTTE HATED THINKING about Evie living in the house with that awful man. Thankfully she'd made it out.

A shudder coursed through her. Only now she'd landed

in the hands of men who might be even worse, men who would sell her to others and force her into sex slavery.

The mere idea made bile rise to her throat.

"Please tell me that bastard is in jail," Lucas said.

"No." Disgust left a sour taste in her mouth. "He's in a wheelchair. The prison system didn't have a facility that could house and protect him from other prisoners, so he's free."

She had no sympathy for the man. Anyone who preyed on innocent children and females deserved to be taught a lesson.

"I'm going to talk to him," Lucas said. "The bastard could have wanted revenge against Evie and found a way to steer the kidnappers in her direction."

"I'd hate to think that he was that evil," Charlotte said. "But I suppose it's possible."

A knock sounded and a male voice said, "I'm ready for duty." Deputy Bronson, Charlotte thought.

"Great," Lucas said. "I need to leave for a while."

Charlotte rubbed her hand over her eyes. "I'm being released today."

"Are you ready for that?" Lucas asked.

Was she? No. But she had to face it sometime. "Yes. The doctor has arranged for the vision-rehabilitation therapist to meet me and help me acclimate."

"What time?"

"I don't know yet," Charlotte said. "Sometime late afternoon." She needed to call Honey and ask her to pick up some clothes for her.

"I'll be back to drive you home."

Charlotte tucked a strand of hair behind her ear. "That's not necessary. Deputy Bronson can drive me."

"No, I'll do it."

Lucas's firm voice indicated the discussion was closed.

Charlotte bit her lip. Did she really want Lucas to witness her clumsy attempts to get around in her own home?

Worse, how would she stand being in her house once his scent invaded her space? Already, at night, she'd begun to associate it with comfort. Safety.

She'd even begun to imagine that he wanted to protect her because he cared about her.

That was foolish. She was simply a witness in a case he needed to solve. He probably hoped that she'd eventually remember something helpful.

She closed her eyes and willed that to be true.

But her mind was an empty void, dark and blank, just like the space in front of her eyes.

LUCAS SHIFTED AND jammed his hands in his pockets. Why didn't Charlotte want him to drive her home? Did she dislike him for some reason?

That thought made his gut churn.

Deputy Bronson would easily handle the task. Yet for some reason, Lucas wanted to do it himself.

He wanted to be the one to protect her. He wanted to be there if she needed someone...

Whoa... What the hell was wrong with him? He knew better than to get involved with a witness in a case he was investigating.

The last two nights when Charlotte had awakened in the throes of nightmares, reliving the shooting/kidnapping, he'd held her in his arms and she'd relaxed against him. He'd told himself he simply wanted to comfort her.

But the hard truth was that he liked holding her. He liked the way she felt against him. He liked the soft, sweet scent of her skin and the way her hair felt when it brushed his cheek, and the whisper of her sultry voice rasping his name as she drifted back to sleep.

Deciding he definitely needed some air and space from

Charlotte, he told Bronson he'd be back and headed outside. He phoned Keenan on the way to his car and asked for the address for the Scogginses.

The house was about twenty miles from Dead Man's Bluff.

The summer heat had lifted, the temperature was cooling to the sixties, and the first signs of fall were showing in the leaves as he drove toward the address. Soon the colors would be vibrant reds, oranges and yellows before fading to brown.

Would Charlotte get to see them?

He followed the GPS and turned onto a narrow dirt road that led out to farmland and mountain. Thirty miles later he reached a dilapidated wooden house that sat by a rotting barn. A rusted black pickup was parked beneath a dilapidated carport that was tilting to the right.

He parked and waited until the dust settled around his vehicle before he walked up to the porch. The boards squeaked as he climbed the steps, and he knocked on the screen door.

It took five minutes and knocking three more times before the man's wife answered.

"Mrs. Scoggins," Lucas said as he flashed his badge. "I need to talk to you and your husband."

"What the hell for?" She folded her bony arms and glared at him.

"Five minutes, that's all I'm asking," Lucas said.

She huffed, opened the door and grabbed a cigarette pack as she led him through a run-down kitchen to a living room that reeked of old furniture and dust. Every imaginable surface was covered in dirty clothes, yellowed newspapers, cigarette wrappers and overflowing ashtrays.

The woman lit up, then sank into a rocker beside her husband. Scoggins puffed on his own cigarette from his wheelchair. The man narrowed his eyes and sneered.

Lucas identified himself. "I'm sure you've heard that four girls were kidnapped from the art studio in Tumbleweed a few days ago."

The old man shrugged. "So. What's that got to do with us?"

"One of the girls was named Evie. She lived with you for a while." He glanced pointedly at the wheelchair. The man's wife stiffened and stubbed the butt of her cigarette into a coffee cup.

The old man snarled. "That's a mean one. Can't say I feel too sorry for her."

Lucas's blood ran cold. He scanned the room for a computer, but the only electronic thing in the room was the television and it was ancient. The phone was an old rotary. "Do you own a cell phone?" Lucas asked.

The couple exchanged confused looks. "You drove out here to ask me if I have a cell phone?" the man snarled.

"Just answer the question. Do you have a cell phone or a computer?"

"Do we look like we do?" Mrs. Scoggins said sarcastically. "Hell, since they took the kids away, we can barely afford to keep the electricity on."

Pure rage shot through Lucas. He hated people who used the system. They took money under the guise of caring for children, yet they spent the money on booze or cigarettes or drugs, not the kids.

"You're lucky you're not in jail." Lucas leaned over the old man in an intimidating stance. "Now, tell me what the hell you know about the human trafficking ring that kidnapped those girls?"

Chapter Nine

"Either leave or I'm calling my lawyer," Mr. Scoggins said sharply.

"That's what cowards like you do," Lucas said. "Hide behind the law when you have no respect for it in the first place."

"Get out," Scoggins shouted.

Lucas folded his arms, then faced the wife. "If you or your husband had anything to do with the kidnapping in Tumbleweed, I'll find out, and you'll pay. But if you co-operate and tell me what you know, I'll see that you get a deal." It wouldn't be a good one, but he'd find some piddly compensation.

"Look at us," Mrs. Scoggins said. "We live in the middle of nowhere. We have no computer or internet. We can't live in town because Dick had to register for that damn stupid sex-offender list. And we sure as hell don't have company. That hateful girl cost us all our friends."

"You and your husband abused innocent children," Lucas said through gritted teeth. "Your behavior is what cost you friends."

"You don't know anything about us," she hissed.

"Oh, yes, I do. I've met others like you. You and your husband use the foster system to support your habits. You abused the children, then blamed them. You hated Evie, and the entire foster system. Maybe you sold out Evie to get revenge."

She cut her eyes away from him and stared out the back window.

Scoggins wheeled his chair in front of Lucas. "I told you to get out, and I meant it."

Lucas glared at him. "I'm leaving, but if I find out you're lying and that you had something to do with the abduction in Tumbleweed, I'll be back." He put his hands on each side of the man's wheelchair and leaned into his face. "And this time, I'll make sure you're locked away. This place will look like a resort compared to where you'll be going."

Mrs. Scoggins flinched, but her bastard husband lifted his chin in a dare. "You ain't got nothing on me."

Lucas dropped a business card on the table in front of the wife. "Call me if you decide to do the right thing."

With a derisive look, he turned and headed back to the door.

"If you come back, I'll call the sheriff and tell him you're harassing us!" Scoggins yelled.

Lucas chuckled to himself. Let him call the sheriff.

Harrison had a baby on the way. He'd always felt responsible for Chrissy, and for Lucas and his two other brothers.

Just like him, Harrison had no tolerance for predators and pedophiles.

CHARLOTTE RUBBED A finger over the stitches on her forehead, blinking in a futile attempt to alleviate the throbbing in her head. She despised taking painkillers. They made her sleepy and put her in a fog.

She needed to be clearheaded, to remember details about the kidnapper.

And she had to concentrate on learning to survive in a sightless world.

She and the vision therapist, Rebecca Cain, had been working for what seemed like hours. Rebecca explained tips that would help her manage her life at home and agreed to meet her there to help her get oriented.

"It will be important to keep your furniture and belongings in a specific place," Rebecca said. "Once you master maneuvering the house on your own, a chair or food item in the wrong place could throw you off."

"I understand," Charlotte said. "Although I like to be creative in my art, I am an organizer."

"Good, that's half the battle." Rebecca paused. "The real work will take place when we get you home. But for now, I want you to visualize the interior of your house. Picture the rooms, the layout, the location of the doors and closets."

Silly for her to close her eyes, but it was a habit she utilized when mentally picturing places, objects and scenes she wanted to paint.

"You're at the front door," Rebecca said. "What do you see?"

This was easy compared to forcing herself to remember the kidnapping. "My friend Honey renovated the house." Charlotte smiled as she remembered the two of them poring over the plans. "She gutted the interior and created an open concept. Hickory floors, a big open room with a living area to one side, a kitchen with an island and bar stools connects to the living area. There's a fireplace on the far wall in the den with a vaulted ceiling."

"And your furniture?" Rebecca asked.

Charlotte could feel the soft leather of the camel-colored sofa. "A sectional sofa with a coffee table made from reclaimed wood. I…whitewashed it myself."

"Sounds lovely," Rebecca said. "Go on."

"I mounted a TV above the fireplace." She paused, emotions fluttering in her chest. "I guess I won't need that."

"You can still listen to it," Rebecca pointed out.

"I like music," Charlotte said. "My Bluetooth speaker connects to my playlists. I usually listen to that instead of the TV anyway."

"Good. Imagine yourself walking through the living area. Where is your bedroom from there?"

"When you enter the house, there's a wide hall that leads to my room and an en suite. A guest bathroom opens to the hall and a guest room. A third room with floor-to-ceiling windows and French doors leading to the backyard lets in natural light. I use that room as my studio. You can see woods and the mountains in the background."

"Sounds beautiful," Rebecca said. "Do you have a back deck or porch?"

"A deck," Charlotte said. "I like to sit outside and watch the sunset in the evening." Her voice cracked. She would miss those sunsets and the view of the mountains and the trees and…the colors. It was fall and soon the leaves would be changing.

She mentally formed a snapshot from past memories but already the image seemed muddy.

Would she eventually forget the subtle nuances and shades of colors?

LUCAS STOPPED BY Harrison's office after he left Scoggins. Too bad the man had survived that gunshot wound. He deserved to be six feet under.

He relayed his conversation with the couple to his brother.

"They do live on the outskirts of town," Harrison said. "Unless they managed to use a computer elsewhere, I don't see how Scoggins could have made contact with the kidnappers."

Unfortunately, he didn't, either. Which pissed him off. He almost wanted the old man to be involved so he could punish him for what he'd done to Evie and that other child.

"How about the library or bookstore?" Lucas asked. "Do they have computers for public use?"

Harrison adjusted his Stetson. "Yes. I'll talk to the owner of the bookstore and Carmella Jones at the library and find out if Scoggins used their internet."

"Better get warrants, so we can search the computers," Lucas said. "If we find something, we sure as hell don't want to have to let that pervert walk."

"True." Harrison stepped aside to call the judge and Lucas walked to Harrison's office. A corkboard above his brother's desk held flyers and pictures from other cases across the state and nation.

The mountains and wilderness areas of Texas provided a perfect refuge for those wanting to live off the grid and hide.

Another board held photos of the missing teens.

The young faces spoke to Lucas and made his heart ache. How many times had they looked at his sister's picture over the years and prayed she was still alive? How many times had he imagined the worst?

Although her life had been taken way too soon, at least Chrissy had had family who cared for her. Family who'd never given up looking for her.

In cases of human trafficking, oftentimes the girls were runaways or homeless and no one missed them enough to report them. Eventually, the search went cold and the cops and feds moved on to other cases.

"I promise you—Evie, Mae Lynn, Adrian and Agnes— that I won't give up. I'll keep looking until we rescue you."

Footsteps echoed behind him, and Harrison appeared. "Getting the warrants. The owner of the bookstore said she hadn't seen Scoggins, but she's pulling records of everyone who used the public computers and will send me the list. I'm still waiting on Carmella to call back about the library."

"We may be chasing false leads," Lucas said, his tone gritty. "But we have to do something."

His phone buzzed. The medical examiner's office.

Lucas quickly connected. "Special Agent Hawk."

"I have an ID on the girl you found."

"Who is she?" Lucas asked.

"Her name is Louise Summerton. She's from Sky Falls, fifteen years old."

Sky Falls was a small town about an hour away. "Was she in the system?" Lucas asked, wondering how he'd IDed her so quickly.

"Yes, but not for a crime. Her parents reported her missing a month ago, said she ran off with her boyfriend. They provided a DNA sample when they filed the report."

Lucas heaved a wary breath. The boyfriend could have killed her, meaning she wasn't related to their current case. Or…he could be involved in the trafficking ring somehow. He couldn't discount any possibility.

"What was cause of death?"

"Blunt-force trauma. Looks like she fell and hit her head on a rock."

"Or someone smashed her head with one."

"That's possible, too."

"Gunshot wound?"

"No."

If she'd been shot with the same gun used on Charlotte, they could have linked the cases.

"Did she have defensive wounds? Any DNA under her nails?"

"There were bruises on her wrists."

"Have the parents been notified?"

"Not yet."

"The sheriff and I will handle it," Lucas said. "Maybe the parents can tell us more about this boyfriend."

For all they knew, he could have sold her to this group.

AN HOUR LATER, Lucas and Harrison drove to the Summertons's house. Death notification was one of the worst aspects of the job.

"When is the baby due?" Lucas asked. They both needed a distraction from what they were about to do.

"March. She'll probably be showing soon."

"Are you excited about being a father?"

"Yeah, but I'm a little nervous, too," Harrison admitted.

"That's probably normal," Lucas said.

"Honey's going to be an amazing mother."

His brother's love for his wife was obvious. "You'll make a great dad, Harrison. God knows you fathered me and Dex and Brayden after Dad left."

Harrison clenched his jaw. "I still can't believe he never contacted us."

"I know. I thought for sure when the news aired about us finding Chrissy that we'd hear something."

Lucas drove through a small neighborhood of older ranch homes and parked in front of a redbrick house overgrown with weeds and bushes.

"Guess that's one mystery that may never be solved," Harrison muttered.

Lucas nodded. When he'd first joined the Bureau, he'd searched for his father, but had turned up nothing. He wished to hell he could sit down and talk with him.

But he had no leads. As time passed, he'd decided either his father was dead or he just didn't want to be found.

He opened his door and climbed out, and he and Harrison walked up to the house. Harrison knocked while Lucas scanned the property. He didn't know what he was looking for, but the job had taught him to always be alert.

A male voice yelled that he was coming, and a minute later, the door opened. A stout-looking man, probably in his forties, stared back at them, a hammer in his hand.

"Mr. Summerton?"

The man's bushy eyebrows formed a unibrow as he frowned. "Yeah."

Harrison was wearing his sheriff's uniform, but he introduced himself anyway, and Lucas did the same.

The man's face paled. "You have news about Louise, don't you?"

Lucas nodded grimly, and the man stepped back and opened the door. "Let me get my wife."

He followed Harrison inside, dread curling in his belly.

Mrs. Summerton appeared, her eyes haunted, as if she already knew what they'd come to tell her.

She fiddled with the collar of her blouse, her hand trembling. "You found our daughter?"

Lucas nodded, and Harrison offered her a sympathetic smile. "Yes, ma'am. I'm sorry," Harrison said.

Her face crumpled, tears filling her eyes as she reached for her husband. He put his arm around her and the two of them walked over to a threadbare sofa and sank onto it, hands clenched together.

Lucas and Harrison followed, giving the couple time to absorb the news.

"Where?" Mr. Summerton finally asked.

"Not too far from Dead Man's Bluff," Harrison said. "We're investigating the kidnapping that happened in Tumbleweed and were checking out abandoned properties. We believe the kidnappers are part of a human-trafficking ring and thought they might be keeping the girls at a ranch or farm in the area until they could move them. That's how we found Louise."

Mrs. Summerton gasped, horror darkening her eyes. "You think they're the ones who took Louise?"

"We don't know," Lucas said quickly. "But we will find out what happened to her, I promise you that."

Tears trickled down the mother's face. "My poor darling... When can we see her?"

Lucas exchanged a look with Harrison, and Harrison spoke. "She's at the medical examiner's office at the moment. I'll let you know when he releases her body so you can make arrangements."

The couple nodded, grief riddling their faces.

Lucas knew they needed time to process the news, but the other girls were still alive. If the cases were related, these people might have information that could help save them.

He cleared his throat. "We understand this is difficult, and we're sorry for your loss." He paused. "But we need to ask you some questions."

"You said that you thought Louise ran off with a boyfriend," Harrison began. "What can you tell us about him?"

Mrs. Summerton swiped at her tears. "I thought we were close, but I didn't even know she had a boyfriend."

"I never believed she'd run off like that," Mr. Summerton mumbled.

Lucas narrowed his eyes, confused. "Then why is it in the report?"

The couple looked at each other as if silently debating how to respond.

"Please tell us what you know," Lucas said.

Footsteps sounded, and a young boy of about ten shuffled into the room, his face drawn. "I told him she ran off."

Mrs. Summerton bit her lip. "This is Roger, Louise's brother."

Lucas angled himself toward the kid. "Roger, why did you think your sister ran off with a boy? Did you see her with him?"

The kid shook his head. "He never came here, but she talked to him on the computer."

Lucas softened his voice. "Is that computer here?"

Roger nodded.

"I need to examine it." Lucas glanced at the parents. "It would be best if we took it with us."

"My daughter was not promiscuous," Mrs. Summerton said. "She was a good girl."

"I'm sure she was," Lucas said. "And I promise that whatever we find on the computer will remain confidential. We are not here to disparage your daughter, only to find out who took her from you."

The couple nodded, and Mr. Summerton gestured for them to follow him. Roger bolted ahead.

Lucas's heart ached for the woman. It had only been a short time since he and his brothers had had to deliver bad news like this to his mother.

They'd thought that having answers would help them heal.

They'd finally found Chrissy's killer.

But it hadn't brought Chrissy back. Just like nothing he could do would bring the Summertons's daughter back to them.

But four other girls' lives were at stake.

And that computer might hold the key to finding out who'd taken them.

Chapter Ten

Lucas followed Roger to Louise's bedroom, where he gestured toward a laptop on an oak desk in the corner. "We're supposed to share, but Louise always used it at night when I went to bed. She didn't want Mom or Dad to know."

Although the boy had obviously taken it over since his sister's disappearance.

"We would like her computer returned when you're finished," Mr. Summerton said from behind him.

Lucas nodded. "Of course." He glanced around the boy's room, noting the basketball posters on the wall along with posters of superheroes. A typical preteen boy's room. Tennis shoes on the floor, dirty clothes piled on top of a hamper, a collection of model airplanes the kid had put together on a shelf above his bed.

"I'd like to see Louise's room," Lucas said.

Harrison exchanged a knowing look with him, and they followed the father to the girl's room. Mrs. Summerton stood in the doorway, tears trailing down her cheeks as she stared at the room.

"I haven't changed a thing since she left," the woman said, her lower lip quivering. "I kept thinking she'd come back."

Lucas's chest tightened. "I understand," he said quietly. "My family lost my little sister years ago, but her room is still the same." He couldn't stand to go in it, but holding on to Chrissy's things obviously gave his mother comfort, as if part of Chrissy was still with them.

Lucas held the computer to his side while he walked through the room. Harrison went straight to a white wicker desk and checked the top, then inside the drawers.

"What are you looking for?" Mr. Summerton asked.

"Something that might indicate where your daughter met this guy when she left," Harrison said.

Lucas opened the closet door, looking for a treasure box or journal, something private that held the girl's secrets. "Did she have a cell phone?"

Mr. Summerton nodded his head. "Yeah, we finally caved. Only because we thought she might need it for an emergency." He made a sarcastic sound. "Look what good that did."

He stepped from the room and returned with a pre-paid phone and handed it to Lucas. The phone was dead. Keenan could retrieve whatever was on it.

Harrison turned, a small diary in his hand. "Mind if we take this? Maybe Louise wrote something about the boy in it."

"She didn't," Mrs. Summerton said, her expression sad. "I read through it. Mostly she talked about how she wanted to get out of this town, away from us."

"That's not uncommon for teenagers," Lucas said, although it was obvious that the girl's statement hurt her mother.

"I know," Mrs. Summerton said. "We weren't perfect, Agent Hawk, but we loved our daughter."

"I don't doubt that," Lucas said. Although if there had been tension within the home, Louise might have written about it in that book or on her computer. You never knew what really went on behind closed doors.

"We'll return the journal, phone and computer when we're finished," Lucas said.

"Just find out who took our little girl from us," Mrs. Summerton said. "He has to pay."

CHARLOTTE TOWEL-DRIED HERSELF in the bathroom. She felt almost human again. Although showering in the dark was daunting, at least she was clean again.

Unfortunately, nothing could wash away the stain of the kidnapping from her mind.

A knock sounded at the bathroom door. "Do you need help?" Honey asked.

Charlotte bit her lower lip. How humbling to think that she might. "No, I've got it. Thanks."

"I hung your clothes on the hook on the back of the bathroom door."

Charlotte had no idea where the towel bar was, so she dropped the towel on the floor by the shower, then felt along the wall until she reached the door and the clothing.

She ran her fingers over the garments in search of tags to determine if they were inside out and where the neck of the shirt fit.

Frustration knotted her insides, but she chastised herself. Coping with her vision loss was nothing compared to what the girls were going through right now. She *would* learn how to manage on her own.

And she wasn't going to whine.

She fumbled with the clothing but managed to finally get dressed. The nurse had given her a toothbrush and toothpaste so she ran her hands over the sink vanity, found them and brushed her teeth. She reached for a cup for water, but couldn't find one, so she used her hand as a cup to rinse.

She felt again for a hand towel and discovered a wall-mounted paper-towel holder and dried her hands.

She searched the sink for a comb or brush. Her hand

hit something and knocked it to the floor. Water sloshed onto her feet.

There went the cup of water.

Annoyed, she tried to find the towel to clean it up, but banged her leg on the toilet.

"Charlotte?"

"I'll be out in a minute," she said through gritted teeth. She finally found the towel but was so disoriented she didn't know if she was drying up the water or making it worse.

Finally, she opened the bathroom door. "I spilled a cup of water on the floor," she said, derision lacing her voice.

"Don't sweat it. It's not a big deal." Honey took her hand and led her back to the bed, then disappeared for a minute to clean up the spill. Charlotte fiddled with the bedding as she settled on top of the bed.

A second later, Honey's footsteps padded from the bathroom toward her. She slipped a brush into Charlotte's hand.

"I figured you needed this now."

Charlotte nodded, silently reminding herself not to whine.

"Harrison texted," Honey said as Charlotte brushed her hair. "They found a female body near Dead Man's Bluff."

Charlotte gasped. "No, please…not one of my students."

"No," Honey said quickly. "The medical examiner identified her already. She disappeared about four weeks ago. Her parents thought she ran off with her boyfriend."

"Do they think her death is related to the trafficking ring?" Charlotte asked.

"They don't know yet," Honey said. "They went to talk to the parents."

Fear threatened to paralyze Charlotte. She'd comforted herself by thinking that the kidnappers wouldn't hurt the girls, not if they intended to sell them.

But what if that wasn't their intention?

Or what if one of the girls fought or tried to escape?

If they'd killed one girl, they wouldn't have qualms about killing another.

The girls might be in more danger than she thought.

LUCAS AND HARRISON carried the computer and phone to the lab for analysis. While he watched Keenan run a preliminary search on the phone, Harrison called Honey.

"What can you tell by analyzing her phone?" Lucas asked.

"The same number popped up numerous times, but it belonged to a burner phone as well so there's no way to trace it."

Lucas cursed. "How about the computer?"

Keenan checked Louise's search history and social-media sites.

"She was active on Facebook," Keenan said. "But the stuff she posted is tame." She clicked on the girl's Facebook page and Lucas noted pictures of Louise and her family, then Louise and two other teenagers.

"Who are those girls?" he asked.

Keenan scrolled through the posts and Louise's friends. "A girl named Phyllis and another named Connie. Looks like they attend school together."

"I need the police reports from when Louise first went missing, I assume the detective or sheriff who investigated spoke with them."

Keenan gestured to another computer, and Lucas used it to access the files while Keenan searched for other sites Louise had visited.

Lucas quickly skimmed the file on the initial investigation into Louise's disappearance. The investigating officer had cleared the family of suspicion. He'd also questioned Phyllis and Connie, who both claimed that Louise met a guy online and had become secretive.

Neither knew the boy's name or if they actually hooked up in person.

Lucas rubbed a hand over his face. Could have been a pedophile or stranger, not involved in the trafficking ring. Predators were everywhere.

"I've got an address for a contact Louise made via a teenage singles site," Keenan said. "She and someone who called himself Devon were corresponding for weeks."

Lucas moved over to look at the computer screen with Keenan. "He was flirting with her," Lucas said.

Keenan nodded. "Judging from her posts, Louise wasn't confident around boys. I'm sure this guy's attention flattered her."

Disgust gnawed at Lucas. If the guy was simply a normal teen looking for a friend, that would be all right, but his gut instinct warned him that wasn't the case.

"Did they meet in person?" Lucas asked.

Keenan tilted her head to the side with a sigh. "They were supposed to meet the day she disappeared."

"This secret boyfriend has to be involved." He'd bet his life that he wasn't a boy, either. That Louise had been lured by a stranger, perhaps one of the trafficking ring.

Keenan nodded. "The IP address leads to an office building in El Paso."

"I'll get someone in El Paso to check it out. Anything else?"

"Where were they supposed to meet?"

"He suggested a teen center about ten miles from the girl's house."

"How was she going to get there? The parents didn't mention that she had a car."

Keenan frowned. "He was supposed to pick her up at the computer café near her house."

"Good God."

"I know," Keenan said softly. "You'd think with all the

crazy, scary stories on the news that young girls would be more careful. Unfortunately, teenage hormones over-power common sense."

Especially if a girl was needy or felt homely and was starved for attention.

"Give me the address. I'm going to canvass the people at the café and see if anyone saw or heard anything." He stood, anxious to check out the shop.

Harrison returned and Lucas explained what Keenan had found. "I have a feeling they never made it to the teen club," Lucas said. "But it's on the way to the computer café so we'll stop there first."

CHARLOTTE WAS ANXIOUS to go home. Honey wanted to stay until Harrison and Lucas arrived, but she insisted her friend leave. The last thing she wanted was to put her pregnant friend in danger.

Her head was throbbing so she took a couple of pain-killers, then laid back against the pillows and closed her eyes. Images of those men barging into her studio filled her mind. She struggled to see something helpful, but the masks covered their features.

All except for the cold eyes. They were men without a conscience. Men who killed. Who took children and teen-agers and sold them like cattle.

Reliving it was hell, but she had to push herself...

She felt the hard whack on her head as the brute slammed the butt of his gun into her forehead. Stars swam and she swayed, clawing to remain upright. Screams filled the air.

One of the men spoke. She struggled to understand, but the gunshot blasted.

Another voice. She was on the floor. Blood soaked her shoulder. Pain splintered through her.

She stared up at the chaos. Her students fighting to

get away. Evie running. The brute speaking into a mic on his shirt collar.

She strained to hear what he was saying. Something like Shep... Shet... Shetland...

She sat upright, eyes wide open. Except the darkness greeted her again. Grays and blacks.

She had to focus on the voice. Thick, gravelly, into the mic... Yes, he said Shetland. Like Shetland pony?

Her pulse pounded. What did it mean? Were her memories confused because of the drugs?

No. The man was talking to someone else. Maybe they were discussing where they would meet?

Shetland... Was there a Shetland pony farm somewhere nearby? If so, the girls could be there...

Chapter Eleven

Lucas and Harrison scanned the area surrounding the teen center as they parked. On the drive, Lucas phoned the deputy director, who'd assigned another agent to check out the warehouse in El Paso.

The teen center was a freestanding concrete structure with art deco-style sketches on the sides that had probably been painted by the teens.

A strip shopping center sat behind it, housing a pizza joint, ice-cream parlor, karate studio and western mercantile.

"Someone could easily have parked in the shopping center and scoped out the teens," Lucas said as they walked up to the entrance.

"Yeah, but in the last three instances, groups were taken. Louise supposedly disappeared by herself."

True. Lucas reached for the door and opened it. Noises echoed through the front entry as they entered. Signs indicated a gym, basketball courts, a swimming pool and exercise equipment. Rooms were designated for teen classes, including dance, aerobics, Zumba and spinning. A sign pointed down the hall toward a rec room for special events, a snack area, a media center with a big-screen TV and a stereo system.

Lucas introduced himself and Harrison to the receptionist. He flashed a photograph of Louise.

"We need to know if this girl was a member," Lucas said. "Her name is Louise Summerton."

The young woman studied the picture then shook her head. "I don't remember her, but let me check our members' and visitors' lists."

Harrison looked through the glass windows at the pool area, where several teens swam laps.

"I don't have her name on either list," the young woman said.

"Do you mind if we talk to some of the other teens?" Lucas asked. "Maybe one of them remembers her."

"Sure. But why are you asking about her?"

Lucas lowered his voice so as not to create alarm. "Because she disappeared a few weeks ago. According to her computer, she planned to meet a guy here."

The young woman's eyes widened. "That's awful."

"Have there been any problems at the center?" Lucas asked.

"What do you mean?"

"Any unwelcome guests? Fights between teens? Perhaps an older man stopping by or watching from outside?"

Fear darkened the woman's face. "No one has reported anything like that."

Harrison glanced at the camera in the corner. A wall-mounted TV displayed various areas of the center, along with the entrances and exits.

"Can we look at your security tapes?"

"Let me call the manager." She punched a button and paged a man named Jordan Lansing. Seconds later, a tall, broad-shouldered man in shorts and a T-shirt appeared. He looked like a football coach, tough and big, and greeted them with a friendly smile.

The young woman quickly explained the reason for their questions, and the man's expression changed to concern. "You think this girl disappeared from the teen center?"

Lucas shrugged. "We don't know yet. According to her social media, she planned to come here with someone she met online." Lucas showed the man a photograph of Louise. "Do you recall seeing her?"

An odd look passed over the man's face, then he shook his head. "No, but she could have come on one of my days off."

Lucas pulled up the calendar on his phone to show him the date the girl went missing. "I'd like to see the security tapes from this date."

Harrison cleared his throat. "While you're doing that, I'll talk to some of the other teens. Maybe one of them knew the girl."

The receptionist called one of the teen counselors to the front to escort Harrison through the center while the director led Lucas to a security office, introduced him to a guard named Juan Perez and explained what he needed.

"We have cameras on all the entrances and exits, along with the stairwells," Perez said.

Lucas was impressed that they were trying to make the center as safe as possible. The guard scrolled through the tapes and located the one for the day Louise disappeared.

He, the guard and Lansing studied the footage, watching as teens came and went. A group of girls had congregated for a swimming class, but Louise wasn't among them. A few teenage boys gawked at the girls and made crude comments about them before disappearing into the locker room.

But no one stuck out as suspicious.

After scrolling through the tape twice, then searching through other tapes from that same week, Lucas sighed. "She wasn't here. He must have met up with her at the coffee shop." Or in the parking lot or on the street nearby.

He gave the director his card and asked them to call if anything suspicious turned up, then went to meet Harrison.

His phone buzzed just as he joined Harrison outside the teen center. The hospital.

His breath caught. He hoped to hell Charlotte was all right.

Nerves on edge, he punched Connect and said hello.

"Lucas?"

"Charlotte, is everything okay?"

"Yes, but I may have remembered something."

His pulse jumped.

"It might not be anything, but I was thinking about when the men burst in… One of them spoke into a mic attached to the collar of his shirt."

"Coordinating with the team," Lucas said.

"That's what I thought. I couldn't hear everything they were saying, but I think he used the word *Shetland*."

Lucas frowned. "Like Shetland pony?"

"Yes. I know it sounds crazy, but I was wondering if there's a Shetland pony farm nearby. Maybe they took the girls there."

Hope budded inside Lucas. "I'll find out. And, Charlotte?"

"Yes?"

"Thanks. Harrison and I have one more stop to make and I'll come to the hospital to drive you home."

"Just find the girls," Charlotte said. "I can get another ride."

He knew damn well she could. But he wanted to take her home.

Wanted to make sure she got settled into her house and that she was safe tonight.

CHARLOTTE SAT ON the edge of the bed, hands knotted as she waited on Lucas. For once she was grateful that she didn't normally wear makeup. At least she didn't have to worry that she'd smeared mascara across her nose or cheeks.

She repeatedly racked her brain for other details about the kidnappers. If she had her sight back, she'd research Shetland pony farms herself, but until she adapted her house and computer and her lifestyle to accommodate her vision loss, she was at the mercy of others.

A knock sounded at the door and she tensed, then listened for it to open.

"Charlotte, it's Lucas."

Relief surged through her. Deputy Bronson was nice, but there was something about Lucas's deep voice that soothed her soul.

She fiddled with her hair, smoothing it down. "Yes?"

"Are you ready to go home?" Lucas asked.

She turned toward his voice, wishing she could see his expression, but she had to rely on memory.

His deep-set brown eyes had looked serious in the photograph, intense, just as she imagined them to be now. His cleft chin, thick five-o'clock shadow, and gruff voice added to his masculinity She was surprised he wasn't taken.

Then again, Honey had confided that the Hawk men harbored guilt over their little sister's disappearance and had remained single, devoting themselves to law enforcement. Until Harrison had fallen in love with Honey, that is.

"Charlotte?" Lucas's footsteps came closer. "Did the doctor release you?"

She slipped off the bed and stood, steadying herself by placing one hand on the edge of the mattress. "Yes. I'm ready to go." She straightened her spine, searching for courage.

"The nurse is bringing a wheelchair," Lucas said.

Charlotte lifted her chin. "I don't need it."

"Whoa." Lucas's voice gentled as he touched her arm. "It's hospital policy. Every patient leaves in a chair."

She suddenly felt silly. "Of course." She should have known that. But her pride smarted.

Another knock, then Haley's voice. "I'm here to take you downstairs."

Charlotte nodded. The vision therapist planned to meet her at the house, after Charlotte arrived and called her. All she had to do was make it to the car and get in her house, then she could start learning how to lead her life.

Haley guided her to the wheelchair and she sank into it. She held her head high as Haley rolled her down the hall toward the elevator, certain people were staring at her.

Noises echoed around her. A laugh. Voices. A loud beep. A shrill screech.

Someone was crying.

With every strange voice and sound, the reality of her situation struck her. She was in the dark, didn't understand what was going on, who was talking, how far they were from the elevator or what floor she was on, or if someone was watching her.

For all she knew, the kidnappers could be waiting at her house to ambush her, and she would have no clue.

LUCAS WAS TEMPTED to help Charlotte into the car, but he fought his instinct. Charlotte was fiercely independent. Leaning on others would be difficult for her.

He understood the feeling. He would hate it if he was in her shoes.

Still, part of him wanted to sweep her into his arms, hold her and take care of her every need.

She fumbled for the seat belt, and he kept his hands by his sides to keep from fastening it for her. The nurse offered him an encouraging smile and he returned it, but the moment the door closed and he was alone with Charlotte, nerves set in.

"I appreciate you driving me," she said as she clicked the seat belt.

"No problem." He shifted into gear and drove from the hospital parking lot.

"I live in that neighborhood Honey developed," Charlotte said.

"Honey texted me the address."

Charlotte angled herself toward the window as if she could see out, and his heart ached for her. "What time is it?" she asked softly.

He checked the clock. "About six o'clock," he said. "Almost dinnertime. Why don't I stop and pick up something?"

A heartbeat of silence passed, tense and raw with emotions she obviously wanted to suppress.

"I guess that would be good. I like to cook, but...that's not possible at the moment."

He couldn't help himself. He reached out and covered her hand with his. "Give it time. You've just suffered a terrible trauma, both physically and emotionally."

"I will cook again," she said stubbornly. "Now, talk to me."

Lucas smiled at her spunk, then relayed his visit to the teen center. "Are you familiar with that facility or the director, Jordan Lansing?"

It had occurred to him that Lansing could possibly be involved. But he'd seemed like a nice man, interested in helping teens and protecting them.

Hell, he'd been fooled before though.

What better setup for preying on young girls than a facility where they gathered in droves?

"I've heard of it and Lansing," Charlotte said. "The program is legit. God knows, the teens need it. Lansing is a good guy. He lost a child of his own and is trying to help save others."

So he could most likely strike Lansing off the suspect list.

He explained about the email exchange between Louise and the alleged boy who wanted to meet up with her. "We stopped by the computer café, though, and no one recognized Louise or remembered anyone suspicious hanging around."

"You think it was a setup to lure her away so the boy could take her?" Charlotte said.

"It's possible. We're airing her photo on the news with her story. Hopefully if someone saw something, they'll speak up."

"I keep wondering what's happening to the girls," Charlotte said. "If the same group killed Louise, how do we know they'll keep the girls alive?"

Lucas opened his mouth to offer her encouragement, but a gunshot pierced the front right side.

"Get down!" he shouted.

She screamed, and he shoved her head to her lap as he swung the car onto the shoulder.

The glass shattered as another bullet hit the passenger window.

Chapter Twelve

Charlotte covered her head with her hands, her body jerking as Lucas swerved off the road. The brakes squealed, and the tires were grinding as they bounced along the shoulder of the road, then he straightened so quickly that she was thrown against the console.

Another bullet pinged the car, and Lucas cursed and sped up.

"Lucas?"

"Just stay down. I'll lose the son of a bitch."

Another quick jerk of the car, and she banged her elbow on the door. She raked shattered glass from her hair, her breathing choppy as she fought panic. The car sped up, flying and bouncing across rugged terrain.

She clung to the seat as he swung the car around and screeched to a stop.

"What are you doing?" she cried.

"I want to find out who this SOB is." He stroked her hair. "Listen to me, Charlotte. We're at the edge of a ravine, so do not get out of the car. Do you hear me?"

Her head was buried in her arms, but she lifted it slightly and nodded.

"Stay down and don't move until I return."

She blinked, fighting fear. "Where are you going?"

"I parked behind a boulder. I'm going to fight back."

She gulped back a scream of protest as the car door slammed, and she was left alone in the dark.

LUCAS CURSED. HE'D managed to get ahead of the damn shooter, but the bastard was coming for them. Dust spewed to the right where a dark Jeep sped down the dirt road.

Lucas ducked behind the boulder, then quickly glanced back to make sure Charlotte was still in the car. The door was closed. Thank God she'd listened.

Wiping perspiration from his brow with his sleeve, he pulled his gun and took aim.

The Jeep barreled around the corner, then slowed as if searching for them. Lucas counted the seconds, waiting until the car was close enough to hit, then fired. The bullet skimmed the top of the Jeep, and the driver wove to the side. Damn. The windows were tinted. He couldn't see inside.

A second later, the Jeep spun around and headed straight toward the boulder, where he was hiding. Lucas cursed, then fired another shot and another as it roared toward his vehicle.

His bullet hit the windshield and pierced the glass, making the driver swerve to the left. He hit rocks and dust, and gravel flew in a cloud around the Jeep. But it didn't stop.

The driver straightened, then accelerated and roared over the terrain, cutting to the right to go around the boulder. It was heading straight toward his car. Dammit, was he going to push it over the edge with Charlotte inside?

He raced to the right and fired, sending bullets into the driver's window. The driver jerked sideways. The Jeep went into a skid and raced over the edge of the ravine.

Lucas jogged to the edge and looked down. The Jeep flew nose-first, slamming into rocks along the side, then careened into the rocks below. A loud crash reverberated in the air, then the gas tank exploded.

Lucas scanned the area surrounding the Jeep in case the shooter managed to escape. Nothing.

Flames burst into the air, smoke billowing as orange, red and yellow streaked the sky.

Another explosion and the rest of the vehicle turned into a ball of fire. Flames engulfed the Jeep, and smoke curled into the sky in a gray fog.

Satisfied the shooter couldn't have survived, he jogged back to his car. One glance confirmed that Charlotte remained inside.

His heart pounded as he opened the car door. "It's me, everything's all right."

She looked shell-shocked and shaken. Tears tracked her cheeks and her pale face looked haunted.

"Where is he?" she asked in a choked voice.

Lucas slid into the driver's seat, then pulled her up against him. "Dead. He crashed over the ravine."

Her body trembled against him, and he wrapped his arms around her, stroked her hair and held her.

Dammit, it could have been them going over that ravine. Charlotte could have been shot.

"I won't let anything happen to you," he whispered. "They won't get you, Charlotte."

Not as long as he had a breath left in his body.

CHARLOTTE LEANED INTO LUCAS, grateful he was alive and they were safe. But the reality that someone had tried to kill them—her—sank in, driving fear deeply within her.

She wished she could stop shaking, but she was trembling from the inside out.

Lucas rubbed circles over her back, a comforting gesture that she savored. He could have been killed trying to protect her.

But he hadn't hesitated.

It's his job. Nothing personal.

The reminder made her take a deep breath. Still, for a moment she laid her hand against his chest, drinking in his warmth and strength.

Lucas was the most honorable man she'd ever known. No wonder Honey had fallen in love with his brother and his family.

"Are you okay?" he murmured against her ear.

She nodded, then lifted her head. She wished she could look into his eyes, see what he was thinking. If he pitied her or…found her attractive.

She silently chastised herself. It didn't matter if he did. He had a job to do and she refused to be a demanding, needy female.

"Did you get a look at him?" she asked as she leaned back against the seat.

His breath rushed out. "No, the windows were tinted. Once it went over the edge and crashed, he didn't get out."

He'd probably died on impact. Either that, or he was trapped and burning in his car.

A shiver rippled through her. She hated to think about anyone suffering. But if he was one of the kidnappers, he deserved what he'd gotten.

"I need to call CSI," Lucas said.

Charlotte nodded. "Go ahead. I'm fine now." Although she wasn't fine and they both knew it.

But she was alive, and for now, that was all that mattered. The girls were going to need her once they were found.

THE NEXT HOUR dragged by. Lucas helped Charlotte from the car and led her to a group of rocks to sit while the CSI team processed the car.

They gathered the bullet casings from the side, and the one on the floorboard that had shattered the window. The breeze picked up, swirling dust and leaves across the terrain and blowing Charlotte's hair around her face.

He couldn't help but stare at her for a moment. She was so damn beautiful. Even with her porcelain skin discolored with bruises and the stitches evident on her forehead, her long black hair framed delicate features that accentuated high cheekbones, a small button nose and eyes that were so blue they reminded him of the gulf.

She thumbed her hair back from her face, and lifted her head to the wind. His chest clenched. Charlotte was an artist.

It must be especially painful for her not to be able to see colors.

A car engine rumbled, and Lucas glanced up as his brothers approached. He'd called Dexter and asked him to bring one of the ranch vehicles for him to drive.

Dexter glanced at the smoke billowing in the sky, and then at Charlotte. Brayden strode to the edge of the ravine, then whistled as he returned.

"No way the shooter survived that."

"I just hope there's enough left for the ME to make an identification. We need every bit of help we can get on this case."

Dexter gestured toward Charlotte. "How's she holding up?"

"She's actually been amazing," Lucas said, wishing he'd phrased his comment differently when his brothers graced him with curious looks.

"I mean, she's strong," Lucas said.

Dexter simply nodded, but Brayden gave him a sideways grin. "Honey raves about how much time and love Charlotte put into that art studio. A damn shame those men shot up the inside."

"It can be fixed," Lucas said, making a mental note to talk to Honey about it. Although first he'd have to ask

Charlotte if she wanted to return to the space. The trauma might drive her to close the studio or move away.

"Thanks for the SUV," Lucas said.

"You want us to stick around?" Brayden asked.

Lucas shook his head. "No need, CSI has this."

Dexter elbowed him. "Let us know how we can help."

Lucas nodded. "I will. Thanks."

His phone buzzed just as they drove away. Keenan. He quickly connected. "Agent Hawk."

"I've been researching the Shetland reference," Keenan said "There's a Shetland pony farm about fifty miles from Tumbleweed."

Lucas's pulse jumped. "Send me the coordinates. I'll check it out."

He hurried toward Charlotte and told her about the call. "I'll drop you at home then drive out there. Let me make sure someone can stand guard."

"That's crazy," Charlotte said. "You don't need to waste time driving me home. I'll ride with you to the property."

Lucas hesitated. They'd already had one close call today. What if they drove to this farm and found the kidnappers on the premises?

NERVES RATTLED THROUGH CHARLOTTE. She wanted to go home and curl up in her bed.

But if Lucas had a lead, they had to follow it. "Please, Lucas. I'll stay in the car. I don't want you to waste time if there's a chance you might catch these guys and find my students."

A tense heartbeat passed. "I promised to keep you safe. I'm not sure having you ride with me out there will accomplish that."

"Don't treat me like an invalid," Charlotte snapped. "The fact that one of the ring shot at us means the group hasn't moved too far. Maybe they're at that ranch."

Another tense silence. "That's true." He helped her up, and she stood, brushing at her jeans. "But if it looks like someone is there, you have to promise to stay in the car. I can't protect you and chase them if they try to escape or fight back."

"I'll do whatever you say," Charlotte said with a shiver. "Let's just go."

"All right."

The scent of smoke filled the air, a reminder that they'd barely escaped death today.

She curled her fingers around Lucas's arm, slowly checking her footing as she walked.

"My brothers dropped off one of the ranch SUVs for me to drive," Lucas said as he coaxed her into the passenger seat.

She fumbled for the seat belt, cursing her clumsiness as her fingers brushed Lucas's.

"I've got it," he said. "Just try and relax."

Relax? How could she possibly do that knowing someone had just tried to kill her?

LATE AFTERNOON SHADOWS painted the road with gray lines as Lucas drove toward the Shetland pony ranch. According to the text Keenan had sent, the business had folded a little over a year ago.

Abandoned and remote, it would make the perfect place to house the kidnap victims. It was also close enough to Tumbleweed for the kidnappers to come back for Charlotte.

Charlotte lapsed into a strained silence as he drove, the tension between them palpable. He admired her strength and resilience.

But she had to be afraid.

The desert land gave way to farmland and dry brush, a testament to the remote location of the ranch. Charlotte's eyes were closed, although her fingers worried the hem of her T-shirt in a nervous gesture.

"What brought you to Tumbleweed?" Lucas asked, striving to help her relax.

"Honey's renovation project," Charlotte said. "I saw a write-up about her plans and was drawn to her sketches. I drove out to meet her the next day."

"Honey has revived this town," Lucas said, remembering how badly the town had treated her as a child. His mother had been one of the worst. Although now she loved Honey like a daughter.

She would probably like Charlotte, too.

Where had thought come from?

Worried he was getting too close to Charlotte, he clamped his mouth shut and allowed the silence to stand between them for the next half hour. He could not get personal with Charlotte.

She was a victim, a witness, for God's sake.

She needed him to be clearheaded and do his job.

The sign for the ranch slipped into view, the wooden post tilting sideways.

"Where are we?" she asked.

"We passed Dead Man's Bluff and turned west. We're pulling down the drive to the ranch now. The ranch went out of business a while back." His gut churned as he surveyed the land. "Damn, it's not only deserted, but all the buildings on the property have also been torn down."

He parked, punched Keenan's number, put her on speaker and explained that the place was deserted. "Keenan, Shetland is also a type of cattle. See if there are any Shetland cattle farms around."

"Okay, hang on."

The sound of keys clicking echoed in the background. She returned a few moments later. "There is a Shetland cattle ranch about forty miles from where you are now. The property's in foreclosure. I'm sending you the coordinates."

"Thanks, Keenan." He ended the call, checked the text, then turned around and headed toward the cattle ranch. If it was in foreclosure, the ranch was probably abandoned now. A good place for the kidnappers to hide.

"Shetland cattle?" Charlotte said. "I've heard of those. They're working cattle."

"Right." Just like the girls would be made to work. Lucas grimaced, and they fell into a tense silence as he drove. Miles of farmland spread in front of him, then the houses became more sparse.

He found the road leading to the Shetland cattle ranch and turned, following it toward the main hub of the ranch.

This property looked deserted as well, although some of the outbuildings and stable fencing remained.

He scanned the land in search of a vehicle or any sign that the kidnappers were around, but nothing stuck out.

Two run-down barns and a large stable occupied the front of the property, and a dilapidated farmhouse sat on a hill.

Abandoned farm equipment had been left rusting in the pasture, and a dented pickup without wheels was parked in the bushes.

Charlotte seemed to sense they were getting close. "Is anyone here?"

"It doesn't appear so. But they could have locked the girls in the barn or somewhere on the property until they returned."

Charlotte shivered. "How can people treat each other so cruelly?"

"I ask myself that all the time."

He cut the engine, then laid his hand over Charlotte's. "I'm going to lock the door then search the property. I need you to stay inside." He took her hand and placed it over the horn. "If you hear anything, make some noise and I'll come running. And stay down."

Charlotte sucked in a breath and nodded, and he squeezed her hand to reassure her, then grabbed a flashlight from the dash and climbed out.

He squared his shoulders, senses alert as he scanned the ranch again. No activity. Still, he held his gun at the ready as he strode to the barn door and peered inside.

A stench hit him—something was dead inside.

He clenched his gun, praying it wasn't one of Charlotte's students.

Chapter Thirteen

Lucas yanked a handkerchief from his pocket and pressed it over his mouth and nose as he entered. The interior space was dark. Stalls on both sides of a center walkway appeared empty, but he had to check them out to make sure.

Dammit, he had to find the source of that stench.

Shining his light along the floor and into the stalls, he found rotting hay and animal feces. A dead coyote lay in the last stall. Flies and insects swarmed the space. He swatted them away with his hand, gagging at the intensity of the foul odor.

Satisfied no one was being held inside, he exited the back of the barn and noticed a storage shed behind it. He scanned the area. No cars or signs of life.

Using his flashlight, he checked the ground for footprints and tire marks, and spotted boot prints near the storage shed.

He aimed the flashlight over the boot prints and followed a trail of them that led to a graveled area where the men might have parked.

Heart racing, he hurried to the door of the storage shed, expecting to see a lock, but there wasn't one.

If the girls were here, the men would probably have padlocked the door.

Disappointment flared inside him. He pushed open the door then swung the flashlight in a wide arc across the interior. Metal shelves hung on one side of the building while a large metal cage sat on the other.

Bile rose to his throat as he approached it. This cage was big enough to hold a large animal. Or…several small humans.

Anger hardened his jaw, and he aimed the light on the floor of the cage to examine it. It was dirty and blood was smeared on one corner. A broken fingernail sat by the blood.

He lifted the flashlight and studied the wall that the cage was jutted up to.

Several scratches marred the surface, scratches made by a nail or some other small metal object.

In the top corner there were more indentations. This time the scratches formed two words.

Help us.

CHARLOTTE JUMPED AT the sound of the wind blowing. The vision therapist said that her other senses would become more acute, that she'd notice sounds and smells that she normally didn't pay attention to.

Or maybe it was just her nerves. Knowing someone had tried to kill her and that she was alone and helpless in the car made her strain for sounds of a car or footsteps or the kidnappers' voices…or the girls' voices screaming.

Hopefully with joy that Lucas had found them.

But only the shrill whistle of the wind filled the awkward silence. She tried to calm herself by imagining the fall leaves fluttering to the ground in the breeze. Red and yellow and orange would dot the land and create a rainbow of colors.

Footsteps crunched on gravel. Outside the car.

She froze, holding her breath. Lucas? Or could one of the kidnappers have been hiding somewhere on this ranch and snuck up to kill her?

A gentle tap at the window and then the car door was opening. "It's me, Lucas," he said softly.

Relief surged through her, and her breath rushed out. "Did you find anything?"

"They aren't here," Lucas said. "But they may have been." He slid into the seat beside her. "I found a cage where someone was held," he said, his voice laced with disgust. "Someone scratched the wall beside the cage and spelled 'Help us.'"

Charlotte bit back a cry, her heart aching.

"I'm calling CSI," Lucas said. "There might be DNA in the cage. Then at least we'll know if it was your students in there or someone else."

The image of a cage holding humans struck Charlotte with a wave of nausea. She'd known sex trafficking was a huge problem. But like most people, she'd felt it at a distance.

Now that it had touched her life personally, she not only wanted to find her students, but she also wanted to do something to prevent it from happening to others.

WHILE LUCAS WAITED on CSI to arrive, he phoned the deputy director. "Any word from Hoover or the agent in El Paso?"

"Hoover hasn't turned up anything concrete. And the agent in El Paso said that office space was empty."

"Any sign the kidnappers or others involved in the trafficking ring had been there?" Lucas asked.

"It was cleaned out. Not a desk or chair left, or any electronics."

"Sounds like professionals who didn't want to leave any trace of themselves behind." Lucas spotted the CSI van approaching. "Keep me posted." He ended the call, then spoke to Charlotte. "The CSI team is here. I'll be back in a minute."

She nodded and leaned her head against the headrest. Lucas hurried over to the team and explained what he'd found. "Look for traces of blood and DNA. I want to verify who was held in that cage."

Lucas pointed out the storage shed where he'd found

the plea for help and took photos of it for his own references. The CSI team dispersed to search for evidence and process the scene.

Then he joined Charlotte in the SUV. "They're processing the property now. I'll take you home."

She toyed with the end of her hair as he drove, a nervous gesture that made him want to reach out and hold her hand and calm her.

But he clenched the steering wheel instead. Touching her stirred feelings inside him.

Feelings he didn't have time for.

"I'm supposed to let the vision therapist know when I arrive home," Charlotte said. "But I don't have my cell phone. I left it on the corner desk in the front room at the studio."

"CSI took it for evidence," Lucas said. "We'll stop and buy you a burner one until you get yours back."

She dug in her pocket and removed a business card. "Here's the number for the therapist. Do you mind calling her?"

The edge to her voice told him how difficult it was for her to ask for help. "Of course not. By the way, Charlotte, I arranged for a crime-scene cleanup crew to take care of your studio after CSI finished in there." He certainly hadn't wanted her to return to that bloody scene.

"I hadn't thought about the studio." A shudder rippled through her as if she was reliving the shooting and kidnapping. "I hope we can salvage the girls' art."

"When you're rested and up to it, I'll go in with you and we can assess the damage."

Charlotte's lower lip quivered. "I'm not sure what difference it'll make. If my sight doesn't return, I don't know what I'll do. I won't be able to teach art anymore."

Lucas's chest squeezed. She was facing a lot of challenges. "There are other mediums you could try. How about sculpting?"

Charlotte pressed her lips into a thin line. "I don't know. We'll see."

The fatigue of her surgery must have worn on her, or maybe she simply couldn't deal with the thought of losing her art, because she closed her eyes and drifted to sleep. The sound of her quiet breathing soothed his own anxiety as the vehicle ate the miles back to town.

If this trafficking ring was international, as he suspected, sooner or later something had to break.

He stopped at a convenience store and bought her a burner phone, keeping his eye on the vehicle from inside as he paid.

She was still asleep when he climbed inside and started the engine. Although even in sleep, turmoil strained her features, and the bruise on her forehead looked stark.

The quiet strength emanating from her twisted his insides, though, and he phoned the vision therapist and left a message that Charlotte would be home soon.

An hour later, Charlotte roused from sleep as he pulled into her driveway. "We're here."

She heaved a wary breath, her body stiffening as if she dreaded going inside.

"One step at a time," he said softly. "Just take it one step at a time."

She nodded and reached for the door.

CHARLOTTE STOOD BY the SUV, nerves fluttering through her. She'd parked in her drive a hundred times, but today she was disoriented.

This is your home. You helped build it, you know the layout. You've made happy memories here.

She'd loved watching the sunset over the back deck, had hung ferns on the front porch. There were three, or was it four, steps leading to the front porch?

The idea of finding her way to the front door suddenly seemed daunting.

"The vision-rehabilitation therapist will be here in a few minutes." Lucas lifted her hand and placed it on his arm. "Are you ready to go in?"

Was she? No.

But she would learn to adapt.

"Yes."

He patted her hand, and she curled her fingers around his arm, her stomach fluttering as she felt the muscles in his biceps. He guided her to the porch, pointing out a loose rock and an uneven patch of grass as they walked.

"Your house is beautiful," Lucas said. "Did you choose the blue paint color?"

Charlotte smiled as she remembered the conversation with Honey. She wanted a pale blue like the ocean. "Yes. Blue is my favorite color."

"I like the porch and porch swing," Lucas said. "It looks very homey."

"Honey did a great job remodeling the place," Charlotte said. "There's a back deck, too. A good place to watch the sunset."

Except now she wouldn't be able to see the sun setting or rising.

It didn't matter. All that mattered was finding Evie, Mae Lynn, Agnes and Adrian.

"We're at the steps," Lucas said.

Charlotte nodded, carefully feeling her way. One step. Two. Three.

"Last one," Lucas said.

"You must have done this before," she said, appreciating his patience.

"No. If I was in your shoes, I'd be pissed right now."

"I am," she said. "But it's taking all my energy not to fall apart." And not to fall all over him. But she bit back that thought.

He chuckled. "I'll try to keep you from falling."

"Don't worry about me," Charlotte said, one hand on the rail. "Just find my students and bring them home safely."

"I'll do my best." He paused and she realized they were at the door. Harrison had given Honey her purse from the studio, and Honey had brought it to the hospital so Charlotte fished out her keys and handed them to Lucas.

The wind picked up, ruffling her hair and stirring the wind chimes. They tinkled and clanged, music to her ears. She imagined leaves raining down to the ground, the fall colors swirling.

The sound of the door opening dragged her from her thoughts. Charlotte froze, listening for other sounds inside, determined to orient herself. The entryway led to an open-concept living room with an island and kitchen decorated in blues and whites. She'd positioned her sectional sofa facing the fireplace. French doors led to the porch.

"It's nice," Lucas said. "You have a talent with color. I like the abstract on the wall above the sofa. Did you paint it?"

"I did, I was excited over finally having a home of my own."

"It shows in the splashes of color," Lucas said.

She gave a sarcastic laugh. "Now everything is black."

A tense heartbeat passed and she regretted her comment. She hadn't meant to complain.

"Don't give up hope," Lucas murmured. "The doctor said it'll take time for your body to heal."

Outside, a car engine rumbled. "Who is that?"

"Probably the vision therapist," Lucas said. "I'll let her in."

"Thanks." She envisioned the furniture placement and felt along the wall until her leg bumped the sofa. She raked her fingers along the edge until she found her favorite spot.

She sank into the cushions, exhausted and terrified of her new life.

Lucas's phone buzzed just as the vision-rehabilitation therapist entered the house. She was a brunette with a warm smile named Rebecca.

He escorted her inside and over to the sofa, where Charlotte was sitting. "I need to take a call. I'll be on the front porch."

"We'll be fine. We have a lot of work to do to make Charlotte feel at home here again," Rebecca said.

The strain on Charlotte's face made his gut clench. "Let me know if you need anything."

She nodded and quickly turned to Charlotte.

He checked the message. Keenan.

Hoping she had a lead, he stepped outside and quickly returned her call.

"I traced an IP address from a computer to the Summerton girl's laptop," Keenan said.

"Who does it belong to?" Lucas asked.

"The computer leads to a banker in Tumbleweed. Fifty-year-old Herman Stanley." She paused. "Lucas, Charlotte Reacher got the loan for her studio at that bank."

Lucas's mind raced. The banker in town had access to money, knew the comings and goings of the business leaders in town. Knew Charlotte personally. He'd also know how to hide money if he was being paid to provide information to the trafficking ring.

He checked his watch. The bank would be closed now. "Send me his home address."

"It's on its way."

They ended the call, then Lucas phoned Harrison to fill him in. "Bronson can guard Charlotte while we talk to Stanley," Harrison said.

Lucas agreed. If Stanley had intentionally set up Charlotte's studio for attack, he would make sure he paid big-time.

Chapter Fourteen

Lucas rushed to tell Charlotte and her therapist he needed to follow a lead. They were counting the steps from the sofa to the kitchen.

A pang went through him. Charlotte shouldn't be suffering like this.

"I have to check out a lead, Charlotte." He turned to Rebecca. "How long will you be here?"

"A couple of hours," Rebecca said. "We're making progress."

"Bronson is on his way over to watch the house," he said. "Stay inside, Charlotte, and keep away from the windows."

The therapist looked alarmed for a moment. "I'll close all the shutters."

"Let me check all the locks on the windows first." Lucas combed through the house, checking the security aspects. Harrison had said that Honey installed dead bolts on all the doors in her houses. She'd wanted to add a security system but had left that decision up to the owners.

He examined the windows and made sure each one was locked, then returned to the living room. "You should have a security system installed right away, Charlotte. Do you want me to set it up?"

A tense second. "I suppose that would help."

Lucas left his card on the table by the front door. "If you need anything, Rebecca, call me."

Rebecca handed him a business card with her number on it as well. "Don't worry, Agent Hawk. I'll take care of her."

"Charge up her phone and put my number in so she can easily find it."

"I will. And I'll make sure it's voice-activated so she can call whoever she wants," Rebecca said.

"Deputy Bronson should be here any minute. I'll wait outside until he arrives."

He stepped out front just as Bronson pulled up. "Thanks for coming, Deputy."

The deputy gave a quick look around the property. "How's the access in the rear?"

"Back deck with a door to the inside. All the windows are locked and so is the dead bolt on the back door. I'm going to arrange for a security system to be installed."

Lucas jumped in his SUV and drove to the sheriff's office to pick up Harrison. "I have the warrant," Harrison said as he climbed in the passenger side.

Lucas plugged the address into his GPS and drove through town, then followed the road to the lake where the banker lived.

"What do you know about Herman Stanley?" Lucas asked.

Harrison grimaced. "He's a shrewd businessman. He practically ran the home owners in Lower Tumbleweed into foreclosure. Collected on all the debts and made himself a small fortune."

"Did he give Honey a hard time when she bought the property?"

Harrison's mouth tilted into a smile. "Yeah, he wanted her to work through him, but she didn't trust him. She found backing from an investor she'd worked with in Austin."

"Good for her."

Harrison nodded, his smile fading into a grim line as Lucas wove down the tree-lined drive to Stanley's estate home. The house was a large brick Georgian complete with columns, a circular drive and ranchland that stretched for miles and miles. A swimming pool and tennis court were visible from the driveway.

A black Cadillac sat in the drive along with a white Mercedes and a sleek gray BMW convertible.

Lucas parked in the circular drive, and he and Harrison walked to the door. A loud chime echoed through the house and exterior as Harrison punched the doorbell.

Night had descended and the sky was dark with storm clouds, obliterating the stars and moon. Looking up at the black night made him think of Charlotte and how difficult it would be to live in the dark.

The door opened, and a short, rail-thin lady in a maid's uniform answered the door. "Stanley residence. How may I help you?"

Harrison gestured to his badge, and Lucas flashed his credentials. "We need to talk to Mr. Stanley."

"I'm afraid he's not here. Do you want me to give him a message?"

"Where is he?" Lucas asked.

The woman narrowed her eyes. "In Austin on business."

Harrison pushed the warrant in her hands. "We need to look around."

The maid gasped. "What's going on?"

"Hilda," Lucas said as he read her name tag, "we have reason to believe Mr. Stanley may be involved in the disappearance of a young girl named Louise Summerton, and possibly the kidnapping that occurred in Tumbleweed. Do you know anything about that?"

The woman's eyes widened, and she shook her head vigorously.

"If you know something about his business and the missing girls, tell us. If you don't, and we find out you lied to us, you'll go to jail as an accomplice."

CHARLOTTE FORCED HERSELF to concentrate on the tips Rebecca offered. They mapped out the interior of her house, giving her a mental picture of where everything was placed. Rebecca provided her with a cane to help her maneuver the rooms, and she counted steps from each piece of furniture to the next.

Together she and Rebecca organized her bathroom toiletries so she could locate her toothbrush, toothpaste, hairbrush and towels.

Even the simplest task seemed overwhelming. She'd made so many mistakes already that her head was spinning. The first thing she'd done when she tried to maneuver the kitchen was break a glass.

Rebecca suggested plastic glasses at first to help prevent breakage, and Charlotte agreed.

"You're doing great, Charlotte," Rebecca said. "I realize this may be overwhelming at first. You can't learn everything in a day, but you've made a lot of progress."

Charlotte sank onto the sofa with a cup of hot tea Rebecca had made for her and sipped it. "I used to love to cook, but I don't think I'll ever feel comfortable using the stove or oven. What if I catch something on fire?"

"One step at a time," Rebecca said. "I was told that your sight loss might be temporary. You may not need to learn to use the oven, but if you do, we'll master it."

"You're so positive," Charlotte said. "How long have you been doing this?"

"About five years. But I grew up with a blind sister, so I already understood the complications of living without sight and how important it is to keep your environment in order. You'll have to tell people not to move your furniture or your remote or the contents of your cabinets. Once, I wasn't thinking and left a tube of antibiotic ointment on the bathroom counter. My sister mistook it for toothpaste. I felt terrible afterward."

"You sound like an amazing sister," Charlotte said.

"My sister is the amazing one. Not only is she self-sufficient, she teaches visually impaired children."

"It must be nice to have a close family," Charlotte said.

"It is." Rebecca hesitated. "How about you? Do you have parents or siblings close by?"

Charlotte shook her head. "No, I grew up in the system. That's the reason I chose to work with the teenagers through my art studio."

Another awkward moment passed. "I'm sorry about what happened. But it sounds like the sheriff and Agent Hawk are doing everything they can to find the man who shot you and abducted your students."

"They are." Charlotte took another sip of her tea. She just hoped it was enough.

"Tomorrow I'll come back and help you organize your cabinets and pantry. We can also tag your clothing so you can pair items that match."

Charlotte nodded. "Maybe I should just buy twenty white T-shirts and jeans so I don't have to worry about confusing them."

Rebecca laughed softly. "That's an idea. But judging from the gorgeous artwork on your walls and your dishes, I think you like color."

"What difference will it make if I can't see it?"

Rebecca's breathing rattled in the air, and the sofa cushion dipped as the woman sat down next to her. Charlotte startled when Rebecca took her hand, then placed it over her heart. "You've been through a terrible ordeal and a shock, Charlotte. But you are still the same loving, kind person who likes art and colors and who devoted her life to those teenagers. Nothing can change that. Not the kid-napping or the shooting. Not even the loss of your sight." She paused. "So keep fighting, okay?"

Charlotte's throat clogged with emotion. She bit down on her lip, hating that she was on the verge of tears.

"Promise me," Rebecca said.

Charlotte laid her free hand over Rebecca's and nodded. "I promise."

"Good. Now, you have to be exhausted. So let's get your room and you prepared for the night before I leave. I can also set up your coffeepot so you can make coffee in the morning."

Nerves mingled with relief. Lucas had said he'd stay over, but she didn't want to depend on him. She wanted to do things for herself. "Thank you. I'd appreciate it."

They spent the next half hour practicing how she would manage coffee and breakfast, then Rebecca helped her think through her clothing arrangement so she could find her pajamas, and clothing for the next day.

"It helps that you're already organized," Rebecca told her.

"I guess it's a control thing," Charlotte said. Although now she felt totally out of control and she didn't like it.

Rebecca's phone buzzed. Charlotte heard her step away, then she returned a moment later. "I have to go."

"Is everything okay?"

"Yes. I promised my sister I'd pick her up." She squeezed Charlotte's hand again. "You're going to be okay. I promise. I'll make sure that deputy is still outside."

Charlotte forced a smile, but inside her nerves kicked in. Rebecca's footsteps echoed across the wood floor, then the front door shut. The sudden silence enveloped her, igniting her fears.

Don't panic. Remember what she taught you.

Exhaustion tugged at her, and she took a deep breath

and decided to put on her pajamas. Outside, an engine rumbled. Rebecca leaving.

She used her cane and counted the steps to her bathroom, then washed her face and looked where she knew the mirror hung. How many times as a kid had she stared at that port-wine birthmark and wished it gone?

Now it was gone, but since she couldn't see herself, it didn't matter.

But the scars and ugly taunts she'd received from kids still reverberated in her head. Those taunts had shaped her. Changed her.

Just like the shooting and her vision loss would.

Determined to stay strong, she stretched out on her bed to rest while she waited for Lucas to return.

Seconds later, she fell into a fitful sleep. The men were storming her studio, the girls were screaming, she was trying to save them but she was bleeding…

She jerked awake, her breathing erratic, then heard a noise outside. A car?

No…a loud thump. Then low voices.

Voices… Men's voices. Not the deputy's or Lucas's or Harrison's.

Terrified, she reached for her phone. Rebecca had set certain numbers on speed dial for her, so she pressed the number for the deputy. A second later, the phone rang. Once. Twice. Three times.

He wasn't answering.

Another noise.

Heart pounding, she clutched her phone to her chest. She had to call Lucas. But first she needed to hide.

She and Rebecca had practiced how to get to her den and the kitchen. But the best place to hide was the attic.

She gripped her cane in one hand and slid off the bed, then counted the steps to the hall.

Fear pushed her forward, and she felt along the wall for the attic door. Hands shaking, she fumbled with the lock.

Another noise. This time out back. Someone was trying to get in.

She bit back a scream, then threw open the door and felt for the wall and steps. Adrenaline kicked in, and she closed the door behind her and locked it from the inside, then crawled up the stairs to hide.

LUCAS SEARCHED THE banker's office while Harrison strode to the man's bedroom. He combed through desk drawers, looking at files Stanley had brought home. Dozens of business files, portfolios, stock and investment information and personal records.

He flipped through one file and noted several large cash deposits. Stock investments and dividends didn't pay out in cash.

Where had the money come from?

The man's laptop was missing. He probably had it with him. But he had a desktop. Password-protected.

Dammit. He texted Keenan to get a tech analyst to come out, open it and search the man's browser history and files. If he had pictures of girls/conquests on the computer, they could nail him.

Hoping he had hard copies, something that would confirm they were on the right track, he dug into the file cabinet and combed through dozens of folders.

Dammit, no incriminating pictures.

That didn't mean he didn't have some. The man hadn't made his fortune because he was stupid. He obviously knew how to hide what he was doing.

Determined not to leave without searching every corner, he opened the closet and scrounged through file boxes. He found information on the property Honey had bought back after Stanley had foreclosed on it. Just as he'd suspected, Stanley hadn't given the families any leniency. He'd forced them into taking out second mortgages and upped the interest rates so high that the owners couldn't possibly make their payments.

Harrison strode down the steps, boots clicking. "Did you find anything?"

"Just a boatload of financial material. You?"

"So far nothing that links him to the trafficking ring."

"I called the Bureau to send someone out to get into his computer. We'll have to find him and confiscate his laptop as well." He checked his watch, suddenly uneasy. "Let me call Bronson and check on Charlotte."

He punched Bronson's number, and let it ring but it rolled to voice mail. The hair on the back of his neck prickled. Something was wrong.

He called Charlotte's number, but she didn't answer.

Panic stabbed at him, and he tried Bronson again.

"Something wrong?" Harrison asked.

"No one's answering. I have to go."

"I'll wait here on the tech team."

Lucas nodded and hurried toward the door. The maid was hovering over the glass figurines in the curio in the foyer, dusting them, her eyes flickering with nerves.

He didn't bother to stop and talk to her. He jogged to his car, jumped in and sped toward Charlotte's.

Fear threatened to consume him as he barreled down the drive and onto the road leading back to town. He needed a damn siren, but the ranch SUV didn't have one.

He blew his horn and flashed his lights at traffic, waving the drivers to move aside as he careened around them and flew through town. By the time he reached Charlotte's home, terror choked him.

He slowed as he approached her house, scanning the property. No cars in sight. Maybe someone had parked in the woods down the road.

He swerved into the driveway, his headlights illuminating the front bushes and porch. A shadow caught his eye. Movement.

To the right.

Someone was out there. Bronson?

No, this guy was wearing all black and he was skulking along the side of the house.

Rage and fear seized him. He pulled his weapon, threw the SUV into Park and jumped out.

Chapter Fifteen

Where the hell was Bronson?

Lucas glanced in the deputy's car, but Bronson wasn't inside. He scanned left and right, then spotted him lying face down near the porch, his body half-hidden by the bushes.

He stooped down and eased toward him, then felt for a pulse.

Low but thready.

He quickly checked for injuries—a nasty gash on the back of his head. He turned over his body. No bullet wounds.

The bushes rustled to the right, and he spotted the shadow again. Men were going through the back door.

He punched 911, then gave them the address and shoved his phone in his pocket. Slowly he inched around the side of the house, careful not to make noise. If he could catch these guys alive, he could force them to tell him where the girls were.

Inside the house, a light glowed in the kitchen, but no other lights were on. Did Charlotte know there were men outside? Was she in the kitchen?

He inched closer to the kitchen window, but Rebecca had closed the shutters and it was difficult to see inside. Charlotte could already be in bed.

He mentally recalled the layout of the house. The master bedroom was on the opposite side of the house from the kitchen.

A noise made him quicken his pace. One of the men was inside.

Dammit.

He closed the distance to the back deck. The door to the inside was ajar. The dead bolt hadn't stopped the bastard or even slowed him down.

He eased toward the steps, but leaves rustled behind him and the barrel of a gun dug into his back. "You're not going to stop us," a man growled.

Lucas froze. Dead, he couldn't save Charlotte. But he sure as hell didn't intend to let this bastard stop him.

"Leave her alone. She can't identify you."

"Orders. We never leave witnesses behind."

Lucas didn't hesitate. He spun around, jerked the gun into the air and slammed his fist into the man's stomach. Rock-hard. Muscular.

He might be ex-military.

The gun went off, the bullet hitting the porch rail. The man fought back, threw his leg up and kicked Lucas in the knees. Pain knifed through him, and he dropped to the porch floor, struggling for air.

Dammit, he didn't have time to waste. His assailant lowered the gun again and aimed it at Lucas. He quickly rolled to the side to dodge the bullet then raised his own weapon and fired.

The bullet caught the man in the chest. His eyes widened as he realized he'd been hit, then he charged toward Lucas with a rage-filled roar.

Lucas fired again, then again. A bullet pierced the man dead center in his heart. Blood gushed and the man collapsed on the porch then tumbled down the steps and landed in the bushes.

Lucas kept his eyes trained on the bastard as he grabbed the man's weapon and tucked it in his jeans.

There was still one man inside. He couldn't let him hurt Charlotte.

Gritting his teeth at the throbbing in his left knee, he grabbed the railing and dragged himself up then staggered through the door. Footsteps echoed from the back room. Charlotte's bedroom.

A wave of cold fear washed over Lucas.

He swallowed back a growl and crept down the hall toward the intruder.

CHARLOTTE BURROWED BENEATH the quilts in the trunk she'd stored in the attic, fear nearly paralyzing her. The sound of gunshots reverberated in her ears.

Had the intruder shot the deputy?

Footsteps pounded below. Then someone was trying to open the attic door.

She held her breath and clenched the quilt edge, digging her fingers into the soft material. More footsteps. A hard slamming sound—someone kicking in the door?

She pressed her fist to her mouth to stifle a cry. Where was the deputy? Was he alive?

Another noise. In the kitchen, not the attic stairs. Were there two of them?

Her lungs squeezed for air. God help her.

She didn't want to die.

Footsteps, the stairs squeaked. Then a voice.

"Stop right there."

Her pulse jumped. Lucas. He was here to save her.

A gunshot sounded. She jumped, choking on a sob, then forced herself to lie still. A bang, then a grunt. Then a body hit the floor.

Lucas shouted something, then she heard banging and

grunting as if the men were scuffling. Tumbling down the stairs.

She closed her eyes and prayed Lucas won the fight.

LUCAS SLAMMED HIS fist into the man's jaw, then his stomach. This brute was bigger than the other one. Muscular, too, with a thick neck like a linebacker. Although his face was covered with a black mask.

He wanted to see his face.

But the brute knocked Lucas backward. Lucas lost his footing and tumbled down the stairs. His gun hit the floor a few feet away. The man pulled his weapon, but Lucas lurched to his feet and ducked sideways. He reached for this gun, but the man came after him. Lucas caught him around the knees and knocked him back onto the steps. The man grunted and raised his gun, but Lucas slammed his wrist and sent the gun flying onto the steps.

They traded blows, rolling across the floor and fighting to retrieve Lucas's gun. The intruder kicked Lucas in the stomach with his boot, but Lucas rolled toward his weapon and snatched it. He spun around and aimed, but the man had disappeared.

Footsteps pounded, then the back door slammed. Lucas lurched to his feet and gave chase. He ran through the hall to the kitchen, then outside, but the sound of a motorcycle engine came from the woods behind the house.

He raced down the porch steps, aimed his gun and fired at the motorcycle as it ripped across the backyard toward the street. Panting, he chased it, firing again and again.

But the man was too fast, and the motorcycle sped onto the road and disappeared.

He wanted to go after it. But Charlotte was inside somewhere. At least he didn't think the men had gotten to her.

Heart hammering, he glanced over at the dead man then raced inside. "Charlotte, it's me, Lucas. He's gone!"

He combed through the downstairs, searched her bedroom and closet and her studio, then made his way back to the attic.

Fear crowded his chest as he entered the stairwell again. "Charlotte, it's Lucas. Are you in the attic?"

He eased up the steps, praying she was safe, his heart in his throat. She had to be okay.

Only there had been four men who'd stormed into her studio. And no telling how many more were involved in the trafficking ring.

What if another one had gotten to her before he'd arrived?

CHARLOTTE TREMBLED AS she cowered inside the trunk, her instincts warning her not to move or make a sound. The world was a blur, the darkness a tunnel that sucked her into its endless vortex.

She shoved her fist against her mouth again, choking back a sob. A squeak of the stairs. The wind outside banged against the roof. The upstairs door into the attic rattled.

"Charlotte, I'm here, it's Lucas! The intruders are gone. Are you in there?"

Relief whooshed through her, and she heaved a ragged breath. Perspiration trickled down the side of her cheek, as tears she didn't know she'd shed blended with the moisture.

"Charlotte, please tell me you're all right."

Lucas. His voice, deep and comforting. Worried.

She had to pull herself together.

"I'm here," she called, although her voice was muffled in the fabric of the quilts. Realizing he couldn't hear her, she pawed her way through the covers, pushed open the lid of the trunk and gasped for air as she climbed out of it.

She was dizzy. Disoriented. Which way was the door?

"Charlotte?"

"I'm in here," she said, her voice raw with emotion. "I locked the door. Give me a minute to find it."

"I can pick the lock or break the door if you want."

She sniffed and wiped her sweating palms on the legs of her pajamas. "No, I'm coming. Just talk to me so I can find the door."

She forced herself to stand still and listen, not to run blindly through the space. An antique dresser she'd planned to refinish stood on the wall near the dormer window, a few boxes of art supplies stacked beside it. The trunk... she'd left it on the opposite side of the dormer window facing the door.

Feeling along the edge of the trunk for the lock, she swung her hands out to feel her way. She'd dropped her cane somewhere on the stairs.

"Charlotte, I'm right here," Lucas said, his voice gruff. "Talk to me."

"I'm okay," she said, although that was a lie. She'd been terrified she was going to die and never see him or her students again.

"You were smart to hide," he said in a low voice.

"What about the deputy?" she asked as she found the wall and inched along beside it toward his voice.

"I called an ambulance. He was unconscious but breathing, a knock on the head but no gunshot."

His voice was so reassuring that her breathing began to steady, and she picked up her pace.

"The ambulance should be here soon, Charlotte. Are you hurt?"

"No," she said, grateful her voice didn't completely falter. She stumbled over an object on the floor and reached for something to steady herself.

"Charlotte?"

"I'm fine." She straightened her spine and bumped the wall, then realized she was at the door. Her breath whooshed out. She felt for the lock and turned it, then pulled at the knob.

"I've got it," Lucas said. "Step back."

Still trembling from the ordeal, she inched to the side. A second later, the door opened and Lucas's masculine scent filled the air. Her head swam with relief, and she reached out to touch him.

He instantly drew her into his arms, her breathing erratic. She fell against his chest and drank in his warmth and strength as he wrapped his arms around her and held her close.

LUCAS RAKED HIS hands over Charlotte's back, desperate to know that she was unharmed. "Did they hurt you?" he said against her hair.

She shook her head, one hand flat on his chest as if she needed to hold on to him to stand up. She was trembling, her breathing erratic, her fear bleeding into his.

"I heard a scuffle outside and called the deputy, but he didn't answer so I decided to hide."

"I'm glad you did," he murmured, hugging her closer, so close he felt her breasts rising and falling against his chest. Unable to help himself, he stroked her back, then lifted one hand and threaded his fingers through her hair. Needing to see that she was unharmed, he tilted her head back and studied her face.

She was terrified, but holding on to her courage. Her eyes were blank as she struggled to see him. His heart ached for her. For him.

He wanted to look into her eyes and see if she felt the same chemistry he felt. He was drawn to her like he'd never been drawn to another woman.

His breath whispered out. She murmured his name. "I want to see you," she said so softly he almost didn't understand her.

Then he realized what she was asking.

He cradled her hands in his then lifted them to touch his face. A smile curved her mouth, and she ran her fingers up the side of his face to touch his hair. He held his breath while she planted her fingers in it, stroking the top, then down the sides.

"I keep it short for the job," he said, feeling awkward as hell.

She nodded, then traced her fingers over his forehead, over his eyes and nose. She inhaled sharply, his own breath quickening as she traced her fingers over his cheek. His breath caught as she touched his lips with one finger.

She wet her lower lip with her tongue, stirring every male primal instinct within him, and he couldn't resist.

He cupped her face in his hands, lowered his mouth and closed his lips over hers.

Chapter Sixteen

Charlotte clung to Lucas, savoring the feel of his lips against hers. It had been a long time since she'd been held by a man or kissed like this.

Maybe she never had.

Because Lucas's kiss felt hungry, needy, as if he wanted her. But she felt safe at the same time.

He was gentle, as if he thought she was a delicate flower whose petals would fall off if he became too aggressive.

That gentleness made her want more.

She slid her arms around his neck and pulled him closer, deepening the kiss, silently telling him with her mouth and her body that she wanted him.

He stroked her hair with one hand, glided his other hand to her waist and coaxed her into the vee of his thighs. With a whisper of her name, he teased her lips apart, then plunged his tongue into her mouth, stirring erotic sensations to flutter in her stomach.

Passion ignited inside her, making her feel tingly inside, and she moaned softly. She'd simply wanted to feel his face, know the planes and angles of his bone structure, the contours of his jaw, and…just to be close to him.

No, she needed this. Wanted this and more.

She could have died at the hands of those awful men. So could he have. But he'd rushed into danger to protect her.

Another deep kiss left her breathless, then he trailed

kisses along her neck and ear. She wanted more. Wanted to feel his bare chest and his body heavy on top of her. Wanted to feel her legs sliding against his, his thick sex stroking her and giving her pleasure.

A siren's wail burst into the night, jarring her from the euphoria of his arms. The deputy was outside, hurt. Her students were still missing, terrified, fighting for their lives.

She and Lucas didn't have time to indulge in sating their selfish desires.

She lowered her hands just as he eased away from her.

"I'm sorry, Charlotte, that shouldn't have happened."

Instantly, she tensed and stepped backward. She wished she could see his face, read his expression, but that was impossible. She had to rely on the tone of his voice and it was laced with guilt.

She didn't want to talk about it, though. "You'd better see about the deputy."

He took her hand, but she jerked away.

"I'm just going to help you down the stairs," he said gruffly.

Heat climbed the back of her neck. She should have realized that. But she was too shaken and confused to think rationally. Worse, her body still tingled, ached for his touch.

She took a deep breath, held out her hand and ignored the desire rippling through her as she allowed him to lead her down the stairs.

Lucas silently cursed himself for losing control. He shouldn't have kissed Charlotte.

Dammit, he wanted her. Wanted to touch and taste every inch of her. Wanted to make her *his*.

That sounded barbaric, even in his own mind. But hell, it was true.

He'd never wanted a woman like he wanted Charlotte. And a first kiss had never affected him the way that one had.

Her hand trembled as she placed it in his, and he cursed himself again. She'd been frightened and vulnerable and he'd taken advantage of the moment.

He wouldn't do it again.

She deserved better. A protector who didn't act on the lust that was driving him crazy.

He forced a calmness into his voice as they left the attic. An image of her, terrified and feeling her way up those stairs, taunted him, rousing his anger.

One man had escaped. One was dead outside.

Dead men didn't talk. But hopefully they could learn something from his body. An ID might lead them to the man's background, his contacts, how he'd gotten involved in this trafficking ring.

And to who else was involved.

The siren wailed closer, lights flickering in the front yard as it screeched to a stop.

"We're in the hall now," he told Charlotte.

"I'll wait on the sofa while you take care of things."

He nodded, then realized she couldn't see him and guided her to the couch. She felt for the cushions, then sank onto it, and he rushed to the front door to meet the ambulance.

Deputy Bronson was dragging himself up from the ground as Lucas made it onto the porch. He hurried down the steps to him.

The deputy looked confused, and was rubbing the back of his head. "Dammit, they ambushed me. Is Charlotte all right?"

"She is," Lucas said. "How about you?"

"Took a knock to the head. But my pride hurts more than it does."

Lucas guided him over to the steps. "Take it easy, the ambulance is here."

Two medics, one female and one male, approached. "What do we have?"

"Deputy has a head injury." Lucas gestured toward the back of the house. "There's also a dead man out back. He tried to break in and kill the woman who lives here."

The CSI team rolled down the drive, and two investigators jumped from the van.

Lucas explained the situation to the CSI team. One member had worked the crime scene at Charlotte's studio, so he was familiar with the case.

The female medic stooped down to assess Bronson's injury then take his vitals. The CSI team followed Lucas inside the house, and he introduced them to Charlotte. "They'll process the house. Is that all right?"

"Do whatever you need to do to catch these guys and end this," Charlotte said. "I'll wait here."

Lucas wanted to sit with her and comfort her, but there was a dead body out back.

"One of you can start in here, and the other can follow me to the dead man." He gestured toward the hall and rear door. "When I arrived, two figures were sneaking around the house in the bushes. They came around the side of the house and entered the back door. I caught one of the men and we fought, and I shot him. The other man came inside to search for Charlotte. My guess is that he checked the downstairs then found the attic door, broke it and then started up to get her. That's where we tangled." He paused, angry at himself. "Unfortunately, he escaped."

Lucas nodded while the younger CSI started at the back door, dusting for prints and searching for forensics.

The second medic followed Lucas to the bushes, where the dead man was. Lucas and the CSI snapped photographs, then Lucas rolled the man to his back and removed his mask.

He should have looked like a monster. This man had nearly killed Charlotte. He'd taken innocent girls and done God knows what.

Death had been too quick and easy for him.

But he looked like someone Lucas might see on the street.

Lucas snapped pictures of his face, then his body, then dug in the pockets of his black jacket for an ID. Nothing inside. No wallet or ID of any kind.

"Look for identification when you search the property. The one who escaped left on a motorcycle," Lucas said. "If they didn't come together, this guy's motorcycle may still be in the woods. His ID might be there." Still, he sent photos to Keenan to start searching DMV records and facial-recognition software for the dead man's identity.

A car engine rumbled from the front. "Must be the ME," Lucas said. "I'll let him know what we've got."

"Is Deputy Bronson all right?" Charlotte asked as Lucas returned from the outside.

"His pride is hurt more than anything," Lucas said. "He took a blow to the head, but he'll be okay. The medics are going to transport him to the ER for stitches."

"Did he see the men's faces?"

"No, they wore masks and jumped him from behind. I removed the mask from the man I killed. I didn't recognize him, and he had no ID on him, so I sent a picture to our analysts. They'll search databases and use facial-recognition software to ID him."

Lucas had killed a man to save her life. That thought disturbed her. Although the despicable man had kidnapped her four students and planned to sell them, so she tamped down the guilt.

"Are you okay, Lucas?"

A heartbeat passed. "Yes, he took the brunt of the fight. So did his partner before he escaped."

"That's not what I mean. You killed a man. Does that bother you?"

Another heartbeat passed, then footsteps echoed on the wood floor. They stopped in front of her, his masculine scent enveloping her.

She'd never realized how sexy a man could smell.

She felt dizzy, light-headed, from breathing him in.

The sofa cushion dipped as he sat down beside her. Then he took her hands in his.

That simple touch and connection made her want to kiss him again.

But he'd obviously regretted the kiss, so she wouldn't instigate one herself.

"I don't like to take a life, Charlotte. But I came to terms with the fact that sometimes it's a necessary part of my job. This man was evil. He and his group hurt you and four innocent teenagers. He would have killed you if I hadn't killed him first."

She swallowed hard. "I know. But I'm still sorry it came to that."

He murmured that he understood. "I do regret not being able to take him alive," Lucas said. "But only because I might have been able to force him to give us information about the girls."

She squeezed his hands. "What happens now?"

"CSI is processing the crime scene."

She flinched. These animals had tainted her studio and her home.

"Hopefully we'll identify the man I shot and that will give us a lead on the group. The one who escaped left on a motorcycle. We searched the woods and found the second one, so we'll process it as well. I plan to get a security system installed in your house tomorrow."

"I appreciate that," Charlotte said. If Lucas used someone he trusted, she could trust them, too.

"All right, I'll make a call." He released a weary breath. "I'm sure you're exhausted. It's nearly midnight and you were just released from the hospital."

A shudder coursed through Charlotte. She'd been plagued by nightmares since the abduction.

There was no way she could sleep in her house tonight.

LUCAS FELT CHARLOTTE'S shudder rip through him. She was holding up amazingly well.

But at some point, everything was going to hit her. It always did.

Then victims crashed hard.

Right now, she was hanging on to the hope of finding the girls. But each day they were missing meant the chance of finding them alive or unharmed decreased.

"It's going to take the team a while to finish up. I'm sorry, but there'll be fingerprint dust on surfaces. I'll call a cleanup crew to come in the morning."

Charlotte bit her bottom lip and gave a little nod. Her strained expression indicated how she felt about her home being invaded, first by two monsters and now by crime investigators.

This was the home she'd built. Her colorful art pieces hung on the walls. Her furniture and decor was light and airy, bright with the hope of a future.

Now it had been tainted.

He wished he could change what had happened. But all he could do was help her through it.

"I'm taking you to my place tonight," Lucas said. "The kidnappers know where you live. They might come back."

She shivered, emotions darkening her face. "I could stay in a hotel."

"No." The thought of her being in a strange room alone didn't sit well in his gut.

"Our ranch, Hawk's Landing, is secure. No one will think to look for you there."

"I don't want to endanger your family," Charlotte said. "Especially since Honey is pregnant."

"My cabin is on the opposite side of the ranch," Lucas said. "No one will get to you with me there."

He'd die first.

Chapter Seventeen

Charlotte felt disoriented and displaced as Lucas waited on her to pack a bag. She'd worked with her vision rehabilitation therapist to start setting up her house so she could function semi-independently, but now she was being forced from the comfort of her home to stay with Lucas.

It was unnerving in more ways than one. At his cabin, she'd be totally dependent on him, a thought that incensed her.

She didn't want to need anyone. Not now. Not ever.

"Do you need help?" Lucas asked.

Charlotte squared her shoulders and shook her head. There was no way she'd allow Lucas to paw through her underwear drawer. She didn't even want him watching her sort through it.

"Why don't you wait in the living room or check on the CSI team while I gather my things?"

An awkward moment of silence ensued, then Lucas murmured his agreement. "Call me if you need help."

She did need help, but she certainly wouldn't call him. If she wore mismatched clothing, so be it.

Then again, she'd simply pack jeans. They matched everything. No need to pack a dozen outfits. She didn't plan on being at his place long.

She used the cane Rebecca had left and counted steps

to her closet, then pulled out two pairs of jeans to pack, and another one to wear on the ride.

Heat climbed her neck as she realized she was wearing her pajamas and hadn't thought of it until now. Granted, they were modest—light blue cotton pants and a tank top—but she still felt exposed. The bandage on her shoulder where she'd been shot probably stood out in plain view, too.

It hadn't occurred to her to grab a shirt or robe when she'd been running for her life.

She pulled a flannel shirt from the hanger, then found two T-shirts and her overnight bag in the corner of the closet, and carried them to her bed and placed the clothing inside. She moved toward the dresser, silently cursing when she rammed her toe on the corner of the bed.

Remembering Rebecca's advice to stop and take a deep breath when she felt confused or disoriented, she did, then made her way to the dresser and removed two sets of underwear.

Next, the challenge of her toiletry bag. She found her toothbrush and toothpaste along with her brush. No need to take a makeup bag when she couldn't see to apply it. She hardly ever wore makeup anyway. She much preferred the natural look.

She did grab moisturizer and ponytail holders for her hair. For now, that would do.

She packed them in the outside zippered compartment of her bag, then slowly made her way to the living room.

"Ready?" Lucas asked.

No. "Yes. How much longer will the investigators be here?"

"Not too long. I'll have them lock up when they leave."

She turned and glanced across the living room as if she could see it. She could in her mind.

This place had been her sanctuary. Her first real home. She'd decorated it with love.

Would she ever feel safe here again?

LUCAS REMINDED HIMSELF that he had to keep his hands off of Charlotte.

He'd crossed the line earlier. Something he'd never done before.

The realization shook him to the core.

Charlotte lapsed into silence as he drove. Was she worried that he wouldn't behave himself?

Although…she hadn't exactly resisted his kiss. She'd seemed to enjoy it.

Don't go there.

Tonight was about making her feel safe and letting her get some much-needed rest.

His wants and needs be damned.

"Have you ever been to Hawk's Landing?" Lucas asked.

Charlotte tucked a strand of her gorgeous black hair behind one ear. "Yes, I visited Honey at the cabin she and Harrison share. She showed me the plans for the development and my house."

A smile tilted his mouth. He was glad she'd come to his family's ranch, glad she'd seen it so she could picture it in her mind.

"Your land is beautiful," she said. "I didn't go in your family's farmhouse, but I'm sure it's stunning."

Lucas chuckled. "It's homey and lived-in, not a showcase," he said. "But my mother didn't want to change anything after my sister disappeared. When my father left, she fell apart for a while. I think she believed one day he'd come back and she wanted his home to be the way he remembered it."

Charlotte wet her lips with her tongue. "Do you ever hear from him?"

Pain gnawed at Lucas, sucking at his insides. "No, nothing since he left." He didn't even know if his father was dead or alive.

"I'm sorry." She felt along the seat as if searching for his hand and he reached out and took hers. Her skin felt warm, titillating. Her touch was comforting.

They sat in silence until he pulled onto the ranch. "We just passed the gate and sign for Hawk's Landing," he said, hoping to paint a mental picture for her.

The SUV bounced along the graveled road leading past the farmhouse, then he veered to the right.

"Harrison and Honey live to the left of the main house. My place is the opposite direction, but the cabin is laid out the same."

"I know they're excited about the new house they're building," Charlotte said.

"Yeah, they wanted something bigger. I guess for when the baby comes."

Charlotte nodded, but lapsed into silence again. He wondered if she'd ever been married or come close, but refrained from asking.

Best he not go there. She might think he was prying or interested, and he didn't want to give her the wrong idea.

It had never occurred to him to settle down and have a family. But these last few months, as he'd watched his older brother and Honey, he realized it would be wonderful to have someone to love you.

He spotted two horses galloping in the pasture and realized one of his brothers had added to their equine population. They'd talked about ranching again, but he didn't know how they'd manage with all their careers.

"We're here," he announced as he parked in front of the cabin. The rustic wood architecture set against the backdrop of the lush pastures brought a smile to his mouth.

This place was home. His safe haven.

He wanted it to be the same for Charlotte.

But she looked nervous as he led her into the house.

"If you'll describe the layout again, it will help," she said, her voice brittle with emotions he didn't quite understand.

"It's actually similar to your house," he said. "A wide foyer as we enter with a table for keys by the door. Open concept with the den to the right. A fireplace is on the far wall, a dark brown leather sofa facing it. The dining area is to the left of the living room with the kitchen behind it. A hallway is straight ahead and leads to two bedrooms, each with their own bath. The first one is the master and slightly bigger. If you want it, I can take the other room—"

"No, the guest room is fine." She stood ramrod-straight. "I think I'll lie down now."

"Of course." She must be exhausted. He took her hand and led her down the hall past his room to the guest room. She stopped at the door. "Let me count so I can learn my way around."

"Sure. The bed is on the left wall by the window. There's a small dresser by the door, where we are now. The bathroom is to the right."

He guided her through the layout, giving her time to acclimate, then into the bathroom. "There are towels on the hook to your left and a cup for water on the sink. Hand soap is in the dispenser. If you need shampoo, I can bring some in from my bathroom."

"Not tonight," she said. "I showered at the hospital."

The hospital. That seemed like days ago, but was only a couple of hours.

"I can turn the bed down if you want."

"No," she said. "Please just leave me alone. I'll manage."

Her curt tone made him stiffen, but how could he blame her for being short with him after all she'd been through?

The urge to pull her in his arms again teased him, but he fought it off.

He didn't want her to worry that he'd start pawing at her again.

"Call me if you need anything, Charlotte."

She felt her way to the bed, and starting turning down the quilt. "Thank you, Lucas."

He stared at her for a long minute, soaking in her beauty and strength.

"Good night, Charlotte," he said gruffly.

"Good night, Lucas."

Having her in his house, sleeping in his guest room, seemed more intimate than he could ever imagine.

But he forced himself to give her privacy and left the room.

CHARLOTTE HADN'T THOUGHT she'd sleep, but fatigue and her surgery worked a number on her and she fell fast asleep.

The next morning, as she stretched, she realized she hadn't had nightmares. She'd felt safe in Lucas's house.

But with no word from the girls, she didn't want to get up and face the day.

Depression…she understood its call. She'd felt it before.

She had to fight its strong pull.

She rubbed her eyes and blinked, praying that a miracle had happened while she slept and her vision was restored, but no. A flash of light maybe. But then everything went dark again.

Heaving a weary sigh, she forced herself to sit up and mentally orient herself. The bathroom—which way was it?

Frustration warred with the need to talk to Lucas and see if he'd heard any news.

Courage fortified, she slid her legs to the side of the bed, retrieved her cane and mentally focused on finding her way to the bathroom. A quick wash of her face, and she remembered to throw on a shirt over her tank top, then felt her way to the door.

The cabin was quiet. But the scent of coffee wafted toward her, and she followed it to the kitchen.

She paused, unsure what to do. She kept her mugs on the counter by the coffeepot. Where did Lucas keep his?

Tears threatened, but she blinked them back. She was not going to cry over something as unimportant as a cup of coffee when her students' lives were so much more important.

She felt along the counter, hoping to find a coffee mug, but the sound of the door screeching startled her.

She froze. Lucas?

"It's me," he said earning a smile of relief from her. "I went for a run earlier and showered. Just got off the phone with the deputy. He's doing well, went home last night so that's a good sign." A pause and he was walking toward her. "I didn't know if you were a coffee drinker or tea, but I'm addicted to coffee myself."

She relaxed, grateful for his attempt to provide some normalcy to her morning.

He took her hand, and she tensed, fighting the need to lean into him. Lucas certainly wasn't trying to seduce her, but she was seduced by his smell, his voice. His protective, caring touch.

LUCAS SUCKED IN a breath, mentally wrangling in his desires as he moved Charlotte's hand along the counter to the cupboard and his mugs. He could simply get her a cup, but for some reason, it was important to him that she be able to find her way in his house.

Maybe he wanted her here more often...

His phone buzzed.

Thank God. He needed work, not to be alone with Charlotte. He hadn't slept more than an hour for wanting her in his own bed.

"I need to get this. It's Keenan."

"All right."

He poured her a cup of coffee. "Cream? Sugar?"

She shook her head. "No, thanks."

He handed the cup to her, then connected the call.

"We identified the man at Ms. Reacher's house. His name is Damarus Morez. He showed up in the international database. He's wanted as a suspect in several teenage abductions in Mexico."

"What else?"

"We've linked him to a trafficking ring that may have ties in Austin."

"Any specifics?"

His phone beeped in with a text from his brother Dexter. His PI business in Austin had been a help more than once.

Been researching the sex trafficking in the city. May have a lead. An auction is happening tonight.

Lucas's pulse jumped. The idea of an auction sickened him.

But it might be just the lead they needed to catch this damn trafficking ring and find the missing girls.

EVIE WAS BARELY holding it together. She'd lost track of time. They'd been taken two days ago, or was it three or four? Time was all running together.

Her head felt fuzzy from whatever drug they'd forced into her water. So far they'd moved them to two different locations. The first one, that farm, she thought it hadn't been far from Tumbleweed. She'd scratched the words *Help us* on the wall, hoping someone would find it and hunt for them.

She and the others had been kept in the back of the van when they were driving, but there were no windows, so she couldn't see out. She'd listened for sounds of other cars or a city, maybe a bus or train station.

But the van seemed insulated from the sounds outside, and she'd been so tired from the drugs that she'd lost consciousness.

Mae Lynn had that desolate look on her face, as if she'd checked out of the world. She didn't fight or talk or ask questions like Evie did.

They were moving again. She'd heard them talking and they had something planned for later tonight. Something big.

Nerves clenched her stomach into a knot. It didn't sound good.

The van bumped over a pothole and tossed her to the side. She tried to catch herself, but her head hit the metal interior. It wasn't the first time and probably wouldn't be the last. She was bruised and banged up from their rough handling and the ride.

Tires screeched and the van swerved again. She looked over at Adrian and Agnes. They were awake, clinging to each other. Mae Lynn seemed most affected by the drugs, or maybe she just wanted to sleep so she didn't have to face what was happening.

Evie wanted to sleep, too. But she knew better. Sleeping wouldn't stop anything bad from happening. She wanted to be alert, strong, ready to fight if she got the chance.

The van suddenly slowed, gears grinding. Another bump then they turned right and screeched to a stop. Adrian looked at her, wide-eyed.

"What's happening?" Agnes whispered shakily.

Evie held her breath. Their wrists were still bound with zip ties. As much as she'd struggled and tried to break them, she couldn't. Her wrists were bloody from her efforts, a fact that had amused one of the brutes.

The back door opened. Was this one of the bathroom breaks they allowed them? So far, they'd only let them out at isolated areas, where there was nothing around them.

No place to run or hide, or way to call out for help.

She gritted her teeth as the biggest of the men, the animal who'd shot Ms. Charlotte, glared at her. His toothy grin gave her the creeps.

They'd left their masks off the last two times they'd opened the door. She knew what that meant. They wouldn't let her or the other girls live to identify them.

Adrian and Agnes shrank back as he climbed inside. He gave them an odd look then came toward her. Evie bit her tongue. She wanted to kick out at him, but she'd tried that already and gotten a double dose of drugs for it. Besides, he was over two hundred pounds, all muscle and ugliness.

He snatched her arm. "Come on. Time to say bye-bye to your friends."

Evie gasped as his fingers closed around her arm in a viselike grip. "Why are you separating us?" she asked.

"We have a special place for you." His nasty chuckle reverberated through the van as he dragged her to the edge.

"No, don't take her!" Adrian cried.

"Please keep us together," Agnes shouted.

He ignored them and dragged her out of the van. Her friend's screams echoed behind her as he shoved her inside the back of another black cargo van.

He slammed the door shut and she huddled in the dark corner, alone and terrified that she'd never see them or Ms. Charlotte again.

Chapter Eighteen

"I have to go to Austin, Charlotte. My brother, Dexter, thinks he may have a lead on the trafficking ring."

Hope bubbled in Charlotte's chest. "He knows where Evie and Mae Lynn and Agnes and Adrian are?"

Lucas shifted, hesitating long enough to indicate he didn't have the answer she wanted. Odd, even without her vision, she felt connected to him.

She understood the nuances of his voice and movements.

"He didn't mention them specifically."

Charlotte sighed. "Then what did he say?"

Another hesitation.

"Tell me the truth, Lucas. I may not like it, but not knowing is just as difficult.

"I can't bear to think that you'll lie to me or keep information from me."

Lucas stepped closer, captured her hand in his. "I won't lie to you," he said, his voice gruff, full of conviction. "You're too deep in this. You deserve to know the truth."

"The scenarios that keep playing in my mind are too horrible to say out loud."

"I understand. All the years my sister was missing, my family was plagued by nightmares of what might be happening to her. Finding out she was dead was terrible, but at least we could give her a proper burial and finally grieve for her."

Charlotte nodded. He did understand. "So what is the lead?"

"Dexter's a PI. He's made a lot of contacts on the streets. He's heard chatter about an auction tonight outside Austin."

Charlotte's stomach roiled. "An auction? You mean to sell the girls?"

A pained heartbeat passed. "Yes. He's trying to set us up as potential buyers."

"My God." She touched Lucas's arm. "It sounds dangerous."

"Don't worry about me. I can take care of myself."

"Please be careful."

He pressed a kiss to her hand. "I'd like to take you to the main house to stay with my mother while I'm gone."

"Lucas, I don't want to endanger your mother."

"These men have no idea you're at Hawk's Landing. Besides, the ranch hands will watch out for anyone coming onto the property."

Charlotte didn't want any of his men to get hurt protecting her. But she also didn't want to be alone again.

"Come on," he said. "You'll like my mother. And I found a kitten that I brought to the ranch. You can help her with that."

Charlotte knew he was trying to distract her from thinking about the auction and from worrying about her students.

Nothing could keep her from thinking about them, though.

She wouldn't rest until they were found safe and sound.

LUCAS HAD NEVER taken a girl—woman—home before.

Not that Charlotte and he were in a romantic relationship. They weren't.

She was a job. A witness to a crime and he needed to protect her.

Still, it felt odd introducing her to his mother.

Harrison sent a text saying two of the ranch hands he'd recently hired would be watching the entry points to the ranch and that Brayden would watch the house.

Harrison had also instructed Honey's building crew to be on the alert for any strange men lurking near her job sites.

He doubted the kidnappers had made a connection to Honey, but they couldn't be too careful.

This trafficking ring was broadly spread and might have contacts in town or nearby.

He hated like hell to think that one of Tumbleweed's own residents would engage in sex slavery, but it was possible.

"Will you be back tonight?" Charlotte asked.

"I should be. If not, you can stay in the house with Mom."

Charlotte massaged her temple. Her stitches were healing, but she still had visible bruises and discolored skin from the attack.

Seeing the bandage where she'd been shot had done something to him, made him furious and more determined to find the bastard who hurt her.

"I hate to impose on your family," Charlotte said.

"You aren't imposing. My mother gets lonely now we all have places of our own."

"But you're close by," Charlotte said.

"True. And we all have dinner together once a week. Mom insists."

"That sounds nice," Charlotte said. "I can't imagine having a close-knit family."

"There's been tension over the years," Lucas said. "My brothers and I felt responsible for Chrissy's disappearance.

We tried to make it up to Mom, but nothing can take the place of a missing or lost child."

Emotions clouded Charlotte's face, and Lucas wished he'd kept his mouth shut.

He led Charlotte to his SUV and drove the short distance to the ranch house in silence. When he parked, he came around to the passenger side and helped Charlotte from the car.

"There's a porch with five steps leading up to it."

Charlotte nodded and took his arm. The gesture made his chest squeeze. At least she was beginning to feel comfortable with him. Beginning to trust him.

He couldn't let her down.

CHARLOTTE SWALLOWED HER pride and held her head high as Lucas guided her up the steps and into his family's house.

Honey had told her a lot about the Hawks, how Mrs. Hawk had disliked her when she was growing up, had thought she wasn't good enough for the Hawk family.

Charlotte had decided then that she detested the woman. Honey was the sweetest woman and best friend she'd ever had.

But Honey had insisted that she and Mrs. Hawk had a long talk, and had come to an understanding. That now Mrs. Hawk treated her like a daughter.

Footsteps clicked on floors that were made of wood. The scents of cinnamon and vanilla wafted to her, wind chimes from the porch tinkling as Lucas closed the front door.

"Lucas, I'm so glad you came by."

A second passed, and she felt movement, then realized Mrs. Hawk must be hugging her son.

A second later, she shook Charlotte's hand. "It's so nice to finally meet you, Charlotte. Honey and Harrison have talked about you for months."

The woman's skin was soft, her voice low, melodic. "I'm so sorry, dear, for what you've been going through."

Emotions flooded Charlotte. "Thank you. I told Lucas I don't want to stay here if it's going to put you in harm's way."

"Nonsense," Mrs. Hawk said with a light laugh. "I have four sons and trust all of them to keep us safe."

Something soft brushed against Charlotte's leg. Then she heard a tiny purring sound.

"Sandstorm likes you."

"Sandstorm?" Charlotte said.

"The kitten Lucas brought home."

Lucas brushed her arm, then placed a tiny fur ball in her arms.

Charlotte smiled and hugged the little creature. As a child, she'd always wanted a pet, but it was painful to get attached and then to be separated by a move. Her last foster parents claimed they didn't have money to feed stray animals when they had enough stray kids to care for.

"Come in the kitchen with me and let's let Lucas get going." The woman wrapped her arm around Charlotte's shoulders, and Lucas murmured that he'd be back later.

She prayed he'd return with the missing girls.

LUCAS MET DEXTER at his PI office on the edge of Austin.

As a teen, he and Harrison had worried about Dexter. He'd been rebellious and angry and made their family life hell.

The third and last time he'd skirted trouble with the law, he and Harrison had a long hard talk with him.

They hadn't bailed him out of jail. Instead, they'd let him stew for a week. Their mother had been furious at them, but Dexter had started down a road to destruction and they were desperate to steer him back on track.

When he finally got out, Dexter had been forced to do community service. Working at a teen community center for troubled boys had woken him up.

He'd balked at college and when Harrison suggested he

study law enforcement, he'd resisted. Dexter didn't want to play by the rules.

He liked to make them and break them.

But at least now, he was working on the right side of the law. As long as he didn't bend the rules too far, he and his brothers kept their mouths shut.

Last year he'd even tracked down a drug lord targeting kids as young as eight.

Dexter met him at the door to his office. "Come on in and I'll fill you in."

They both grabbed coffee from the credenza in his brother's office.

"What exactly did you hear?" Lucas asked.

"Chatter about a new shipment," Dexter said. "My source said the code word for the operation is Shetland."

Lucas gritted his teeth. "Like the Shetland cattle ranch where we found a carving made by one kidnap victim."

Dexter nodded. "Word is there's an auction tonight at nine. A private select few clients will attend. All wealthy."

"All looking to buy sex slaves," Lucas said in disgust.

"Exactly." Dexter opened a closet in his office and pointed out two men's suits. Expensive. Designer.

"We have to play the part."

"You got us an invitation?" Lucas asked, impressed.

"Damn right." Dexter handed Lucas a folder. "Here's your cover story. You are—"

"Blaine Thorpe, entrepreneur and multimillionaire."

His brother had thought of everything. He just hoped the plan worked.

CHARLOTTE NIBBLED ON the most delicious cinnamon roll she'd ever tasted. Lucas hadn't mentioned that his mother was an excellent cook.

"I know you paint," Mrs. Hawk told Charlotte. "You're probably missing your art right now."

"I am," Charlotte said. "But nothing matters except finding those students."

Mrs. Hawk covered Charlotte's hand with her own. "If anyone can find them, my boys can."

The pride in the woman's voice touched Charlotte. "I know you're proud of them."

"I am. I let them down years ago when my daughter went missing, but they rallied around me and kept me strong."

"They're lucky to have you," Charlotte said and meant it.

A strained silence passed. "I wasn't always so nice to Honey," she said. "I thank God every day that she forgave me and that she's in Harrison's life. Nothing makes me happier than to know he's finally happy."

"Spoken like the best of mothers."

"Not the best, but I try." She took Charlotte's hand. "I'd like to show you something."

Charlotte stiffened. "But you know—"

"That you lost your sight temporarily? Yes."

"It might not be temporary."

"Keep the faith, Charlotte. Sometimes life gives us things we don't think we can handle, but through it we find other precious gifts."

Charlotte wanted to believe her, but worry for her students robbed her of words.

"Come on. Please."

Charlotte nodded. What else could she do?

She stood and allowed the woman to lead her into another room. A cool breeze fluttered through the window bringing the scent of fall.

"What is this room?" Charlotte said.

"It's my secret room," Mrs. Hawk said.

Charlotte wrinkled her brow.

"I haven't shown it to my sons," Mrs. Hawk continued. "It...was my therapy the last few years."

"Like my painting is for my students," Charlotte said.

"Exactly." Mrs. Hawk led her to a table and placed her hands on top of a hard mound. It felt like clay.

"Tell me what you think," Mrs. Hawk said, a sheepish note to her tone.

Charlotte hesitated, but it seemed important to the woman, so she gingerly ran her fingers over the oval shape. It was a bust.

Her heart squeezed as she traced her fingers over the heart-shaped face. A young girl's face. Pigtails. Ribbons in her hair.

"It's your daughter," Charlotte said, touched that she'd shared it with her.

"It is," Mrs. Hawk said. "This may be forward of me, but I thought since you couldn't paint right now, you might like to try the clay."

Charlotte chewed her bottom lip. She hadn't considered another art medium. And how could she possibly make something art-worthy when she couldn't see what she was doing?

"No one ever has to see it," Mrs. Hawk said as if she'd read her thoughts. "I don't show my pieces. But doing it connects me to Chrissy. And I love working with the clay."

"Are you working on something now?" Charlotte asked.

"Yes, it's a surprise for Harrison and Honey's baby. There's space at the table if you'd like to try. You don't have to make anything with it. For a long time I just pounded out my anger and frustration." She gave a self-deprecating laugh. "If you could see the walls, you'd know what I'm talking about."

Charlotte reached out her hands. "Thank you for sharing. I…might give it a try."

Mrs. Hawk guided her to another chair and a clump of clay.

Charlotte gently touched it then settled in the chair and began to pound it with her fist.

THE AUCTION WAS set to take place in the basement of a nightclub called The Silver Bullet, a trendy hot spot for young musicians and groups flocking to Austin.

Newbies wanting to be discovered started out at open-mic night at a neighboring place called the Cactus Café, then built an audience and reputation and earned bookings here.

Inside, dim lights created a bluesy feel and the walls showcased pictures of local artists who'd made it big. A corkboard at the entryway had flyers advertising upcoming acts and appearances of artists at other venues.

The band tonight, a country rock group who called themselves The Bullhorns, was in full swing.

It seemed an odd atmosphere for a sex-trafficking room, which made Lucas wonder if the owners had any idea what was going on in the space beneath them.

Lucas and Dexter made their way to the bar, fending off smiles from interested women. Truth was, Lucas didn't see anyone as attractive or interesting as Charlotte.

Dexter paused to flirt a little. Then again, that was his little brother's style.

Dexter had never met a person he couldn't talk to or charm.

Lucas leaned against the bar, waiting for Dexter to give him the signal that they could go downstairs.

His brother deftly sidled up to a dark-haired, olive-skinned man, who spoke to him in a low voice.

Dexter flicked his thumb, signaling Lucas to follow. He forced nonchalant smiles at a few of the women he passed, hoping to blend in. But he'd never been a ladies man.

The dark-haired man led them down a hallway past the restrooms, then through a sliding door that probably went unnoticed to most. It was dark inside, but the man used his phone to light the way down a stairwell to another hall with several rooms on each side.

He opened one door and gestured for them to enter.

"You both have bidding numbers at your space," the man said. "The bidding starts in five minutes."

Anger coiled in Lucas's belly, but he managed a sly grin. "Thanks."

Dexter's expression was grim as they each located their designated chairs and took seats to watch the show unfold on the computer screen.

Tension knotted every muscle in Lucas's body. He and Dexter had planned a strategy earlier.

They'd bid on the girls then call in reinforcements to make the arrests once they had the girls in sight.

It was possible the Shetland ring was holding the girls in another location. They'd secure payment, then deliver the merchandise.

He rolled his shoulders, checked his assigned number, then braced himself to play the part of an interested buyer as two men led a group of young girls across a stage.

"Promising," Dexter said beneath his breath in case the room was bugged. These men were professionals and might be monitoring the clients, looking for a possible setup.

Lucas's pulse jumped as the girls were told to look up at the camera.

It was Charlotte's students.

The sisters—Adrian and Agnes—clung to each other, both bleary-eyed with drugs. The other, Mae Lynn, stumbled, her face as pale as a ghost.

She wasn't holding up well. She looked drugged or… in shock.

He had to do something.

But one of the girls was missing. The one Charlotte called Evie.

Where the hell was she?

Chapter Nineteen

As soon as he'd learned the location of the auction, Lucas had spoken with Keenan and they'd set up a trace to search for possible phone or internet connections to the men holding the auction.

Backup was on standby, surveilling the club and surrounding area. He wanted eyes on the streets looking for a van or other vehicle that might be used to transport the kidnap victims.

A voice, smooth and polished, came over the speaker and introduced the first girl to be auctioned. He and Dexter exchanged conspiratorial looks.

This one was Adrian. A second later, the same voice relayed that her sister came with her—two for the price of one?

A bargain deal for someone wanting more excitement, or to have an extra girl to share.

The bidding began at $100,000. Dexter jumped in at $125,000. Lucas gritted his teeth and watched the girls hover together. They had been forced to change into sexy, tight outfits to accentuate the female curves still in the infancy stage.

The bidding increased, jumping back and forth from Dexter to another man, then Dexter upped the bid by offering $250,000.

He won the bid.

"When your wire transfer is complete, we will deliver your merchandise."

It took every ounce of Lucas's effort to maintain a cool expression when he was seething inside.

Agnes cried and gripped her sister's arm as a big man in black escorted them from the stage. The camera was careful not to show the man's face.

Next the man dragged a catatonic-looking Mae Lynn onto the stage. The poor girl looked as if she'd vanished into a world of her own. Someone had made an attempt to comb her hair and apply a little makeup and lipstick, and they'd dressed her in a glittery tube top and black spandex skirt that barely covered her essentials.

She stumbled when the man released her arm and swayed on stiletto heels that made her look tall and thin.

She was obviously drugged. Her eyes were bleary and bloodshot. A wide silver bracelet dangled from her arm—it was clearly an attempt by the kidnappers to hide the bruising from the ties that had kept her prisoner.

The auctioneer spoke again, and another male voice started the bid at $50,000. Lucas waited patiently as the man who'd bid on the sisters offered a higher bid. They went back and forth for a few minutes.

When Lucas sensed they were about to end it, he jumped in with a higher bid at $150,000.

The auctioneer tried to push the bidding higher, but the other men declined. Lucas had just bought Mae Lynn.

The auctioneer assured the other two bidders that he had more merchandise on the way and would keep them informed regarding the next auction.

Cameras inside the room prevented Lucas from checking his phone, but he hoped Keenan had traced the origin of the auctioneer.

"Transfer the money now, gentlemen," the auctioneer

said. "Once we have confirmation, you'll receive word where to pick up your purchases."

The dehumanizing language the man used made Lucas's skin crawl.

But he and Dexter used their phones to complete the transactions. Keenan had arranged dummy profiles and bank accounts in advance.

Silence descended as he and Dexter waited.

Five minutes later, the transfers appeared to be complete.

"You should receive notification momentarily as to where you can collect your merchandise."

Just as the man said, a second later, a text appeared on Lucas's phone with an address.

He glanced at Dexter, who nodded, confirming that he'd received instructions as well.

They filed from the room, both feigning cool smiles as they continued to play the role.

The hallway was dimly lit, and the man who'd escorted them to the private room was following, a gun tucked into the holster inside his jacket. He escorted them out a bottom door which led to an alley.

Outside the club, it was dark. Lucas and Dexter quickly circled to the front, both alert in case they were going to be ambushed in the alley.

Patrons parked and headed to the front entrance. Loud music boomed from the speakers, the perfect cover to disguise a cry for help if one of the girls attempted to escape.

He kept his eyes trained, scanning the lot in search of the girls, but as he suspected, he didn't see them.

The men were smart. They kept the girls isolated and tucked away for safekeeping in case the auction turned into a setup.

He and Dexter got in the car and Dexter directed him to the warehouse district, where several abandoned buildings sat, desperate for renovation.

Lucas's lungs squeezed for air as he parked. Seconds later, a black van pulled up by the warehouse.

Dexter tensed, his body braced for trouble. Lucas slid one hand over his weapon. He was ready.

The van door opened and out stepped one of the kidnappers.

Another man in black, armed and muscular, slid from the passenger side, a semiautomatic in his hands.

One of their hired thugs.

The driver walked around to the back of the van and opened the door.

Lucas and Dexter eased from the car, their expressions neutral, guns hidden. They maintained the facade of the interested buyers they'd posed as.

The man with the semi aimed it at them, warning them to say stay back. Lucas held up his hands in a surrender gesture. Dexter folded his arms and leaned against the car, his look nonchalant.

Just another day of buying and selling innocent girls.

Satisfied they were compliant, the driver reached inside the van and dragged Mae Lynn from the back. Next came Adrian and Agnes.

The sisters were trembling, terrified. Mae Lynn looked completely numb.

"Thank you for doing business with us," the driver said.

He shoved the girls forward, and Lucas caught Mae Lynn before she hit the ground. Dexter swept the sisters into the back of the SUV, then grinned at the men as if to indicate he was pleased.

Lucas helped a trembling, weak-kneed Mae Lynn into the back of the SUV, too.

He leaned into the car and whispered. "FBI. We're here to help you. Stay down."

The girls looked at him wide-eyed. He gently shoved Mae Lynn's head down to her knees.

"Trust me. We're going to arrest them."

The youngest sister choked out a cry, then her sister wrapped her arm around her and pushed her head down as well.

Lucas shut the door, then turned just as the driver and man with the gun were getting inside their van.

He spoke into his mic, alerting the backup team at the club that they could move. Keenan had warrants ready.

Then he shouted at the driver. "Wait, man, there's one more thing."

The animal turned to him, suspicion flaring while the brute with the gun aimed it at Dexter.

Before the man could shoot, Dexter drew and fired at him.

Then bullets started flying.

CHARLOTTE ROLLED AND shaped and pounded the clay, uncertain what she was doing, but working with the clay relaxed her and distracted her from her current situation.

First she crafted juvenile things—a snake, a bowl, a teacup—to simply learn the feel of the clay and how to mold it in her hands.

Then she made a big ball, and tried to shape the face of the man who'd shot her.

She made a large oval shape—was his face oval? No, he had a square jaw, beefy neck, wide head… Or was that the other man?

The mask had covered their faces. Really all she'd noticed were those tattoos…

Frustrated, she rolled the clay back into one big ball again and pounded with her fists, working out her frustrations and anger.

Mrs. Hawk's footsteps, lighter than Lucas's, echoed on the wood floor. She also smelled of lavender. "You probably didn't like the first painting you did, either, did you?"

Charlotte twisted her mouth in thought. "I guess not," she admitted.

"What was the first thing you painted?"

"The ocean, but it was a dark stormy day, and it came out looking like a sea monster was rising from the waves."

"Maybe that's how you saw the world then," Mrs. Hawk said.

Charlotte smiled. Odd how she talked to her students the same way. "You're sure you aren't a therapist?" Charlotte said with a small laugh.

Mrs. Hawk rubbed her shoulder. "I spent a lot of time on the receiving side of therapy. Maybe I learned something."

"Thank you for sharing your hobby," Charlotte said.

"Only another artist could understand." She hesitated. "Although, I'm not going to tell you that I understand what it's like to lose your vision, I'll help you however I can."

"I miss seeing people's faces, their expressions. It helps me understand them."

"Body language is important. But you're probably picking up nuances in tone and people's movements now that you never noticed before."

"That's true," she said. "But I still miss the colors." Emotions welled in her throat. "I'm afraid that I'll forget what the different shades and textures look like."

"You won't," Mrs. Hawk said quietly.

Charlotte soaked in her comforting words, then ran her fingers over the clay again.

"I'd better check on dinner," Mrs. Hawk said.

"It smells heavenly," Charlotte said and meant it because it smelled like home.

"It's just my chili and jalapeno cornbread," Mrs. Hawk said. "It's simple, but all my boys love it."

Footsteps echoed again, this time going softer as the seconds passed, signaling that Lucas's mother had left the room. An image of Lucas's handsome, strong face flashed behind her eyes. She was grateful she'd seen a picture of him before she'd lost her sight.

The day she'd run her fingers over his face had ingrained his features into her mind as well.

Taking a deep breath, she felt the clay again. This time she began to shape Lucas's face.

LUCAS'S SECOND SHOT hit the man with the semi in the abdomen while Dexter tangled with the driver.

The brute with the semi dropped to the ground, then fired at Lucas. Lucas dodged the bullet, then fired again. This time he caught the man square in the forehead. He dropped face-forward into the dirt.

The driver shoved Dexter to the ground then staggered toward the van to escape. Dexter fired at him and caught him in the back of his knee.

The man fell with a howl of pain but kept crawling to the van. Lucas rushed him and jammed his pistol into the driver's temple.

"Give me a reason to finish it," Lucas growled.

The man went still. A second later, he swung his fist out to push Lucas's gun away. The gun flew upward, a bullet was released, then pinged the side of the van.

Lucas punched the man in the jaw before he could react, then brought the butt of his weapon down and slammed it against the bastard's head.

The man's eyes rolled back in his head, and he collapsed against the steering wheel.

A siren wailed. Backup had arrived. Lucas handcuffed the man to the steering wheel, then phoned Harrison and filled him in.

"We're transporting the girls to the hospital. Bring Charlotte. They need to see her."

Chapter Twenty

Lucas explained the situation to the medics. "I'm riding with you to the hospital. I want to talk to him the minute he wakes up."

They agreed, and he went to talk to Dexter and the girls. The sisters were huddled together, terrified and wide-eyed, but obviously relieved to be rescued. Mae Lynn sat catatonic on the end of a gurney, looking pale and in shock.

"Where's Evie?" Lucas asked.

Fear darkened the sisters' eyes. "We don't know," the oldest one said. "They dragged her out of the van, put her in another one and took off."

"What about Ms. Charlotte?" the younger sister asked.

"Is she... Did she die?" the younger one asked.

Lucas wanted to soften the blow, but he wouldn't lie to the girls. "She survived and has been worried sick about you."

"We want to see her," the sister cried.

"We'll make that happen," Lucas assured them. "Although the blow to Charlotte's head caused her to experience vision loss. The doctors don't know if it's permanent or temporary." He offered them a sympathetic smile. "She's going to meet you at the hospital. Dexter will drive you."

Lucas climbed in the back of the ambulance with the unconscious driver.

He didn't intend to let the creep out of his sight.

A HALF HOUR LATER, Charlotte paced the waiting room at the hospital, waiting on the doctor to let her visit her students. Mrs. Hawk pushed a cup of coffee into her hands.

Lucas explained that one of the kidnappers was dead, and the other was in surgery. The FBI were watching the club where the auction had taken place, but were waiting to make arrests until they had information on Evie.

From Lucas's report, Mae Lynn wasn't doing well.

Charlotte brushed at tears and felt a soft hand squeeze her shoulder. Mrs. Hawk. She recognized the scent of the lavender that surrounded her.

"What will happen to them when they're released from the hospital?" Mrs. Hawk asked.

Charlotte sighed. Another worry. "I don't know. They'll probably go back into the system." Although Mae Lynn might need psychological help.

"You know I've been thinking," Mrs. Hawk said. "I mean, I haven't met these girls, and they might not be interested, but... I have a big house and a lot of empty bedrooms."

Charlotte rubbed her temple. "What are you saying?"

"I don't know what it takes to become a foster parent, but maybe the girls could stay at the ranch for a while."

Charlotte's eyes burned with tears. Although she'd feared she wouldn't like Mrs. Hawk, she and the woman had connected. And now she was offering her home to Charlotte's students. "That is awfully generous of you. The girls would love the ranch. Adrian and Agnes are obsessed with horses. But I'll warn you. These girls had rough lives, and that was before the kidnapping. There could be deep-seated psychological trauma now."

Mrs. Hawk brushed a strand of Charlotte's hair away from her face. "Then they're lucky they'll have you to help them navigate their way."

Self-doubt plagued Charlotte. "I want to be there for them, but I'm not sure what good I can do now."

Mrs. Hawk cupped Charlotte's face in her hands. Like her touch, her voice was gentle. "You are exactly what they need, dear."

Charlotte clung to the woman's words, hoping she could live up to Mrs. Hawk's faith in her. Then she wrapped her courage around her like a cloak and prayed they'd find Evie.

LUCAS SAW THE worry on Charlotte's face and wanted to comfort her. "We're waiting on the doctors to finish their evaluation, then you can see the girls."

"How did they seem?" Charlotte asked.

"The sisters are shaken, and it was evident that they'd been drugged. Other than that, they don't appear to be physically harmed. They claimed they were not sexually assaulted."

Relief filled Charlotte's sigh. "Thank God. But you said Mae Lynn seemed more traumatized?"

He nodded. He wouldn't speculate on her condition, but she hadn't looked good.

Lucas placed a comforting hand on her arm. "What was going on with you and my mother?"

Charlotte smiled softly. "Your mother is amazing. She offered to let the girls stay at the ranch when they're released."

Lucas gaped at her in shock. "My mother wants to be a foster parent?"

Charlotte smiled. "It was her idea. She said she had a lot of empty bedrooms."

"What did you tell her?"

"I think it's a good idea, but we'll have to go through Child and Family Services."

Lucas's heart warmed. His mother had been devastated after they'd lost Chrissy.

Taking care of these teens might be the purpose she needed in life.

A doctor appeared, his face solemn as he introduced himself. "Do any of the teens you brought in have family?"

"No," Lucas answered. "They're all foster children." He'd made calls to inform those parents that the girls had been found. They had sounded relieved, but all were reluctant to take traumatized kidnap victims back into their homes.

Charlotte extended her hand and introduced herself. "I've been working with the girls in an art-therapy program. They were at my studio when they were kidnapped. How are they?"

"I'm aware of the incident," the doctor said. "How are you doing, Ms. Reacher?"

"I'm just worried about my students," Charlotte said.

"They are traumatized and shaken, but physically okay. They were given Rohypnol, but the effects aren't permanent. I'd suggest they stay overnight for observation."

"How about the girl named Mae Lynn?" Lucas asked.

"I'm concerned about her. So far she hasn't spoken or responded to any of us. The psychologist said she needs time and patience. She also may need an in-house therapy program."

"I have to see them," Charlotte said, her voice strained.

The doctor looked to Lucas for approval, and Lucas nodded. "They witnessed Charlotte being shot. They need to see that she didn't die trying to save them."

LUCAS WAS RIGHT. Charlotte repeatedly reminded herself to be strong as the doctor escorted her to Agnes and Adrian's room.

Mae Lynn was in a private room awaiting more tests.

Nerves rippled through her as she entered the sisters' hospital room. She wished she could see their faces, their expressions.

But a second later, she realized she didn't need to.

"Ms. Charlotte!"

Agnes's voice.

Footsteps sounded as Agnes ran to her and threw her arms around her. Adrian followed, her shriek echoing through the room. The force of the two of them throwing themselves at Charlotte nearly threw her off balance. Lucas caught her, his murmur of reassurance blending with the girls' cries as their tears soaked Charlotte's blouse.

She didn't care about the dampness. She wrapped her arms around them, rocking them in her arms. "I'm so glad you're all right," Charlotte whispered into their hair.

"We were so worried about you," Adrian sobbed.

"I'm sorry you got shot," Agnes cried.

"Shh, it's all right. I'm fine, and you're going to be okay, too."

She held them until their sobs slowly subsided, then with the help of Lucas, she coaxed the girls back to bed. The girls climbed on one bed together, and Charlotte sat on the end, clutching their hands in hers.

"Now talk to me," she said. "I want to know what happened while you were gone."

EVIE FELT DIZZY AGAIN. More drugs. She could have sworn they were driving in circles. She'd heard the same sound, a train, more than once.

Why would they drive in circles? To throw her off and make her think they were farther away from Tumbleweed than they were?

And what had they done with Agnes and Adrian, and poor Mae Lynn? That girl worried her. She needed to be stronger, to fight.

Evie licked her lips, but her mouth was so dry that she could hardly swallow.

Suddenly the van came to a screeching halt. She clawed at the wall to keep from sliding to the other side and hitting her head.

Willing herself to be strong and look for the right moment to run, she stretched her legs, but they felt weak, rubbery.

The back door of the van squeaked as it was opened. She held her breath, blinking back tears. She refused to cry.

Footsteps pounded on the metal floor as the man approached. It was so dark in the van she couldn't see his face, but he was big. The biggest one with the tattoos. The one who'd shot Ms. Charlotte.

She bit back a scream as he shoved some kind of cover over her head so she couldn't see.

Then he grabbed her arm and hauled her to the back of the van. A second later, her feet hit the ground. She fell, hoping to slow him by making herself heavy and limp. That just angered him. He picked her up, threw her over his shoulder and kept walking. She beat at his back with her bound hands. "Where are you taking me?"

"Stop fighting and behave," he growled.

She choked back a response. She would never stop fighting.

Chapter Twenty-One

Charlotte hugged the sisters one more time. "Will you two be all right here tonight?"

"Now we know you're okay and we're away from those men, we will be," Agnes said.

"But we have to find Evie." Adrian sighed, guilt and fear tingeing her voice. "Evie really held it together, she held *us* together."

Charlotte's throat clogged with emotion. "She is special," she said softly. "And we will find her. Agent Hawk and Sheriff Hawk won't give up until they do."

They hugged again. "What about you?" Adrian asked. "Are you going to be okay, Ms. Charlotte?"

Charlotte sucked in a deep breath. She couldn't lie to these girls, not after what they'd been through. "My vision loss may be temporary. We're not sure. But I'm working with a vision-rehabilitation therapist to help me adjust. I... will probably have to stop art classes for a while." And redo the studio if she reopened.

"As long as we can still visit or hang out with you, that's okay," Agnes said.

Charlotte squeezed their hands. "I promise. I'm here for you. Anytime you want to talk, just call."

"What about our foster family?" Adrian asked.

"I'm not certain what will happen yet," she said. "But

I may know someone else who wants to be your foster mother. If it works out, I think you'll love it."

"Who is it?" Agnes asked in an anxious tone.

"I can't say yet. We have to go through the channels, but she's interested." Charlotte stood. "Now, I want to visit Mae Lynn before they throw me out of the hospital tonight." She paused. "I'll be back tomorrow, and I'll talk to your case worker about where you go from here."

She buzzed the nurse and seconds later, Haley appeared and guided her to Mae Lynn's room.

"He's out of recovery and stirring," the doctor told Lucas. "But he needs rest—"

"I don't give a damn what he needs," Lucas said. "The bastard is part of a human-trafficking ring that abducted those four girls from the art studio in Tumbleweed."

"That may be true, but as a physician, my job is to look out for the patient's best interest."

Lucas folded his arms. "Listen to me, one of the girls is still missing. A girl named Evie. She's thirteen years old and in the hands of men who are selling her as a sex slave. Every second we waste means she's getting farther and farther away."

In spite of the doctor's concern for his patient, anger flashed in his eyes. "All right, you can go in."

Lucas thanked him, then stepped into the room and closed the door. The man was on his back, an IV hooked to him, as well as a heart monitor and oxygen tube.

Lucas crossed the room to the bed, and studied the monster who'd terrified Charlotte's students. Knowing the IV fed the man painkillers, Lucas barely restrained himself from yanking it from his arm.

Instead, he inhaled sharply then nudged his shoulder. "Wake up and talk to me, you bastard."

The man moaned, then opened his eyes and blinked, obviously disoriented.

Lucas cleared his throat. "You're in the hospital, and you're going to prison for a long time. If you want any kind of deal, you need to talk."

Confusion clouded the man's face, then awareness as he sorted through Lucas's words.

Lucas placed his fingers on the man's arm in a vise-like grip. "Where is the other girl, the one named Evie?"

The man's eyes flickered with unease, then he shook his head. "Don't know."

Anger hardened Lucas's heart. "One of your partners is dead. Who's calling the shots and what did they do with Evie?"

"Don't know," he mumbled again.

Lucas pressed his hand on the man's knee where he'd been shot and applied pressure until his eyes bulged in pain.

"I'm going to ask you one more time. Who is the leader and where is Evie?"

The man's jaw tightened. "I told you I don't know. We operate anonymously."

Lucas kept his hand on the man's knee, hinting that he would inflict more pain if he didn't talk. "How do you make connections and get your orders?"

"Burner phones. Texts. We get an address where to make a hit, then grab the Shetlands. Then we get word where to deliver the merchandise."

Rage turned Lucas's blood hot. "These are young girls, not Shetlands or merchandise, you sick SOB. Where did they take Evie?"

The man's eyes widened as Lucas applied more pressure. "I told you I don't know," he said between clenched teeth.

"What *do* you know?" Lucas growled.

The man moaned again, his eyes rolling back in his head as if he was going to pass out. "Someone in Tumbleweed gave the orders. He wanted the last girl for himself."

Lucas went still. "Someone in Tumbleweed?"

The man nodded. "He paid in advance."

Lucas was seething. "Where were you supposed to deliver her?"

"One of the other operatives took the message. He took her while we handled transporting the other three to the auction."

Lucas applied more pressure to the man's knee, but he moaned and wailed that he didn't know anything else.

The doctor burst through the door, eyes livid. "Agent Hawk—"

Lucas threw up his hands. "He's all yours, Doc."

Pulse hammering, he strode from the room to tell Harrison. They'd search every house or business in Tumbleweed if they had to.

"Is she awake?" Charlotte asked Haley as they paused at the door.

"Not at the moment. But you can sit with her if you want. They say patients, even comatose ones, can hear when people talk to them."

Charlotte licked her dry lips. "She's always seemed more fragile than the others," Charlotte said. "Her father abused her physically and mentally. She was just starting to open up to me."

"She'll come back to you," Haley said with confidence. "As a matter of fact, you may be just what she needs. Seeing you get shot was traumatic."

Charlotte grasped her courage. She had to assure Mae Lynn she was fine, that she didn't need to worry about her.

Haley patted her hand as she coaxed Charlotte into a chair. "You're sitting beside her bed, on her left side.

There's an IV in her right arm. She was dehydrated, so we're giving her fluids."

Charlotte reached out to find Mae Lynn's hand, and Haley helped her by placing it over Mae Lynn's. "I'll leave you alone for a few minutes." Haley pushed the nurse-call button into Charlotte's lap. "Call me if you need anything."

"Thanks." She waited until she heard the door close, then she cradled Mae Lynn's hand in between hers and pressed a kiss to her palm.

Mae Lynn's breath hitched, then turned choppy.

"I'm here, Mae Lynn. It's Ms. Charlotte. You and Agnes and Adrian are safe. You're not with those men anymore. You're at the hospital in Tumbleweed."

Mae Lynn didn't respond.

"I know you were scared, and that those men treated your terribly, but you're going to be okay. You're stronger than you think, sweetie." She stroked the girl's hand repeatedly. "I'm here, and I won't leave you. I'll be with you every step of the way."

She continued to stroke Mae Lynn's hand and talk to her, relaying stories about when the girls had first met in her class to the art projects they'd worked on individually and together.

"You have real talent, Mae Lynn," Charlotte said softly. "You're strong inside. If you need to rest, that's fine, rest. But remember that you are loved. I love you and so do Agnes and Adrian and Evie."

A strangled sound echoed from the bed.

Charlotte tensed, then squeezed Mae Lynn's hand. "I'm here, honey. I'm right by your side."

"Ms. Charlotte?"

Mae Lynn's voice was weak, raw with pain.

"Yes, honey, I'm here."

Mae Lynn squeezed her hand in return, and relief flooded Charlotte.

"I thought you were dead," Mae Lynn whispered.

"No, sweetie, no way was I going to give up and leave you girls." She leaned over the bed then drew the girl into a hug. "You've been through a bad ordeal, but I promise that we're all going to get past this, Mae Lynn. We can't let those men destroy who we are."

IT WAS NEARLY midnight by the time Lucas drove Charlotte back to his house.

He left a guard to watch the man he'd shot, and he'd asked Keenan to look for possible connections to Tumbleweed.

The fact that Herman Stanley had been in Austin on business the same week the auction was held might be coincidental. Lucas didn't like coincidences.

Harrison was stopping by the banker's house to see if he'd returned, and look for anything suspicious.

Stanley's house was slightly remote. Would he bring Evie to his house, though? That seemed chancy. How the hell would he hide her?

Although there were cases where kidnappers had held women or girls hostage practically in plain sight.

Keenan was researching Stanley's financials and assets, looking for property where he might take Evie.

A nasty taste settled in his mouth at the thought.

Charlotte remained quiet on the drive home. She looked exhausted and worried. He'd give anything to have been able to bring Evie back with the others.

He scanned the property as he drove onto the ranch, then veered down the drive to his cabin. His mother had mentioned that she'd made dinner, but he was too tired to stop by the house. Charlotte said she had no appetite anyway, and had wanted to go back to the cabin and rest.

The wind whistled through the window as he parked, and he climbed out then guided Charlotte to the cabin.

She stumbled on the top step, and mumbled an apology.

"You don't have to apologize, Charlotte. You're doing great."

A long sigh escaped her as they entered. "I don't know if I can be enough for the girls," she said, the self-doubt in her tone eating at him. "Mae Lynn is having a difficult time."

"You are strong and loving and patient. That's what they need." He brushed hair from her cheek as they entered.

"They need us to find Evie," Charlotte said. "They feel guilty that she was separated. They said that she held them together."

Lucas understood that kind of guilt. He and his brothers had lived with it when Chrissy disappeared. "We'll find her. I promise." But would it be soon enough?

What if the man who'd bought her already had her in his clutches?

Chapter Twenty-Two

Charlotte breathed in the masculine scent of Lucas's cabin as she seated herself on his sofa. His woodsy aftershave permeated the space, reminding her that he was not only an FBI agent, but also a tough cowboy.

Emotions welled in her chest, and tears burned the backs of her eyelids. She blinked them back but failed and felt them trickling down her cheeks.

"Can I get you something to drink or do you just want to go to bed?" Lucas asked.

"Maybe a drink. I don't know if I can sleep yet."

"Wine? Beer? Whiskey? Tea?"

"Do you have red wine?"

"As a matter of fact, I do. We had some left from Harrison's wedding, so I brought a couple of bottles to the house."

She nodded, an image of sweet Evie taunting her. A minute later, Lucas tucked a wineglass into her hands. She wrapped her fingers around the glass then sniffed.

"It's a cab," she said. "My favorite."

"Good." The sound of ice clinking in a glass echoed from somewhere near the kitchen, then footsteps, and Lucas sank onto the sofa beside her.

"You're having bourbon," she said with a small smile as she recognized the strong scent.

"My drink of choice," he murmured.

They sat in silence for a moment, the tension thickening.

She had the sudden urge to lean into him, to ask him to hold her. The emotions of the night bombarded her, her fear for Evie blending with worry over Mae Lynn's recovery.

"I'd better go lie down," she said, afraid she was going to fall apart.

Lucas guided her to the guest bedroom, then once again described the layout. She sipped the wine and felt for the bed.

"Call me if you need anything," he said softly.

She needed him. But she couldn't ask…

His footsteps faded and the door squeaked as he closed it. She stared into her dark world, aching to see the colors in the room, to be independent again.

But that was selfish. Evie had bigger problems and so did Mae Lynn.

Still, the day's events overwhelmed her and tears began to fall. She took another sip of wine, then felt for the end table and eased the glass onto it.

She raked her hand across the bed and found her overnight bag, then located her tank top and pajama pants. She quickly changed into them, her fingers gliding over the wound on her shoulder as she straightened her tank. She no longer needed the bandage, but she would probably have a scar.

That would be nothing compared to what the girls had to overcome.

She choked back a sob, but failed again, and the tears began to flow. The door squeaked.

"Charlotte?"

"I'm fine," she said in a raw whisper.

Footsteps echoed on the floor then his hand brushed the hair from her cheek. She swiped at the tears to no avail. They ran down her face like a river.

The bed dipped as Lucas lowered himself beside her, then he pulled her into his arms.

Charlotte didn't want to lean on him or need him. But she did need him, at least tonight.

LUCAS HELD CHARLOTTE, wanting to soothe her anxiety, but the moment she leaned into him and traced her finger over his cheek, it turned into more.

He cradled her face between his hands and closed his mouth over her lips. Her sweetness and strength triggered every protective instinct in him and aroused him at the same time.

She lifted her hand and he expected her to push him away. Instead, she raked her fingers along his jaw again, an intimate gesture that made his sex harden.

He deepened the kiss, then threaded one hand through her hair and slid the other down her back, drawing her closer.

He wanted more. Wanted all of her.

The thought sent a bolt of fear through him.

But she teased his lips apart with her tongue, and fear vanished, hunger stirring in its wake. He thrust his tongue in her mouth and stroked her back, lust driving his fingers lower, to her waist.

She felt delicate and feminine and so damn sexy that he lowered his head and trailed kisses along her neck. She lifted her head in surrender, offering him full rein. He took it, and nibbled and suckled at her throat, dipping lower and lower until he tasted the sweet saltiness of her skin above her breasts.

Her nipples stiffened to peaks beneath that thin tank top, driving him mad. His finger brushed her nipple, and she breathed in deeply.

"Charlotte, I don't want to take advantage of you," he murmured against her ear.

"You aren't." She kissed him again. "I don't want you to do this because you feel sorry for me."

That was the last thought on his mind. He moved her

hand over his sex so she could feel the evidence of his desire. "That is not pity."

Her soft laugh emboldened him, and he kissed her deeper, then trailed kisses down her throat to her cleavage. He massaged one breast with his hand while he teased the other with his teeth.

She moaned softly, and tugged at his shirt. He slipped her tank top over her head, careful not to hurt her wound. It was healing, but the sight of it intensified his rage at the man who'd shot her.

"Lucas?"

"I don't want to hurt you," he whispered as he gently kissed her shoulder.

She pushed at his shirt. "You won't. It feels wonderful."

Smiling at the catch in her breath, he helped her remove his shirt, then she tugged at his belt. He'd left his gun and holster in the living room, and made quick work of shedding the rest of his clothes.

Anxious to feel her skin against his, he eased her back onto the bed and kissed her again, then looked his fill at her plump breasts. She had perfect round globes, heavy and beautiful, with rosy nipples that stood erect as if begging for his mouth.

He complied and suckled the tip of one, then drew it into his mouth. She moaned and pulled at him, stroking his back, as he eased on top of her.

She parted her thighs, then pushed at his boxers until his sex was free, hard and throbbing in her hand.

CHARLOTTE'S BODY HUMMED with desire. She'd never felt anything like the magic Lucas stirred inside her.

His fingers stroked and loved her, his mouth and lips turned her to putty in his hands.

She felt wild with need and raw with hunger.

He teased her nipples until they throbbed and ached

for more. Sensations shot through her core as his fingers dipped to her femininity and he rubbed her through the thin fabric of her pajama bottoms.

She stroked his thick length, urging him toward her, and he pushed her pajamas down her legs then slipped them off. His boxers hit the floor next, then their movements became frenzied and...desperate.

She'd never wanted a man like she wanted Lucas.

She wished she could see his face, see his eyes, know that he wanted her with the same intensity.

"Don't think," he said with a tender kiss to her lips. "You can feel how much I want you, Charlotte. But if you want me to stop, I will."

"No, I want you, too." She wrapped her fingers around his erection, parted her thighs and guided him to her.

He paused a second, and she heard his jeans rustling, then realized he'd grabbed a condom. She wanted to help him but she stroked his bare hips instead, feeling the muscles of his hips flex and harden as he climbed on top of her.

He nuzzled her neck, then her breasts again, then stroked her damp center with the tip of his sex. She groaned, wanting him deeper. All the way inside her, filling her.

"You are so beautiful," he murmured.

She started to shake her head. She'd had a port-wine birthmark when she was younger, had an ugly wound now from being shot. She was...blind.

"Yes, you are," he murmured again. Without giving her time to protest, he slid his thick length inside her. She moaned, parting her legs wider to cradle his body between her thighs, then lifted her hips, inviting him deeper.

He pulled out, teased her wet center, then plunged inside her again, this time driving himself to her core. She clawed at his back, urging him to move faster and faster. Passion built a frantic rhythm, and titillating sensations spiraled through her.

Stars swam behind her eyes, and she felt dizzy, exhilarated. Deeper, deeper, harder, faster, he made love to her. She wrapped her legs around him and clung to his back as he rode her. A million delicious sensations fluttered through her, and she groaned his name as her release splintered through her.

For a moment, a sea of colors burst into a fireworks show behind her eyes. She felt dizzy. Disoriented.

Wonderful.

Tears pricked her eyes as he kissed her again, then he plunged deeper again, growling her name as his release claimed him.

LUCAS CRADLED CHARLOTTE against him. His body tingled with erotic sensations. His heart fluttered with emotions.

Charlotte nestled closer into his arms, her breathing a soft whisper against his chest.

A smile curved his mouth. She trusted him enough that she'd fallen asleep.

He'd had sex with plenty of women, but he'd never actually spent all night in a woman's bed. Never slept with one.

He started to climb from bed, but leaving her felt wrong. He wanted to hold Charlotte all night.

He wanted to listen to her breathe and feel her warm body against his. Wanted to make sure she rested and wasn't plagued by nightmares.

He wanted to love her again.

His pulse jumped.

He understood how Harrison had felt with Honey.

Being in bed with Charlotte felt right, as if they belonged together.

Fear mingled with panic. But he looked down at her and brushed her hair from her cheek. Dim moonlight played off her features, accentuating her beautiful heart-shaped face.

Long dark eyelashes fluttered over her cheeks, her hair a waterfall of black against the white pillowcase.

He couldn't resist. He dropped another kiss into her hair, then another one on her cheek. She made a low murmur of contentment and snuggled deeper into his arms, and he held her tight.

He was in love with Charlotte.

But he didn't know what the hell to do about it.

She'd worried he was making love to her out of pity. What would she think if he confessed that he was in love with her?

It was rotten timing. She had a boatload of problems. He had a job to finish.

She might misread his motives.

He kissed her forehead and closed his eyes, savoring the feel of her in his arms, and decided to wait.

He might feel differently tomorrow.

No, you won't. You fell in love with her the moment you met her.

But what if she didn't love him back?

CHARLOTTE STIRRED THE next morning, feeling sore but languid and safe in Lucas's arms.

She hadn't contemplated the consequences of making love to Lucas the night before. She hadn't thought of anything but being close to him.

The morning after was always awkward. Or it should have been.

But Lucas surprised her by kissing her good-morning, then bringing her coffee in bed.

Self-conscious, she tugged the covers over her. She probably had bed head and needed a shower.

"You look beautiful," he said.

She blushed and sipped her coffee. "We have to do something today to get Evie back."

"Charlotte," Lucas said softly. "We have feelers searching for connections to Stanley and any place he might have taken Evie."

"That's not enough," Charlotte said. Stanley might not even be involved. "I want you to call that reporter and set up a live interview."

"I don't think that's a good idea," Lucas said.

"I understand you want to keep me safe," she said. "And I appreciate it. But if I go on camera and make a plea for help, someone who knows about this trafficking ring might hear the message and call in."

Lucas's footsteps pounded across the floor. "No."

Charlotte squared her shoulders. "It's not up to you, Lucas. If you don't set it up, I'll get Harrison or someone else to help me."

He stalked from the room, and Charlotte felt for the table, put her coffee cup on it, then found her overnight bag and fresh clothes. She felt her way to the bathroom and quickly showered.

By the time she came out of the bathroom, voices echoed in the living room. Lucas's and Harrison's.

"I am not going to stand by and watch her make a target of herself," Lucas said.

"We'll be there to protect her," Harrison said.

"No, she might get hurt."

"Listen, brother, we're doing everything possible to find out who bought Evie, but time is of the essence. This creep may be taking her someplace where we'll never find her."

Charlotte's insides chilled. Harrison spoke the truth. She knew it and so did Lucas.

She struggled to recall the layout of the bedroom, then felt along the wall until she reached the door. It was partially open, so she stepped into the entryway, her chin lifted high.

"He's right, Lucas. Either call the reporter and set it up, or Harrison and I will arrange it without you."

Chapter Twenty-Three

An hour later, Lucas watched Charlotte speak into the camera, his stomach in knots. Even if he understood her need to go public, he didn't like putting her in the spotlight.

The leader of this trafficking ring might send someone after her again—or come after her himself.

On the way to the station, she'd suggested that would be a good thing. He would be close by, catch this bastard and end this nightmare by bringing Evie home.

But it was damn dangerous. A million things could go wrong.

Gerald Ingram, the blasted reporter who'd leaked the story that Charlotte had survived had been reprimanded by his boss. Lucas intentionally asked for someone else to run this interview, hoping to make a point with the creep.

The SOB Lucas had shot and taken to the hospital was on the mend and now in custody. But he still hadn't offered any more information.

"Thank God and thank the FBI and Sheriff Harrison Hawk for working diligently to stop this human-trafficking room. They have made one arrest and rescued three of the students who were taken from my studio." Charlotte paused and cleared her throat, her emotions brimming on the surface. "But one girl, thirteen-year-old Evie Cranton, is still missing." A photo of Evie appeared on the screen. "Evie is sweet and likes to paint sunsets and flowers. She's just an innocent teenager caught in a horrible situation." She paused again, this time for effect to give viewers time to make a personal connection to Evie. "Think about it, folks. This trafficking ring kidnaps young girls and sells them as sex slaves. It could be your daughter or granddaughter or your little sister or your friend who's taken next."

Lucas couldn't help but think about Chrissy and all the parents with missing kids who still had no clue where their child was. The pain was unbearable; it ate at you every day.

"The police believe that someone in our very town of Tumbleweed may be involved in this trafficking ring," Charlotte continued. "If you know anything about the men who abducted the students from Tumbleweed, please call the FBI or your local law enforcement. Let's stop this inhumane practice of stealing children and women and turning them into sex slaves, and make our town safe again."

Lucas and Harrison exchanged looks as the news anchor recited phone numbers for the Bureau and the sheriff's office.

Lucas moved quickly to extricate Charlotte from Ingram, who'd shown up at the interview like a vulture stalking his prey. The minute they'd arrived, he'd accosted her with a dozen questions about her condition and the health of the three girls they'd rescued. Lucas had threatened him with an harassment charge and steered Charlotte to Ingram's competitor.

"Just tell us—"

"That's enough." Lucas shoved Ingram away with a feral look. "Leave her alone." He quickly ushered Charlotte into the hall away from the creep.

"You did great, Charlotte," Lucas said, the pride in his voice sincere.

"I just hope it works and someone calls in. Evie was

strong when she was with the other girls, but on her own, she may crumble."

Lucas escorted her to the elevator, then out the front door. They'd already set up a plan. He would leave her on the sidewalk to retrieve the SUV, but Harrison was watching. They'd also attached a wire inside Charlotte's shirt just in case something went wrong and someone from Shetland tried to grab her.

"Stay on the curb," Lucas said, close to her ear. "I'll get the car."

Car horns blared from the morning traffic, pedestrians' chatter and footsteps adding to the noise.

Charlotte worried her bottom lip with her teeth. "I'm not about to try to cross the street yet."

Her comment reminded him of her limitations and the challenges she faced.

He didn't care. He would be there to help her if she let him.

CHARLOTTE CLENCHED HER hands by her side, silently reassuring herself that she was safe. Lucas and Harrison were professionals. If something went wrong, she was wearing a wire so they could trace her.

She took a deep breath for courage. She just hoped her TV plea did some good. Hopefully someone in Tumbleweed would see sweet Evie's picture and come forward with information to help them.

If not, and someone from the group targeted her again, she'd try to get them to talk and reveal where they'd taken Evie.

She'd do anything to save that girl.

Wind whooshed as cars raced by. Brakes squealed. Someone shouted behind her. A horn honked. Birds twittered from the tops of the trees close by. A semitruck roared past. Loud music blared from another car.

The town was alive and bustling with noise and people.

Someone brushed her side as they passed. She stumbled and clawed for balance.

Tires screeched again. Another horn. Then another push. This time someone touched her back. Not gently either—they gave her a shove.

The sound of car breaks squealing rent the air. Then hard fingers closed around her arm and she pitched forward. Another shove and she tried to scream.

A hand covered her mouth and a pungent odor clogged her nose. Her eyes burned and she gagged, choking for air.

Then the world tilted and spun, and she fell into the darkness.

PANIC SHOT THROUGH Lucas as he rounded the corner with the SUV and spotted a man in black drag Charlotte into the back of a van.

Harrison darted from the overhang of the building at a dead run and tried to stop what was happening. But the men were too quick, and the van sped off.

They had discussed this scenario, but talking about it hadn't prepared him for the visceral fear that engulfed him at seeing Charlotte in the hands of these monsters.

What if they killed her before he could save her?

He braked and slowed just enough for Harrison to jump in the passenger side. His jaw was tight, his eyes focused on the van as it swerved through traffic.

Lucas sped up, weaving between cars to follow. He'd outfitted the SUV with a siren and he flipped it on.

He could not lose Charlotte.

"They're taking a right up there," Harrison said.

"Got it." Lucas slammed on his horn and maneuvered around a fender bender clogging traffic. By the time he made it to the turn, the van had disappeared.

He pressed the accelerator to the floor, determined not

to lose the van as it roared down a side road and sped into the wilderness.

Just as he rounded a corner, a white van pulled out. He swerved to avoid hitting it. A gunshot blasted the side of his SUV, and he cursed and spun the SUV around.

Harrison ducked to avoid being hit and the passenger window exploded, glass spraying. His brother pulled his gun, leaned out the window and fired at the van.

The van backed up, then a shooter fired back as the van roared straight toward them. Lucas jerked the SUV to the right but the van slammed into his side and sent him into a spin.

Cursing, he tried to regain control, but the SUV rammed into a boulder, the front crunching as the vehicle screeched to a stop. He and Harrison acted on instinct, threw their car doors open and jumped out, taking cover behind the doors.

He fired at the van and Harrison did the same. He hit the windshield and Harrison aimed for the tires, but a spray of bullets forced them to take cover again. Then the van's engine roared, the driver backed up and spun in the opposite direction.

Lucas darted from behind the door and fired at the tires, desperate to stop them from escaping, but dust and gravel spewed behind the van and it raced away.

He and Harrison chased after it, repeatedly firing, but a cloud of dust swirled in a blinding fog as it disappeared.

"Dammit," Lucas said. "That was a setup."

"They figured we'd be watching her," Harrison agreed.

Panic ripped at Lucas. "We can't lose her, Harrison."

Harrison wiped dust and sweat from his forehead. "We won't. She's wired."

Lucas nodded, although these guys were professionals. If they'd expected her interview was a setup, they might also anticipate a wire.

He punched Keenan's number. If they found that wire and destroyed it, they'd lose contact with Charlotte.

Then they might never find her.

CHARLOTTE STIRRED, her head throbbing. She blinked, trying to orient herself, but the darkness consumed her.

They were moving. Traffic noises outside echoed loudly. A horn honking. She was thrown sideways and pain ricocheted through her shoulders as she hit the wall of the vehicle. A van.

Was this the same one the men had used to carry Evie in?

Tears of panic and terror burned her eyes. Where was poor little Evie? Had they already sold her and forced her to have sex with the sick man who'd purchased her?

The van careened to the right and she clawed at the floor to keep from sliding, but lost her grip and slammed against the other side.

Fighting panic, she tried to make a mental plan. They hadn't bound her hands or feet, so when they finally stopped she could try to escape.

But…how could she run when she couldn't see where she was headed?

Frustration mingled with fear, but she choked it back. Lucas and Harrison were watching. They had probably followed the van.

When her abductors stopped, they would storm the men and force them to tell them where Evie was being held.

Grasping on to hope, she blinked back tears. The Hawk brothers would save her. Then they'd rescue Evie and bring her back home, and she and the other girls would be reunited.

Tries squealed and the van suddenly lurched to a stop. She hit the side of the interior again, and gritted her teeth to keep from screaming as the back door of the van screeched open.

A faint stream of light filtered through the darkness,

and pain splintered Charlotte's temple. She rubbed her forehead, but the light flickered then faded just as a hard, cold hand jerked her arm.

"What are we going to do with her?"

"Check her for a wire," a second man ordered.

Charlotte bit back a cry as they dragged her from the back. One of them ripped at her shirt. She tried to fight, but he shoved her up against something rough—a tree, she realized.

Then he tore the wire from inside her shirt and pressed the tip of his gun to her head.

LUCAS HAD NEVER been so terrified in his life. They'd lost Charlotte.

"They just stopped," Keenan told him over the phone. "The signal is there, but they're no longer moving."

"Send me the coordinates."

"On the way."

A second later, he received the text and turned to Harrison. While he'd called Keenan, Harrison had worked on the SUV to make sure it was drivable.

"It's a little rough," Harrison said, noting the broken window and dents in the front.

"Doesn't matter. We don't have time to wait on another vehicle. Keenan says they've stopped." Which could mean anything.

They were transferring vehicles. Leaving Charlotte at a specified location.

Or…

No…he couldn't let his mind go there.

"I'm checking out a couple of leads that came in on that tip line," Keenan said. "Maybe Charlotte's interview did some good and prompted someone to come forward."

He hoped so, but more often than not, going public triggered countless crank calls, false leads, even false confessions from attention seekers.

He tossed Harrison the keys. "You drive. Keenan is checking out a couple of leads."

Harrison caught the keys in one hand then slid into the driver's seat. Lucas jumped in the passenger side and buckled up as Harrison sped onto the road.

He gave Harrison directions, and they raced down a side road that seemed to lead nowhere. Rough terrain, then more ranches and farmland spread before them. The mountains stood in the far distance.

It seemed like forever but finally Harrison veered onto a dirt road that disappeared into a wooded section.

Lucas's pulse raced. This remote location wasn't a good sign.

He scanned the area as Harrison came to an abrupt stop. "This is it."

His brother's concerned expression mirrored the fear clawing at Lucas.

Lucas scoped out the area in search of a house or cabin, but there were no buildings in sight.

He and Harrison opened their doors with caution, prepared for another ambush. The trees rustled in the wind as leaves rained down.

His gun at the ready, Lucas glanced into the woods in search of a shooter, but everything seemed quiet.

"There are tire marks," Harrison said, pointing to the ground. "They stopped here, then it looks like they turned around and left again."

"But this is where Keenan traced the wire."

A dark foreboding swept over Lucas.

Either the kidnappers had stopped here and stripped off the wire or…they'd killed Charlotte and dumped her body in the woods.

Chapter Twenty-Four

"We have to make sure she's not here," Lucas said, his throat thick with fear.

Harrison nodded grimly, then they both began to comb the area. Weeds and trees so thick and close together they almost touched made it difficult to see, but in the next hour they searched every inch of space within a mile radius.

Sweat dampened Lucas's forehead, and he swiped at it with his sleeve, relieved that he hadn't found Charlotte's body. If she was still alive, they had a chance to save her.

He *had* to save her. She meant more to him than any woman ever had or ever would.

His phone buzzed on his hip. He quickly checked it and connected. "Keenan, they found Charlotte's wire and dumped it here, but we haven't found her. Please tell me you have something."

"I'm not sure but it's an address you should check out. It came in on an anonymous tip."

"What is it?"

"A ranch about thirty miles from where you are now."

"Do you know who sent you the tip?"

"No, but I'm trying to trace the IP address. I'll keep you posted. I'm sending you the coordinates now."

They ended the call, then Lucas motioned to Harrison to get back in the car. By the time his brother had started the SUV, the directions came through. He relayed the information to Harrison, and a frown marred his face.

"I know where that is," Harrison said as he reached for his phone. "It's another property that Stanley took over when Wilson Channing died."

"That might mean that Stanley is involved."

Harrison nodded, then tossed Lucas his phone. "Call the deputy and tell him I said to pick up Stanley. If he knows something, he's going to tell us this time."

Lucas made the call while Harrison sped onto what appeared to be a deserted road. Scrub brush and cacti dotted the landscape, with an occasional abandoned or run-down house along the way.

Lucas's heart hammered as they finally neared the ranch. Harrison slowed, and they assessed the property from a distance.

Lucas used binoculars to get a better look. "I see a Mercedes and a BMW and a dark van."

"Someone's there then," Harrison said. "Do you see any of the kidnappers?"

Lucas sucked in a sharp breath. "Actually, one just got out of the van. God…he has Charlotte."

Harrison pulled the SUV into the woods between a clump of trees. "She look okay?"

"She's alive," he said when she beat at the man's back with her fists.

He removed his weapon from his holster, retrieved extra ammunition from the glove compartment and reloaded his gun. "Let's go get her."

Harrison checked his own weapon, and they eased from the SUV. They crept through the edge of the woods, senses alert in case the men had surveillance cameras on the premises or someone stationed as a guard.

They inched their way up to the big two-story farmhouse. Three guest cabins were situated on the property. The bastards could be using the cabins as a brothel.

Disgust turned his stomach. Harrison motioned that he would cause a distraction to draw out one or more of the men. They had no idea how many were inside, so Lucas nodded agreement and gestured that he'd go around back and look inside.

Harrison picked up a rock from the ground and threw it toward the van parked by the house. It pinged off the metal, then he threw another one.

Seconds later, two armed men stormed outside. Harrison raised his gun and shouted. "Drop it. You're under arrest."

The men whirled on Harrison and opened fire, and Harrison shot back. Lucas raced around to the back of the house and inched to the door. He peeked through the back window into a large kitchen, which was set up with a bar and plenty of booze.

Shots echoed from the front, and he prayed Harrison was safe as he crept into the house.

A big man with tattoos just like Charlotte had described raced down the steps in killer mode, his gun at the ready.

Lucas aimed his gun. "Move and I'll shoot."

The bastard whipped around and fired at Lucas. He released a shot, nailing the brute in the forehead. His eyes widened for a fraction of a second, then the big lug tumbled headfirst down the steps and collapsed on the wood floor at the bottom.

A scream echoed from above, and Lucas grabbed the man's gun and carried it with him as he raced up the steps. Behind him, the front door swung open.

He pivoted, gun aimed, ready to kill the other men, but Harrison stood in the entrance. "They're down."

Lucas gestured to the man on the floor then pointed up the steps. Harrison followed on his tail as Lucas climbed the steps. A cry sounded from the right, and he veered toward it.

Harrison went left to check the other rooms, and Lucas inched toward the rooms on the right. He peered inside one, and his stomach revolted. Two teenage girls were tied to beds, both drugged and out of it.

Not Evie or Charlotte, though. He would come back for these girls.

He inched toward the next room and heard a sob. Then Charlotte's voice. "Shh, Evie, it'll be all right."

Relief surged through him, and he pushed open the door. Another man stood with a gun aimed at Charlotte and Evie. He glared at Lucas, a warning that he'd shoot them if Lucas made a move.

Lucas didn't hesitate. He put a bullet between the man's eyes. Evie screamed and Charlotte hugged the girl to her and rocked her as Lucas stalked toward them.

"It's me, Charlotte," Lucas said. "The men are all dead."

Charlotte was trembling, soothing Evie, and he dropped to his knees and pulled them both against him.

Her tears came in a rush, and he held her tight. He didn't know what he would have done if he'd been too late and he'd lost her.

CHARLOTTE COULDN'T CONTAIN her emotions. She'd lived in fear the past few days, but the nightmare was finally over and Evie was safe.

She hugged the girl and Lucas at the same time, grateful they were all alive.

When she'd heard the gunfire, she'd been terrified that he'd been killed trying to save her.

He rubbed her back and pressed kisses in her hair. "Are you okay, Charlotte?"

She nodded against him. "I was terrified you'd been shot."

"No, I'm good." He lifted his head. "Evie, are you all right?"

"I am now," the girl said, her voice filled with anger. "What about the others?"

"They're at the hospital, but they're fine," Charlotte assured her.

Footsteps sounded, then Harrison's voice. "I've called for a couple of ambulances and CSI. There are four other girls here."

Lucas helped Charlotte and Evie stand. "Let's go outside and wait for the medics."

"Bronson called," Harrison said. "He just brought Stanley in. Said the man confessed that he knew about the trafficking ring. He's the one who called in the tip. He wants a deal for helping us."

Lucas tensed. "That depends on what else he can tell us."

He ushered Charlotte and Evie down the stairs. Evie winced when she saw the dead man, then stopped and kicked the bastard.

Sirens wailed outside, announcing the arrival of the medics and crime team. Harrison met one of the ambulances and escorted the medics upstairs to evaluate the other girls and arrange for them to be transported to the hospital for evaluation, and then for their families or foster families to be notified.

"I want to see Adrian and Agnes and Mae Lynn," Evie said in a pained whisper.

"We'll take you there," Lucas assured her.

He asked the medics to check out Evie and Charlotte while he went to help Harrison untie the other four girls.

TWO HOURS LATER, after making certain Charlotte and Evie were examined and reunited with Charlotte's other students, and the four hostages they'd rescued were safe and being treated for trauma and drugs in their system, Lucas and Harrison drove to the sheriff's office to speak with Stanley.

The banker was a creep in the worst way. Not only had he swindled people out of their homes, but he'd also been part of this human-trafficking ring.

Lucas wanted to see him rot in jail.

But he sensed another person might be calling the shots.

"We know someone else in Tumbleweed is involved," Harrison said.

Stanley's eyes widened, his ruddy complexion going pale. "I wasn't involved," Stanley said. "At least not directly."

"Then how were you involved?" Lucas asked.

Stanley cut his eyes between them. "I need a lawyer, don't I?"

"You can ask for one if you want," Harrison said.

"But all deals stop when he shows up," Lucas said in a harsh tone. "This ring has to be stopped. And if you take the fall, that's fine by me."

"No, no," Stanley shrieked. "I tell you I wasn't that involved."

Harrison folded his arms. "Then tell us what you know."

Stanley glanced down at his bony hands, which he kept twisting together. The man was pathetic. No way was he in charge of an organization like the men who'd abducted Charlotte's students.

But his silence had endangered countless innocent girls and Charlotte.

Lucas walked toward the door. "Either spill it or I'm throwing the book at you. And when I do, I'll make sure the media circulates the news that you talked."

Stanley lurched up from his seat, a muscle ticking in his narrow jaw. "You can't do that. They'll kill me."

Lucas shrugged. Harrison slammed his fist on the table,

rattling the wood. "Then speak up. Because frankly I don't give a damn if they put your sorry butt in the ground."

"Not a damn," Lucas agreed flatly.

Stanley shoved his fingers through what was left of his thinning hair. "It wasn't me. But I was asked to set up some offshore accounts and I started asking questions."

Lucas returned to stand across from the man. "And you found out about the trafficking ring."

"Not at first," Stanley said, his voice shaky. "But eventually I kept asking and then got a cut to keep my mouth shut."

"Who paid you off?" Lucas asked.

"I don't know. The money—"

Lucas grabbed him by the collar and jerked him so hard the man's feet came off the floor. "I want a name."

"Geoffrey Williams," he shrieked. "He…paid me to keep quiet. He's head of the group in Tumbleweed. He… bought that last girl for himself."

Lucas's blood ran cold. He had gone to school with Geoffrey. Had admired the popular athlete.

But his name had cropped up when they'd been investigating his sister's disappearance. Lucas had remembered then that Geoffrey had pushed his little sister around.

Maybe he had a mean streak with women…

Geoffrey was also part of the town council. He purported to be helping the town, building the economy.

He'd even helped Honey get approval for the renovation of the homes she'd bought.

Dammit. How much of the money that he'd invested had come from sex trafficking?

AN HOUR LATER, Lucas and Harrison arrested Geoffrey Williams.

The cocky creep had no idea they suspected him, much less that Stanley had rolled on him.

He lawyered up immediately. But Lucas and Harrison had already obtained warrants for the man's house, business and personal computers. And the surveillance cameras at the ranch where Evie had been taken showed Williams paying for Evie, then discussing her future as his personal private sex slave.

Keenan also connected Williams to Louise—he had used a fake account to lure her into thinking he was a teenager interested in her. When he'd gotten her alone, though, she'd fought and he'd lost control and killed her.

He'd been furious and then began to look for another young girl to fill his needs. He'd stopped by Charlotte's studio to check on her business and spotted Evie.

Lucas escorted him to federal lockup and made certain that bail was not an option, and that he had no communication with anyone on the outside or in the jail. He didn't want the bastard to be released or call someone to come after Charlotte again.

Harrison left to go home to Honey, and Lucas drove by the hospital to pick up Charlotte. Evie was going to stay in the room with Adrian and Agnes for the night. The nurses had moved Mae Lynn in with them, hoping the four of them being reunited would help Mae Lynn in her recovery.

Charlotte was quiet as they drove back to his house. "I can go home now," she said, her voice soft, questioning.

"Yes, it should be safe."

"Good." She breathed out deeply. "Once I get the girls settled, I need to get my life in order."

Lucas didn't know what that meant, but he hoped to hell he was going to be part of that life.

Chapter Twenty-Five

Worry plagued Lucas as he drove Charlotte back to his cabin to retrieve her overnight bag, then to her house.

"The security company installed the alarm system," Lucas said, glad Brayden had taken care of meeting the company here and overseeing the installation.

"Let me show you how it works."

"Thanks." Nerves fluttered in her voice as he walked her inside and explained the system.

"I hope I can remember to use it and not trip it," Charlotte said.

"You'll get used to it, and you'll learn to appreciate it." He gently touched her shoulder. "I want you to be safe, Charlotte."

"You've been wonderful to me, Lucas," Charlotte said. "You're a man of your word. You found my students and brought them back. I can never repay you for that."

His throat thickened. "You don't owe me anything, Charlotte. It was my job."

Her smile faded. "Of course it was. The world is a better place because of it, too."

She pulled away and stiffened. "Thanks again."

Lucas sensed he'd said something wrong, but he didn't know what it was. But he couldn't leave without telling her how he felt.

He took her hand in his, frowning when she tensed again.

"Charlotte, I know the case is over, but I have feelings for you. I want to see you again." God, he sounded awkward and stilted and should just tell her how much he loved her.

But something about her demeanor made him hesitate.

"You've done everything for me the last few days, and I appreciate it. But you have your life, and… I have to figure out how to live mine now."

"I don't care that you're blind," he said. "If you get your vision back, good, but if you don't, it won't matter to me."

"It matters to me." Her lips tightened into a thin line. "I'm not going to be a burden to anyone. And I certainly don't want your pity." She pulled her hand from his and turned to face her bedroom. "Now, please leave."

Panic caught in Lucas's throat. "That's not what this is," Lucas said. "I don't pity you, Charlotte. I admire the hell out of you. I know we can make it work."

"No, we can't," Charlotte said firmly. "Go home, Lucas. I…just want to be alone."

"But I love you," Lucas said in a rush.

A tense heartbeat passed, then Charlotte lifted her head as if she was looking at him. "We've only known each other for a few days, Lucas. Don't confuse protecting me with love. You did your job, now go home. I'm tired and want to go to bed."

Lucas studied her for a long moment. He loved her, wanted to be with her, to take care of her forever.

But she obviously didn't feel the same way.

He backed toward the door, his heart in his throat. "Call me if you need anything."

She nodded, but made no move to stop him as he closed the door.

CHARLOTTE CRIED HERSELF to sleep. Lucas had said he cared about her, wanted to be with her.

He'd even said he loved her.

She'd dreamed of having love all her life.

But she couldn't be with anyone until she knew how she was going to manage her life.

She refused to be a problem or burden to Lucas. If she gave into the feelings she had for him and allowed herself to rely on him, sooner or later he'd get tired of it.

Of her.

Then he'd resent her.

She couldn't bear that.

Needing to make a plan, she set the security system, then found her phone and called Rebecca. The vision-rehabilitation therapist had told her about a school for the blind.

Sure, she might get her vision back.

But she might not.

Until then, she couldn't rely on others. She would sign up for the school and take charge of her life.

She couldn't contemplate building a future with anyone until she took care of herself.

THE NEXT THREE weeks were excruciating for Lucas. He and Harrison and the other agents at the Bureau had made more arrests in the Shetland operation and had finally located and rescued the last of the original eleven missing girls.

Although they now believed that the real ringleader had escaped, information pointed to a plastic surgeon whom they suspected had given the man a new face.

That investigation was still on going.

He came inside from the horse stable and washed his hands.

He missed Charlotte like crazy.

But he wanted her to be happy so he'd left her alone.

Honey said that Charlotte had asked her to make some adjustments to her house to accommodate her lack of vision.

Meanwhile, his mother had taken steps to become a foster parent and Adrian, Agnes and Evie had moved in. Mae Lynn was making progress and would be moving in with them soon.

The house was bustling with the girls, who adored the horses and ranch life. His mother asked Dexter to buy each of them a horse to ride. In their spare time, he and his brothers were giving the girls riding lessons.

He'd just finished one with Evie. That girl was something else. She reminded him of Charlotte—all sweetness but full of spunk and fight.

His mother had a purpose now and seemed happier than he'd seen her in years. She'd revealed that she had a craft room where she worked with clay and had shown them her bust of Chrissy. He and his brothers had insisted she display it on the mantle near the dining table so Chrissy would be part of their family meals. No one at the table had been dry-eyed when they'd toasted Chrissy.

His mother had also opened up her craft room for the girls to paint.

He washed up from outside, then went to tell her goodnight and found her in her craft room cleaning up.

"Thanks for giving the girls a riding lesson today," she said with a big smile. "They are so excited about being on the ranch."

Lucas hugged her. "You're incredible with them, Mom." She would have been incredible with his sister, too, but she'd been robbed of that.

"I enjoy having them on the ranch," she said with a smile. "This house has been quiet far too long. Besides, it's good practice for all the grandkids I hope to have."

"Harrison and Honey are working on it." They'd made the official announcement at the family dinner last night. His mother was thrilled.

He hadn't realized how much he wanted his own family until he'd watched his brother and Honey talk about their plans.

Charlotte would make a wonderful mother. If only she loved him…

His mother nudged him with a teasing grin. "You and Charlotte can add your own." Lucas clenched his hands by his sides, his gaze straying to the paintings the girls were doing.

"Lucas? You are in love with her, aren't you? I didn't misread the situation, did I?"

"No." He swallowed hard. "I told her I wanted to be with her, but she doesn't feel the same way."

A tense silence stretched between them, then his mother tugged his hand. "Come here for a minute, son. I want to show you something."

Lucas narrowed his eyes, but she led him to a side table, then lifted a cloth to reveal a clay piece.

"When Charlotte was here, I gave her some clay to work with. She was frustrated about everything, worried about the girls and missing her art." She moved the piece around to give him a better view. "Look at it, Lucas."

He studied the piece—it was a head. Deep eyes. A square chin.

"It's you, Lucas," she said softly. "It's the first clay piece she's ever done, and it's you." She wrapped her arm around his shoulder. "One look at the way she created your face, and I knew she was in love with you."

Lucas looked at her in disbelief, then studied the bust again. Was his mother right?

Could Charlotte possibly be in love with him?

THE LAST THREE weeks had been challenging for Charlotte.

"You look fabulous," Honey said as Charlotte seated herself in Honey's minivan.

"Thanks for picking me up."

"Are you kidding? I've missed you like crazy!"

Charlotte smiled. "I missed you, too."

But she was grateful for the education she'd received at the school for the blind. She still missed her sight, especially the colors and her artwork, but at least she'd learned to be independent, prepare her own meals and do daily household chores.

She would always need to rely on a driver and need help grocery shopping, but she would figure things out. Rebecca had recommended a service that would help with some of her needs so she didn't have to rely on friends or neighbors.

Honey started the engine and sped toward Tumbleweed.

"The girls are doing great," Honey said. "They love the ranch and can't stop talking about the riding lessons the men are giving them."

"I know. They wrote me letters about it," Charlotte said. "Mrs. Hawk was so generous to take them in."

"It's been good for her," Honey said. "She spent years grieving for Chrissy. Having these girls around and knowing that they need her has brought a real spark to her eyes."

Charlotte wanted to ask about Lucas, but she bit back the words. She missed him more and more each day. She just didn't know what to do about it.

And as much as she wanted to see the girls, visiting them at Hawk's Landing would be tough.

Although Lucas might have left town for another case by now...

Honey slowed then parked. "We're here. I'll go in and help you get settled if you want."

Charlotte hesitated. She'd missed her friend, but she didn't want to take advantage of Honey. And she had to prove to herself that she could manage on her own. "I can make it by myself, Honey. But thank you for everything."

Honey cut the engine and pulled Charlotte into a hug.

"Listen to me, don't shut me out. I was your friend before all this happened, and I'll always be your friend."

Tears flooded Charlotte's eyes. Good grief. She'd thought she was past all the emotions.

"You'd still love me if I lost my sight, wouldn't you?" Honey asked.

Charlotte pulled back from her friend, Honey's words echoing in her ears. "Of course I would."

"Then don't push me away, because it won't work. You and I connected the first time we met. I've always wanted a sister, and I found her in you."

Charlotte squeezed Honey's hand. "I feel the same way. It's just—"

"I know you're independent and it's hard for you to accept help," Honey said. "It would be difficult for me, too. But I need you, Charlotte." Honey pulled Charlotte's hand over her belly, and Charlotte couldn't help but smile at her baby bump.

"Please say you'll be here for me and my son."

"A son?" Charlotte squeezed Honey's hands. "I bet Harrison and his mother are excited."

"They are. And I want you to be his godmother." Honey's voice softened. "Promise me you will."

How could she say no to that?

She promised she would, then hugged Honey again and allowed her to walk her to the door. Charlotte unlocked the door then Honey's footsteps echoed on the porch as she left.

Charlotte took a deep breath for courage and stepped inside.

A sweet aroma suffused her, and she paused inside the entryway. Someone had been in the house.

Maybe Honey had cleaned?

No, it wasn't cleaner she smelled. It was roses.

Soft music played in the background, then another scent—masculine, woodsy...

Her heart stuttered. "Lucas?"

"I'm here, Charlotte." Footsteps padded as he walked toward her. "I missed you."

Her heartache over him had intensified each day they'd been apart.

His hand brushed her cheek, then he took her hand in his and kneeled on the floor.

"I love you, Charlotte. I hope you don't mind the flowers, but I wanted to surprise you."

Love mushroomed inside her. "You did."

He slowly opened her palm, and she bit her bottom lip as she felt him place something inside.

"I'm not going away," he said. "I want to marry you and have a family with you."

She traced her fingers over the ring in her hand. An oval diamond, thin band with tiny stones inlaid in it. She imagined how it looked, but knew it didn't matter.

It was beautiful because Lucas was giving it to her.

His breath quickened as he closed his hands around hers. "I've dreamed about holding you and kissing you again every night." He brought her hands to his lips and kissed them. "Please say you want to be with me, too."

She clung to his hand, then kneeled in front of him. "I love you, too, Lucas." She looped her arms around his neck, then pressed a kiss to his lips. Her heart was bursting with happiness and love. "Yes, Lucas, I want to be your wife."

He swept her into a kiss that made her tremble Then he slipped the ring on her finger and kissed her again.

A kiss that promised that nothing would ever tear them apart.

Chapter Twenty-Six

"You look beautiful," Honey said, a note of wistfulness in her voice as she dabbed blush on Charlotte's cheeks.

"Thanks, Honey." She squeezed her friend's hand. "And thanks for helping me with my makeup."

"Not that you need anything," Honey said. "You have gorgeous skin."

Charlotte bit back that inner voice reminding her that it hadn't always been that way. She was grateful to the plastic surgeon who'd donated her time to repair Charlotte's birthmark at no cost.

Honey hesitated, and Charlotte imagined a tiny frown crinkling between her eyes. "Are you okay? Nervous?"

Charlotte shook her head. "No, sorry, sometimes the ghosts come back to haunt me."

Honey adjusted Charlotte's veil. "No ghosts today. Only happy thoughts."

"I am happy," Charlotte admitted. Even if she couldn't see her reflection in the mirror, she felt beautiful.

Lucas had given her that gift. As much as she wanted to see his face when she walked down the aisle, she'd learned to feel things with her other senses. She heard the love in his voice when he spoke to her, felt it in his touch, knew it in her heart.

"I wish I could see what you look like today," Charlotte said with a smile. "Your baby bump is growing."

"So are my boobs," Honey said with a laugh. "But Harrison doesn't seem to mind that."

They laughed together, then Honey took Charlotte's hand and she stood.

"Lucas is a lucky man," Honey said.

"I'm the lucky one."

Honey gently touched the end of Charlotte's hair, where she'd curled it around Charlotte's shoulders. "You're both lucky so don't sell yourself short, Charlotte. He needs you. I've seen it in his eyes. Those weeks you were gone, he was lost."

So was I.

But they'd found each other and she didn't intend to let go for a second.

Honey took her hand and guided her outside the big farmhouse. Giggles and whispers from the girls echoed in the background, blending with the guitar music. Finding out that Dexter played had been a surprise.

Having Adrian, Agnes, Evie and Mae Lynn, who was flourishing at Hawk's Landing, present was the icing on the cake.

"Deputy Bronson is here with Haley," Honey said. "I think they may be getting married next."

Charlotte smiled to herself. Since her hospital stay, she and Haley and Honey had become close friends. Rebecca, her vision therapist, had joined them for their weekly girls' night out.

The guitar music strummed softly in the background, and Harrison's gruff voice whispered her name as he stepped up to walk her down the aisle.

"It's gorgeous here," Honey said. "The fall colors are in full bloom. We made an aisle for you with white chairs decorated in rose petals on the ground. Roses are everywhere, too, just like Lucas requested."

Roses reminded her of the night he'd proposed. Of the moment she realized she couldn't live without him.

"Lucas is a jittery mess," Harrison murmured as they started down the aisle. "He's still afraid he dreamed that you said yes."

A smile filled Charlotte's heart. Harrison walked slowly, careful to keep pace with her, but she could have walked the aisle by herself. Her pull to Lucas was that strong.

Harrison paused, and Charlotte inhaled Lucas's masculine scent. Lucas cradled her hand in his and she squeezed his, silently telling him how happy she was.

The reverend cleared his throat and began the ceremony.

His words faded though as she turned to face her groom. The power of Lucas's love bloomed deep within her, healing hurts and pains with its sweet intensity.

She not only felt safe at Hawk's Landing, but she also felt honored to have found this man.

Suddenly a quick pain flashed behind her eyes. Then light.

She tensed, dizzy for a second.

"Charlotte?" Lucas's concern resonated in his voice.

She blinked, then slowly colors began to slip into place. A sea of yellow, the moon, the reds and oranges of the leaves, the soft pinks of the roses, then… Lucas's face.

Lucas cupped her face between his hands. "Charlotte, honey, what's wrong?" She couldn't speak. She was mesmerized by the chiseled shape of his face, by his strong jaw, by the deep brown of his eyes as he looked into hers.

Time stood still. The wind sifted through the trees, creating its own music. Moonlight glimmered off his face.

"Charlotte, talk to me, honey," he murmured.

She lifted her hands and traced his jaw with her fingers. "I can see you, Lucas. I can see your eyes and that tiny scar on your forehead and that mouth that drives me wild."

A slow smile spread on Lucas's face as the truth

dawned. Then he swept her in his arms and swung her around.

No one in the crowd understood what had happened yet, but they cheered and clapped.

Charlotte wrapped her arms around her husband and sealed their vows with a kiss.

Blue had always been her favorite color, but now brown had replaced it—the brown of Lucas's eyes because they were the color of love.

* * * * *

Look for the next book in USA TODAY
bestselling author Rita Herron's
BADGE OF JUSTICE *series*
later in 2018.

And don't miss the previous title in the
BADGE OF JUSTICE *series:*

REDEMPTION AT HAWK'S LANDING

Available now from Mills & Boon Intrigue!

MILLS & BOON®

A sneak peek at next month's titles...

Just can't wait?
Buy our books online before they hit the shops!
www.millsandboon.co.uk

Also available as eBooks.

LET'S TALK
Romance

For exclusive extracts, competitions
and special offers, find us online:

f facebook.com/millsandboon

◎ @millsandboonuk

🐦 @millsandboon

Or get in touch on 0844 844 1351*

For all the latest titles coming soon, visit
millsandboon.co.uk/nextmonth